CARMEN
SANDIEGO™

Based on the Netflix original series
teleplay by May Chan

Designed by Melissa Martin and Sarah Boecher
The type was set in Proxima Nova.
The sound effect type was created by Melissa Martin.

ISBN: 978-1-328-49578-5 (paper over board)
ISBN: 978-1-328-49506-8 (paperback)

Manufactured in China
SCP 10 9 8 7 6 5 4 3 2 1
4500748841

CARMEN SANDIEGO™

THE STICKY RICE CAPER

A GRAPHIC NOVEL

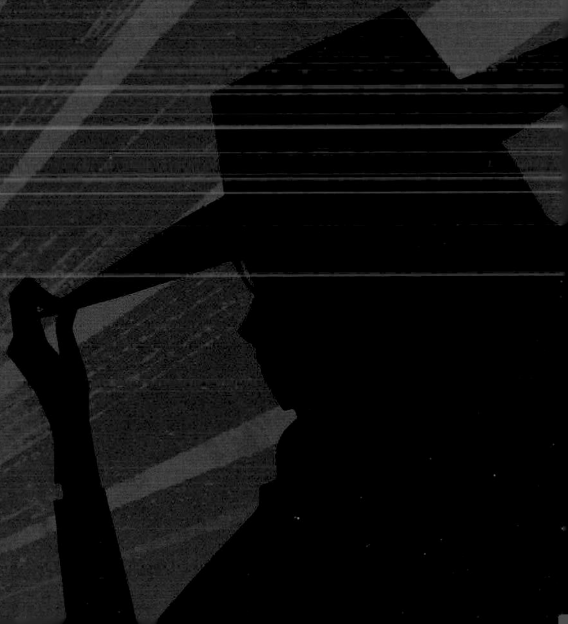

HOUGHTON MIFFLIN HARCOURT

BOSTON NEW YORK

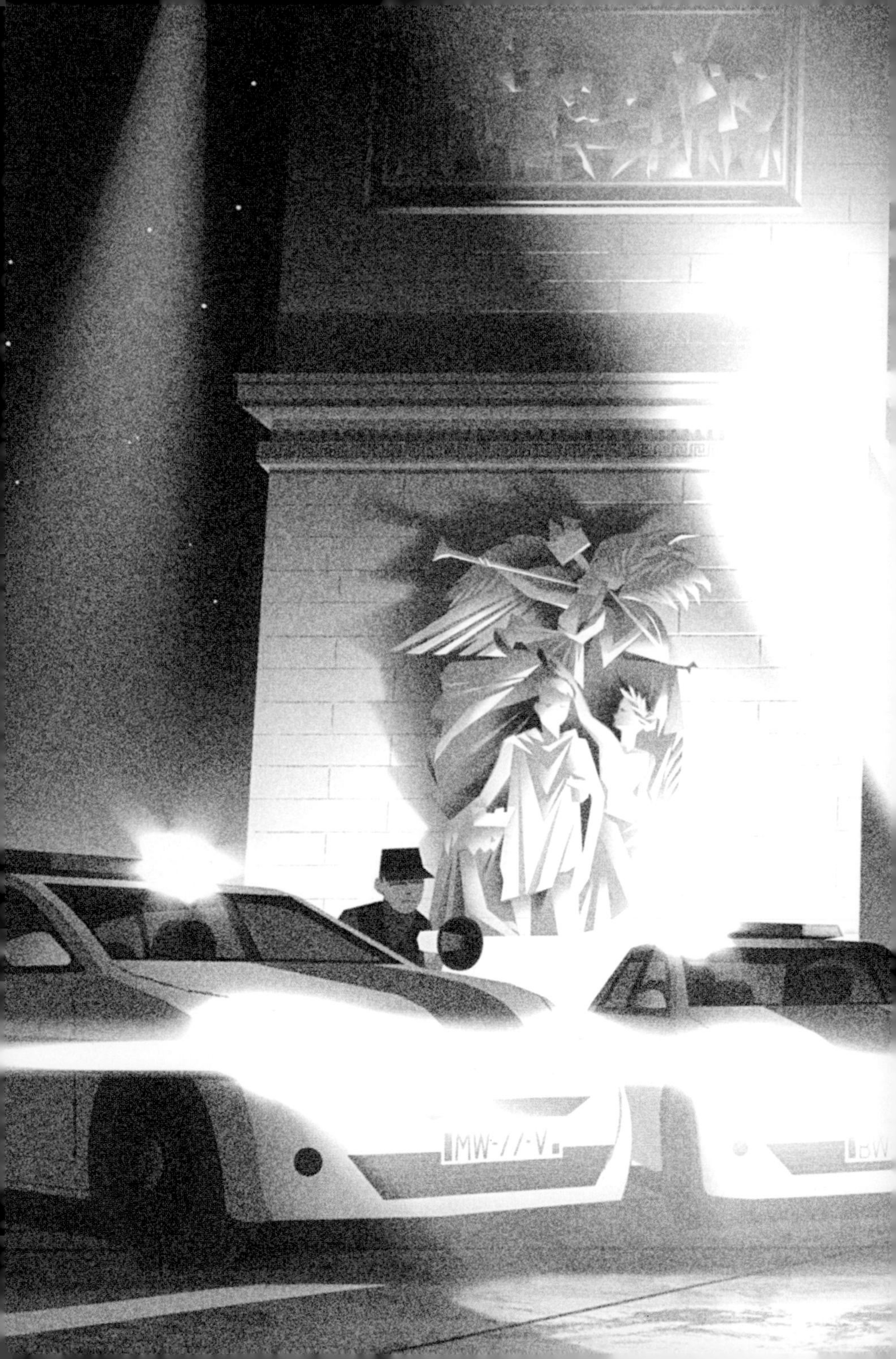
MW-77-V

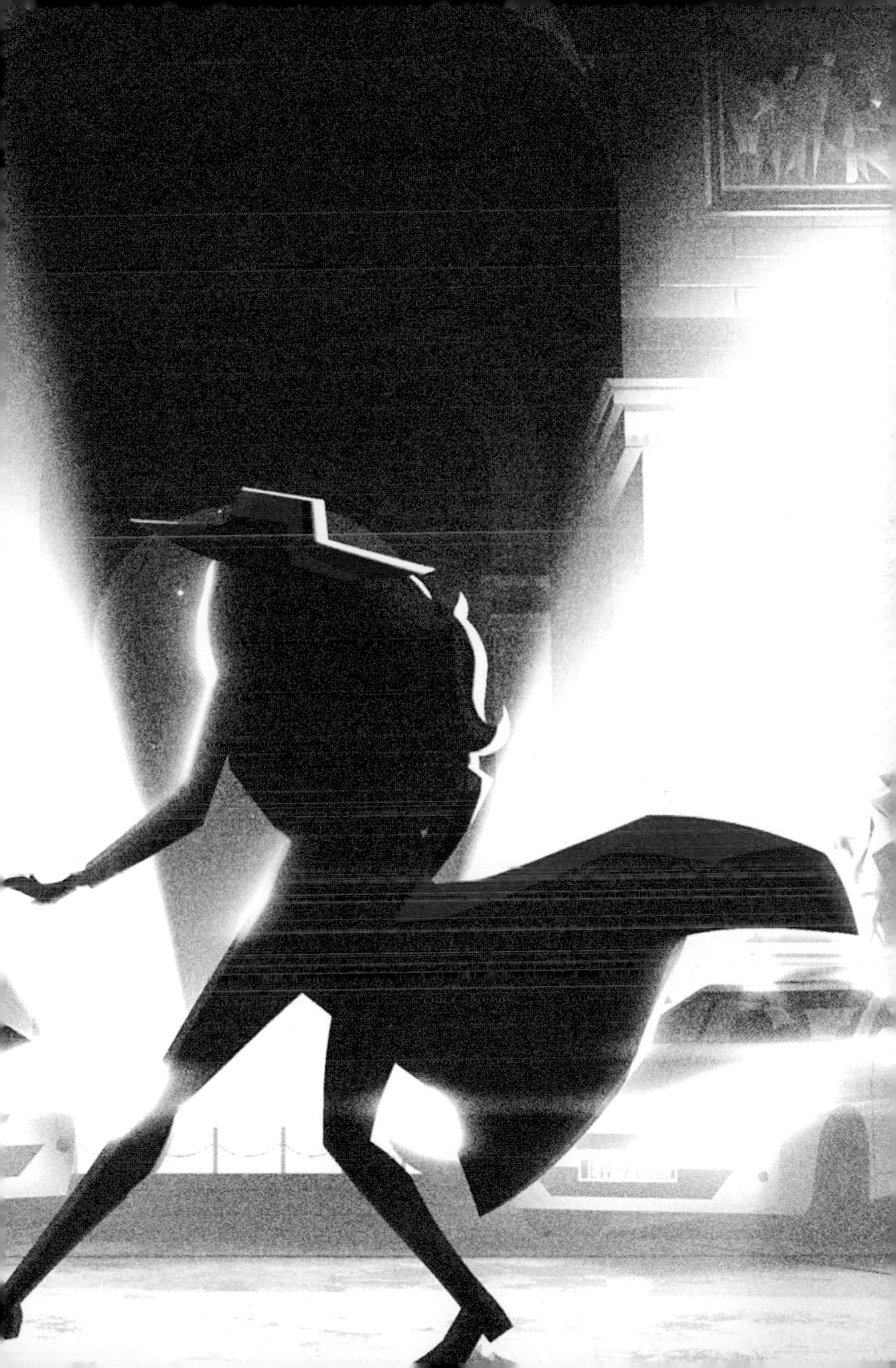

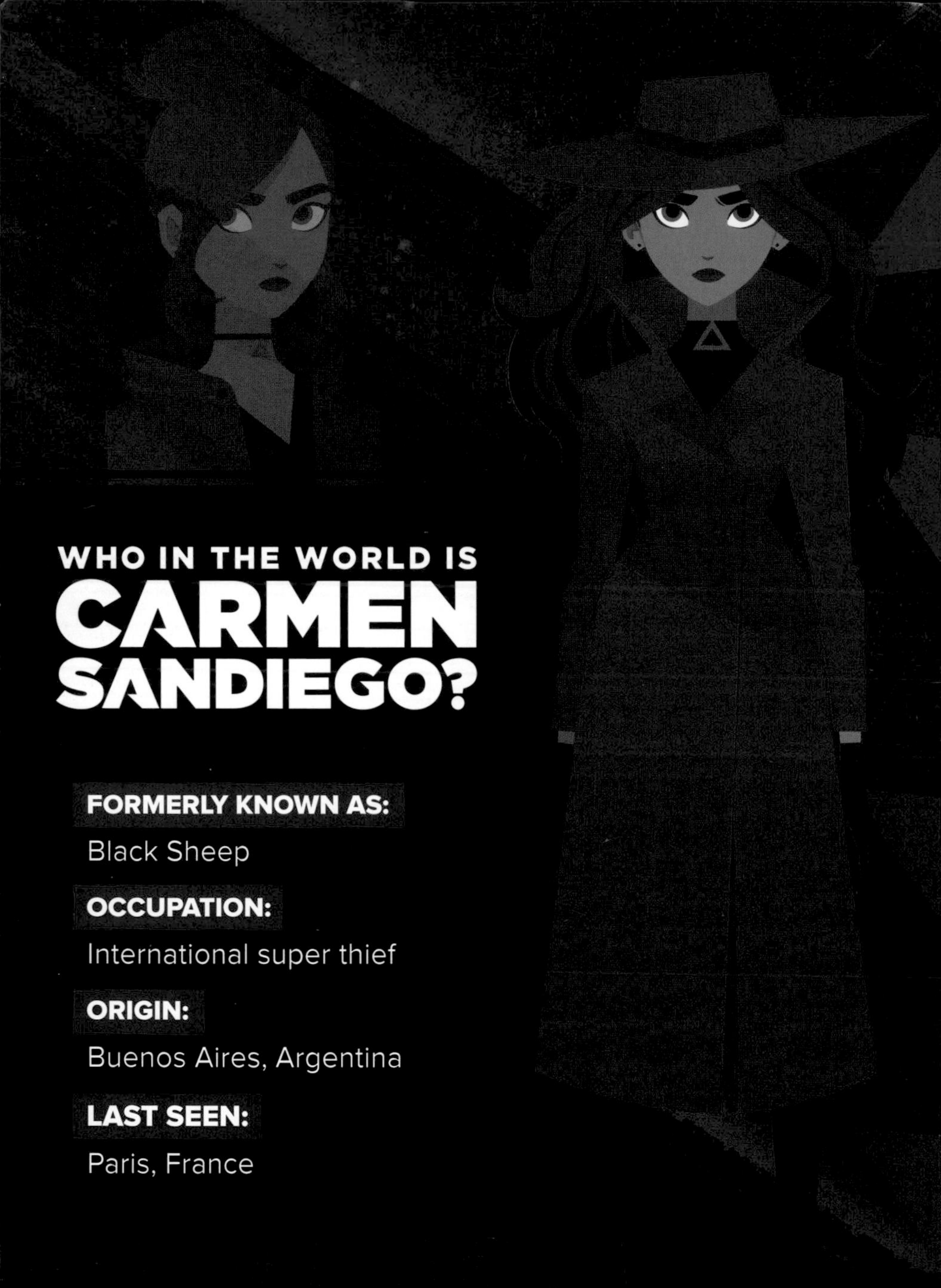

WHO IN THE WORLD IS
CARMEN SANDIEGO?

FORMERLY KNOWN AS:

Black Sheep

OCCUPATION:

International super thief

ORIGIN:

Buenos Aires, Argentina

LAST SEEN:

Paris, France

I was found as a baby in Argentina and raised as an orphan on Vile Island. But I longed to set out and see the world.

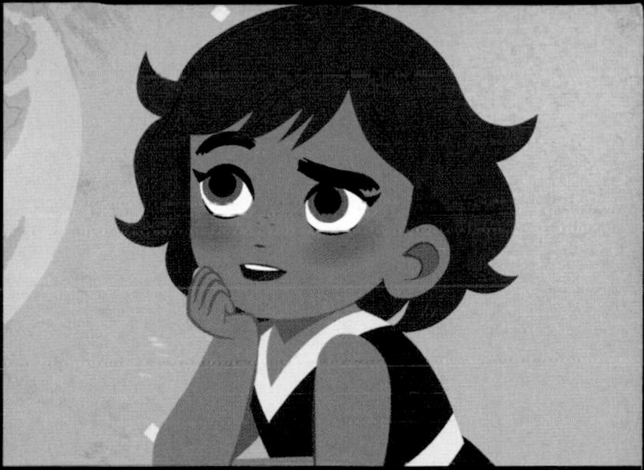

I couldn't wait to train at VILE's school for thieves. I wanted to become a VILE operative, traveling the world to steal precious goods.

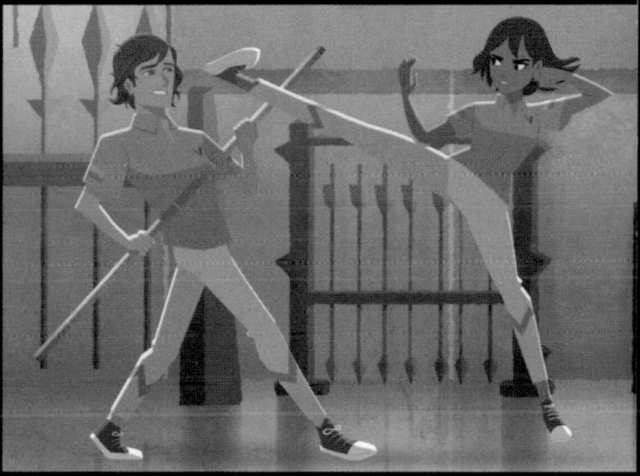

But I knew I had to get out after discovering what VILE really stands for: Villains' International League of Evil!

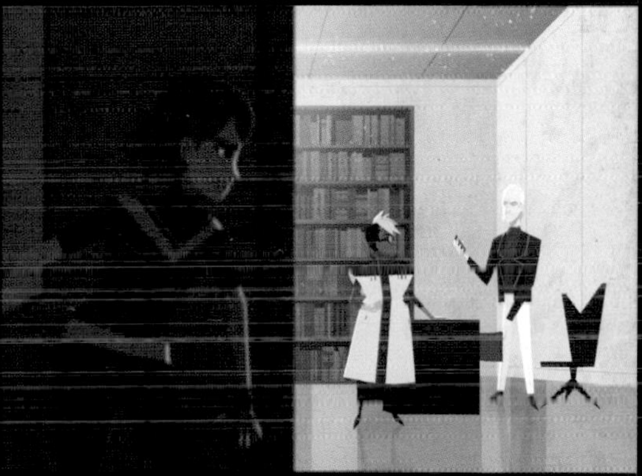

My new mission: take VILE down by stealing from them to give back to their victims.

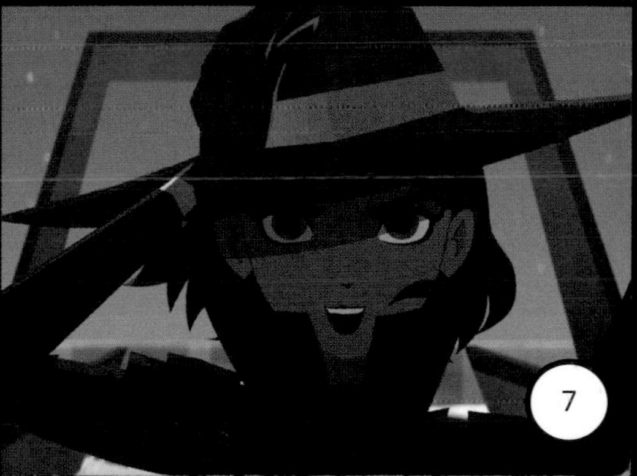

CARMEN'S SKILLS

Super sneak, expert fighter, gadget guru, mistress of disguise

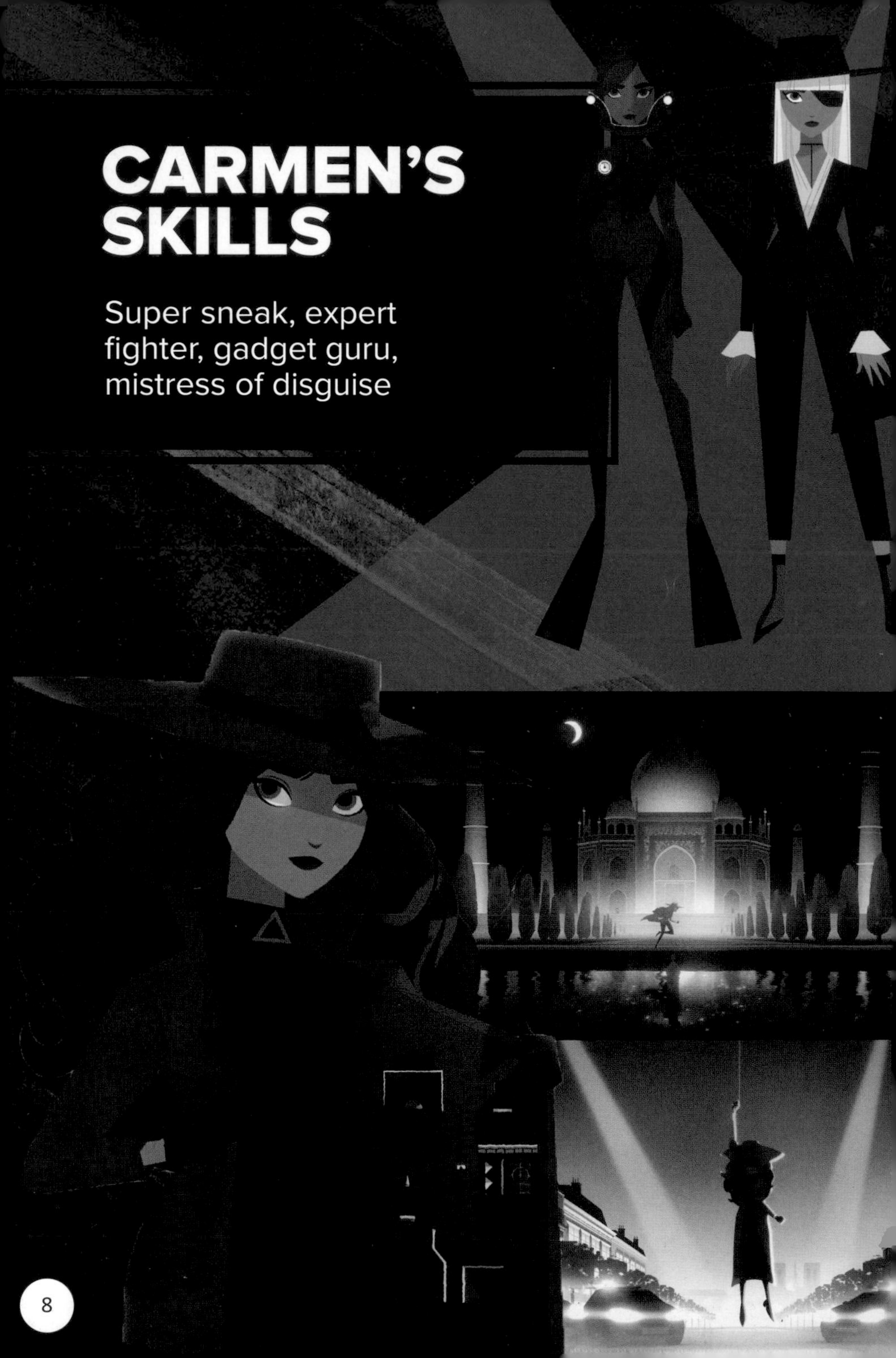

TOOLS FOR A THIEF

Glider Backpack

A collapsible hang glider ready to spring open whenever Carmen needs to make a dramatic entrance or quick escape.

Red Drone

This remote-control flying drone can send a live video feed and can even hack into security systems.

TOOLS FOR A THIEF

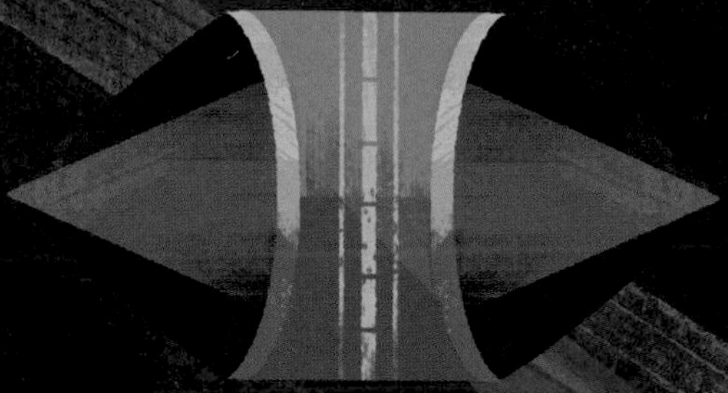

Earring -- Side View   Earring -- Front View

Comm-Link Earrings

Carmen's earrings hide an advanced two-way communications device, which she uses to stay in touch with Player through every mission.

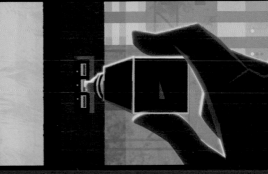

High-Tech Makeup

This lipstick can be used to hack into security systems.

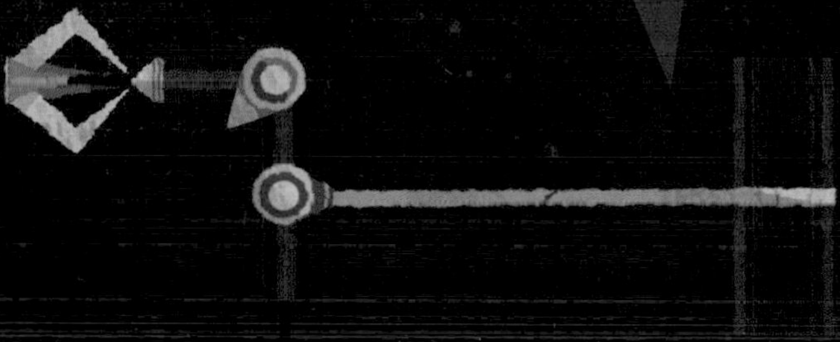

Grappling Hook

A hook on a rope that Carmen shoots from her wrist to reach high places.

CARMEN'S CREW

Player

White-hat hacker

BACKGROUND:

Player is a teenager from Niagara Falls, Canada. He met Carmen by hacking into her phone while she was still at VILE.

SKILLS:

- Learns everything about every place that Carmen goes to help guide her on capers
- Remotely deactivates security systems
- Scours the web for secret signs, coded messages, and hidden clues about VILE's next moves

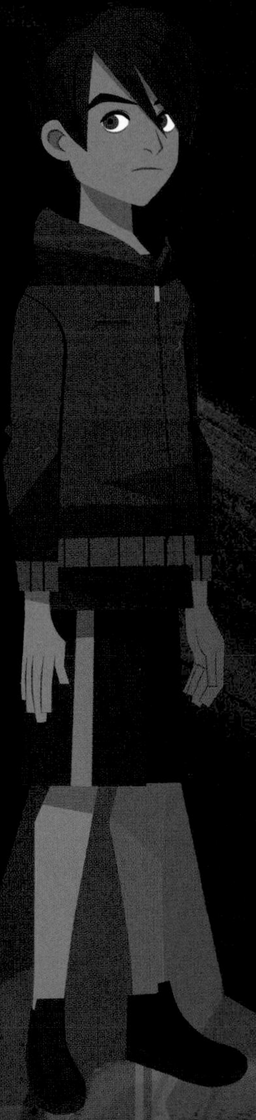

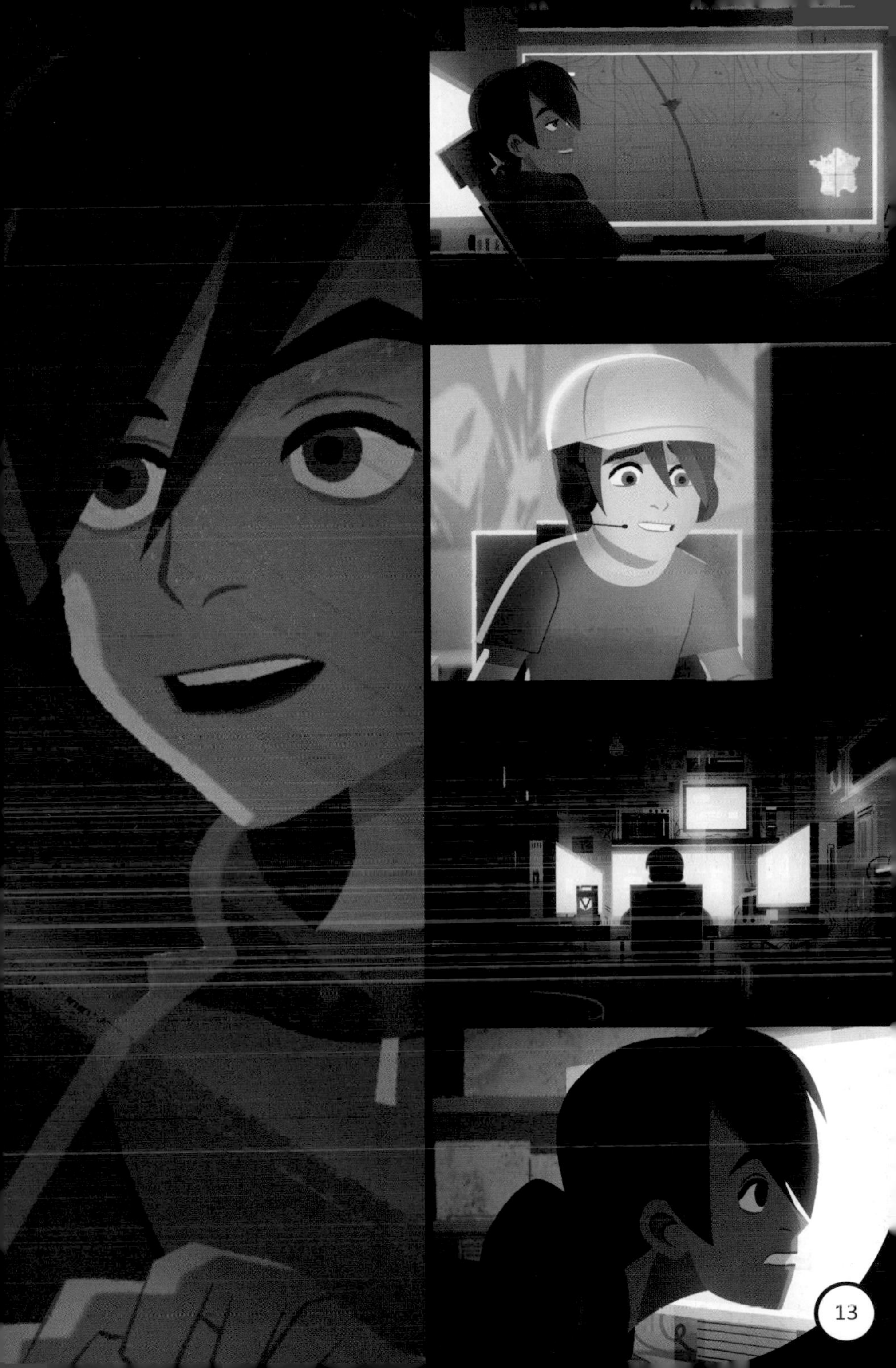

Ivy

Mechanic and tinkerer

SKILLS:

- Operates Carmen's gadgets, like Red Drone
- Great at fixing and making things
- Always has Carmen's back

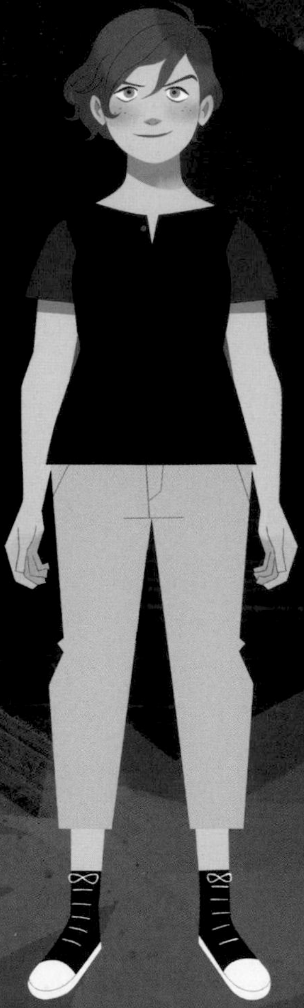

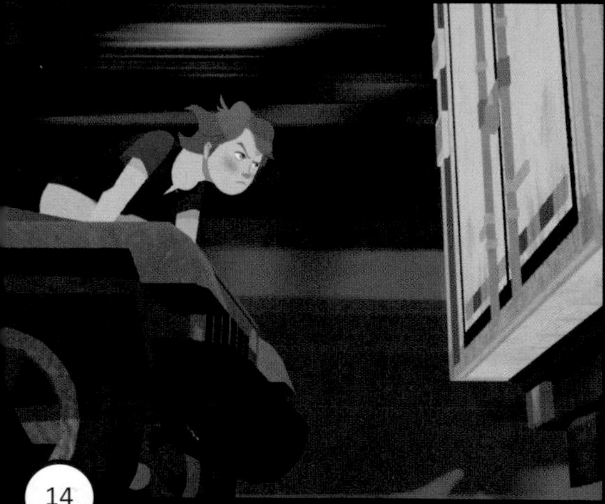

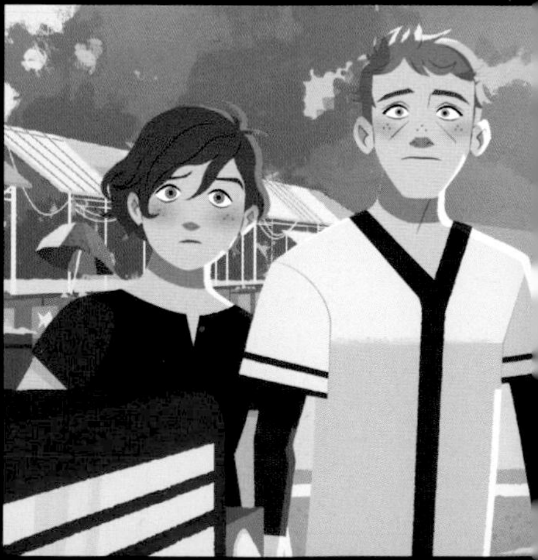

Zack

Driver

SKILLS:

- Great with cars, trucks, motorcycles, speedboats -- anything that goes fast
- Knows how to make a quick getaway
- Always hungry and eats almost anything...except for fish. BLECH!

BACKGROUND:

Ivy and Zack are street-kid siblings from Boston, Massachusetts, USA. They met Carmen when they were robbing the same donut shop, which was owned by VILE.

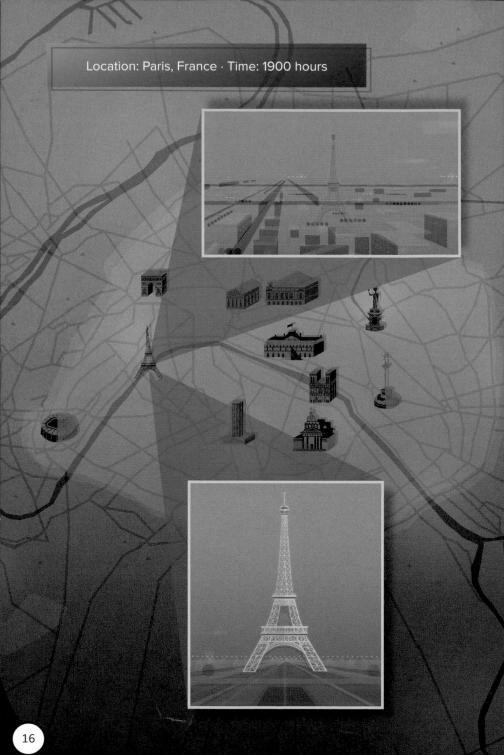

Location: Paris, France · Time: 1900 hours

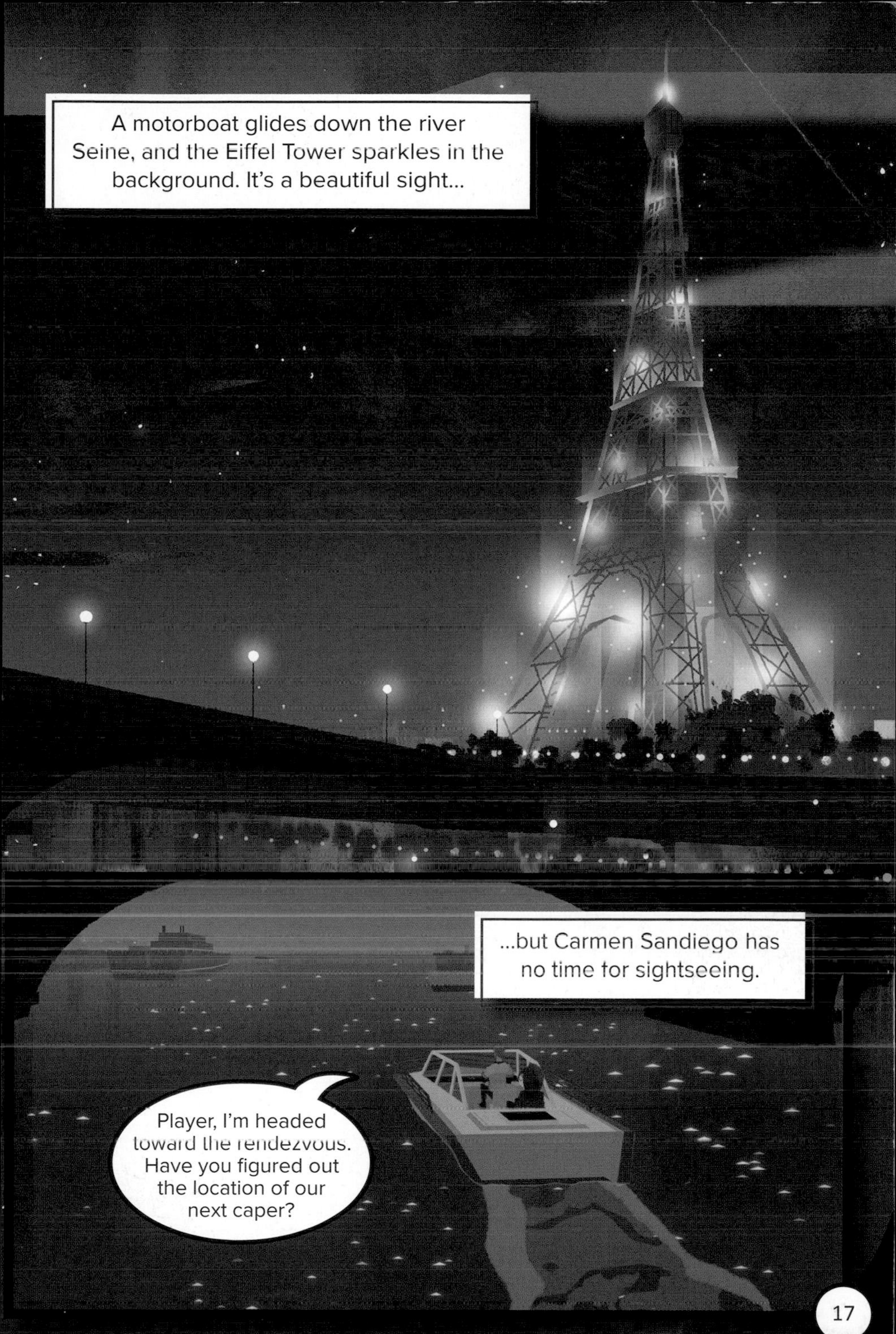
A motorboat glides down the river Seine, and the Eiffel Tower sparkles in the background. It's a beautiful sight...
...but Carmen Sandiego has no time for sightseeing.
Player, I'm headed toward the rendezvous. Have you figured out the location of our next caper?

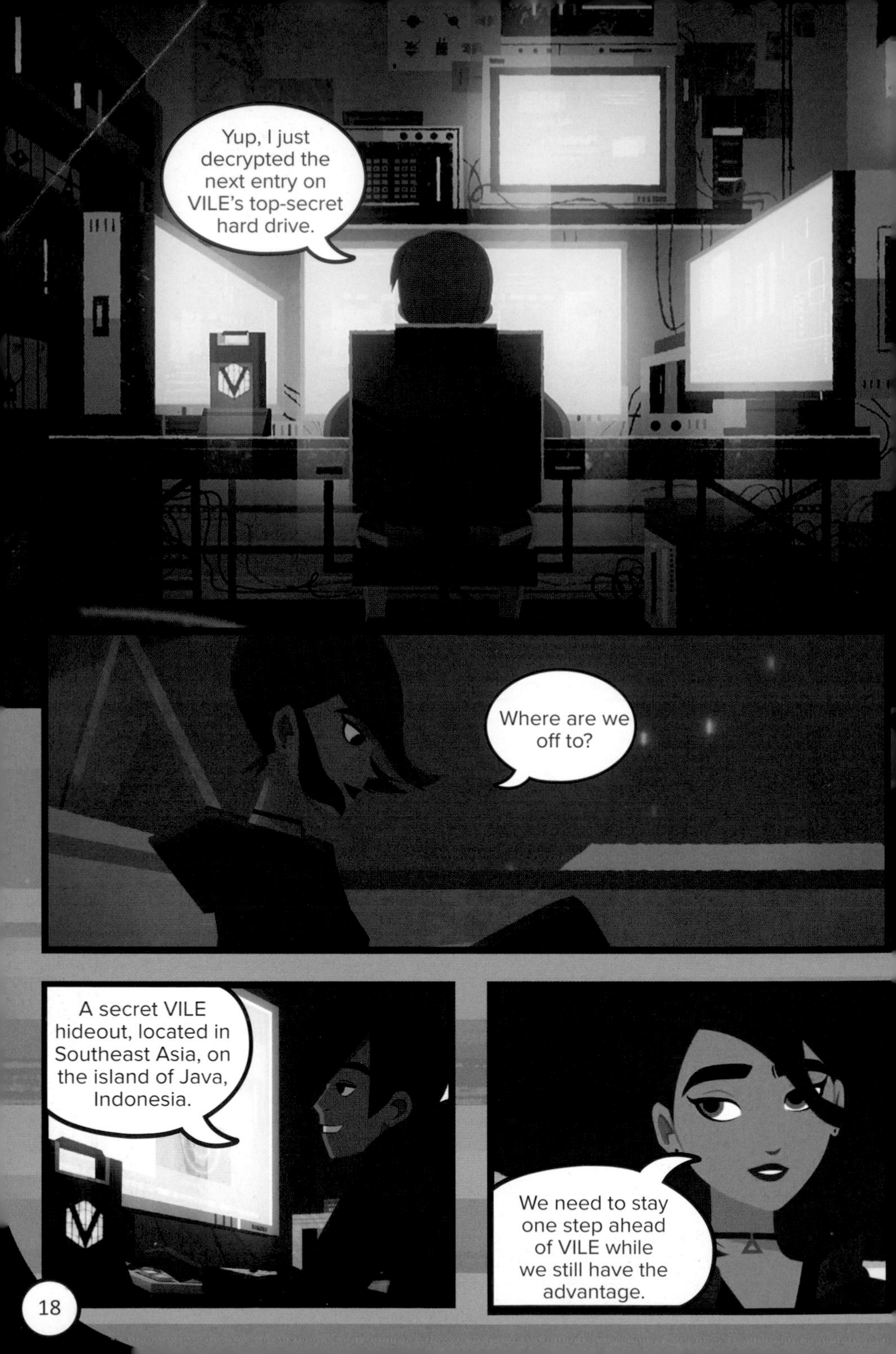
Yup, I just decrypted the next entry on VILE's top-secret hard drive.
Where are we off to?
A secret VILE hideout, located in Southeast Asia, on the island of Java, Indonesia.
We need to stay one step ahead of VILE while we still have the advantage.

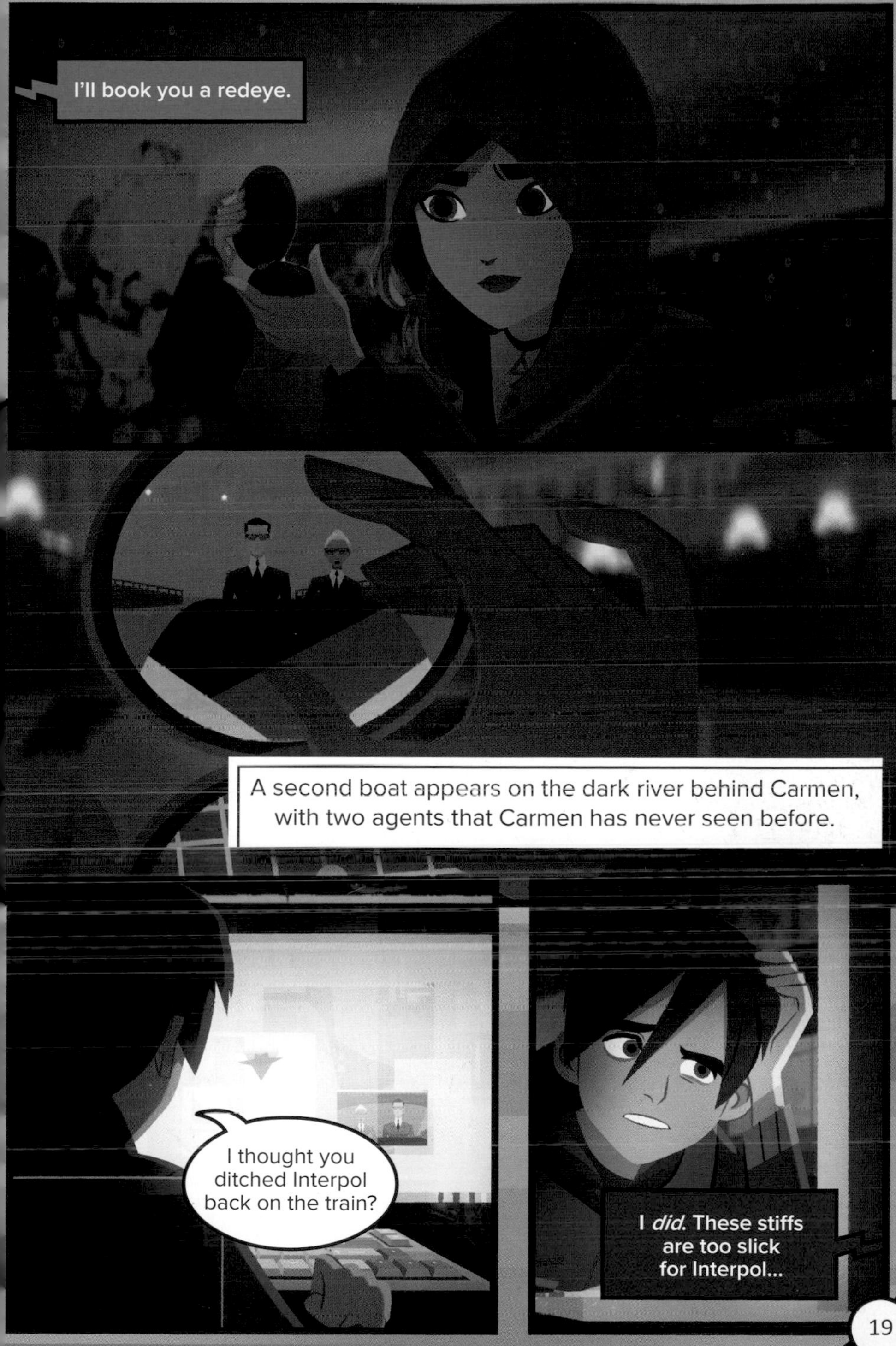
I'll book you a redeye.
A second boat appears on the dark river behind Carmen, with two agents that Carmen has never seen before.
I thought you ditched Interpol back on the train?
I *did.* These stiffs are too slick for Interpol...

...but not sleazy enough for VILE.
Zack! Can you shake the tail?!
I can shake it all night long.

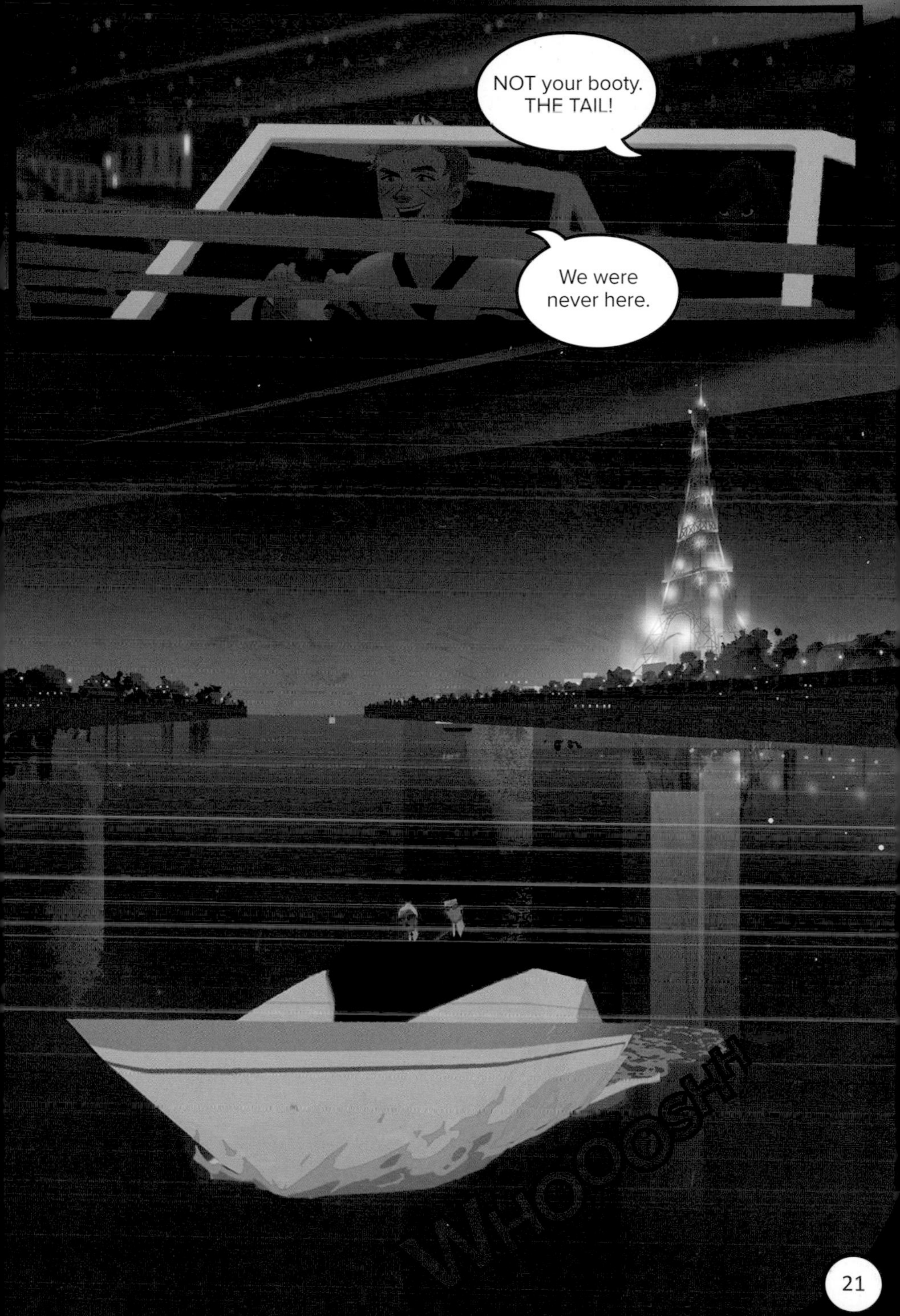
NOT your booty.
THE TAIL!
We were
never here.
WHOOOOSHH

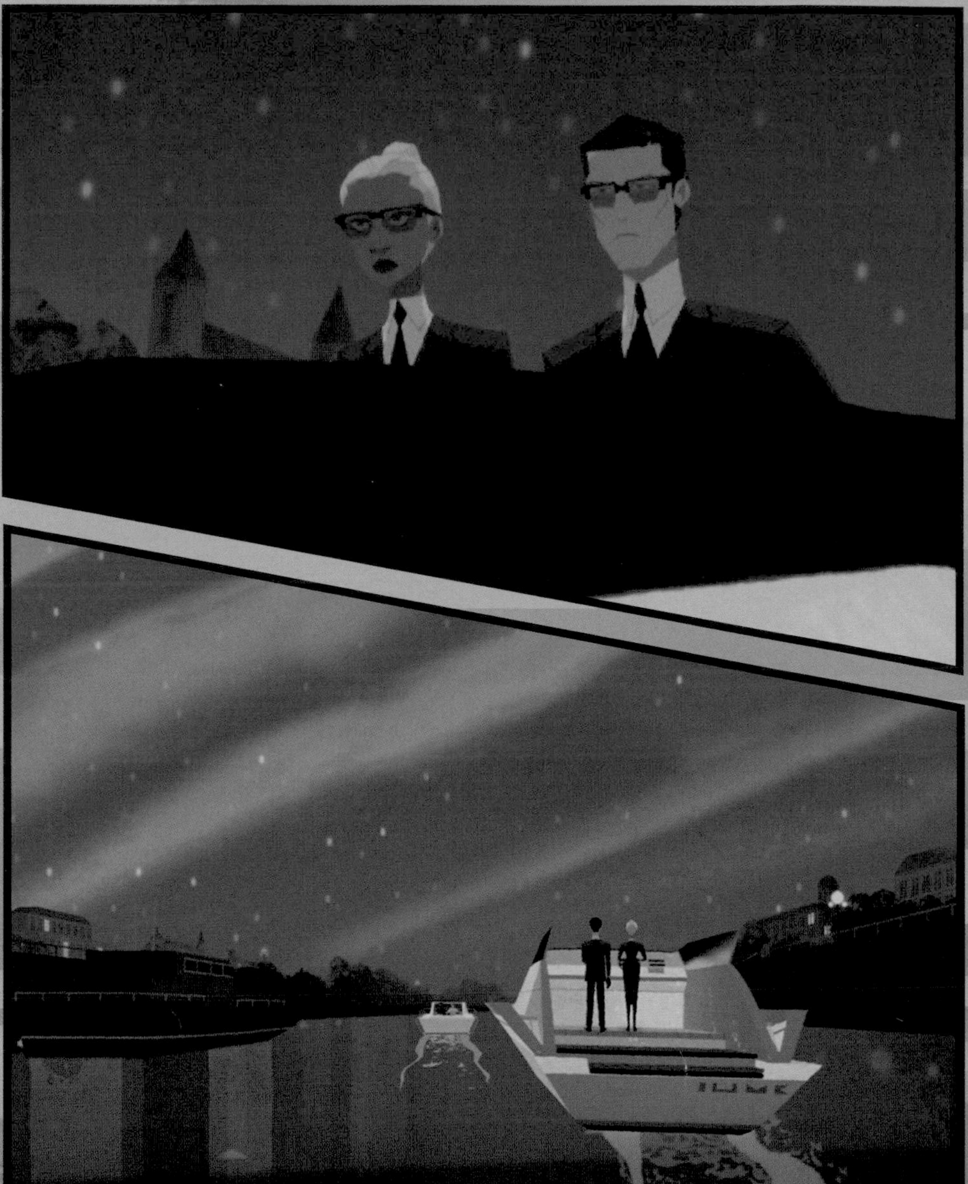

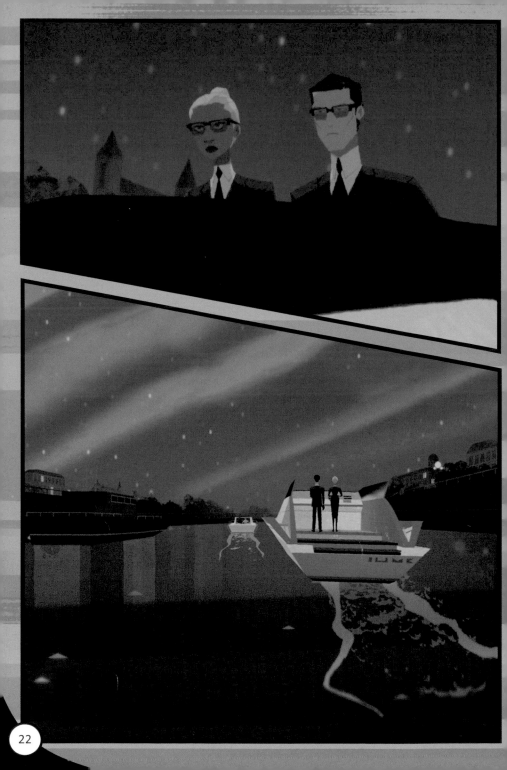

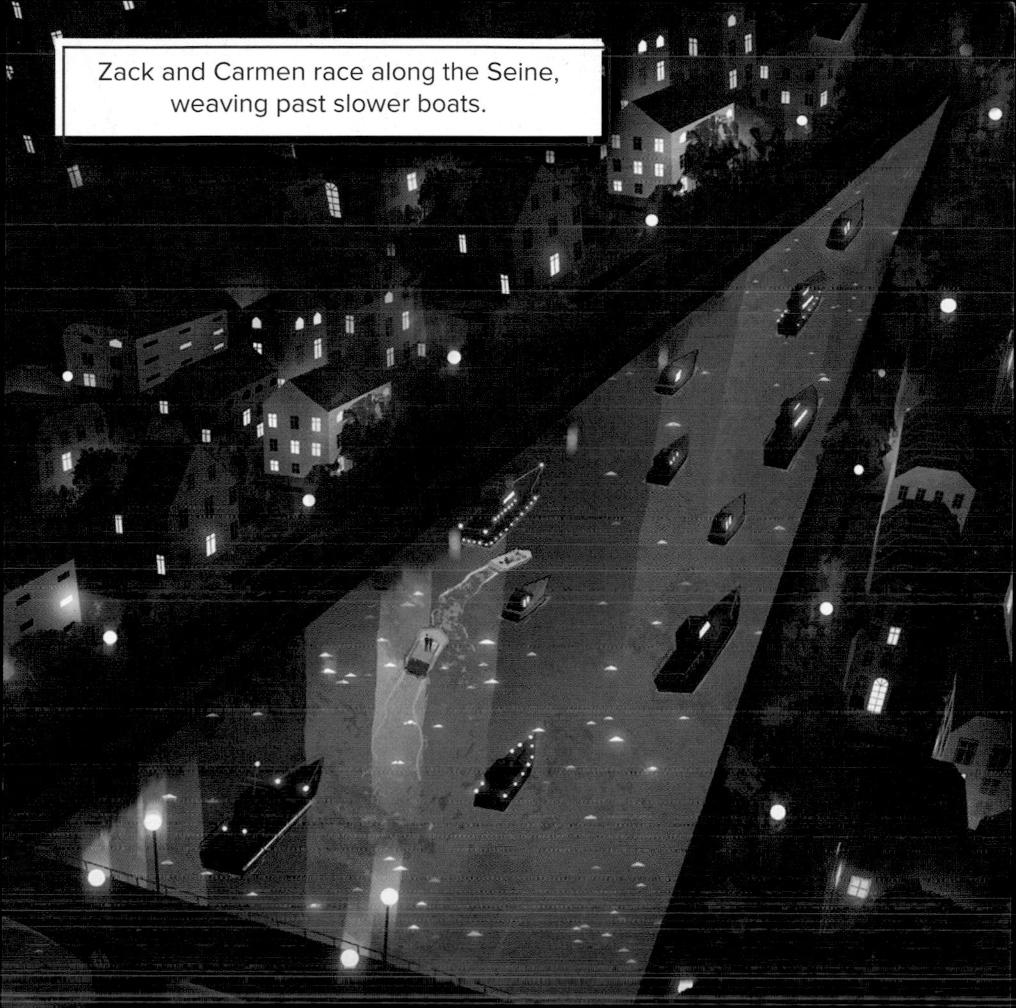
Zack and Carmen race along the Seine, weaving past slower boats.

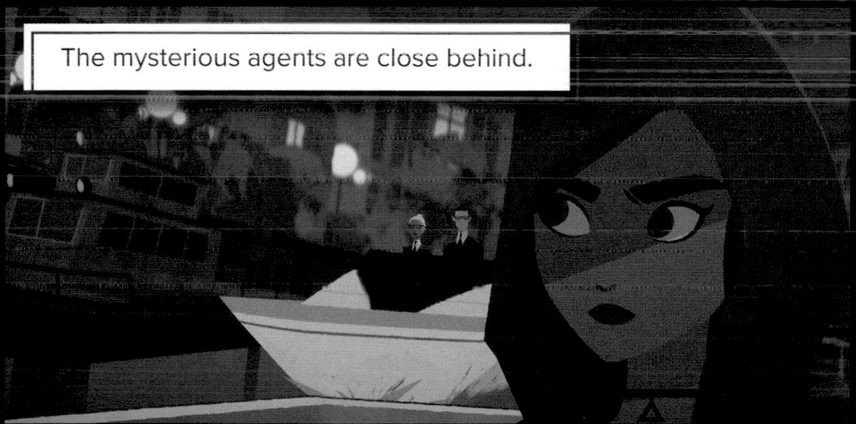
The mysterious agents are close behind.

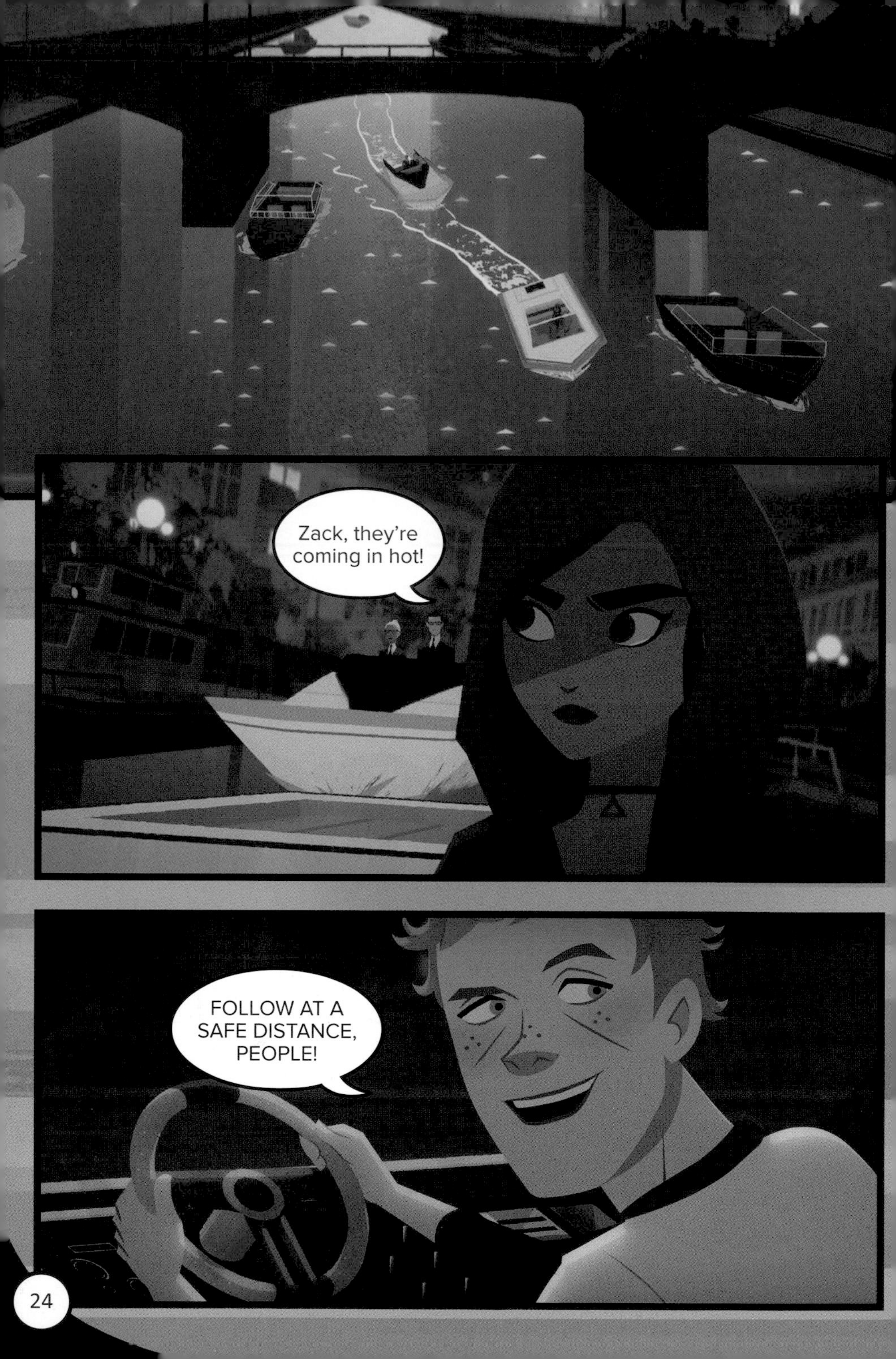
Zack, they're coming in hot!
FOLLOW AT A SAFE DISTANCE, PEOPLE!

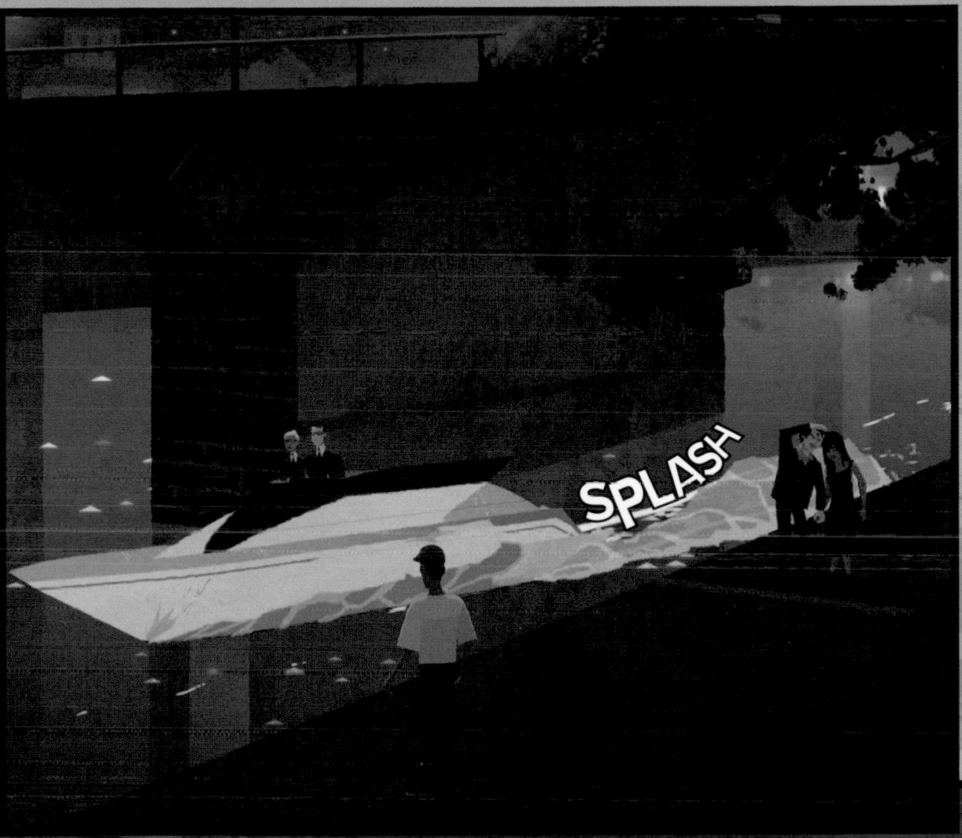
SPLASH

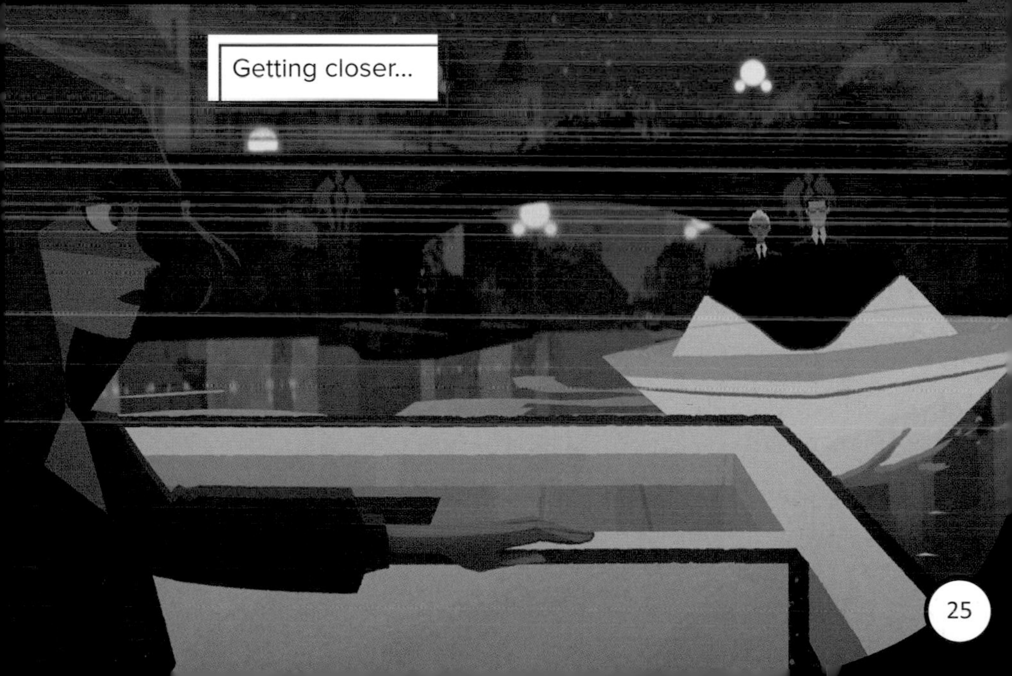
Getting closer...

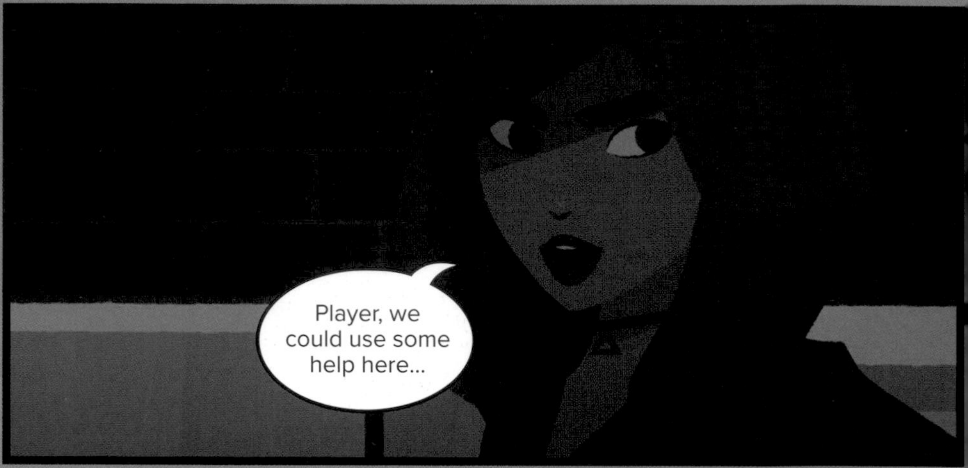
Player, we could use some help here...

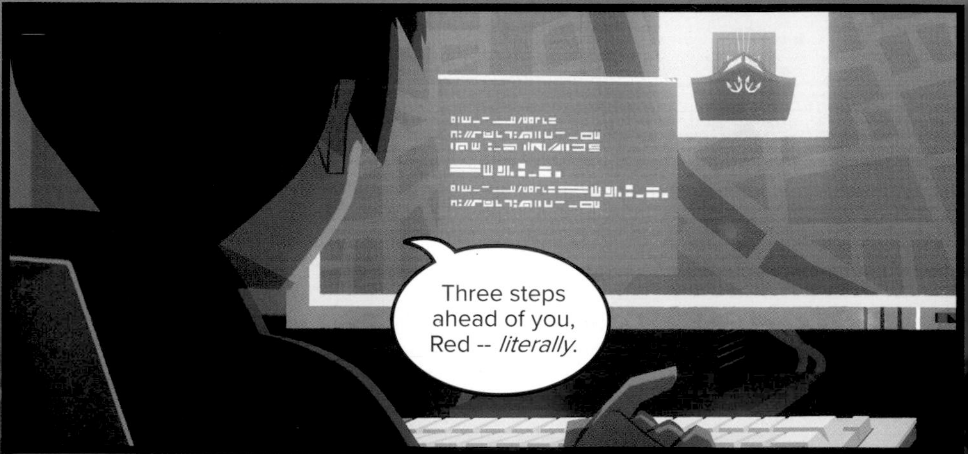
Three steps ahead of you, Red -- *literally*.

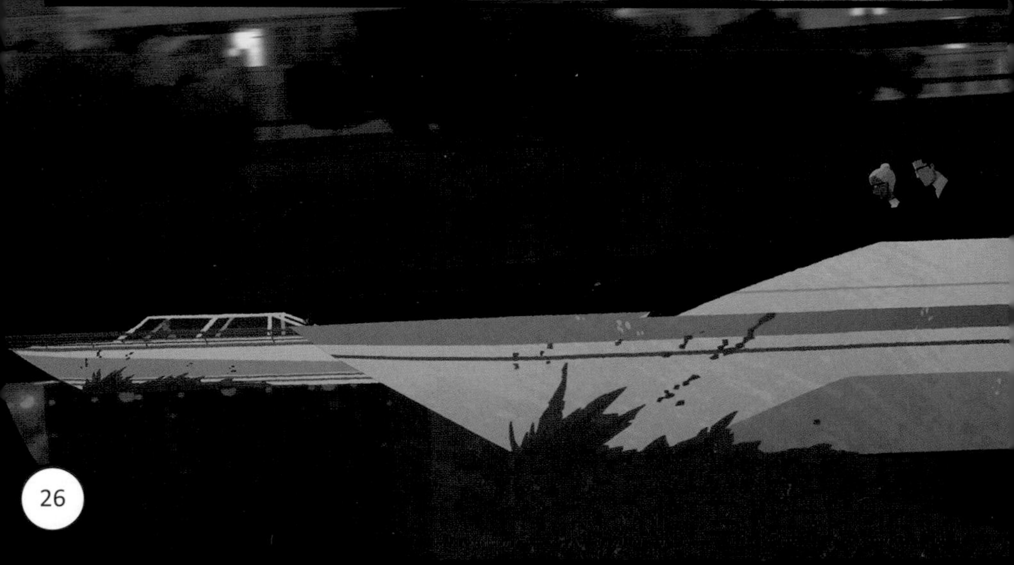

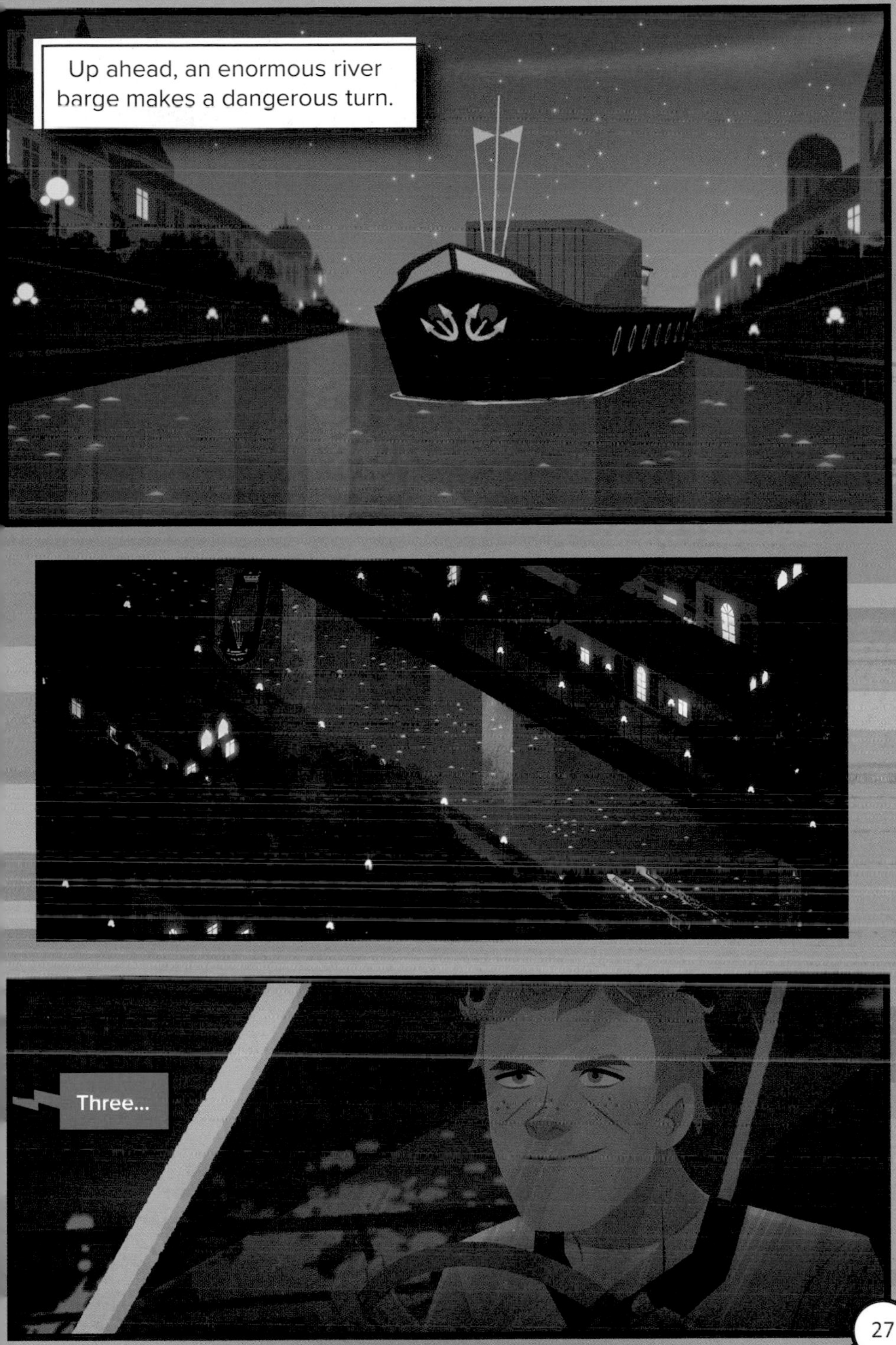
Up ahead, an enormous river barge makes a dangerous turn.
Three...

In a few seconds, the barge will block the whole channel! The two motorboats race toward a collision.

Two...

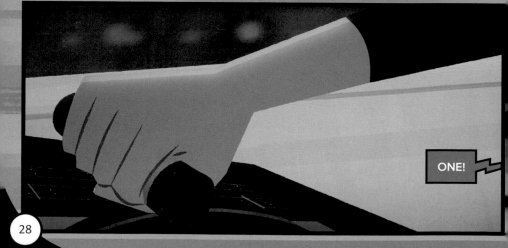

ONE!

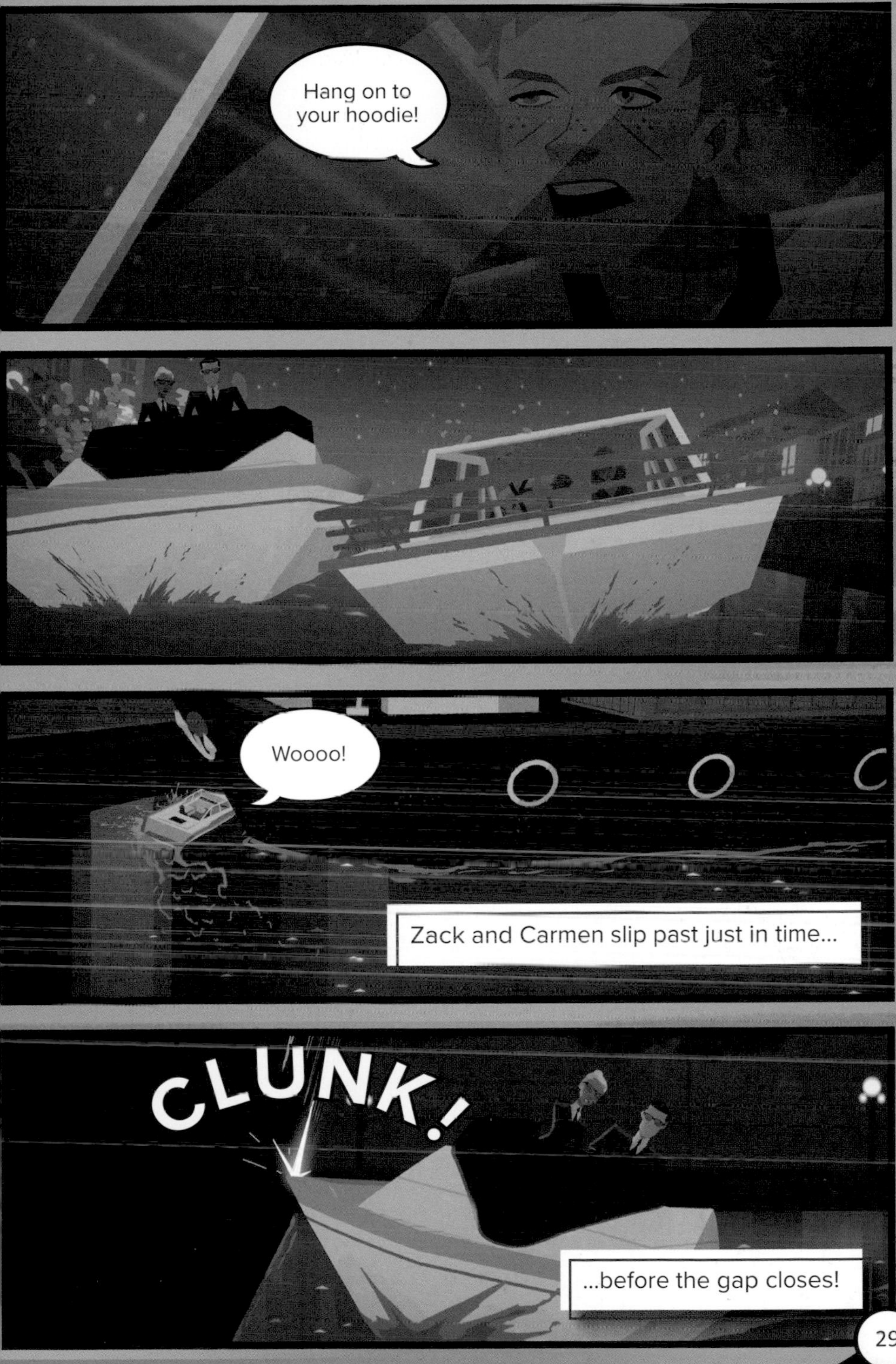
Hang on to your hoodie!
Woooo!
Zack and Carmen slip past just in time...
CLUNK!
...before the gap closes!

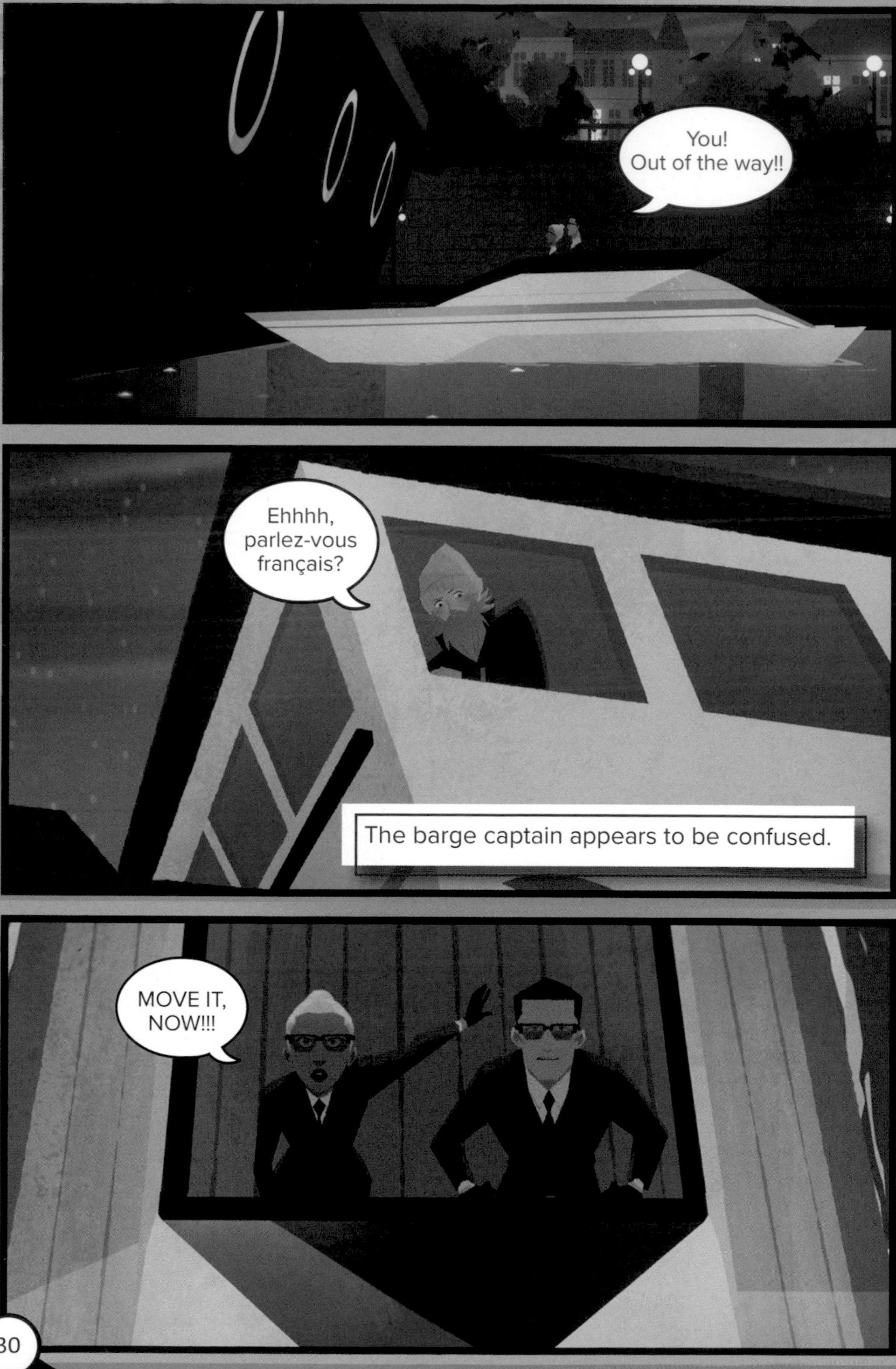
You! Out of the way!!
Ehhhh, parlez-vous français?
The barge captain appears to be confused.
MOVE IT, NOW!!!

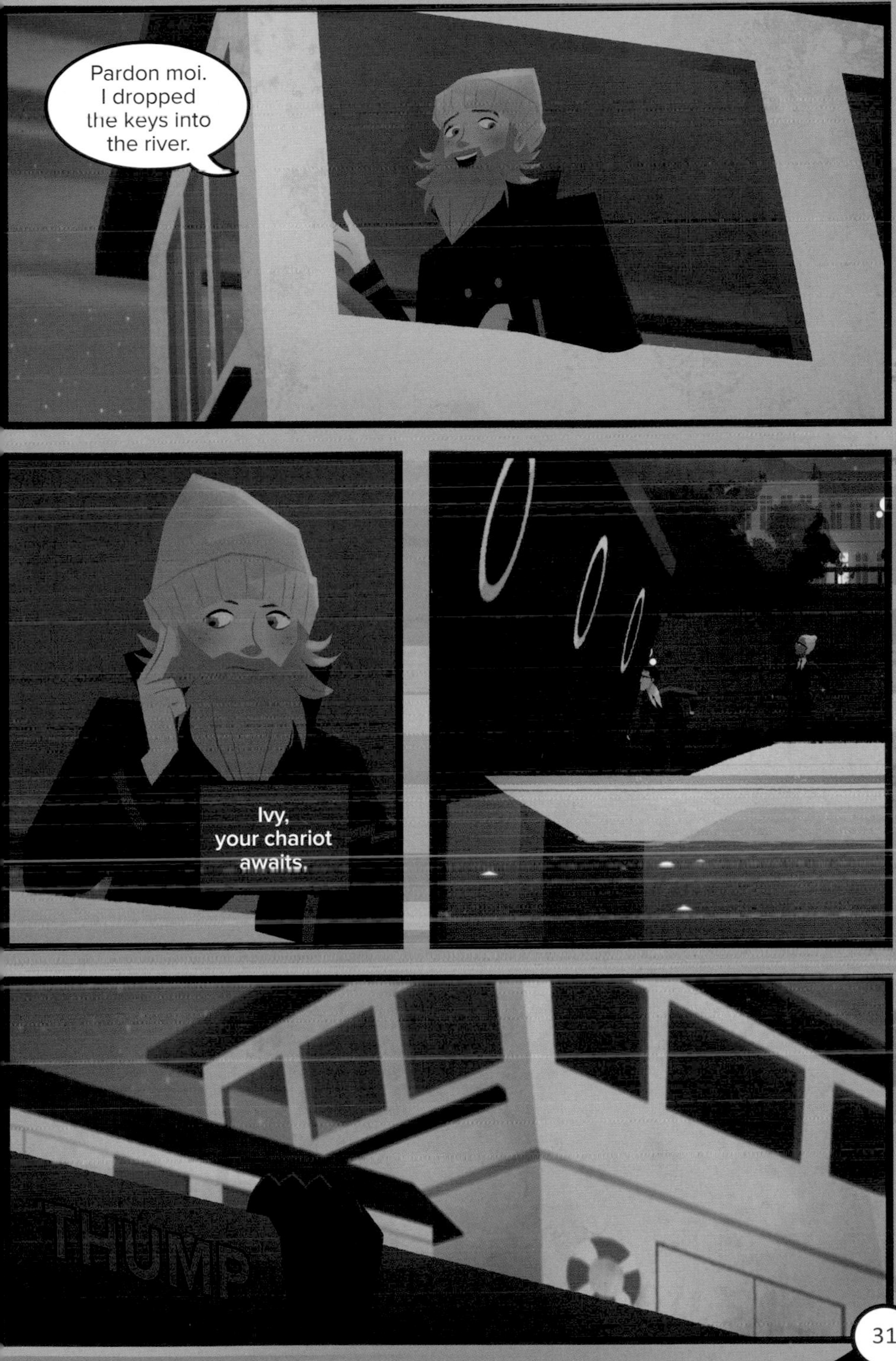
Pardon moi. I dropped the keys into the river.
Ivy, your chariot awaits.
THUMP

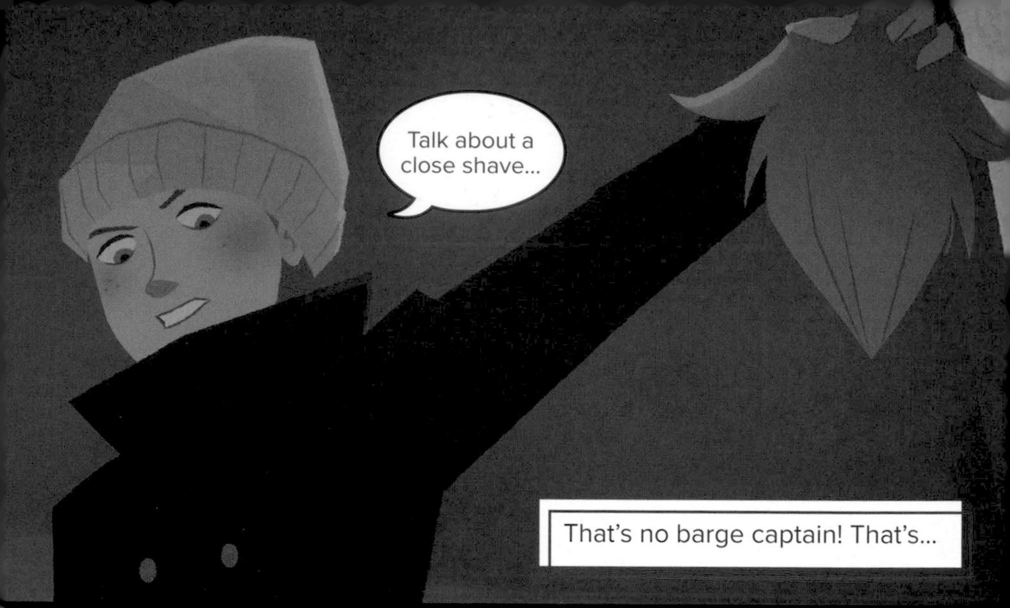
Talk about a close shave...
That's no barge captain! That's...

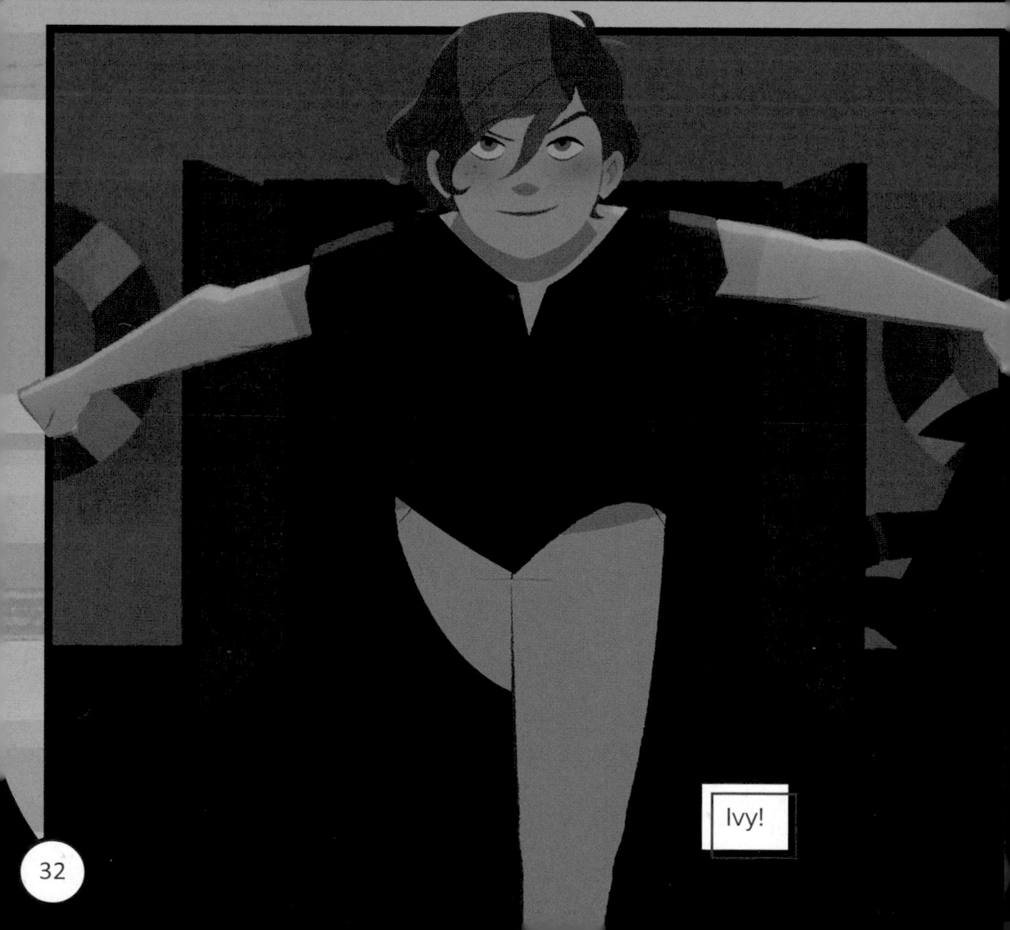
Ivy!

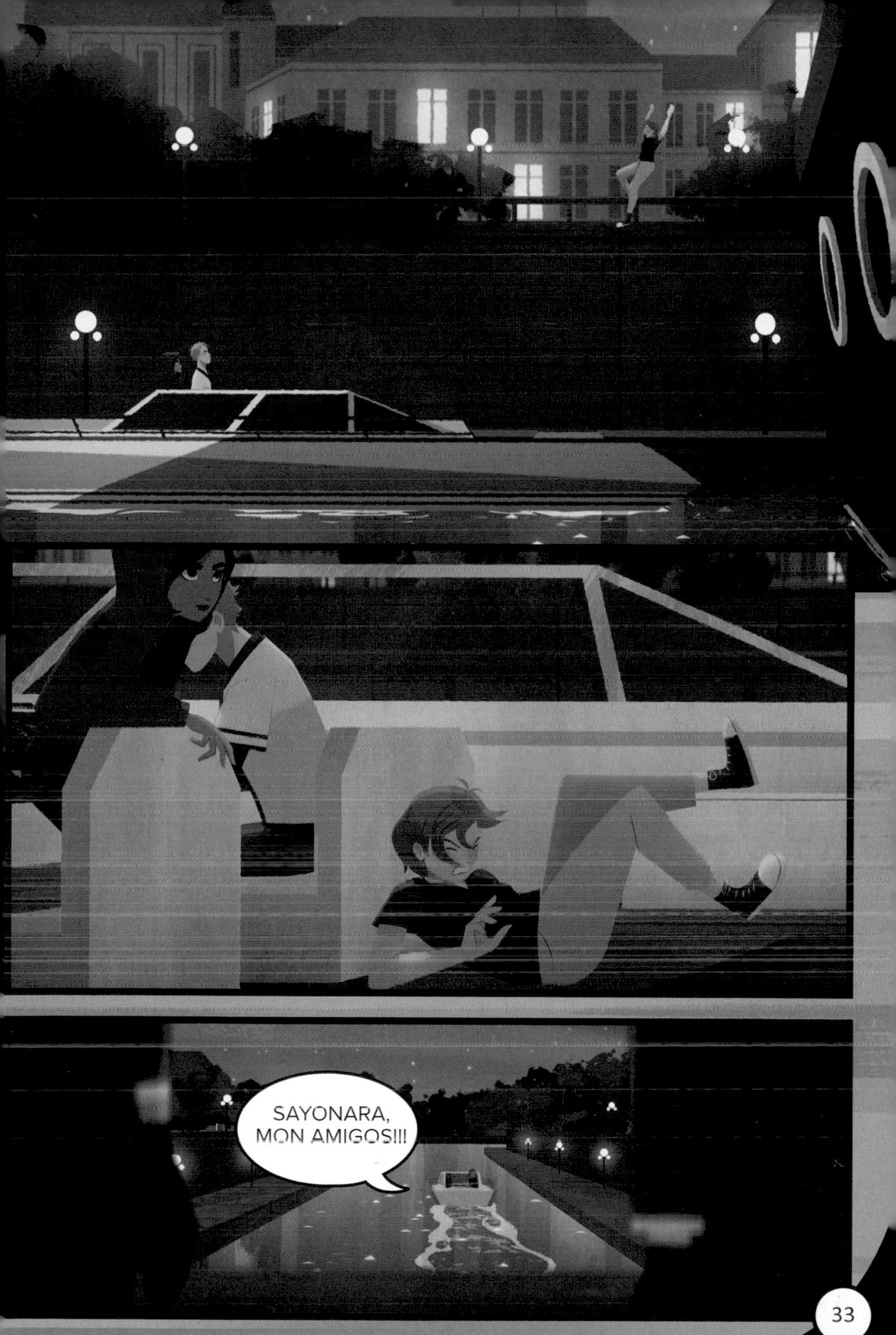
SAYONARA,
MON AMIGOS!!!

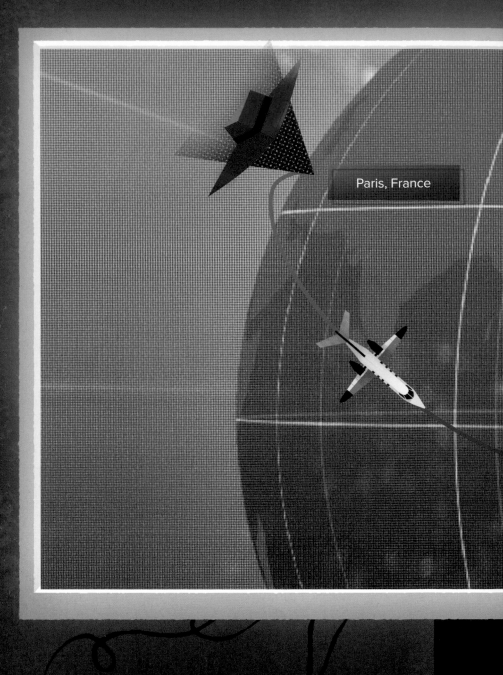

Paris, France

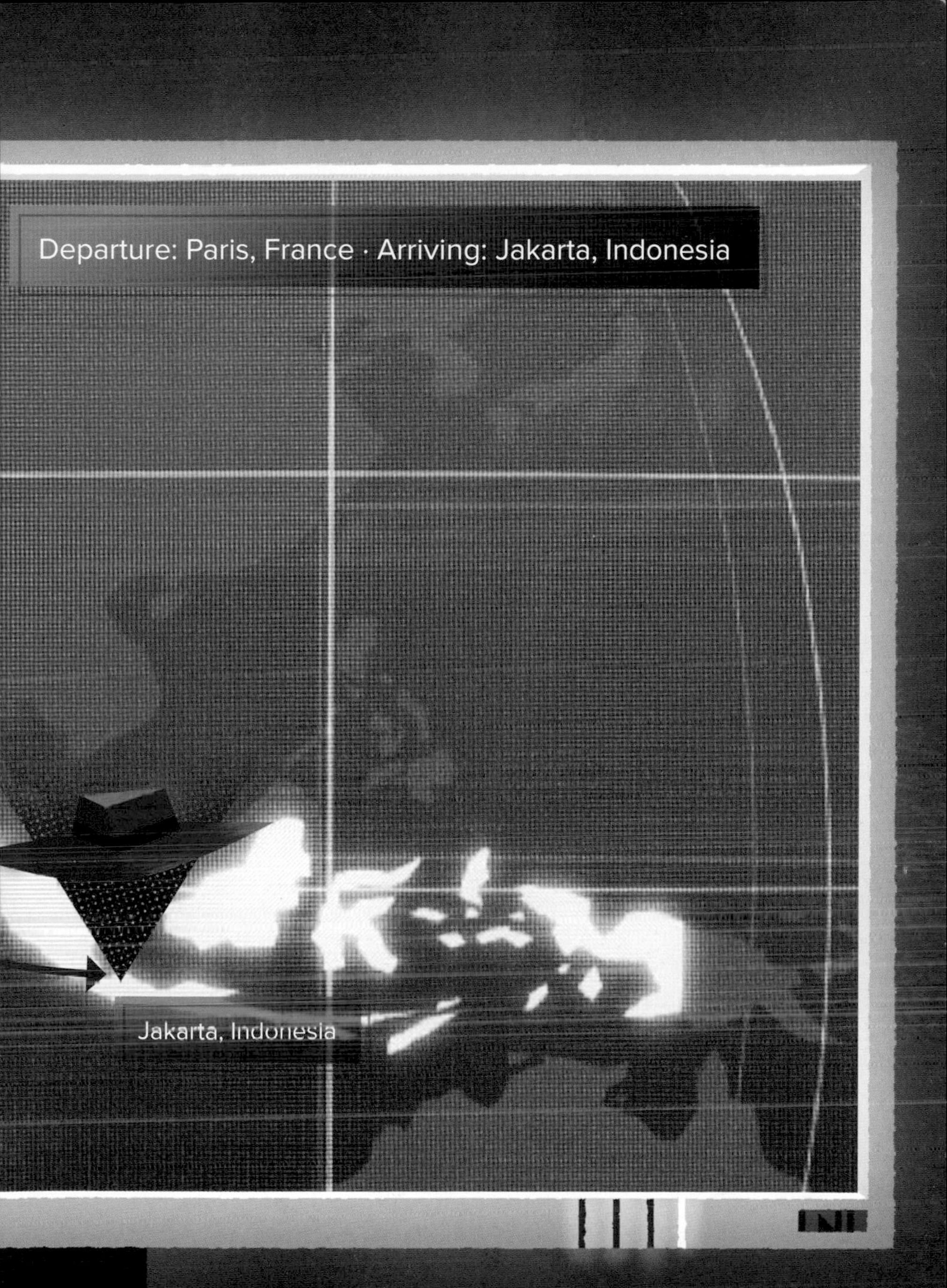
Departure: Paris, France · Arriving: Jakarta, Indonesia
Jakarta, Indonesia

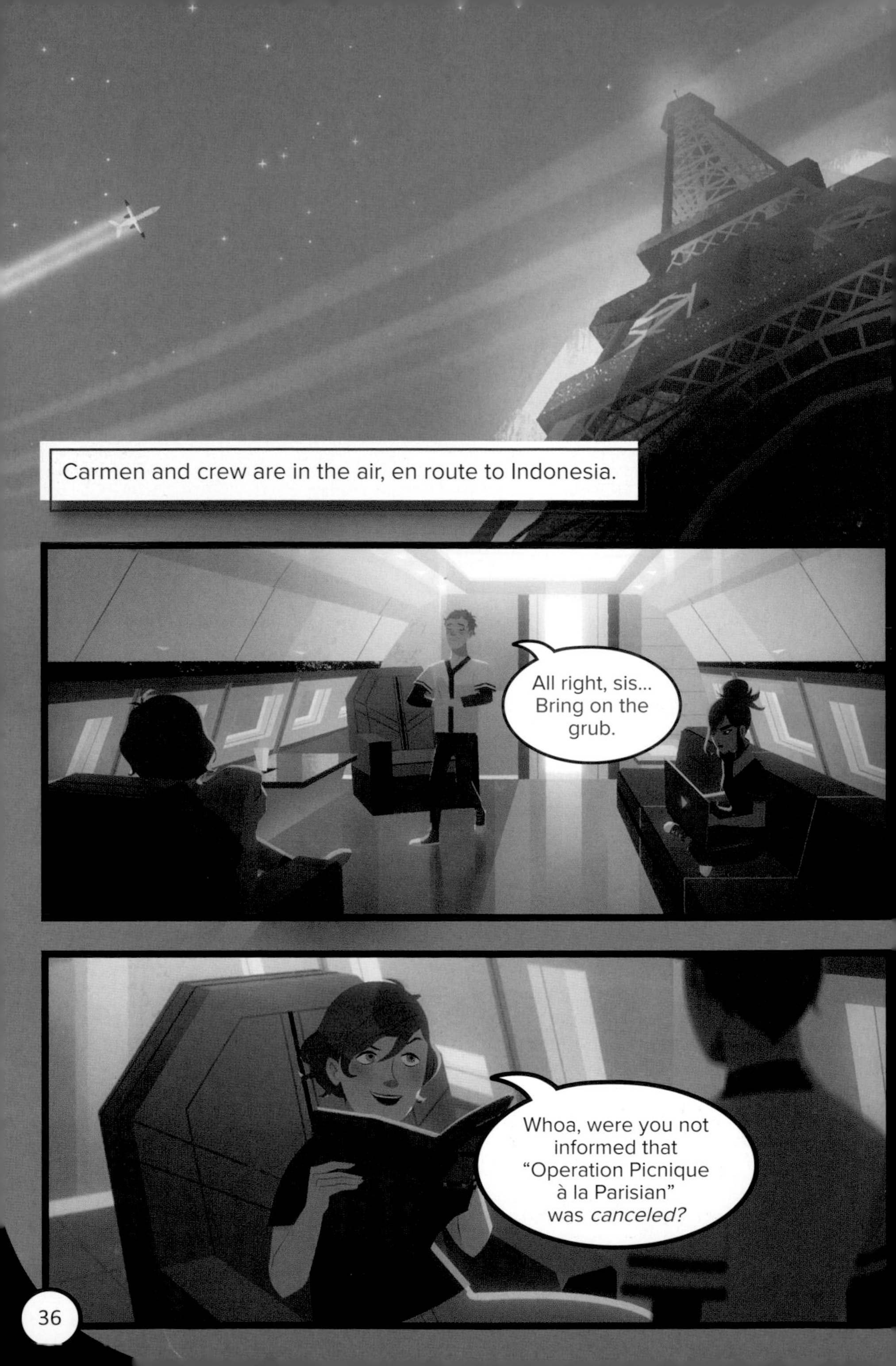
Carmen and crew are in the air, en route to Indonesia.
All right, sis... Bring on the grub.
Whoa, were you not informed that "Operation Picnique à la Parisian" was *canceled?*

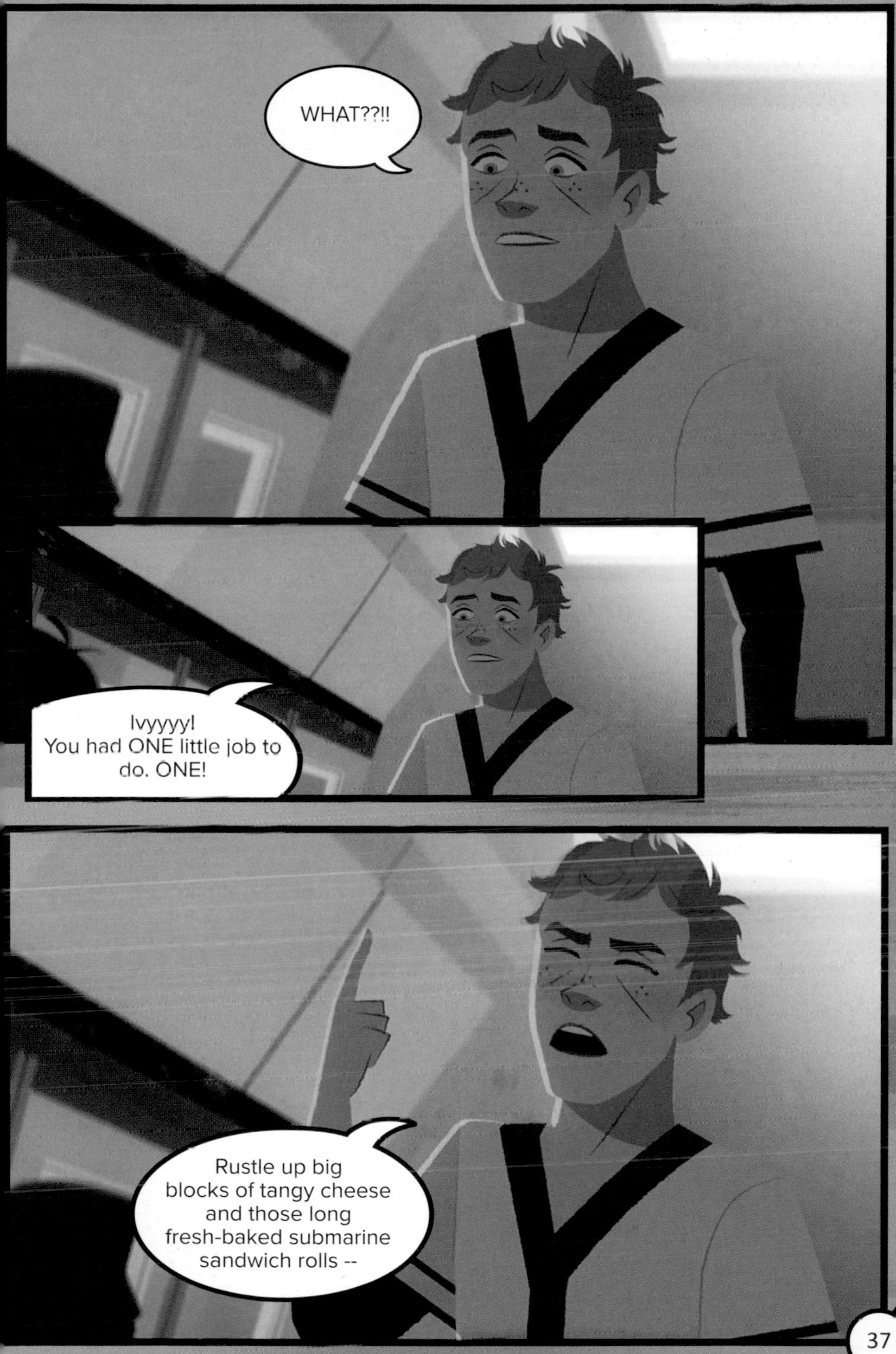
WHAT??!!
Ivyyyy! You had ONE little job to do. ONE!
Rustle up big blocks of tangy cheese and those long fresh-baked submarine sandwich rolls --

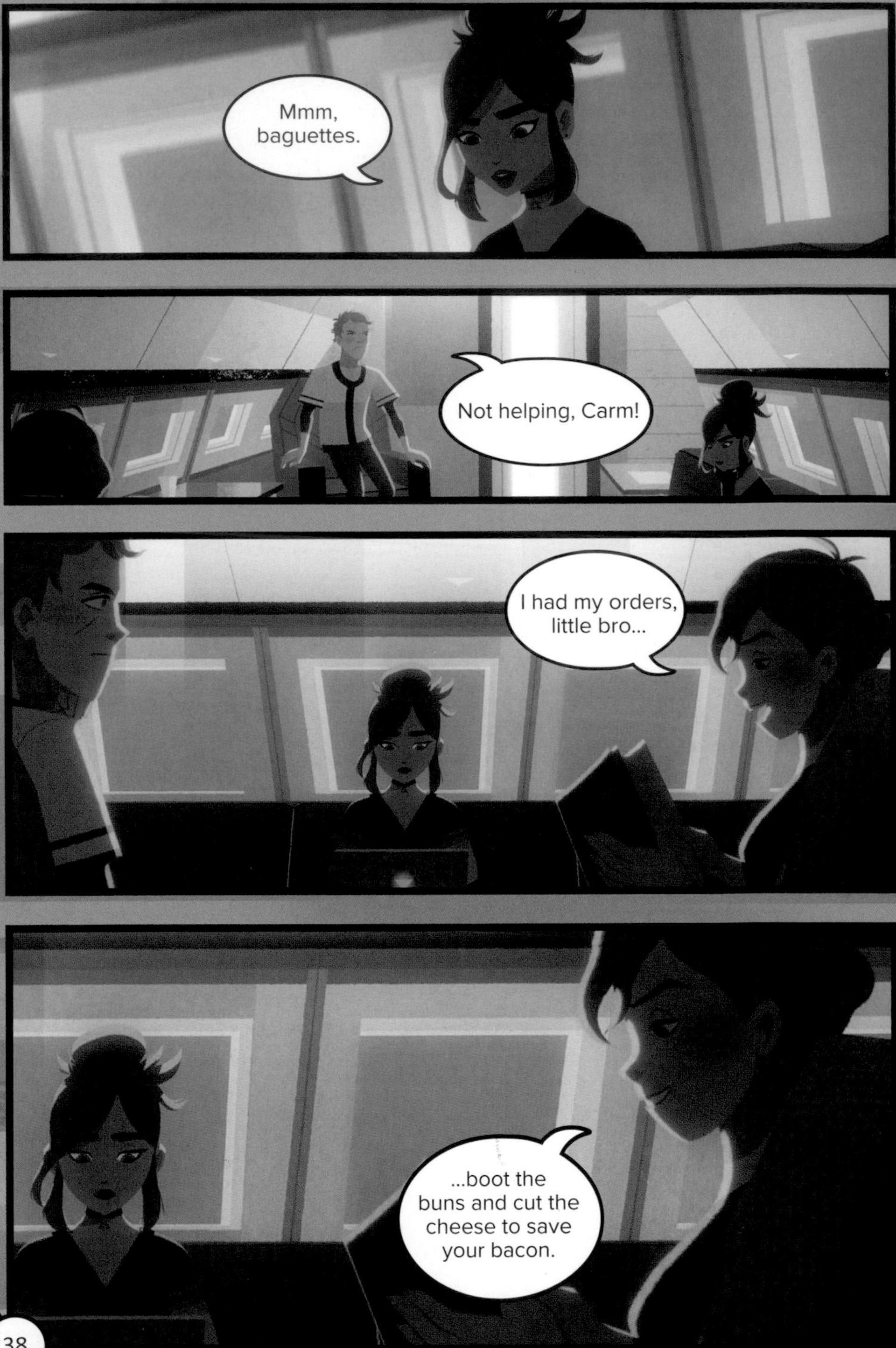
Mmm, baguettes.
Not helping, Carm!
I had my orders, little bro...
...boot the buns and cut the cheese to save your bacon.

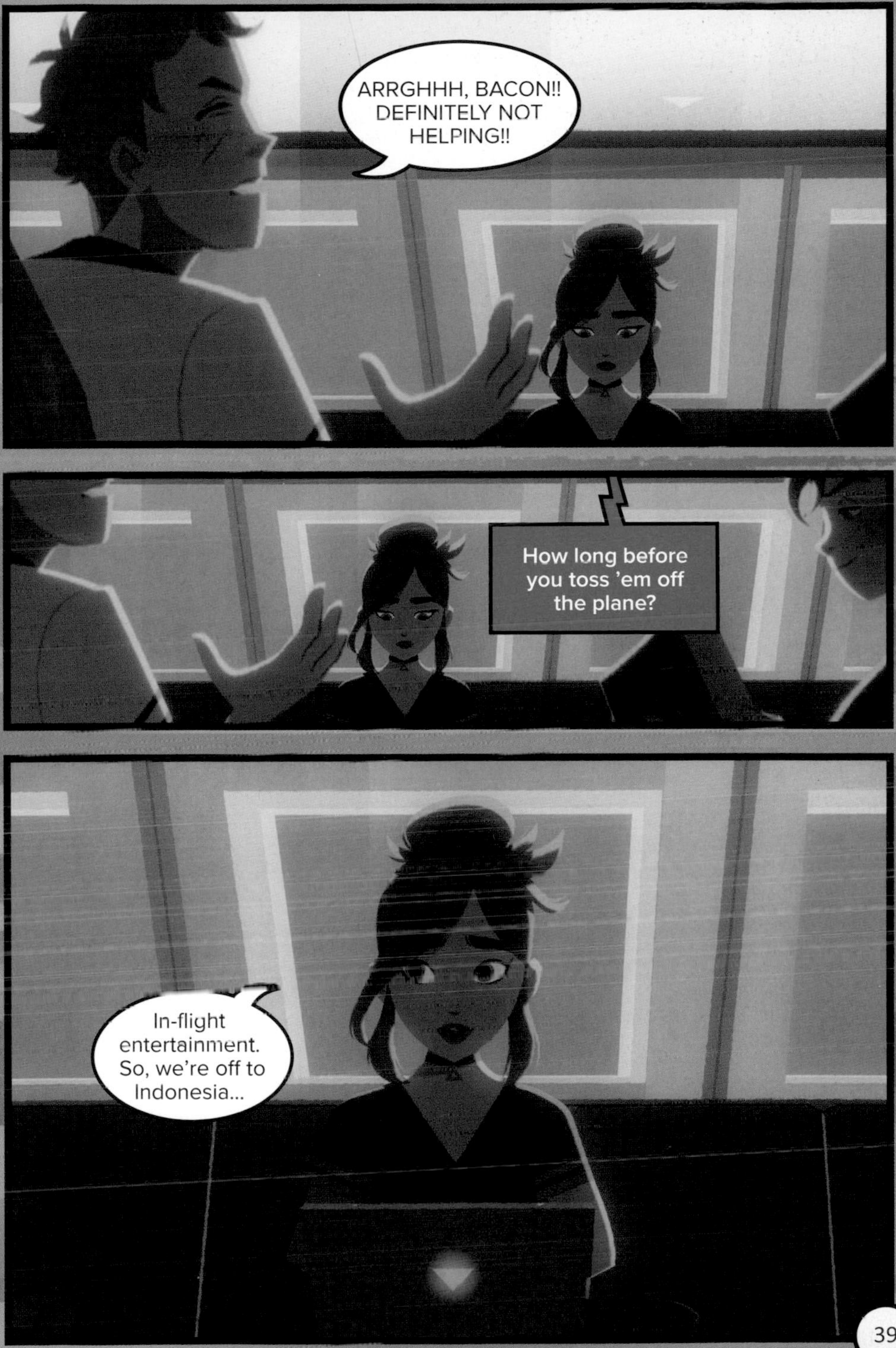
ARRGHHH, BACON!! DEFINITELY NOT HELPING!!
How long before you toss 'em off the plane?
In-flight entertainment. So, we're off to Indonesia...

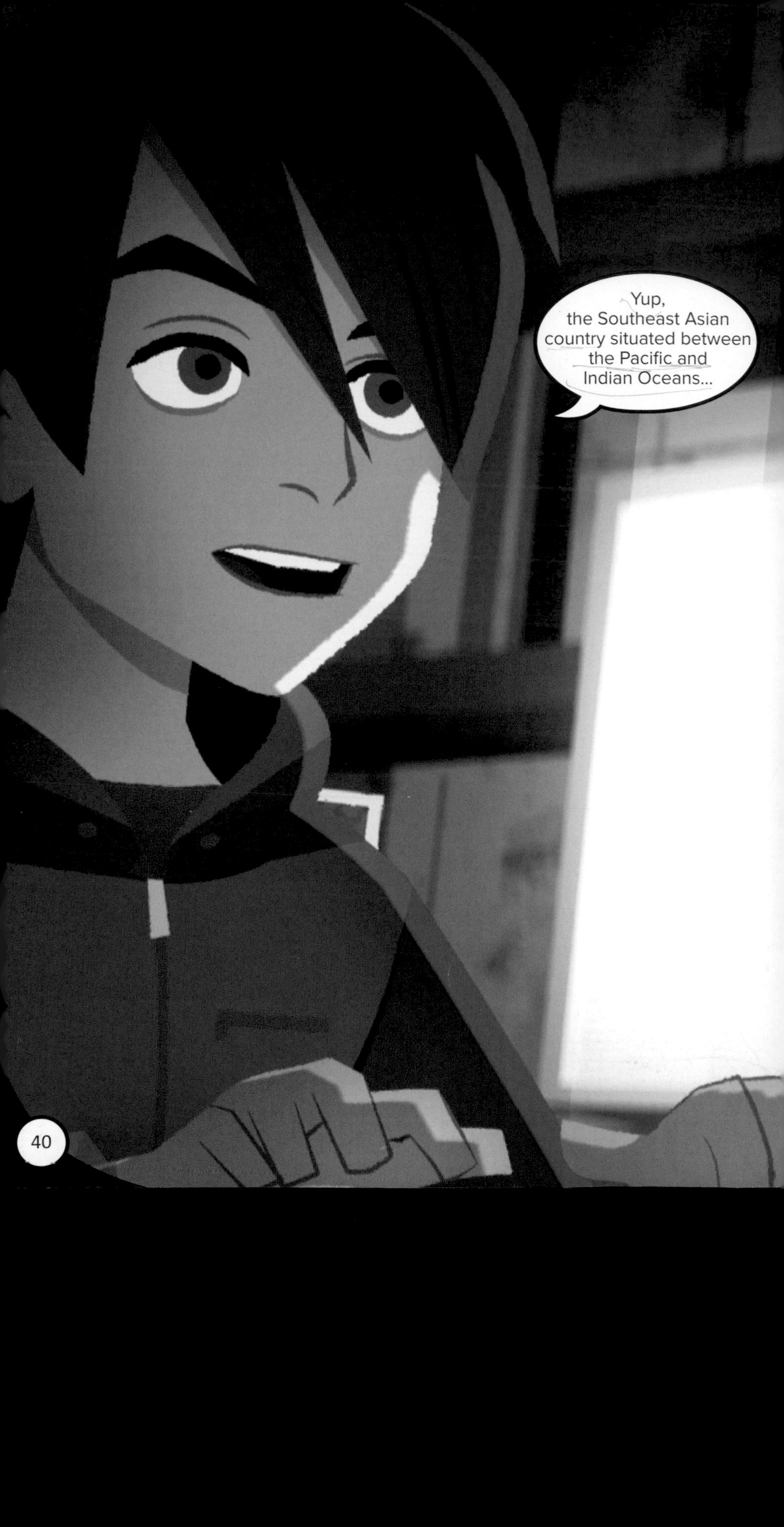
Yup, the Southeast Asian country situated between the Pacific and Indian Oceans...

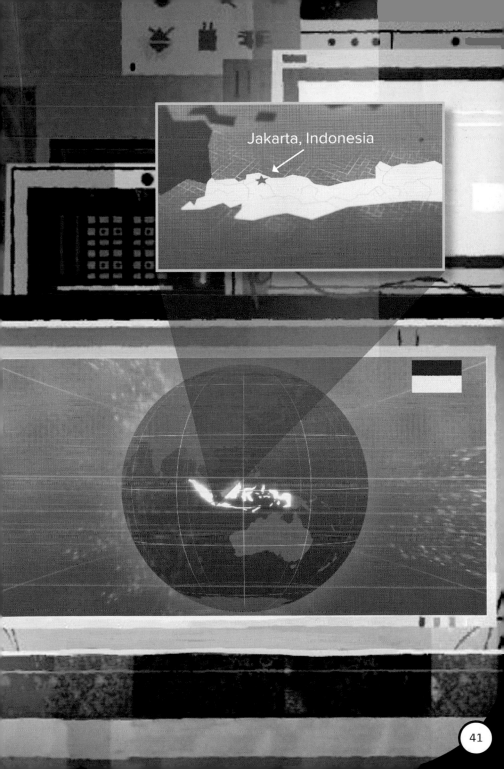

Jakarta, Indonesia

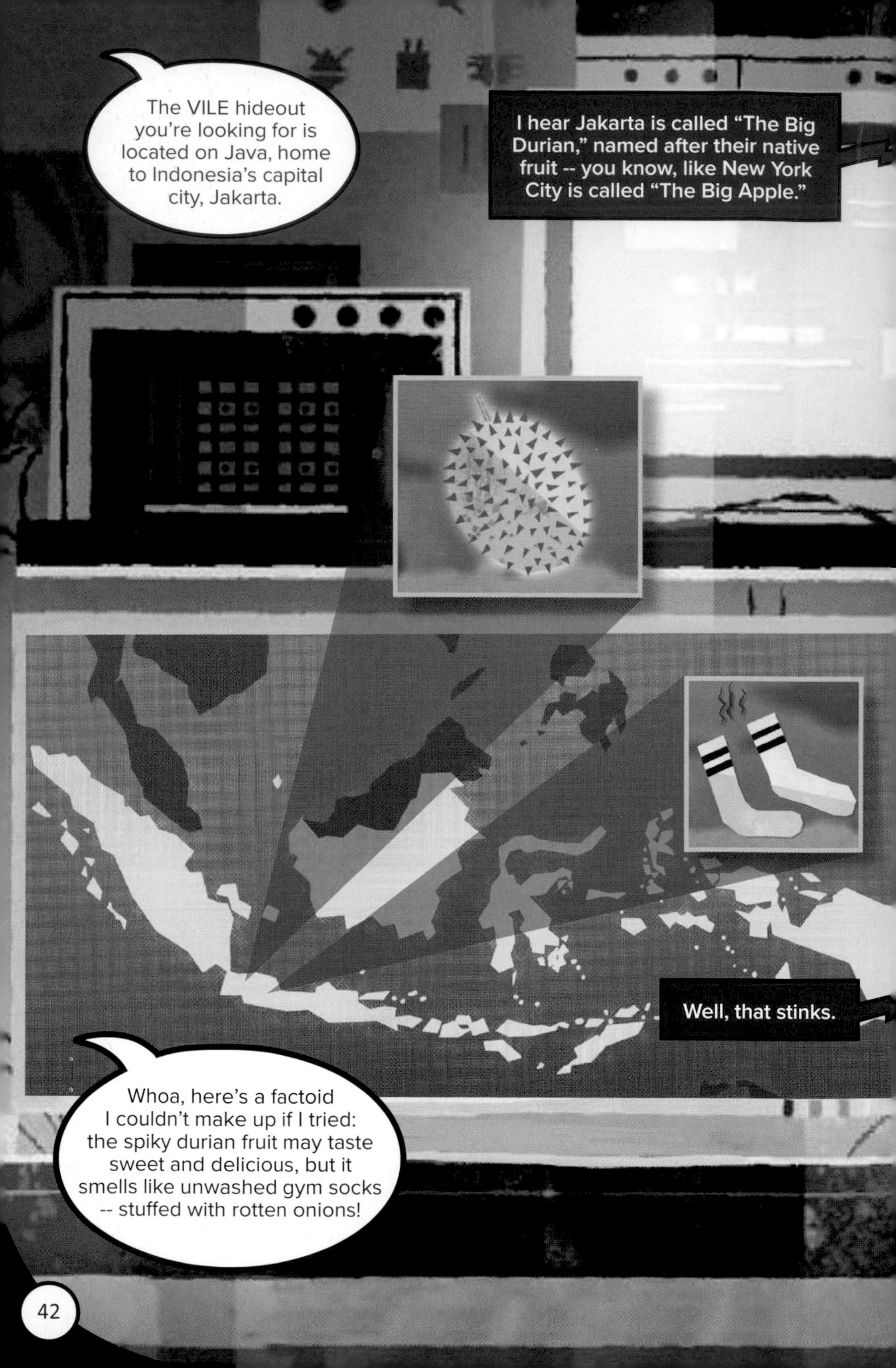
The VILE hideout you're looking for is located on Java, home to Indonesia's capital city, Jakarta.
I hear Jakarta is called "The Big Durian," named after their native fruit -- you know, like New York City is called "The Big Apple."
Well, that stinks.
Whoa, here's a factoid I couldn't make up if I tried: the spiky durian fruit may taste sweet and delicious, but it smells like unwashed gym socks -- stuffed with rotten onions!

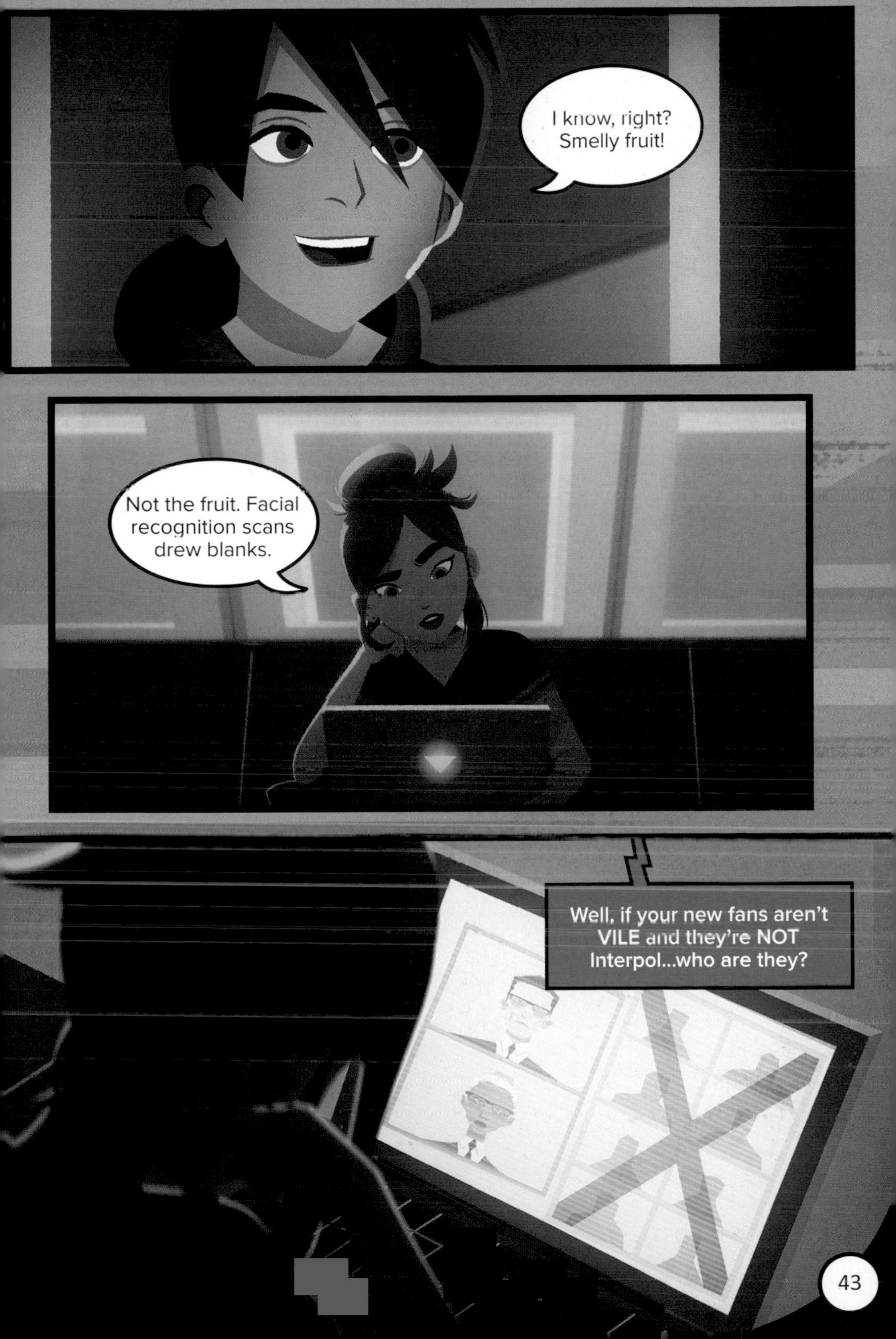
I know, right? Smelly fruit!
Not the fruit. Facial recognition scans drew blanks.
Well, if your new fans aren't VILE and they're NOT Interpol...who are they?

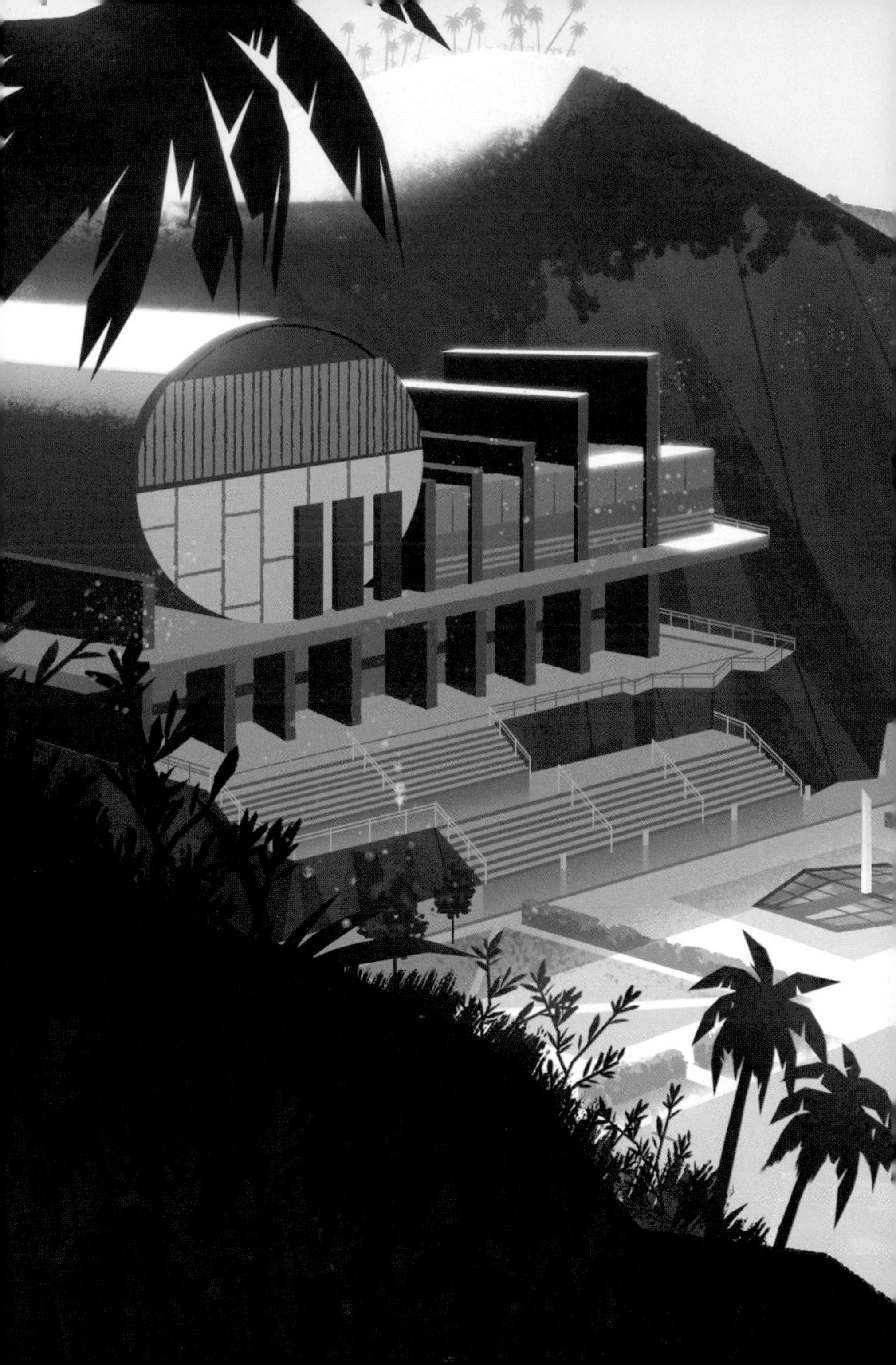

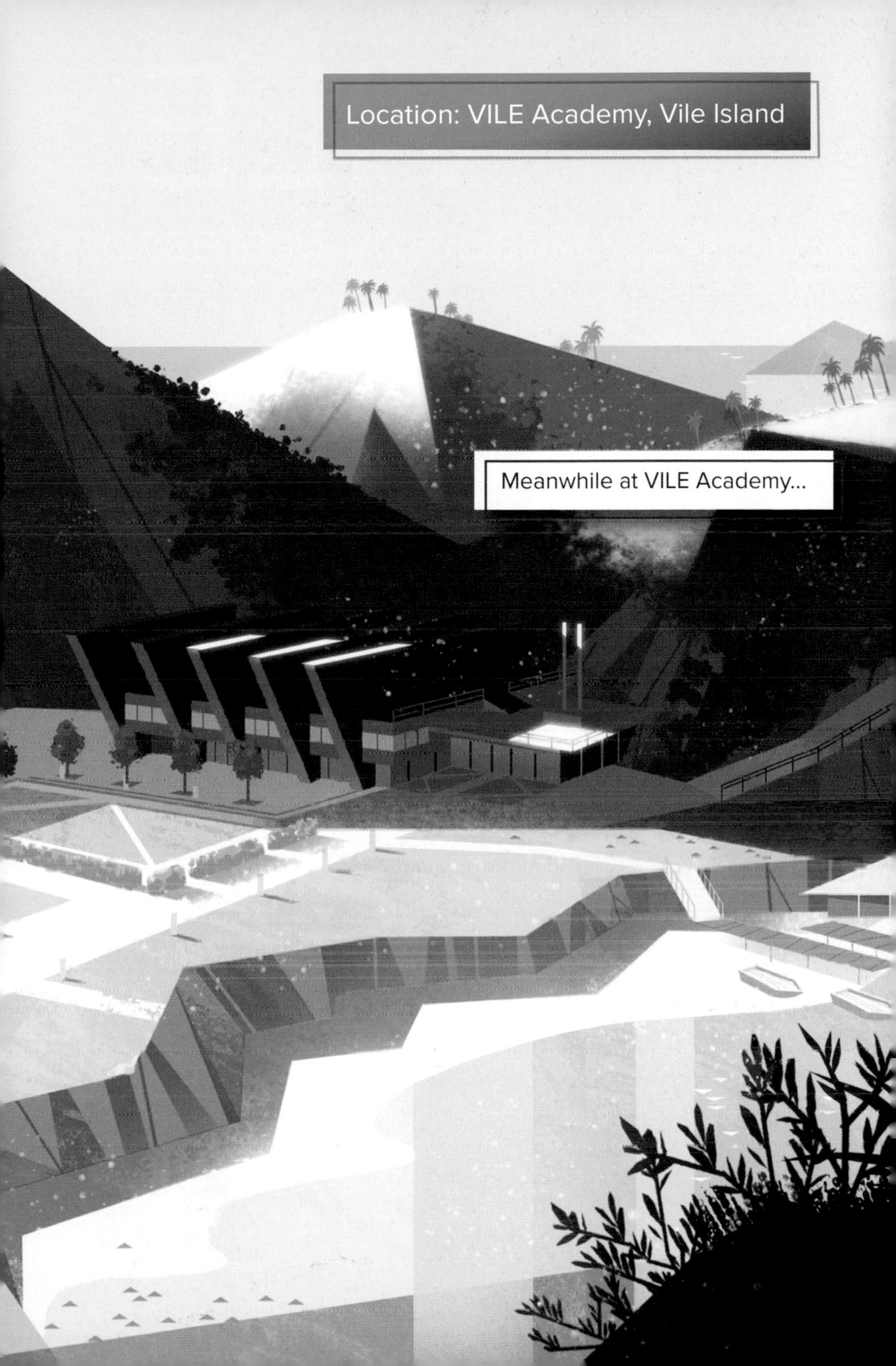
Location: VILE Academy, Vile Island
Meanwhile at VILE Academy...

VILE
Academy Professors

Gunnar Maelstrom

A psychological genius, Maelstrom learns your weaknesses and twists your mind.

Countess Cleo

Cleo believes that ultimate wealth is ultimate power. She adores expensive everything.

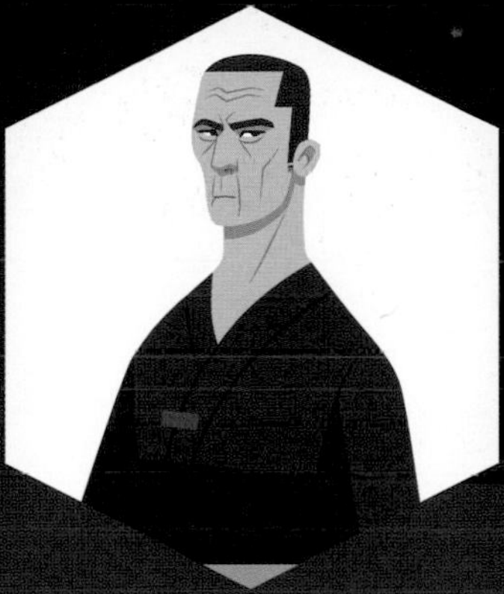

Shadowsan

A real-life modern ninja, Shadowsan teaches the criminal power of stealth and discipline.

Dr. Saira Bellum

Death rays, invisibility fabric, brain-wiping machines -- these are Bellum's favorite things.

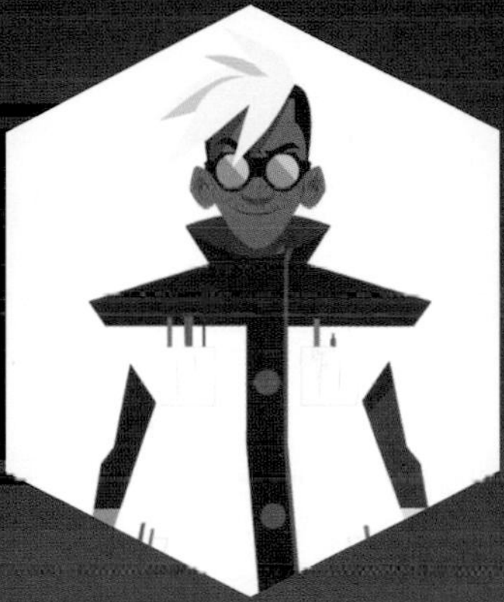

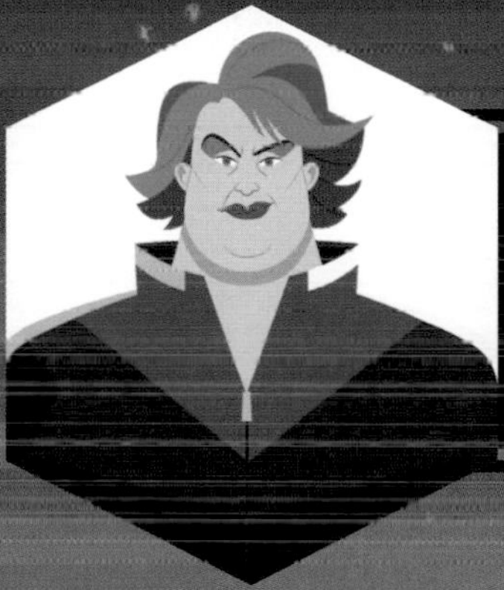

Coach Brunt

Master of hand-to-hand combat, Brunt believes a butt-whooping is the solution to everything.

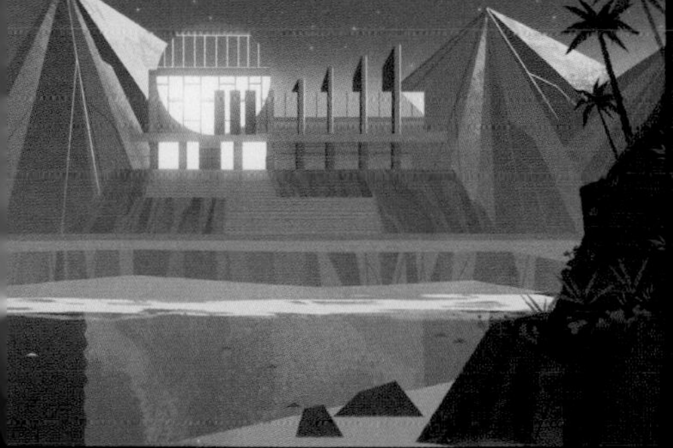

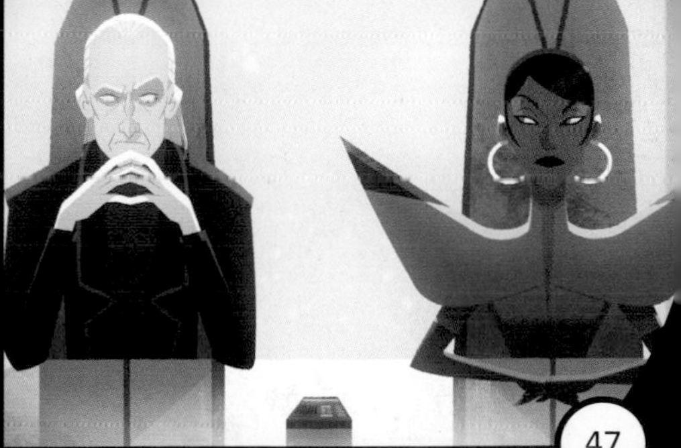

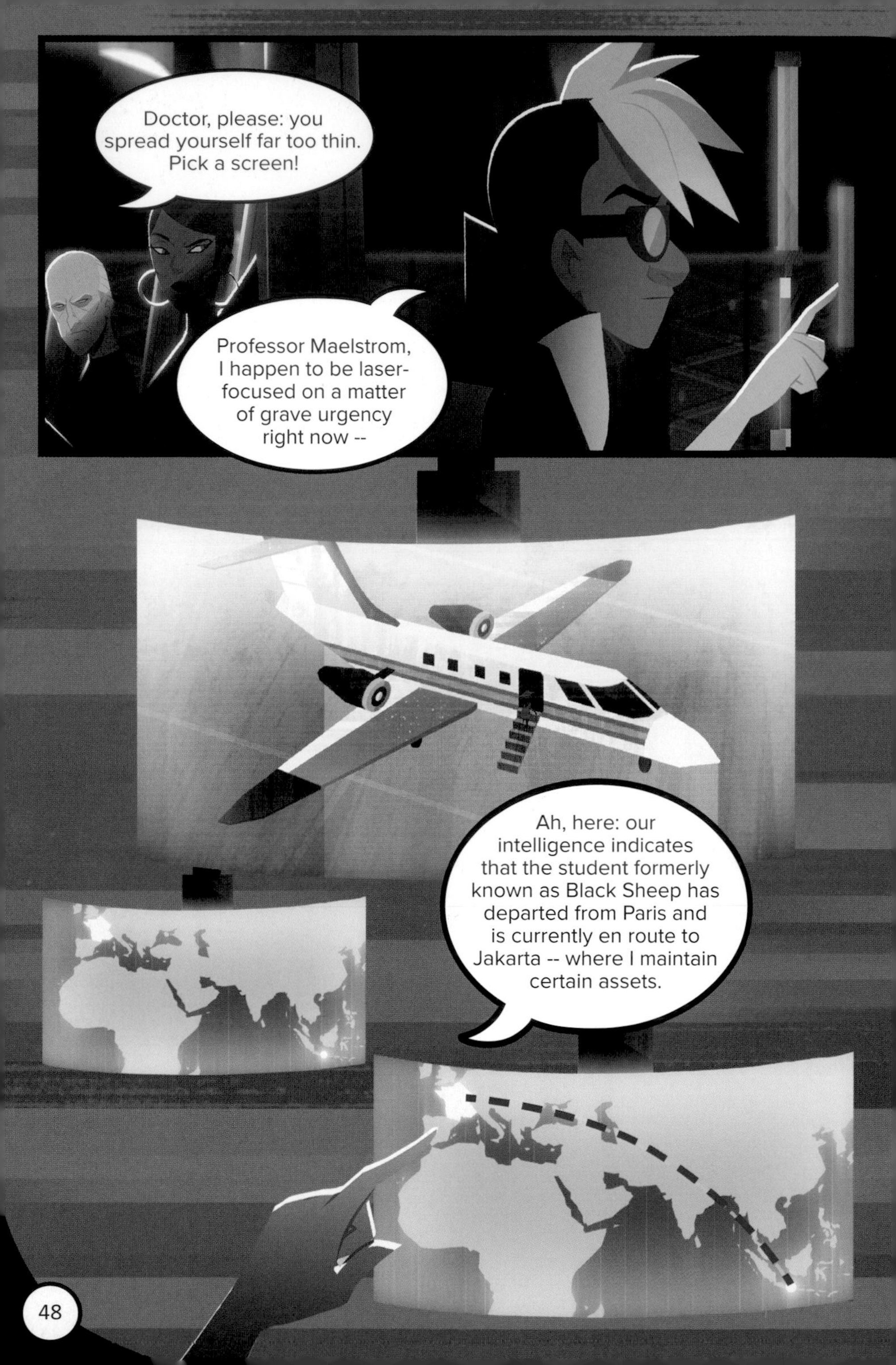
Doctor, please: you spread yourself far too thin. Pick a screen!
Professor Maelstrom, I happen to be laser-focused on a matter of grave urgency right now --
Ah, here: our intelligence indicates that the student formerly known as Black Sheep has departed from Paris and is currently en route to Jakarta -- where I maintain certain assets.

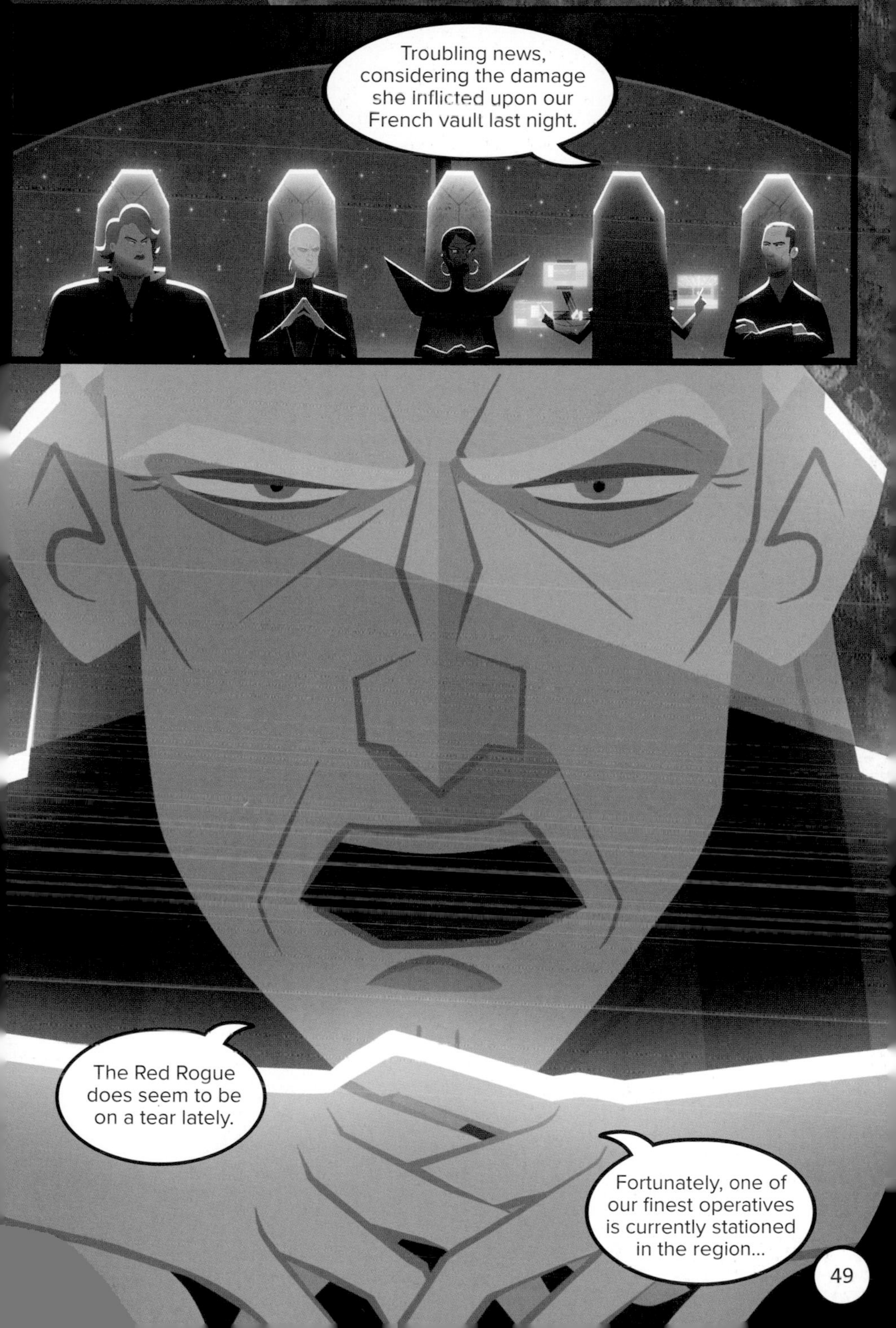
Troubling news, considering the damage she inflicted upon our French vault last night.
The Red Rogue does seem to be on a tear lately.
Fortunately, one of our finest operatives is currently stationed in the region...

Tigress

- Razor-sharp claws and a temper to match
- Loves bling and shiny things
- Master of quick cat-like moves and gymnastic-style stunts
- Carmen's former classmate and school rival

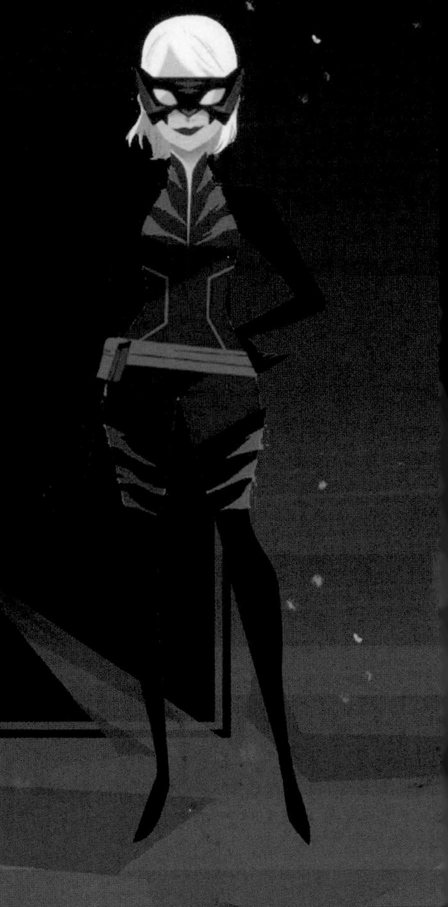

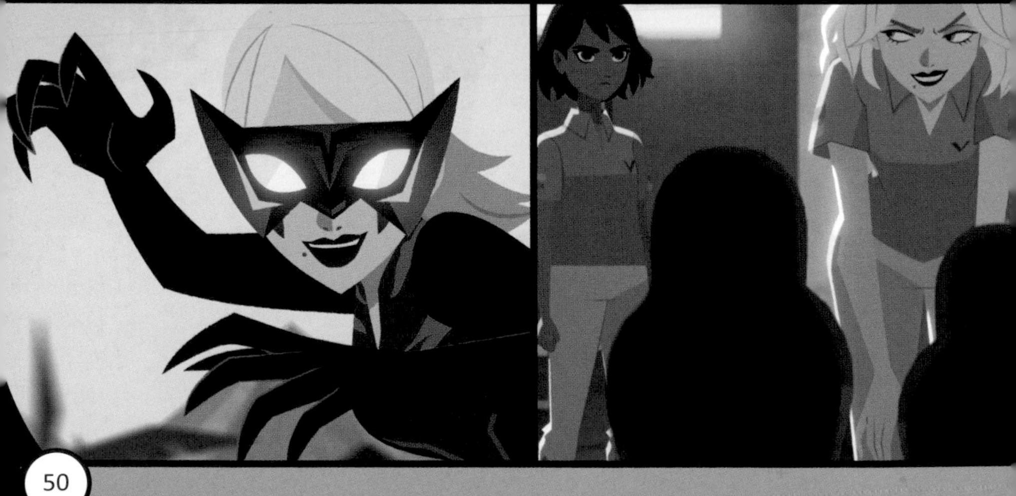

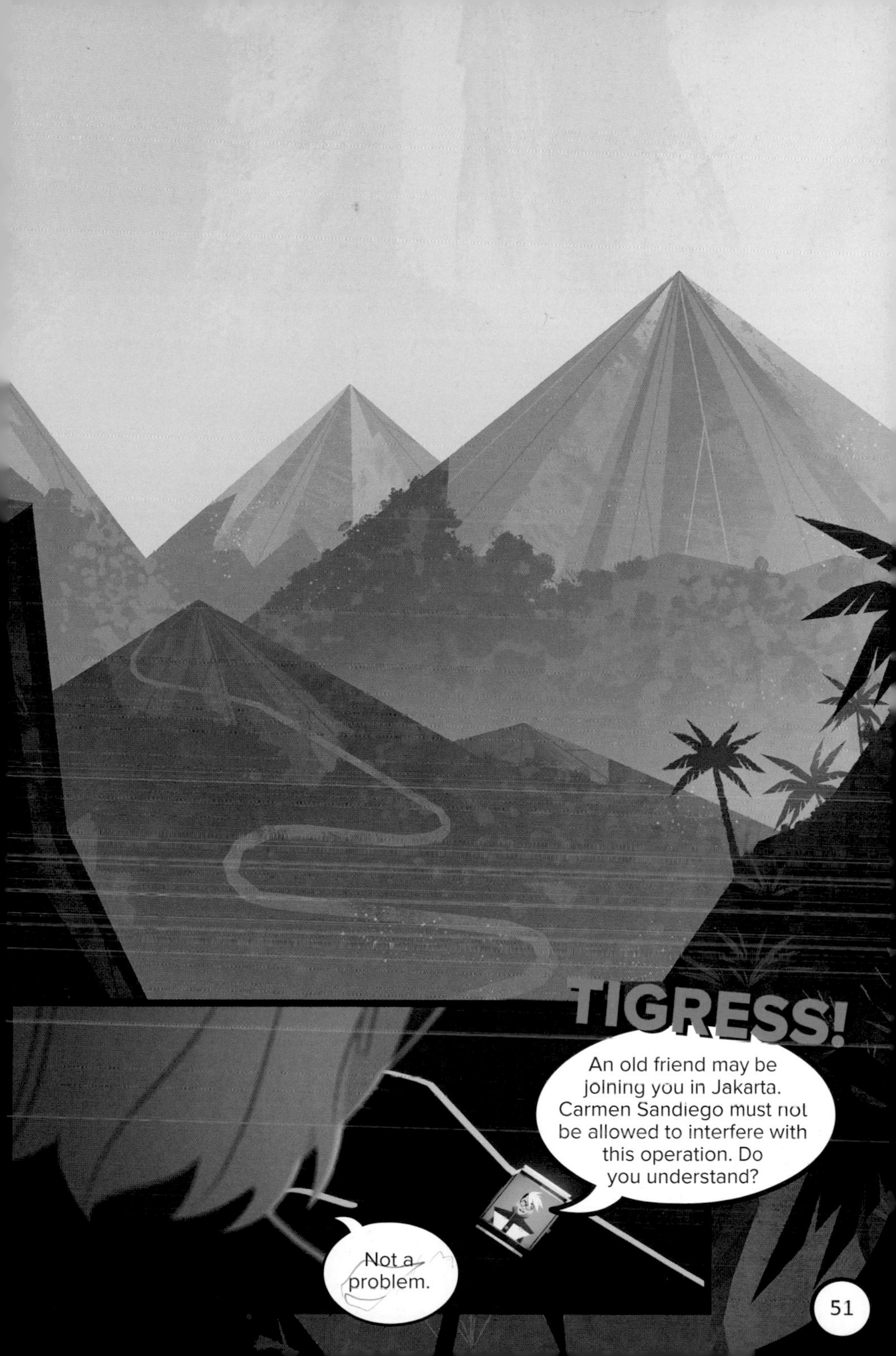
TIGRESS!
An old friend may be joining you in Jakarta. Carmen Sandiego must not be allowed to interfere with this operation. Do you understand?
Not a problem.

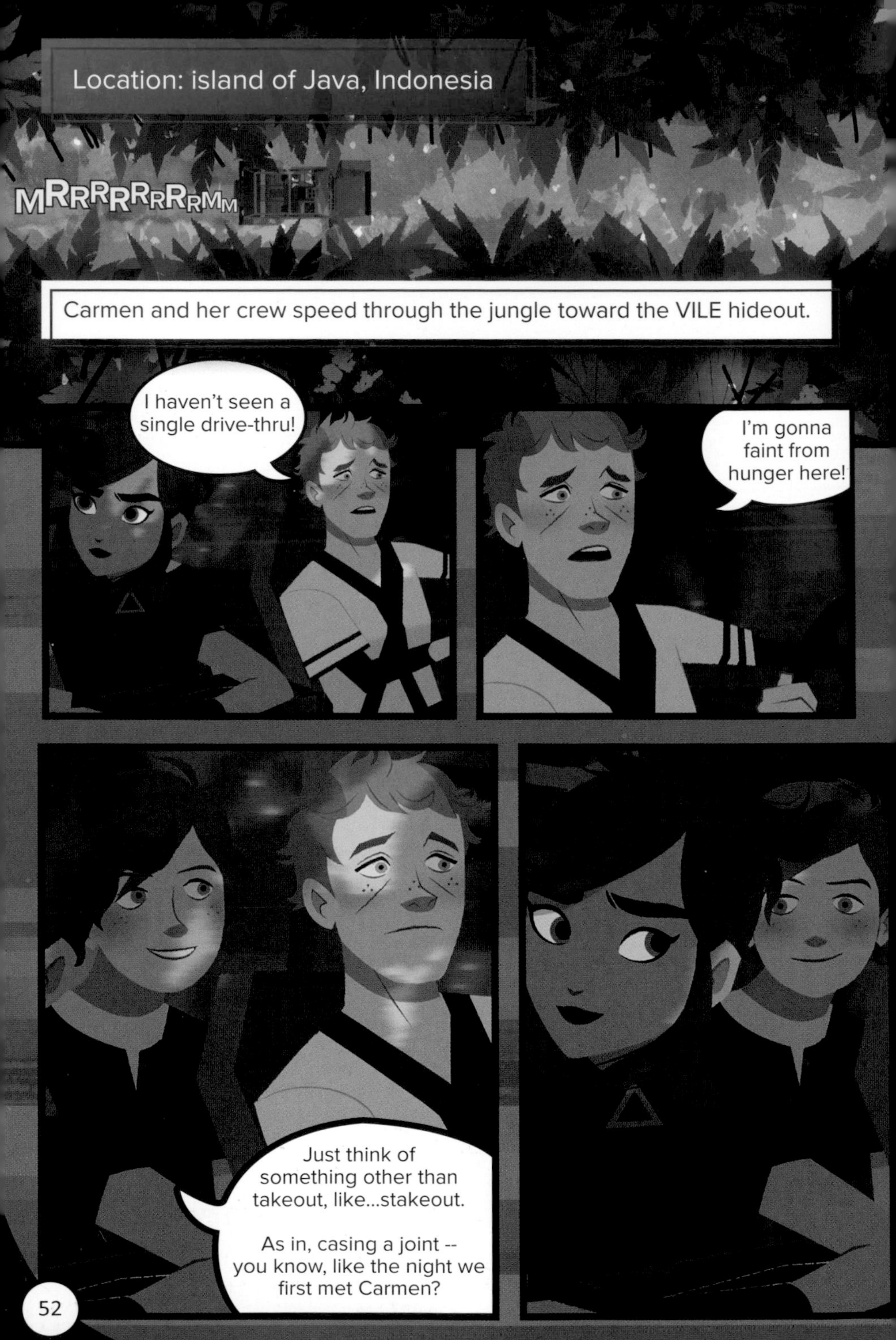
Location: island of Java, Indonesia
MRRRRRRRRMM
Carmen and her crew speed through the jungle toward the VILE hideout.
I haven't seen a single drive-thru!
I'm gonna faint from hunger here!
Just think of something other than takeout, like...stakeout.
As in, casing a joint -- you know, like the night we first met Carmen?

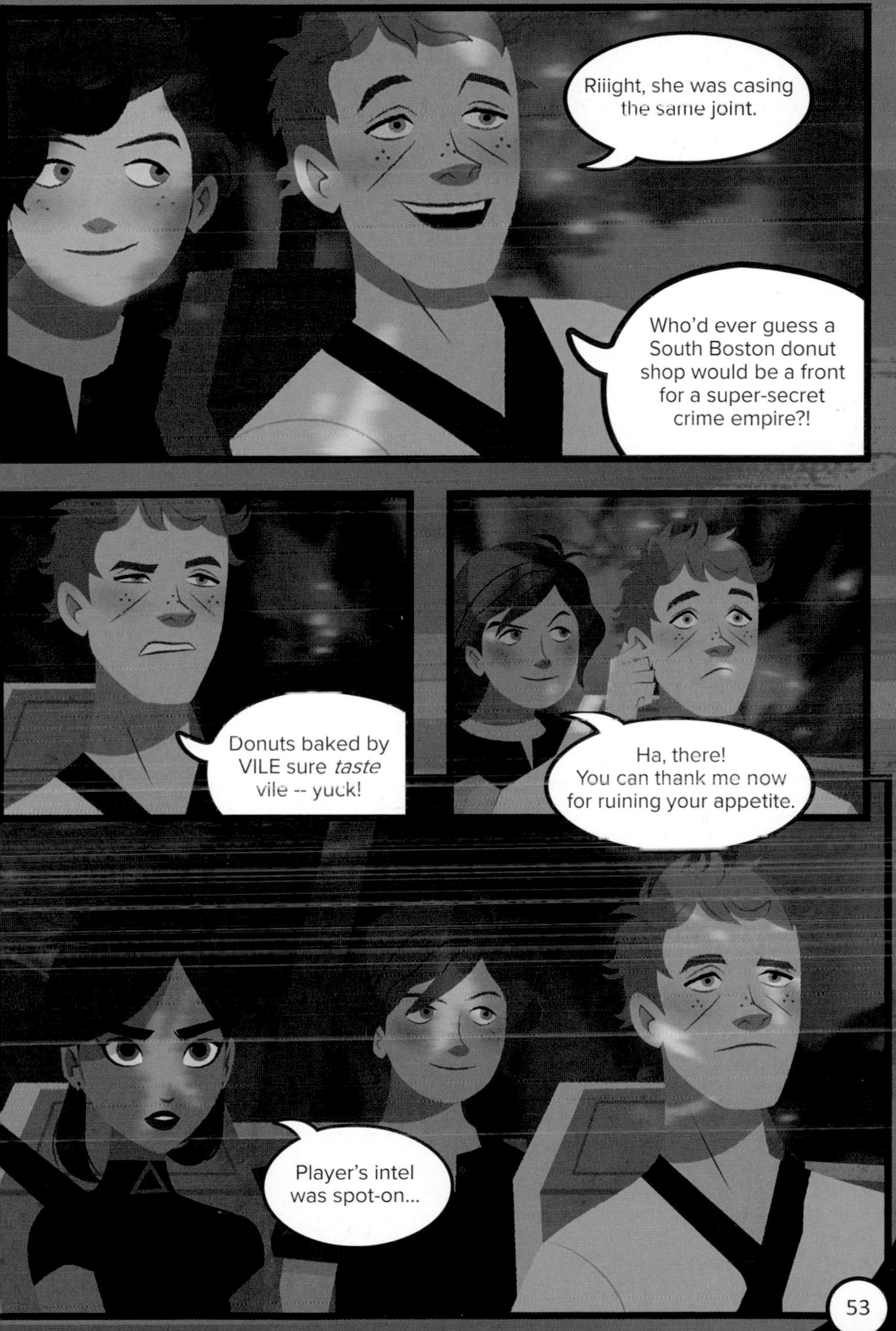
Riiight, she was casing the same joint.
Who'd ever guess a South Boston donut shop would be a front for a super-secret crime empire?!
Donuts baked by VILE sure *taste* vile -- yuck!
Ha, there! You can thank me now for ruining your appetite.
Player's intel was spot-on...

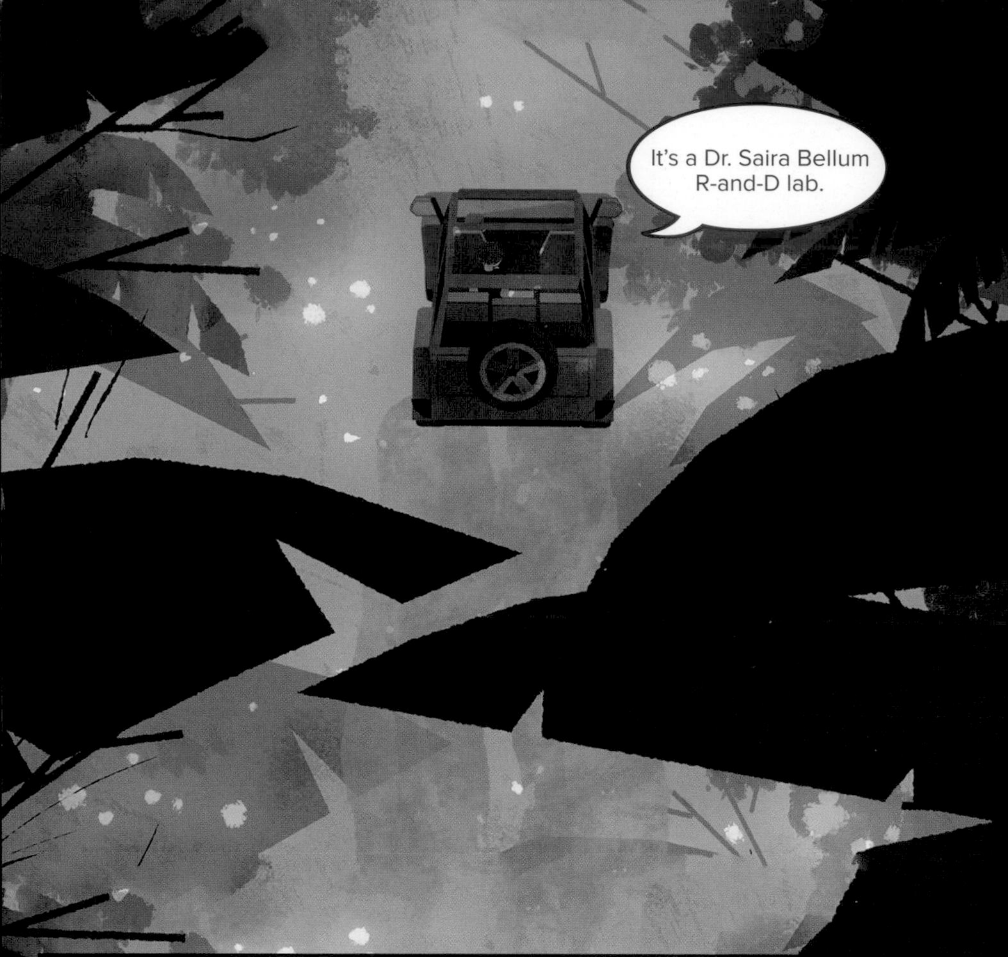
It's a Dr. Saira Bellum R-and-D lab.

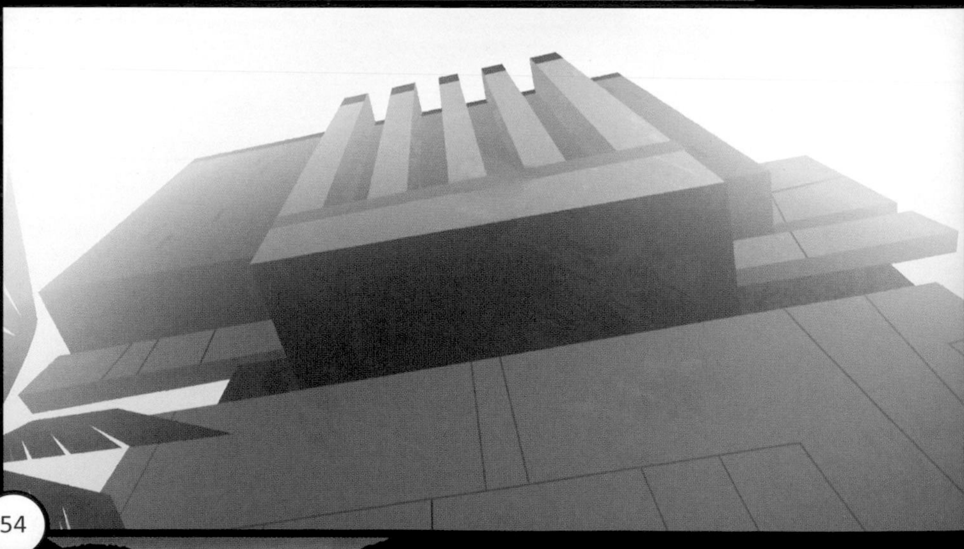

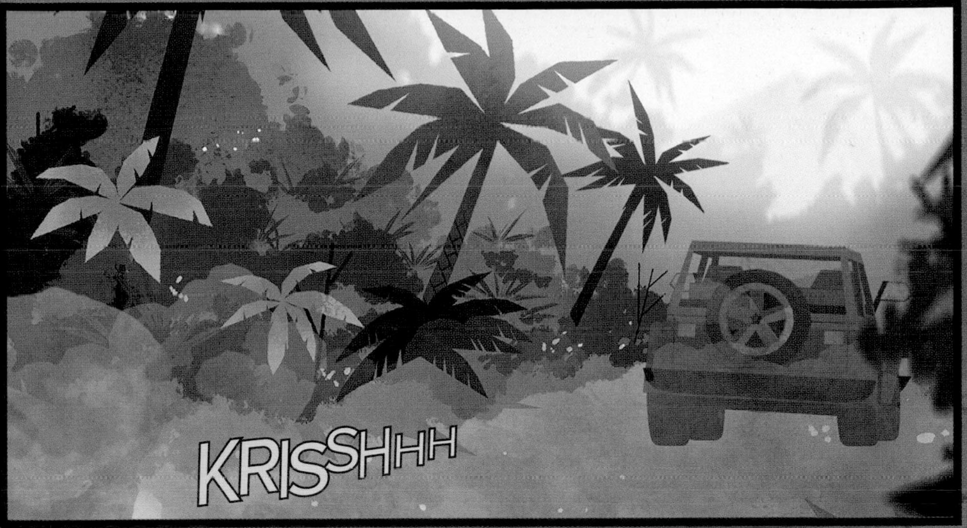
KRISSHHH

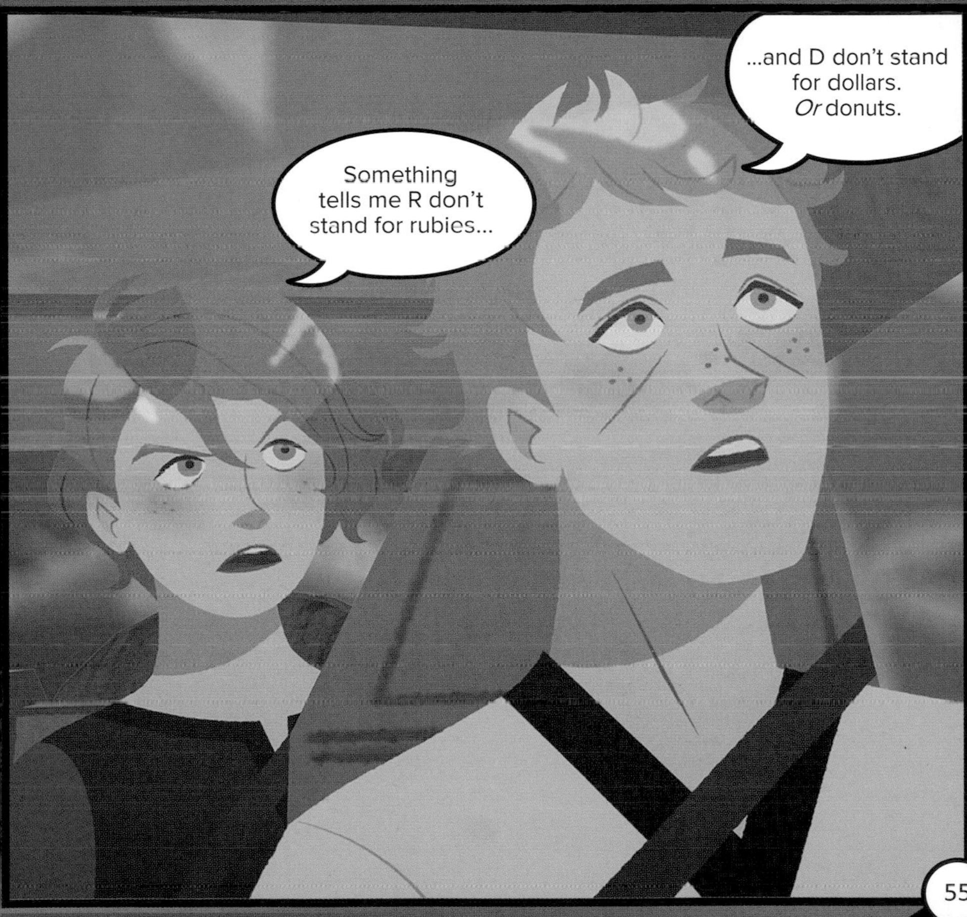
Something tells me R don't stand for rubies...
...and D don't stand for dollars. *Or* donuts.

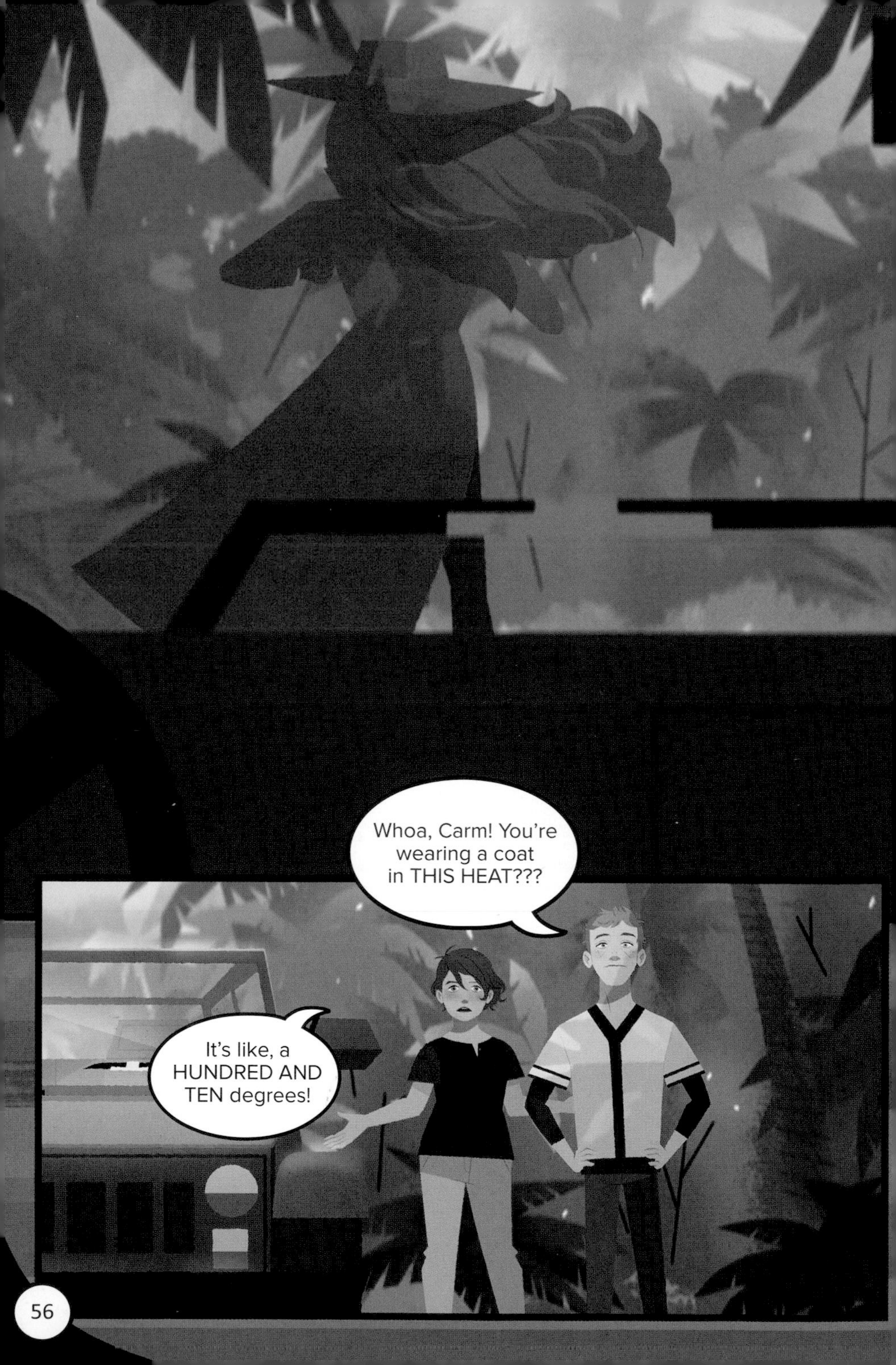
Whoa, Carm! You're wearing a coat in THIS HEAT???
It's like, a HUNDRED AND TEN degrees!

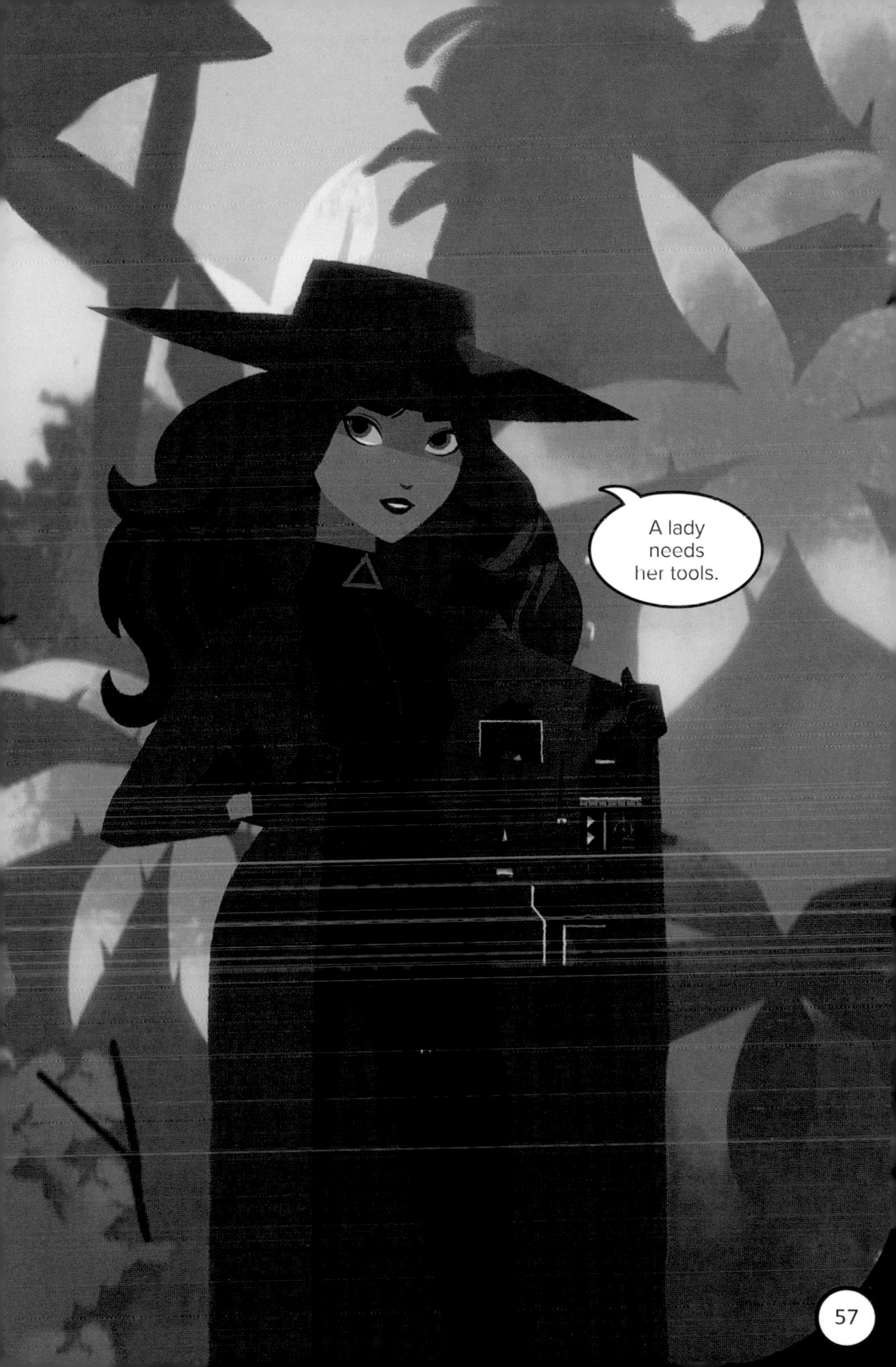
A lady needs her tools.

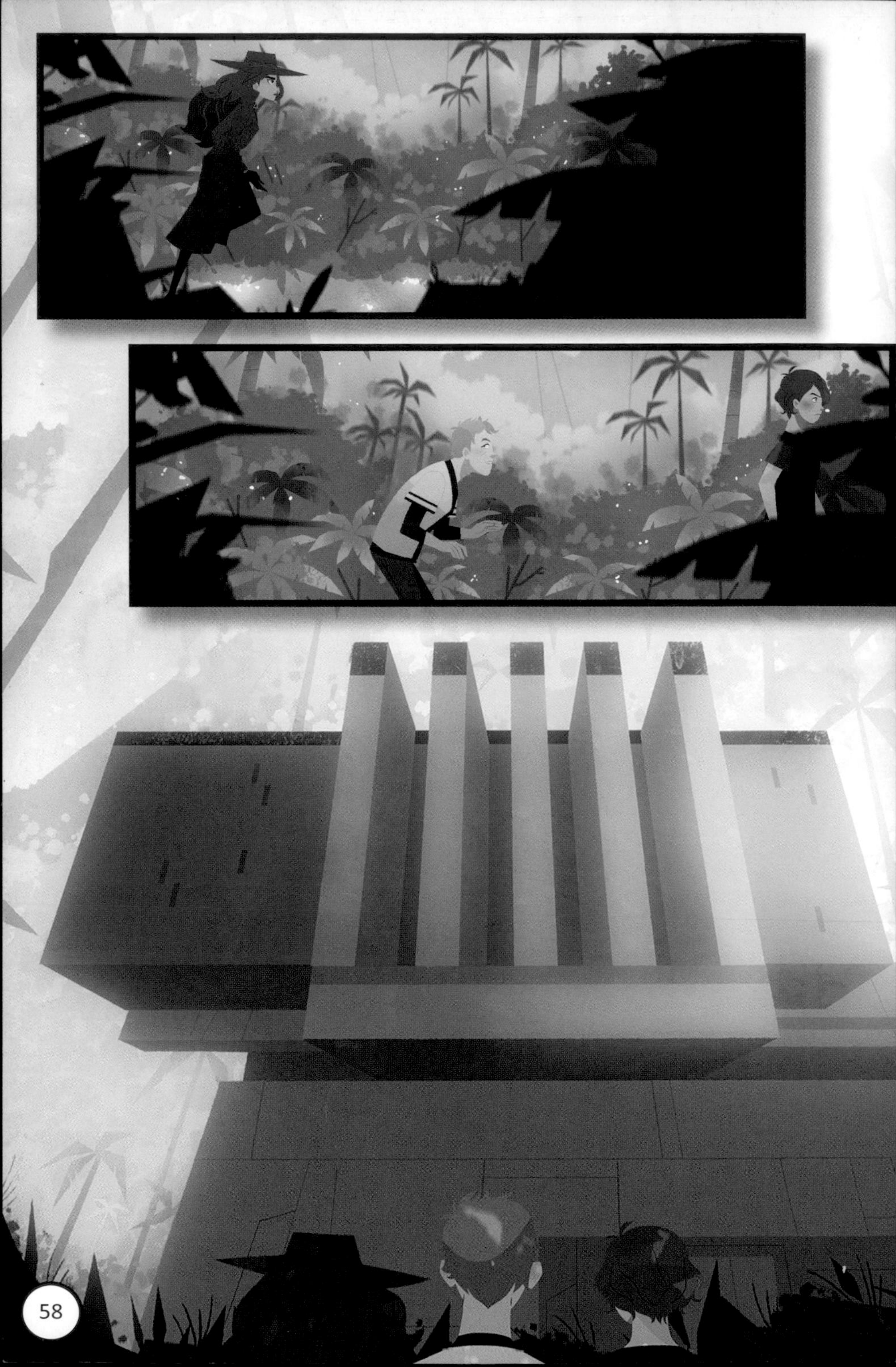

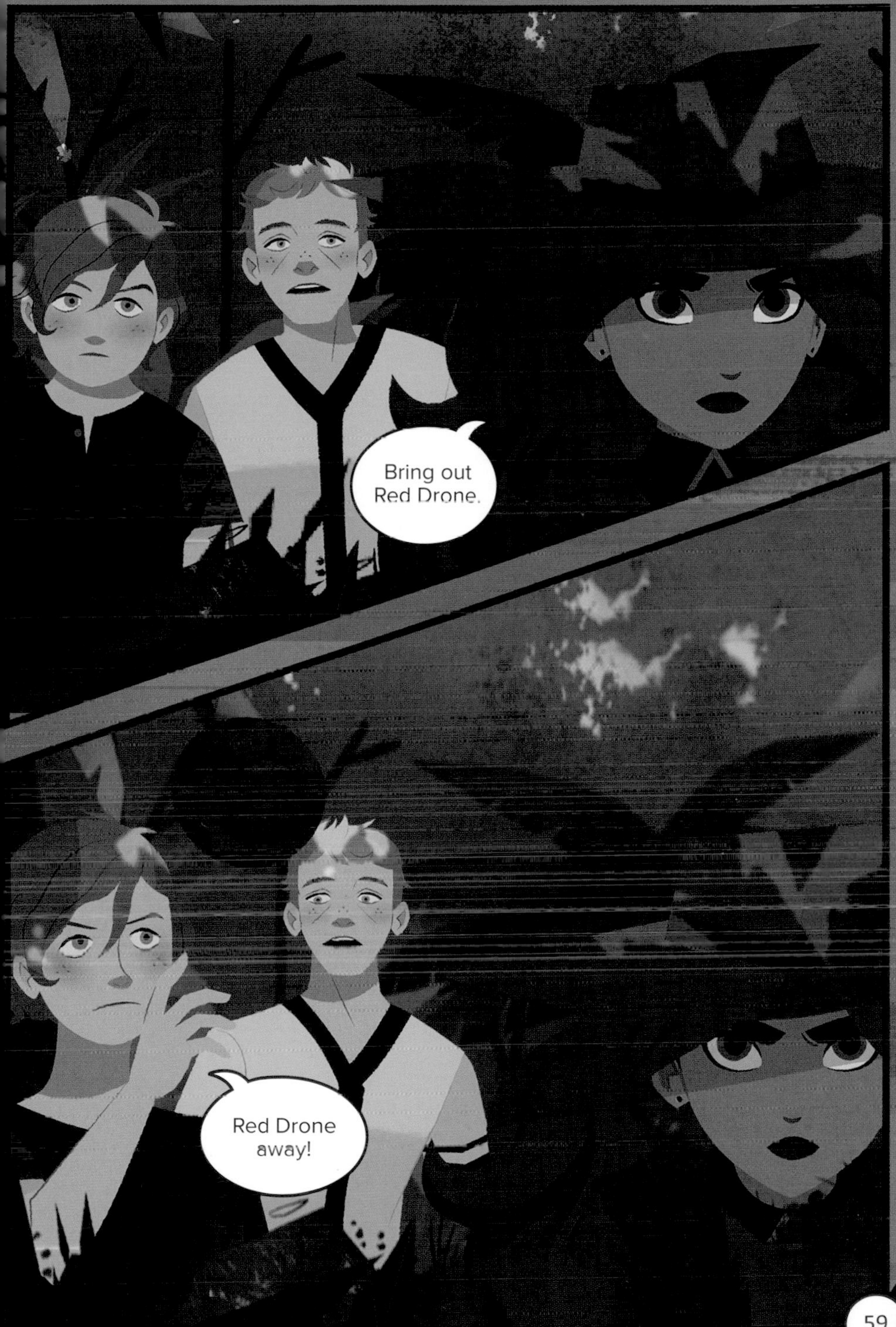
Bring out Red Drone.
Red Drone away!

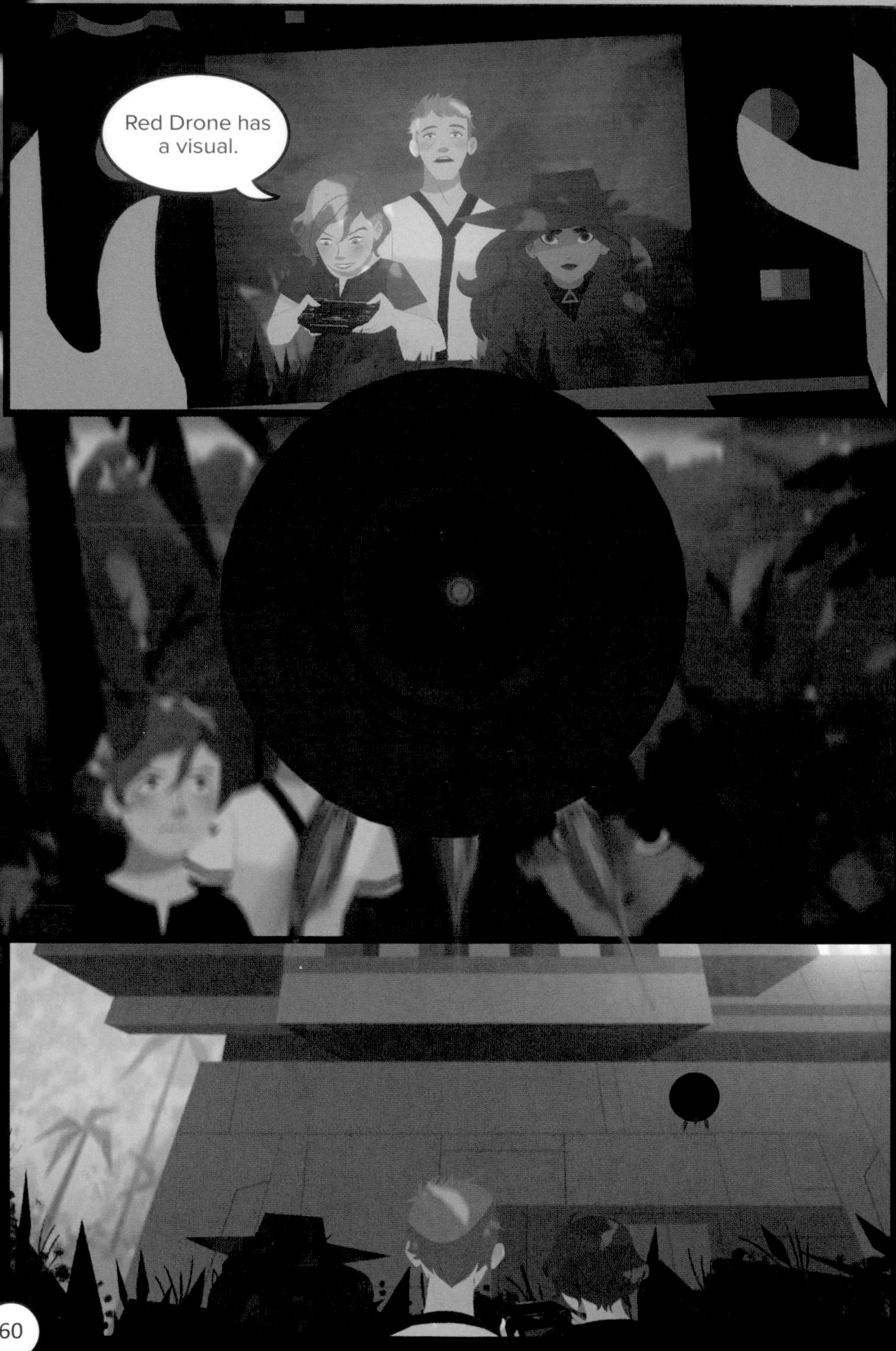
Red Drone has a visual.

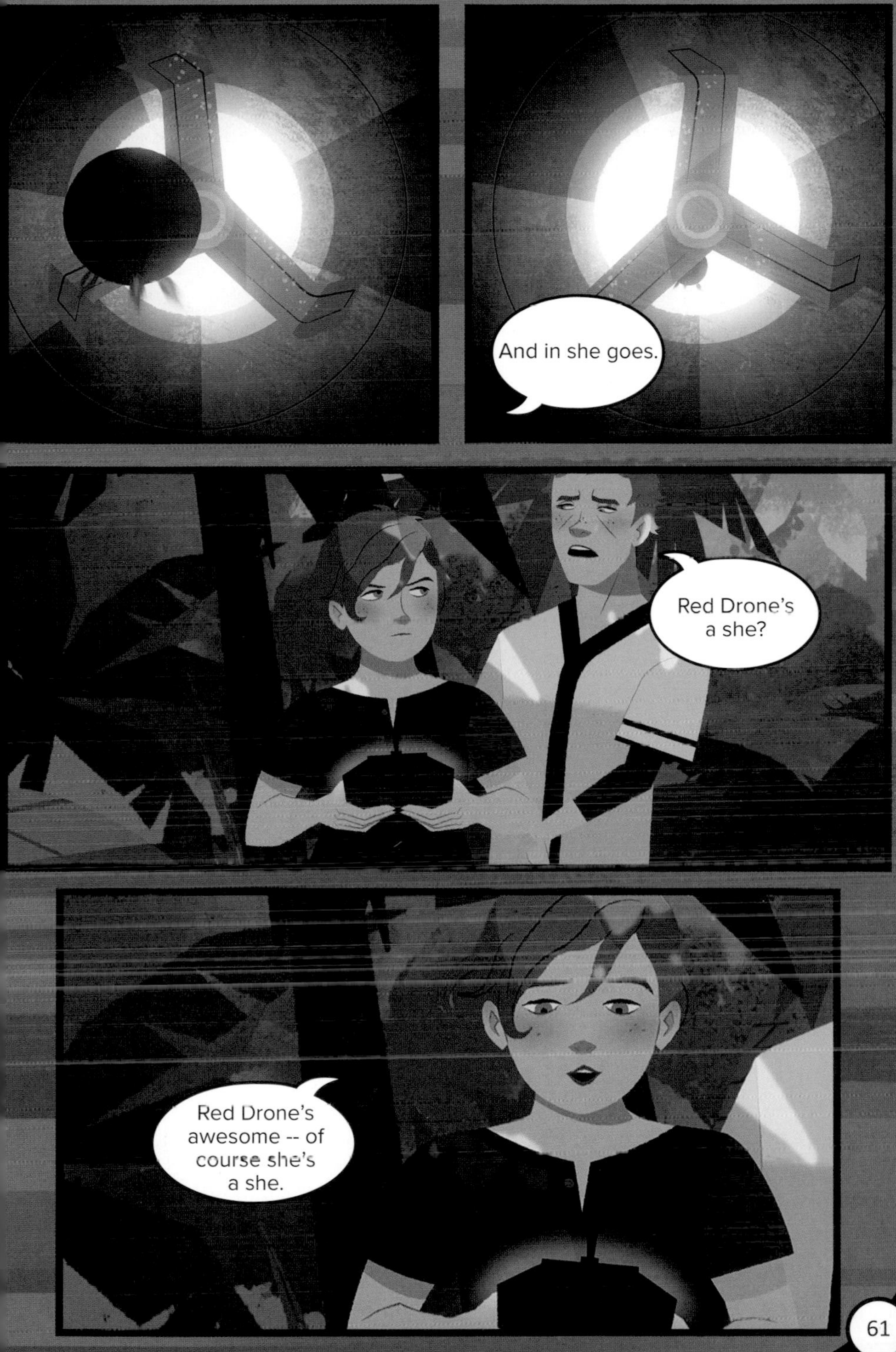
And in she goes.
Red Drone's a she?
Red Drone's awesome -- of course she's a she.

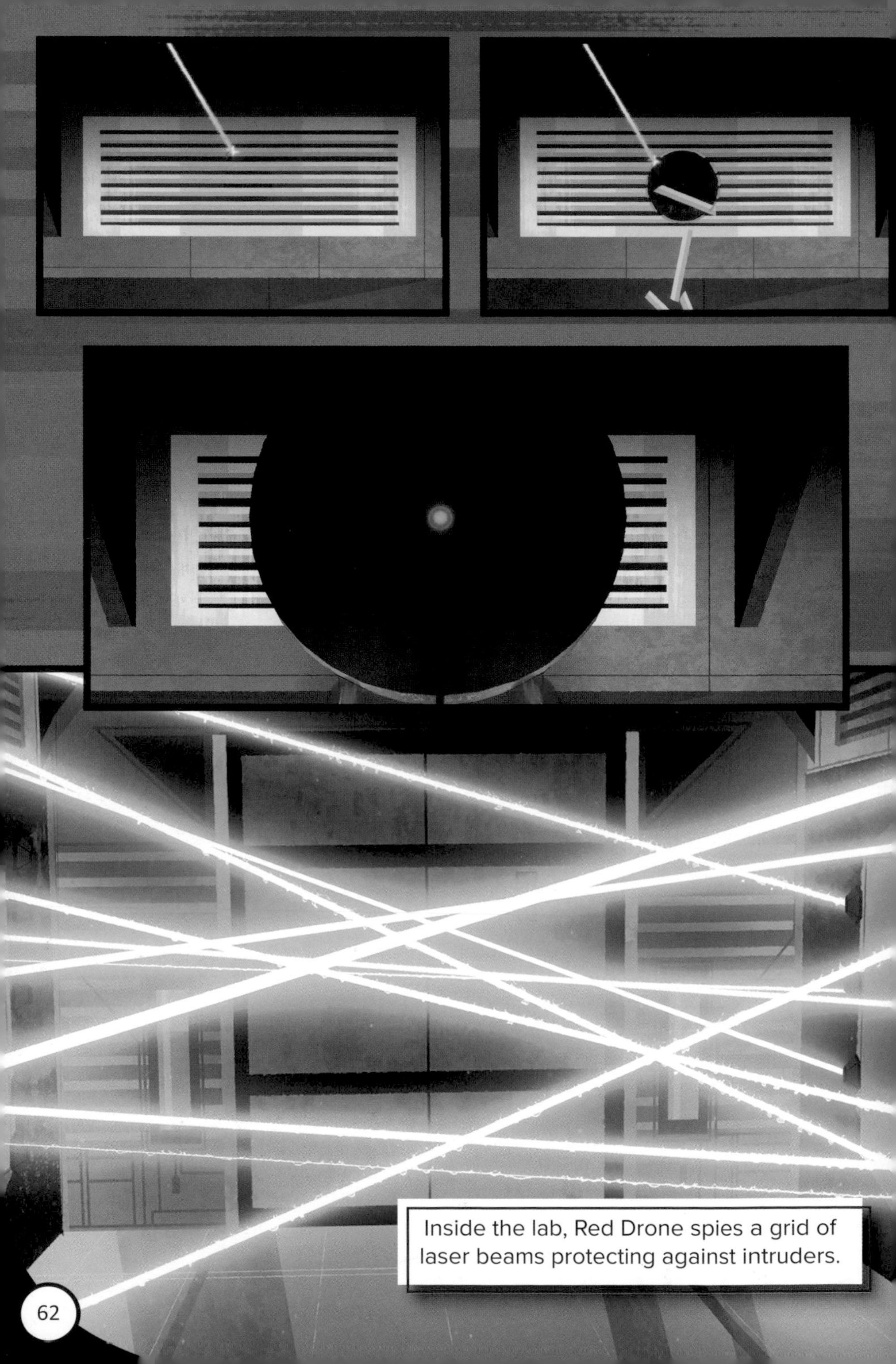
Inside the lab, Red Drone spies a grid of laser beams protecting against intruders.

Whoa!

Hey, how can anyone walk around in there with laser beams pointing all over the place?

Nobody's home.

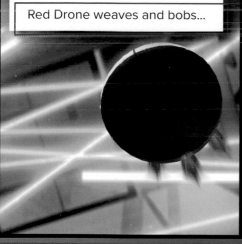

Red Drone weaves and bobs...

...past the deadly beams.

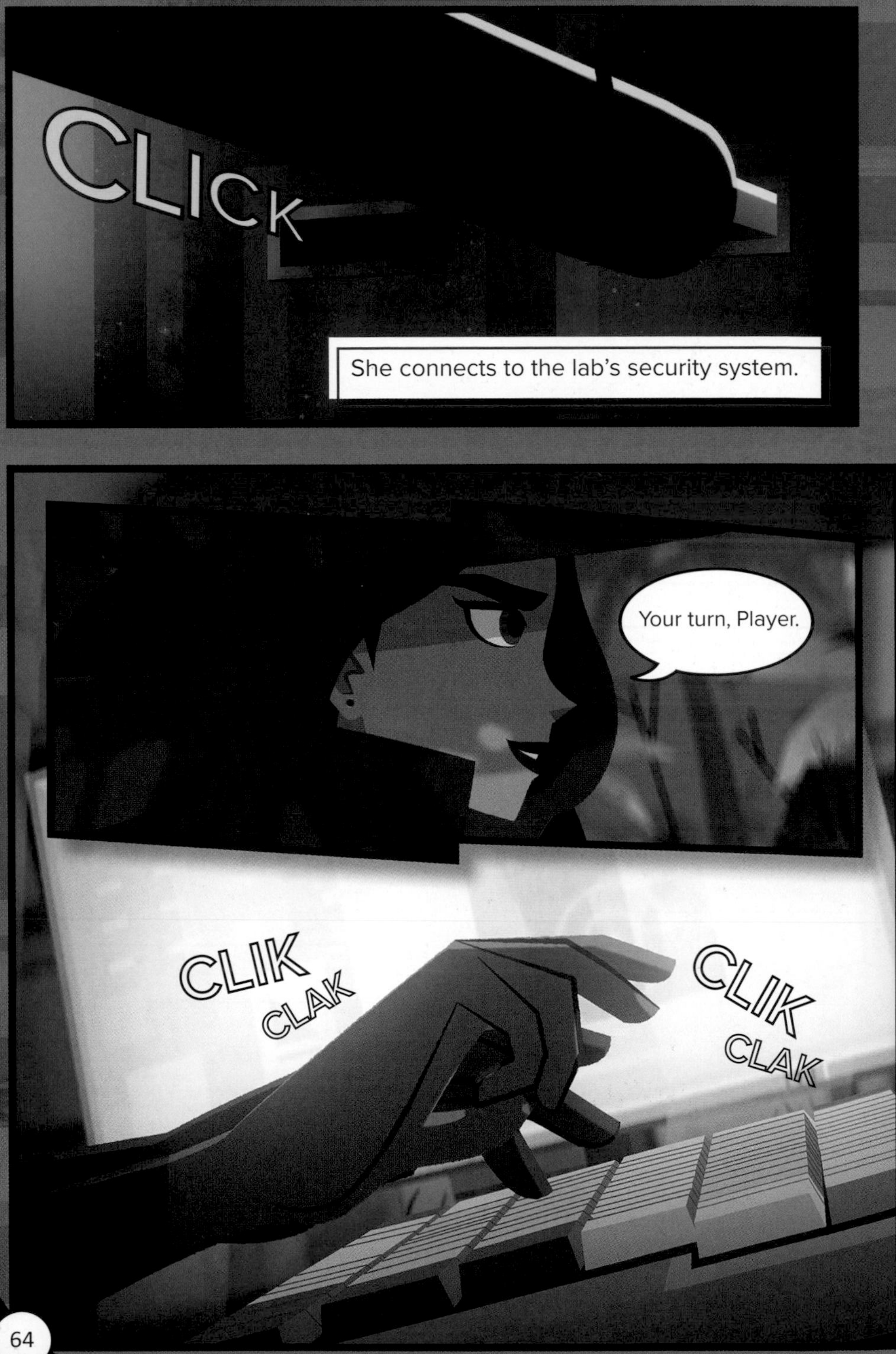
CLICK
She connects to the lab's security system.
Your turn, Player.
CLIK
CLAK
CLIK
CLAK

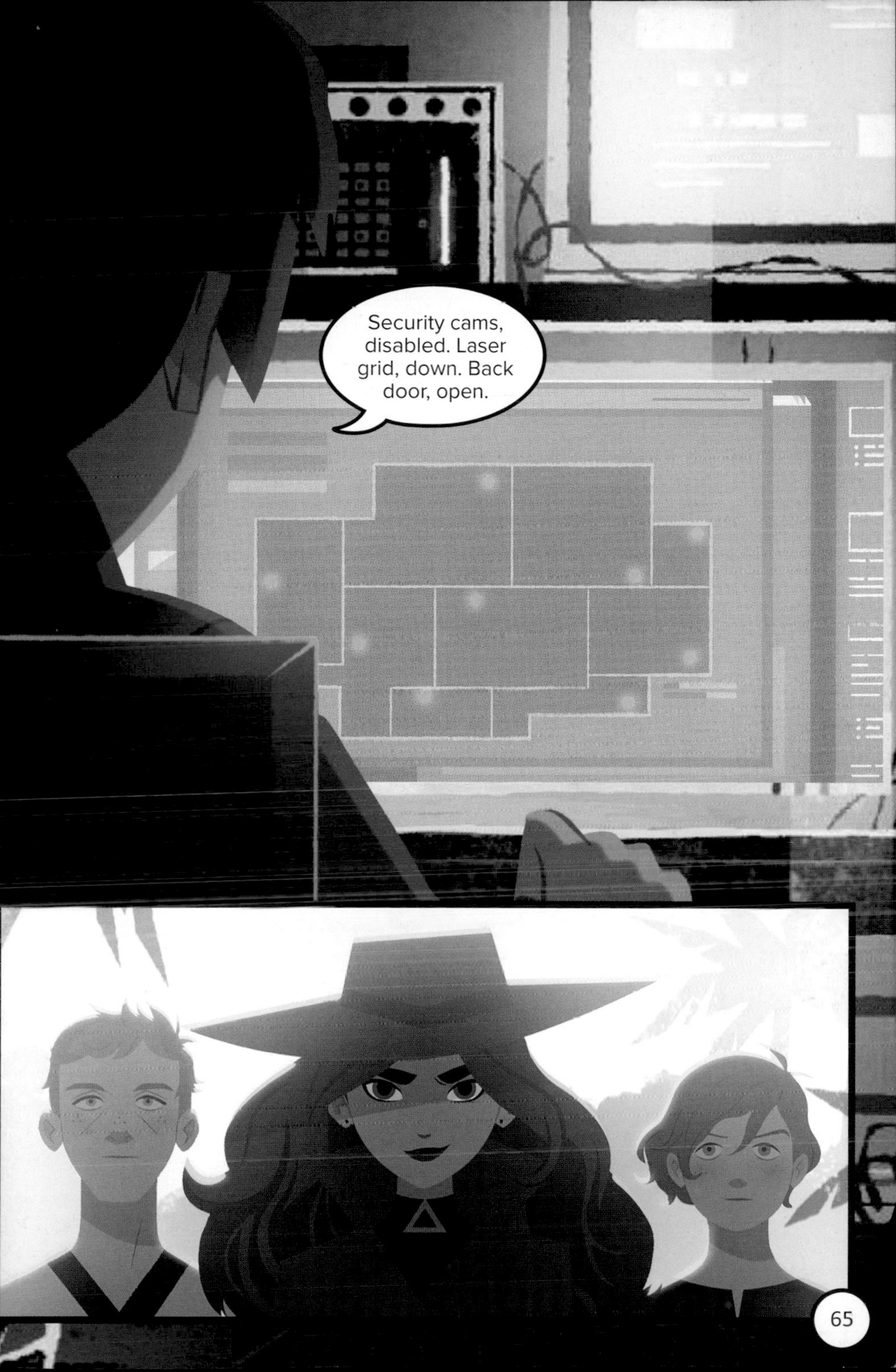
Security cams, disabled. Laser grid, down. Back door, open.

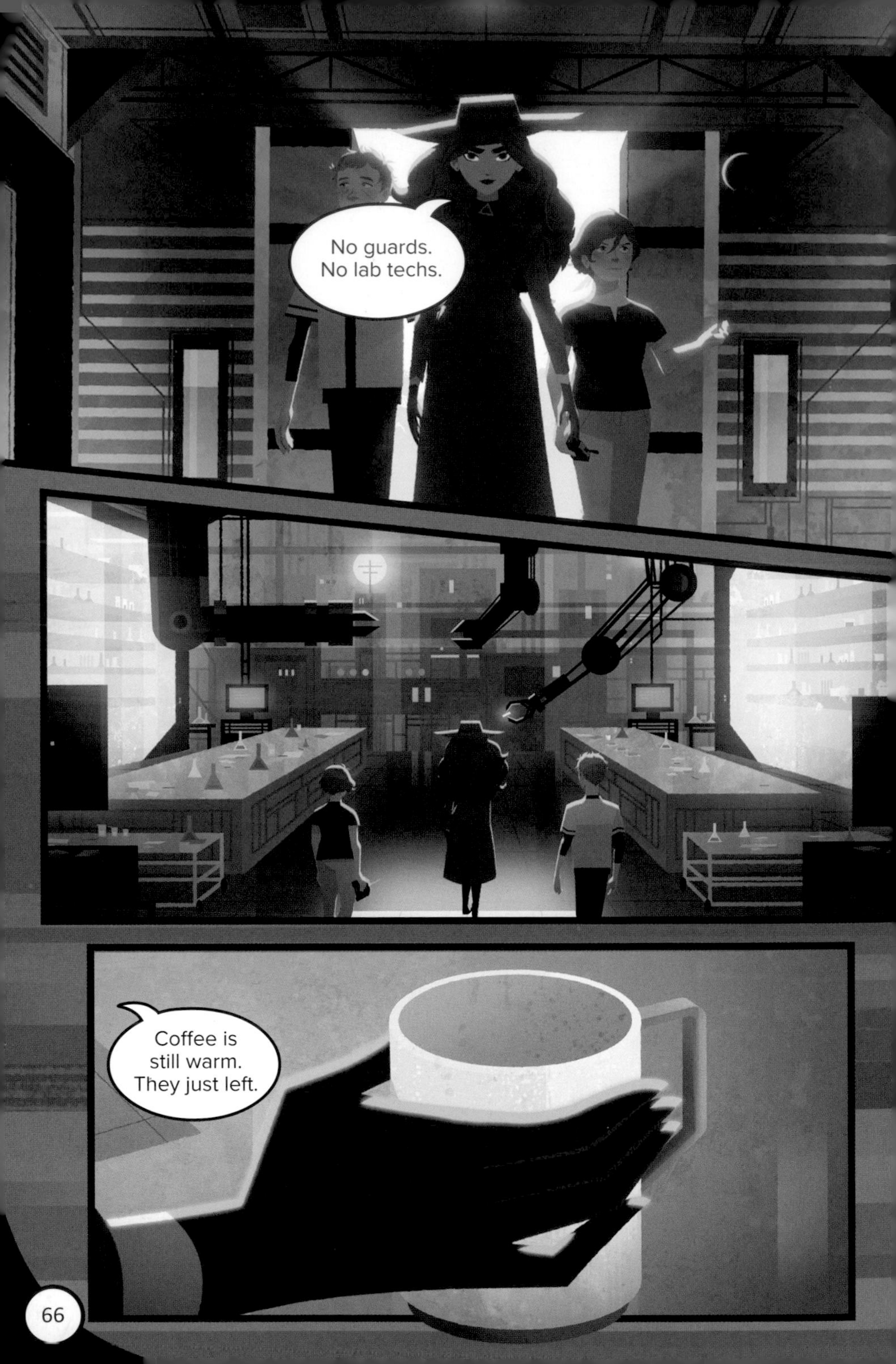
No guards.
No lab techs.
Coffee is
still warm.
They just left.

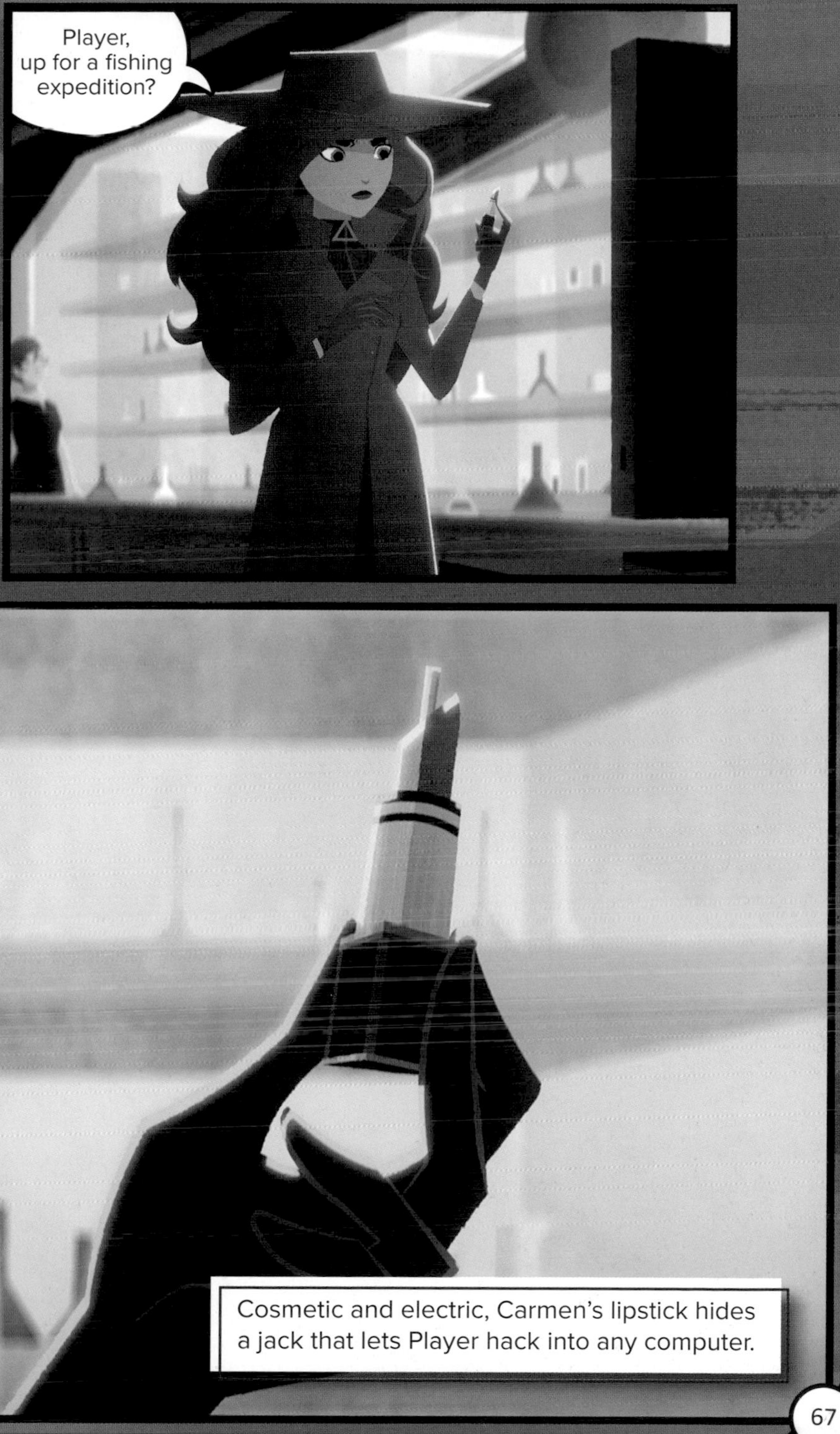
Player,
up for a fishing
expedition?
Cosmetic and electric, Carmen's lipstick hides
a jack that lets Player hack into any computer.

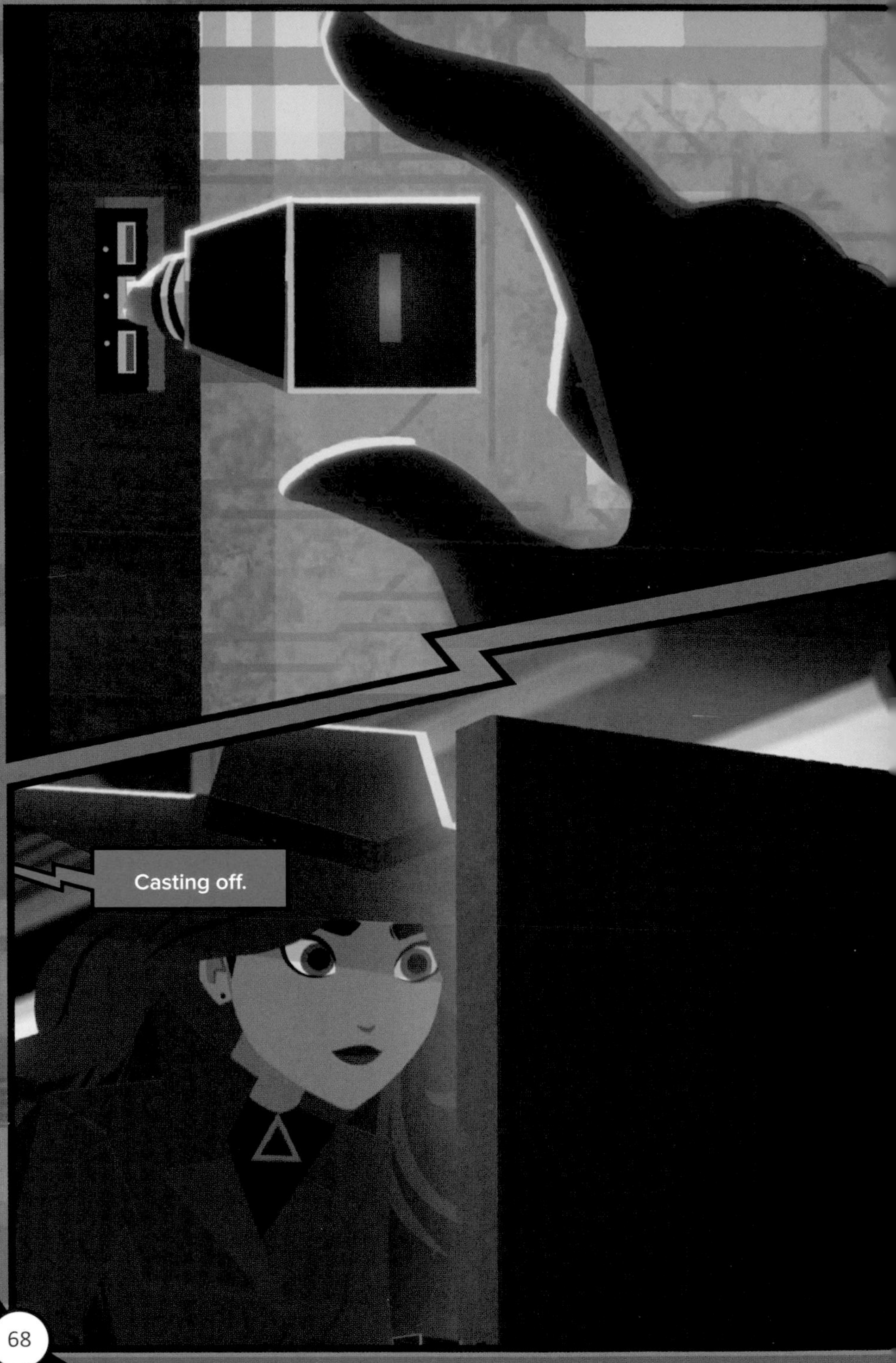
Casting off.

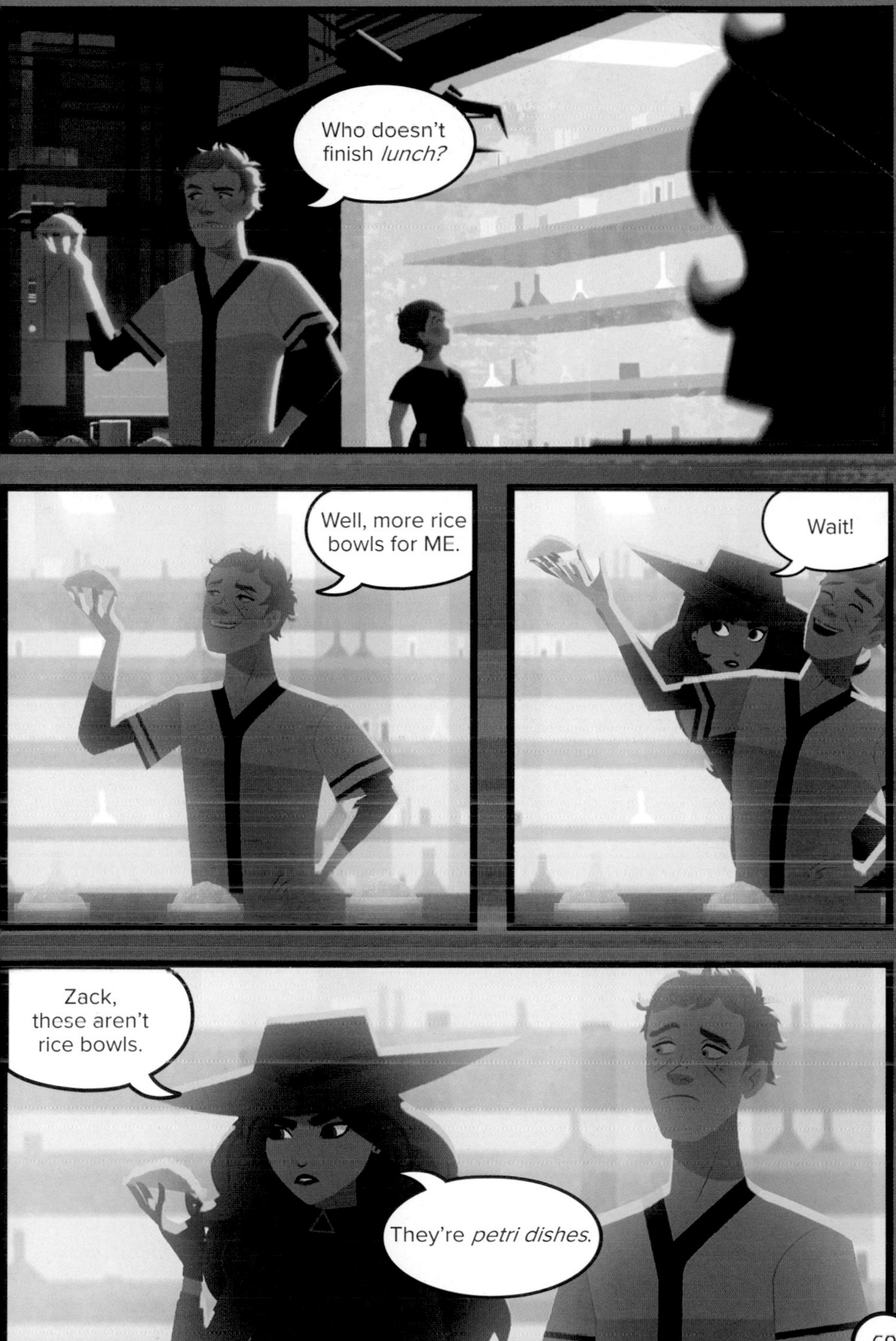
Who doesn't finish *lunch?*
Well, more rice bowls for ME.
Wait!
Zack, these aren't rice bowls.
They're *petri dishes.*

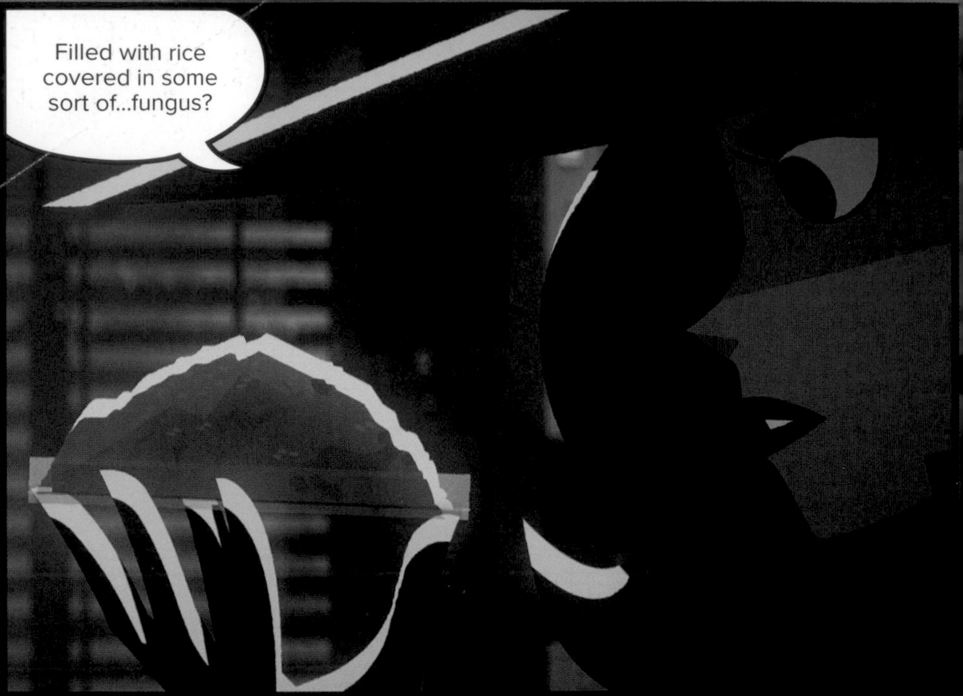
Filled with rice
covered in some
sort of...fungus?

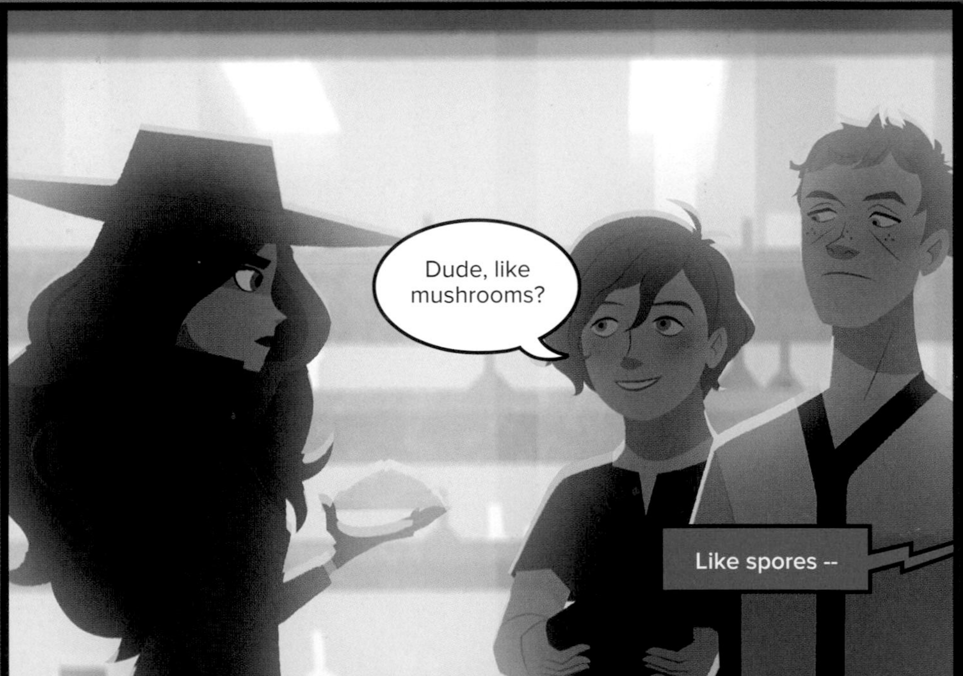
Dude, like
mushrooms?
Like spores --

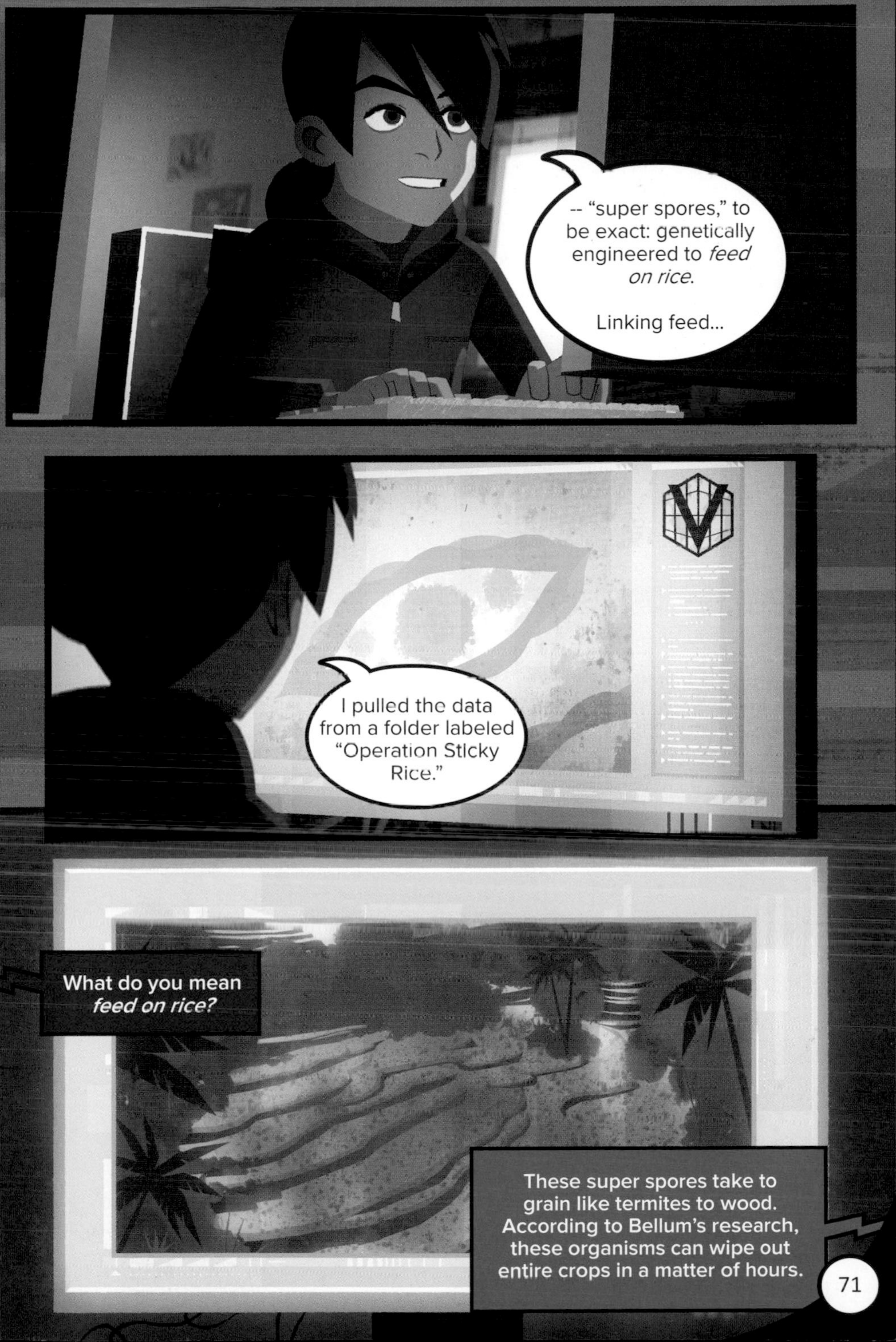
-- "super spores," to be exact: genetically engineered to *feed on rice*.
Linking feed...
I pulled the data from a folder labeled "Operation Sticky Rice."
What do you mean *feed on rice?*
These super spores take to grain like termites to wood. According to Bellum's research, these organisms can wipe out entire crops in a matter of hours.

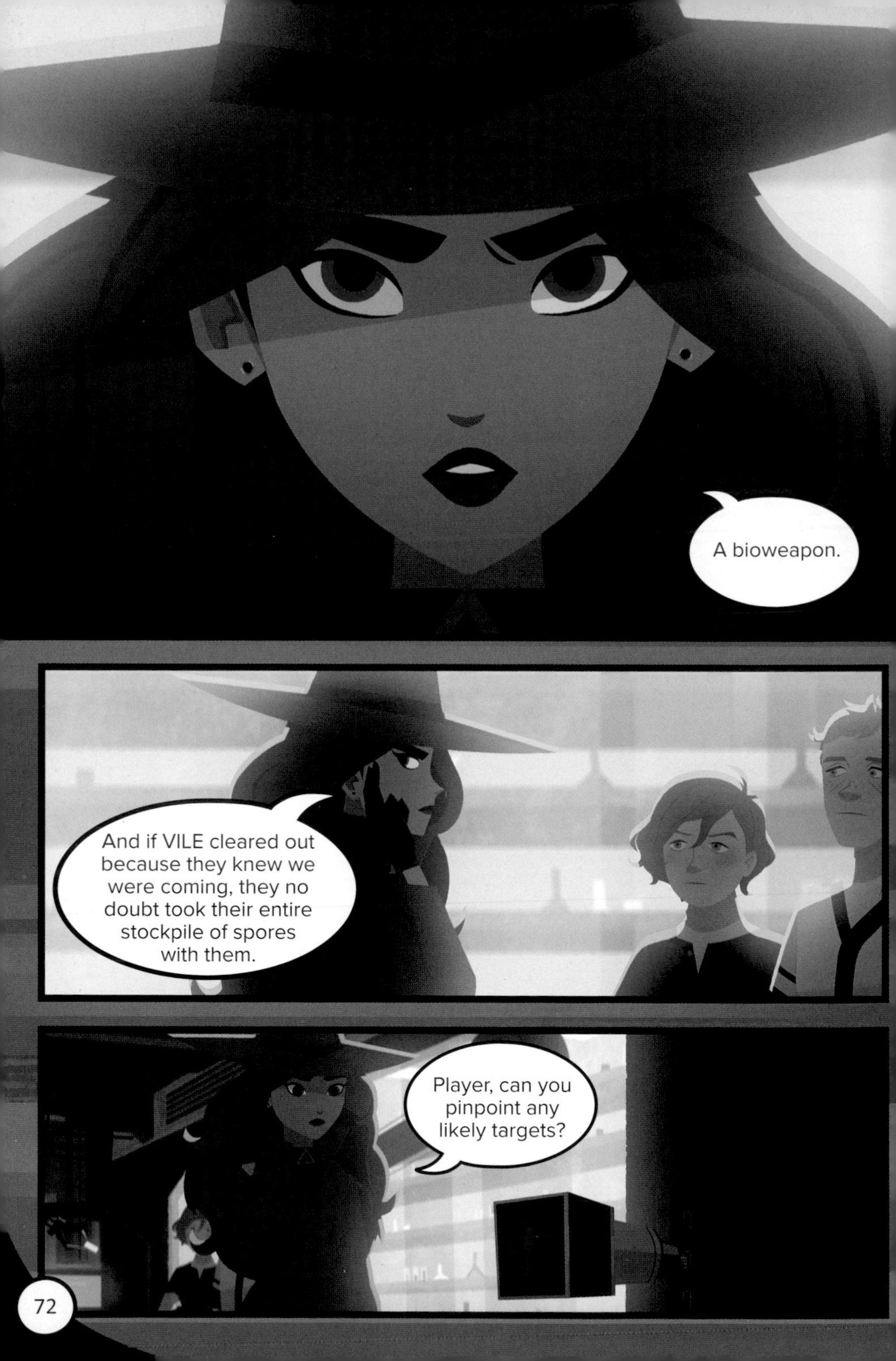
A bioweapon.
And if VILE cleared out because they knew we were coming, they no doubt took their entire stockpile of spores with them.
Player, can you pinpoint any likely targets?

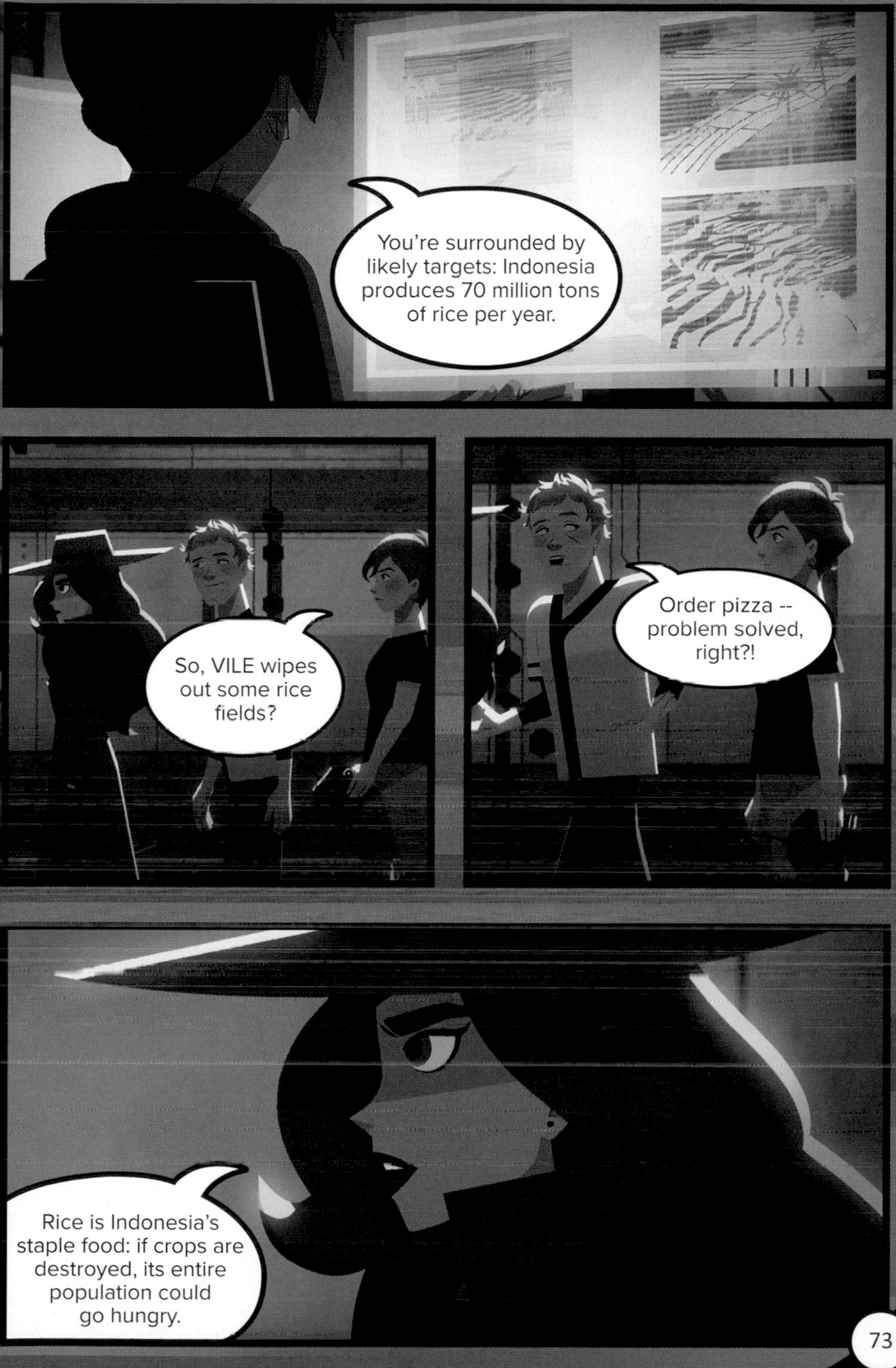
You're surrounded by likely targets: Indonesia produces 70 million tons of rice per year.
So, VILE wipes out some rice fields?
Order pizza -- problem solved, right?!
Rice is Indonesia's staple food: if crops are destroyed, its entire population could go hungry.

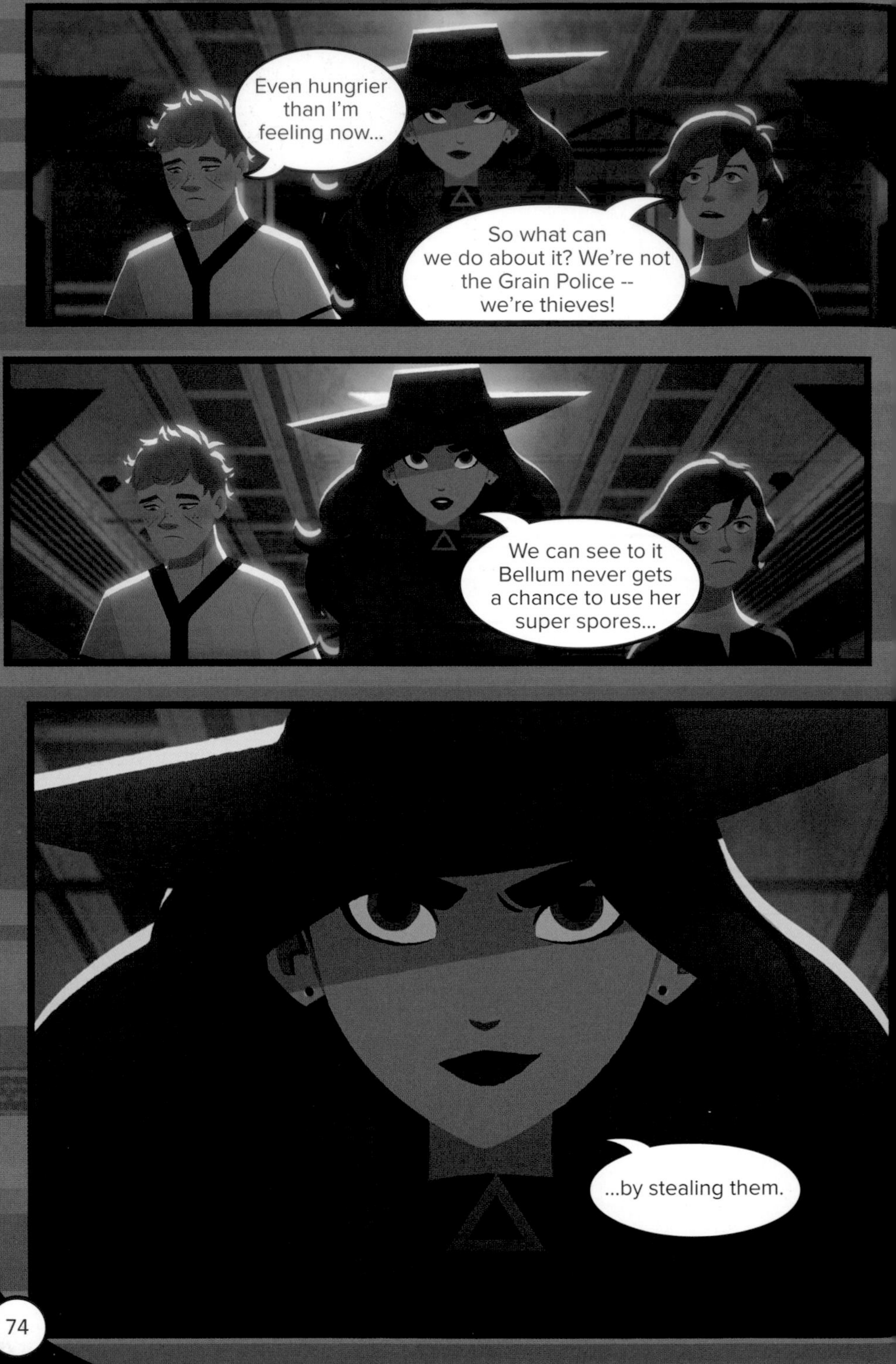
Even hungrier than I'm feeling now...
So what can we do about it? We're not the Grain Police -- we're thieves!
We can see to it Bellum never gets a chance to use her super spores...
...by stealing them.

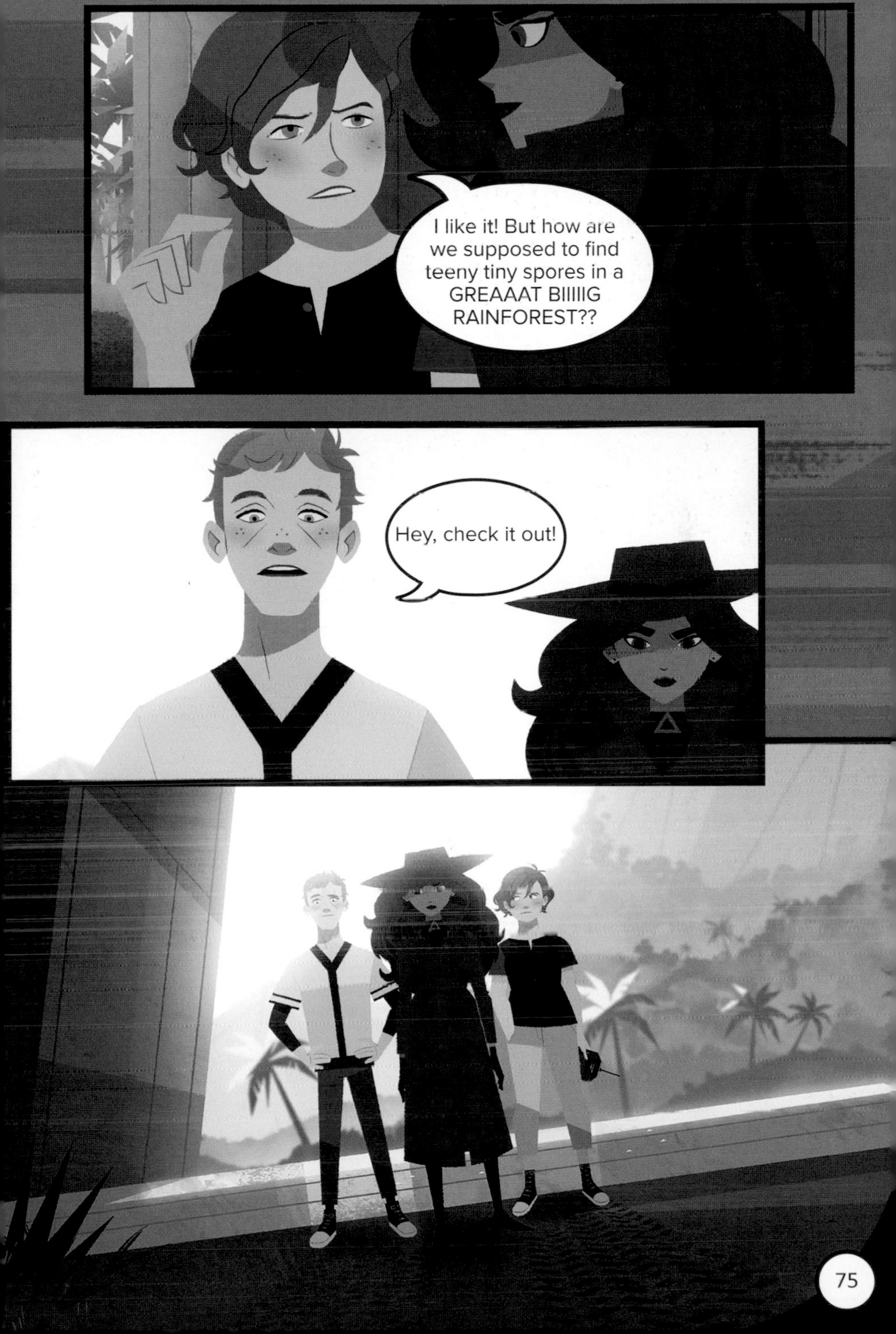
I like it! But how are we supposed to find teeny tiny spores in a GREAAAT BIIIIIG RAINFOREST??
Hey, check it out!

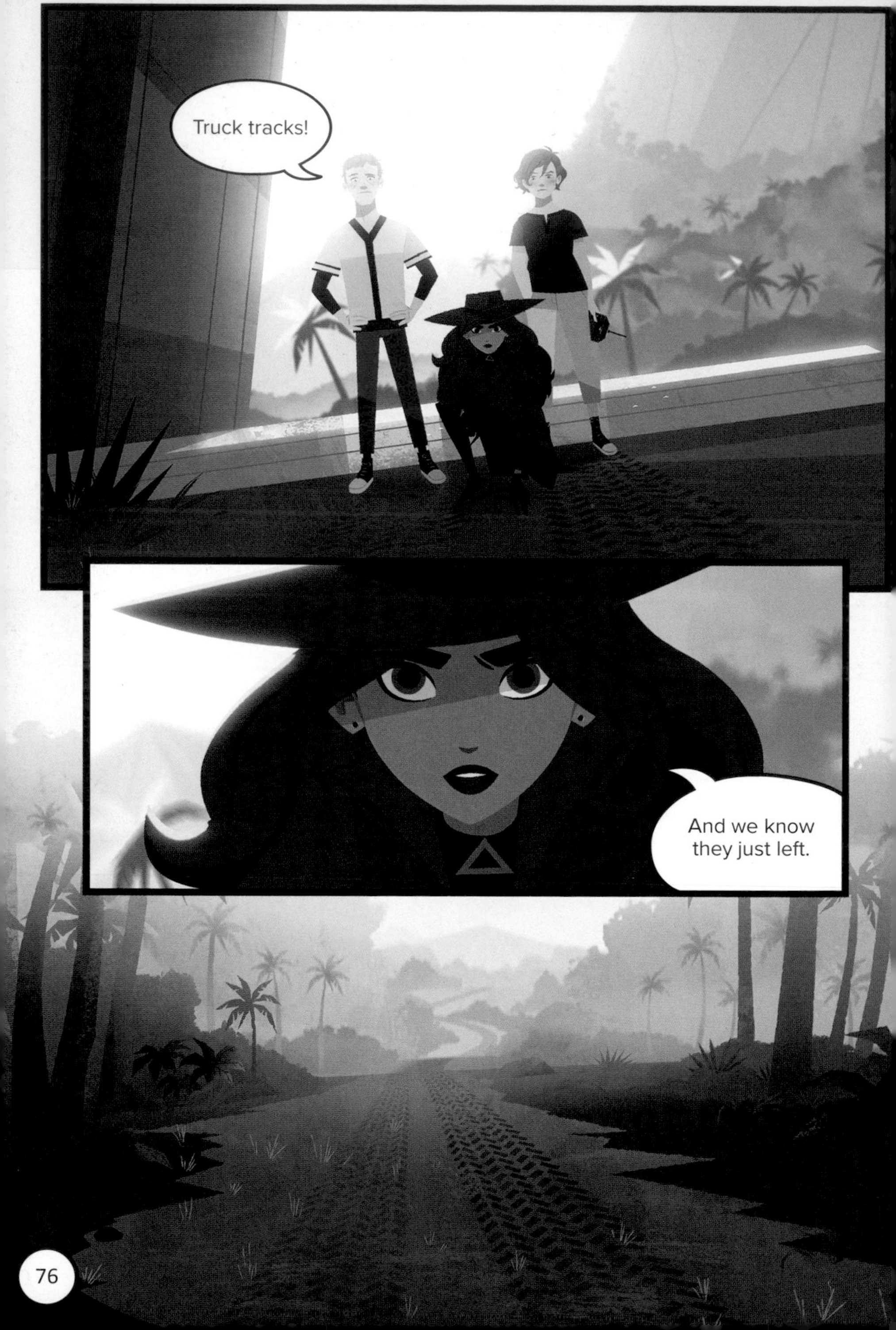
Truck tracks!
And we know they just left.

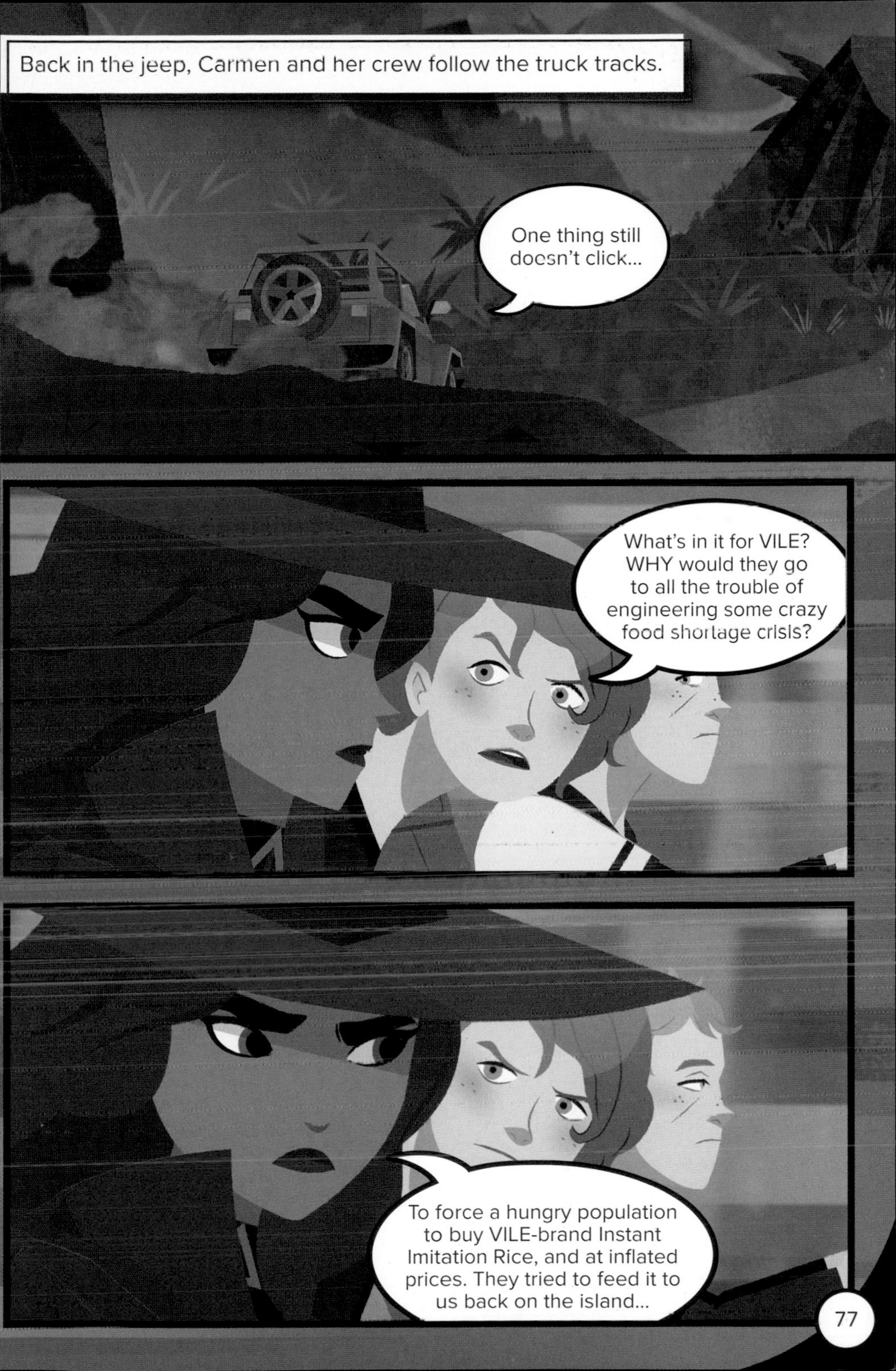
Back in the jeep, Carmen and her crew follow the truck tracks.
One thing still doesn't click...
What's in it for VILE? WHY would they go to all the trouble of engineering some crazy food shortage crisis?
To force a hungry population to buy VILE-brand Instant Imitation Rice, and at inflated prices. They tried to feed it to us back on the island...

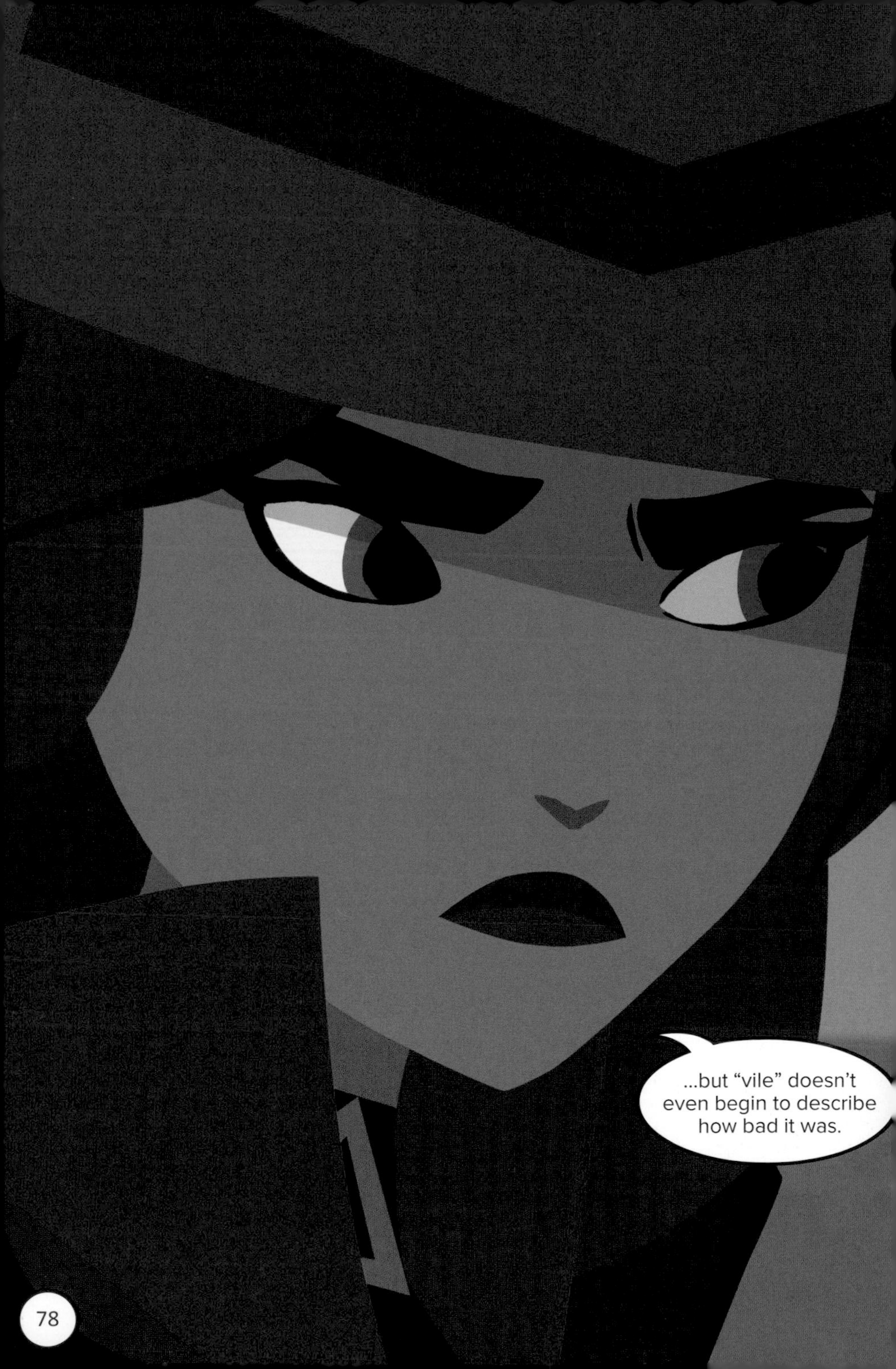
...but "vile" doesn't even begin to describe how bad it was.

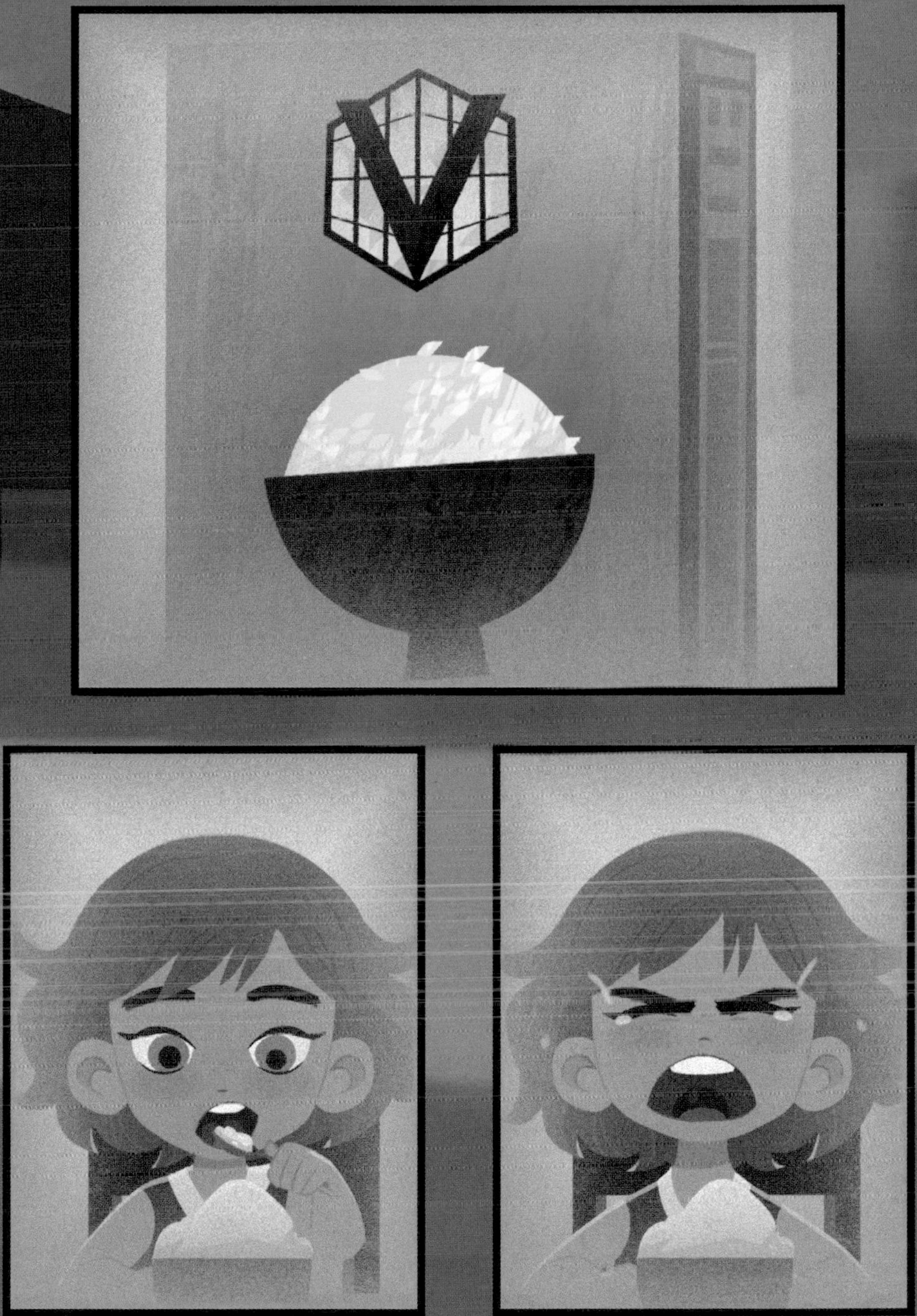

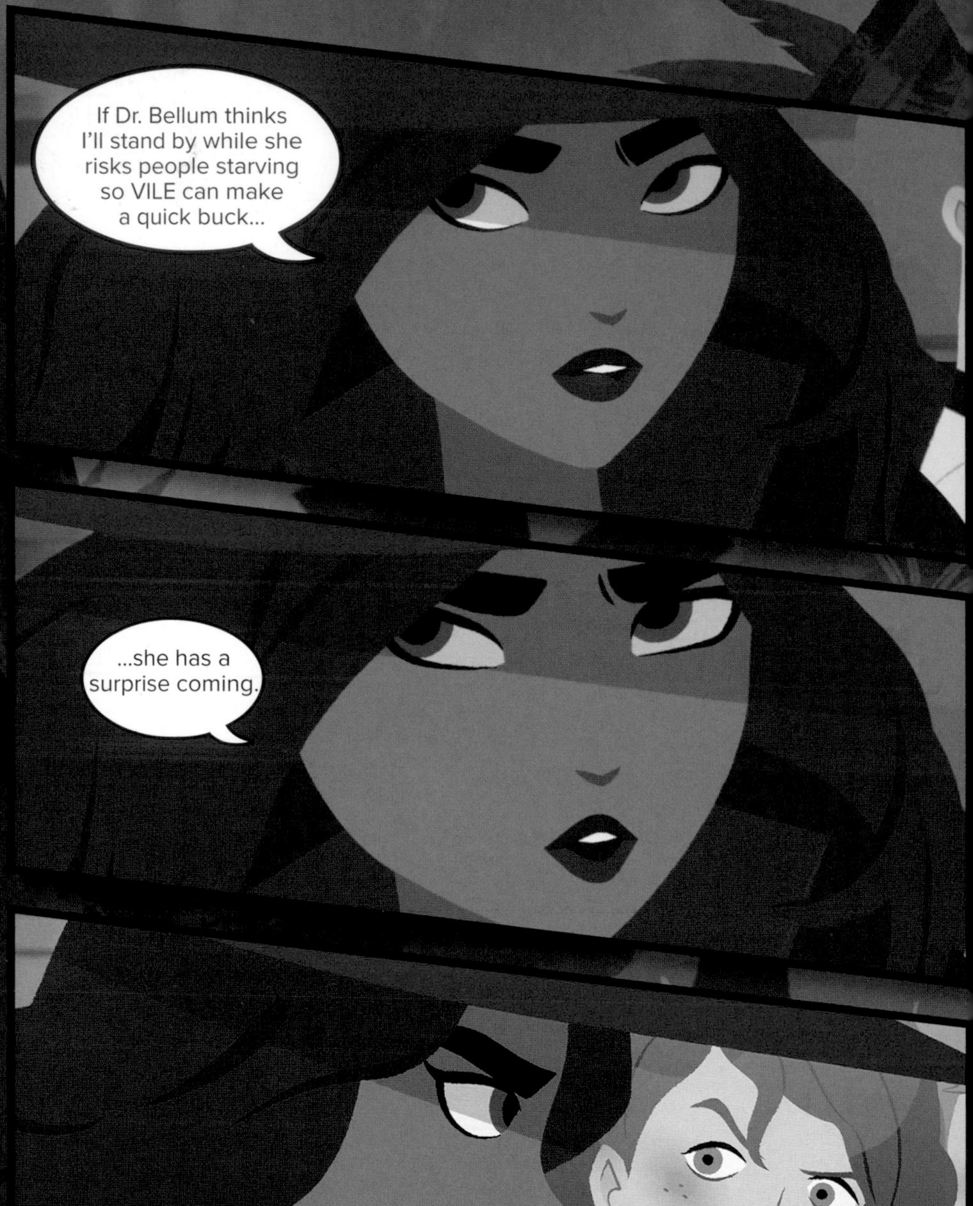
If Dr. Bellum thinks I'll stand by while she risks people starving so VILE can make a quick buck...
...she has a surprise coming.
Carm...

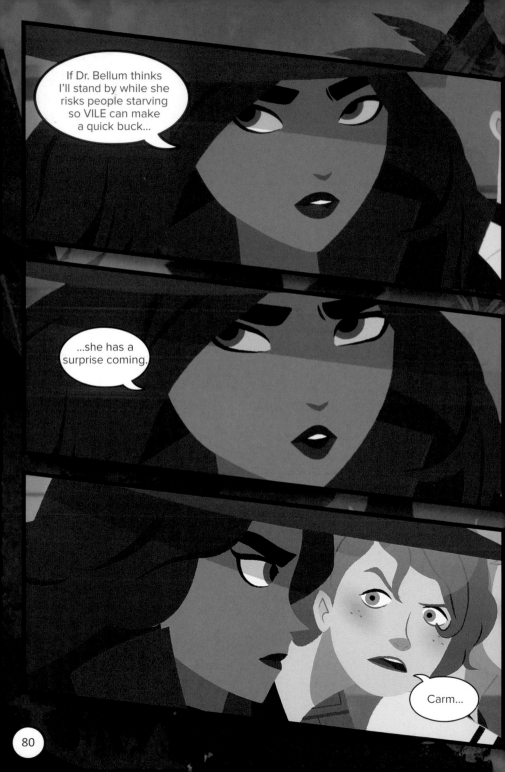

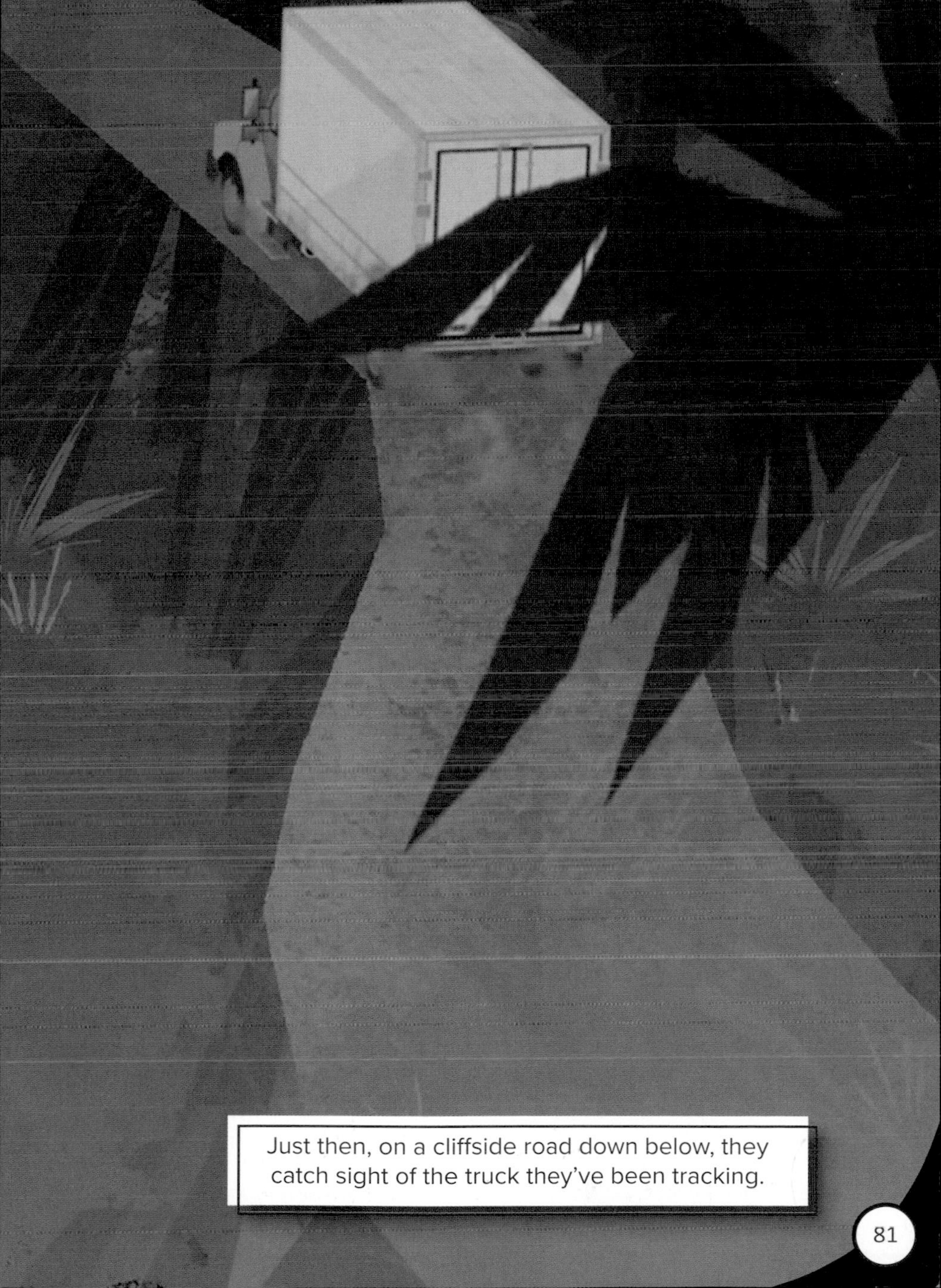
Just then, on a cliffside road down below, they catch sight of the truck they've been tracking.

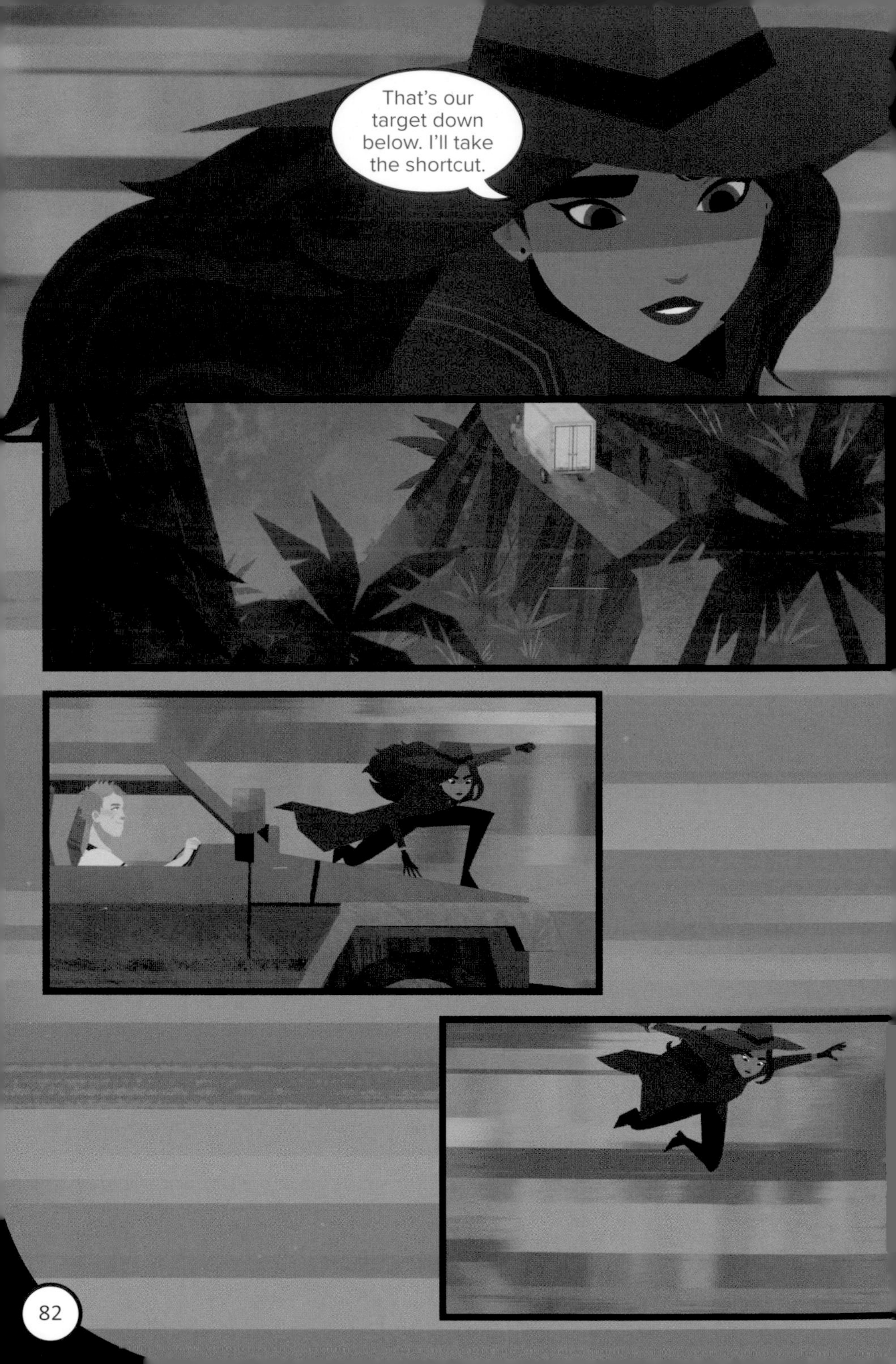
That's our target down below. I'll take the shortcut.

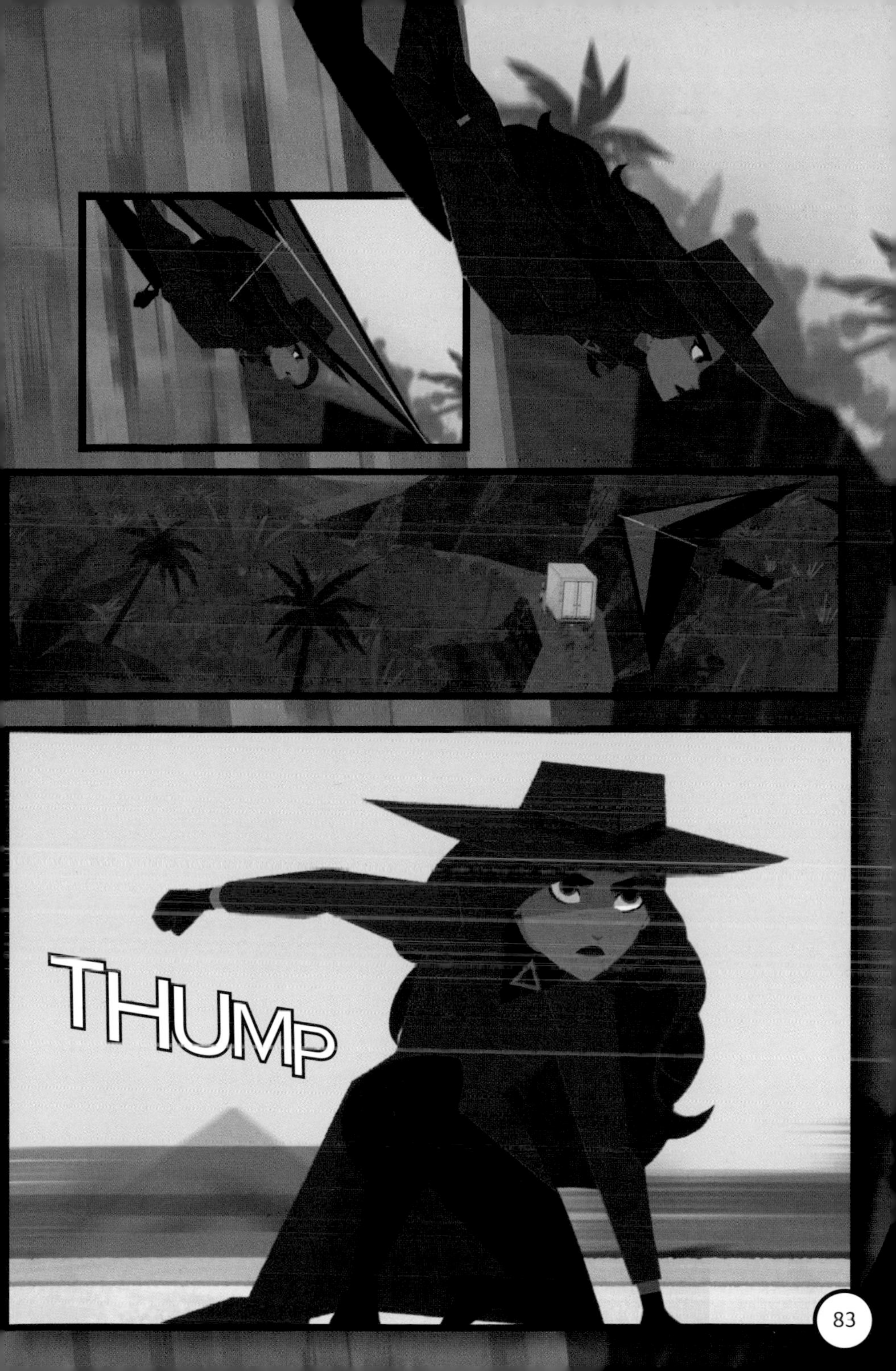
THUMP

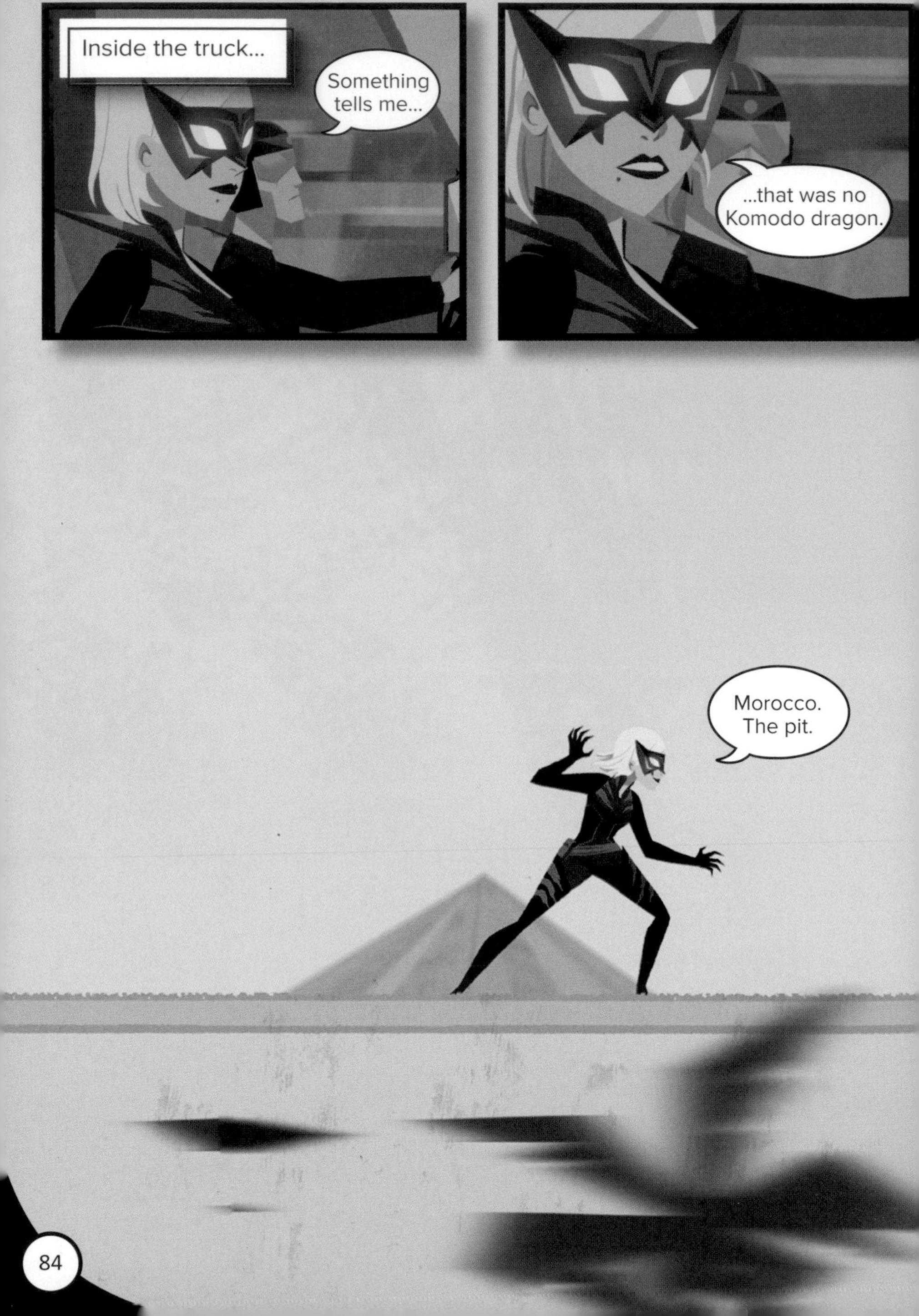
Inside the truck...
Something tells me...
...that was no Komodo dragon.
Morocco. The pit.

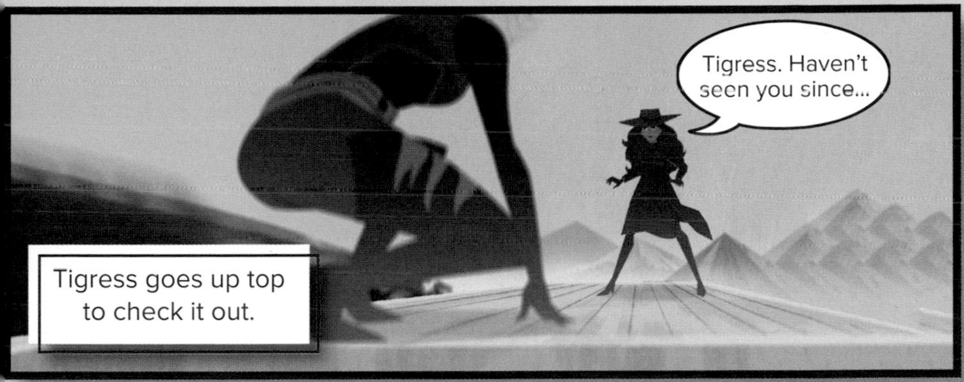
Tigress goes up top to check it out.
Tigress. Haven't seen you since...

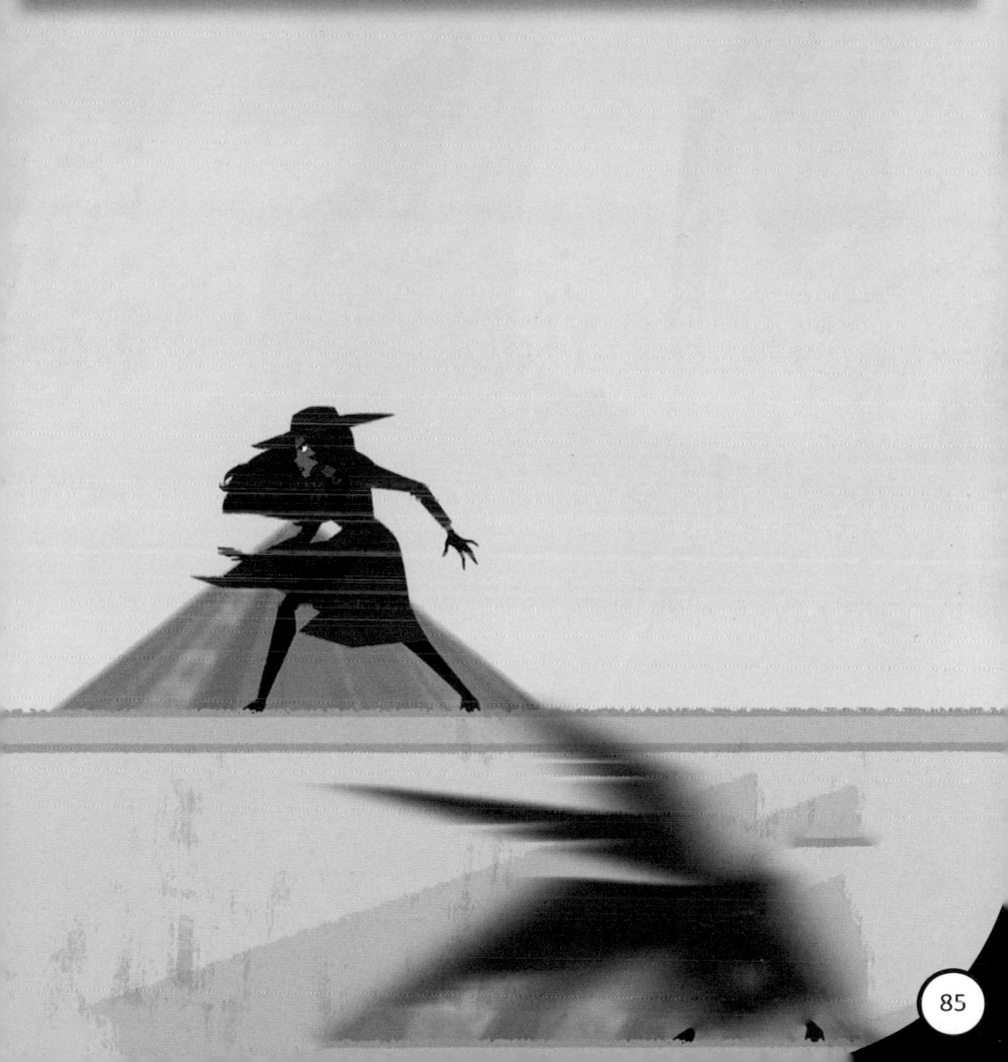

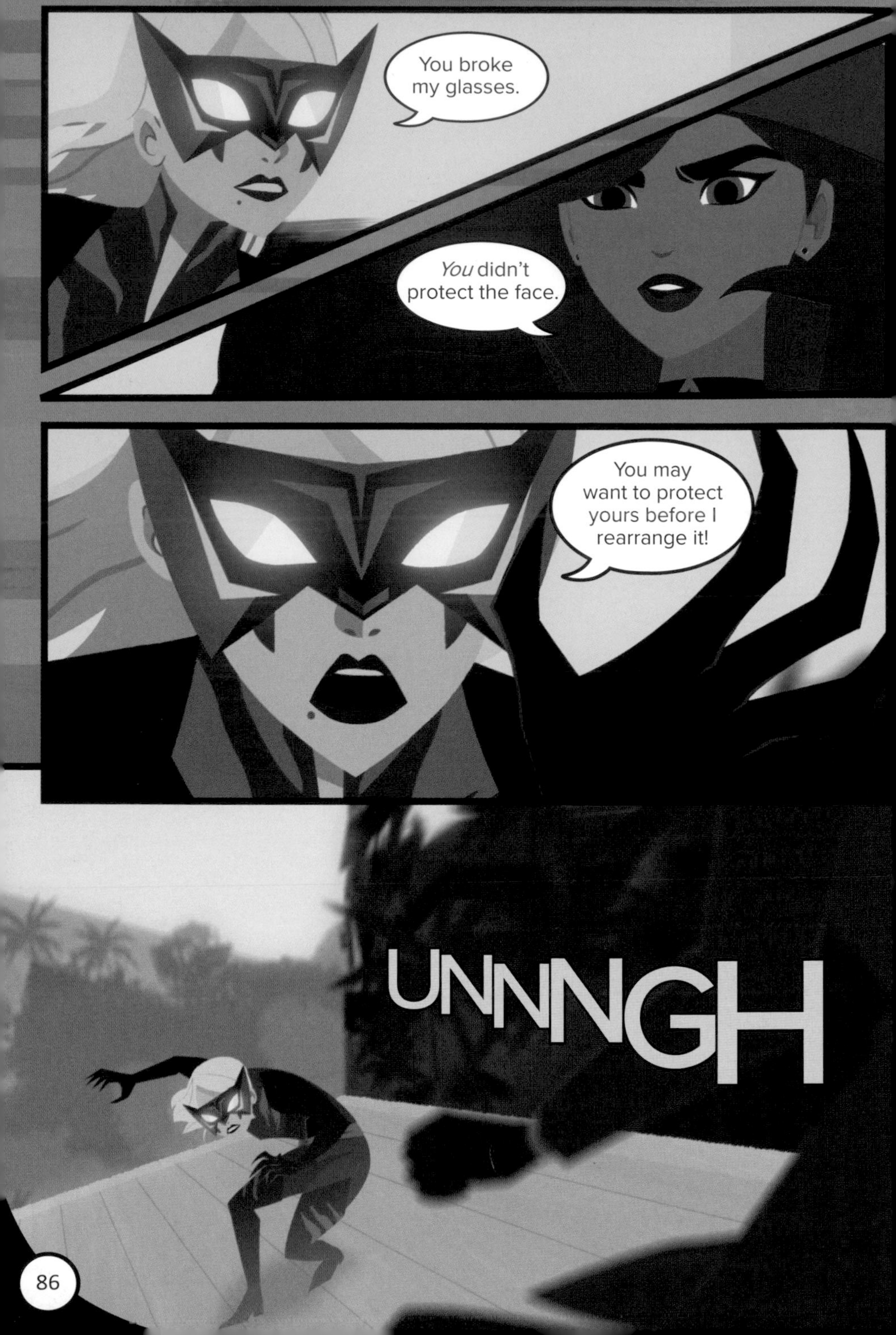

You broke my glasses.
You didn't protect the face.
You may want to protect yours before I rearrange it!
UNNNGH

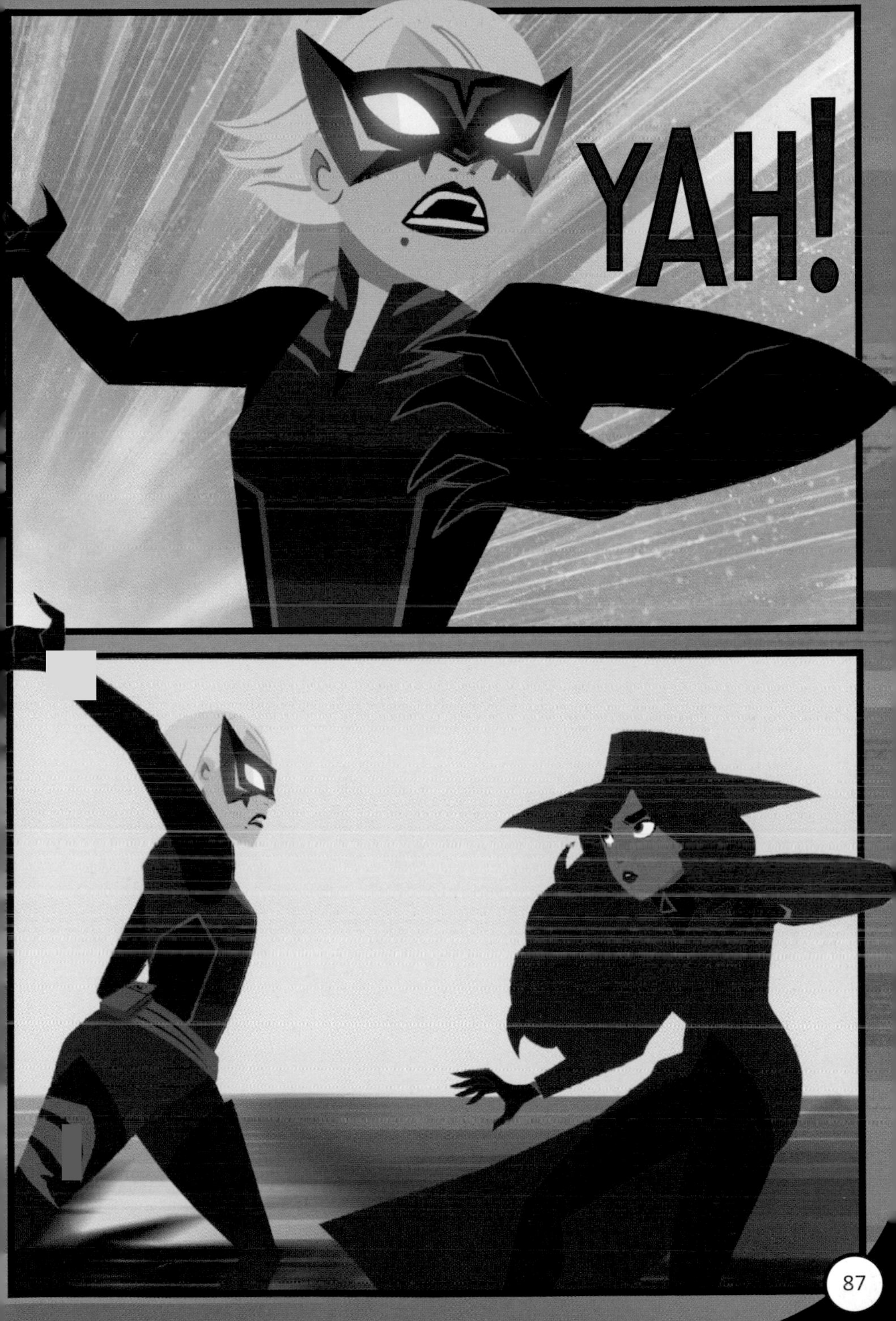
YAH!

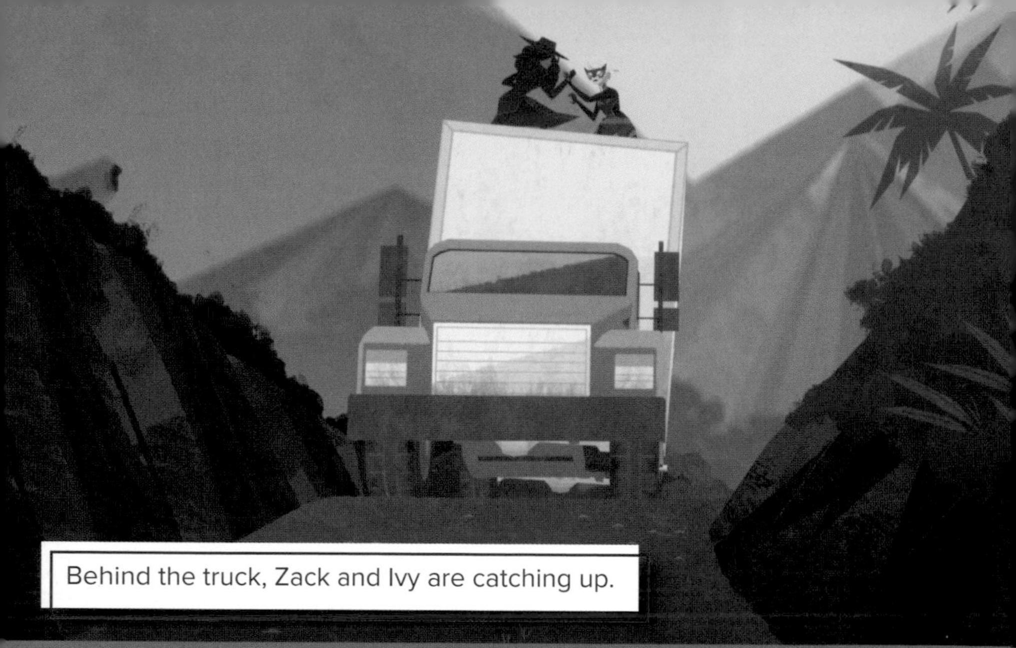
Behind the truck, Zack and Ivy are catching up.

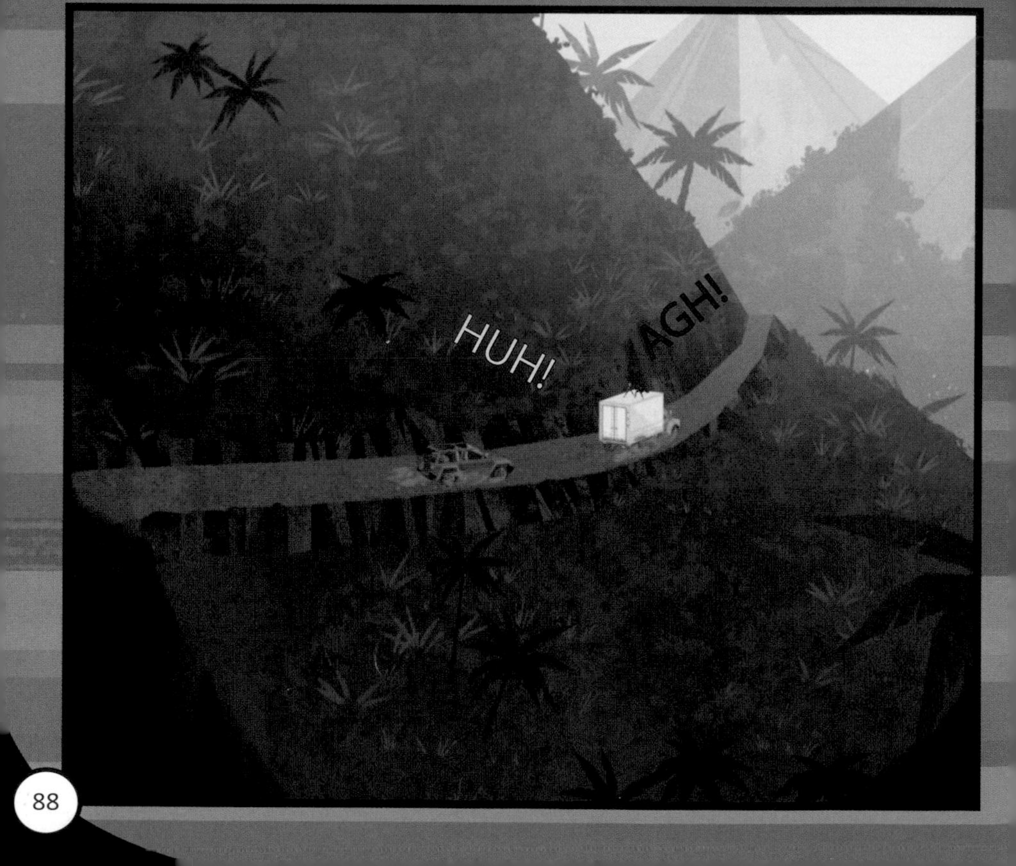
HUH!
AGH!

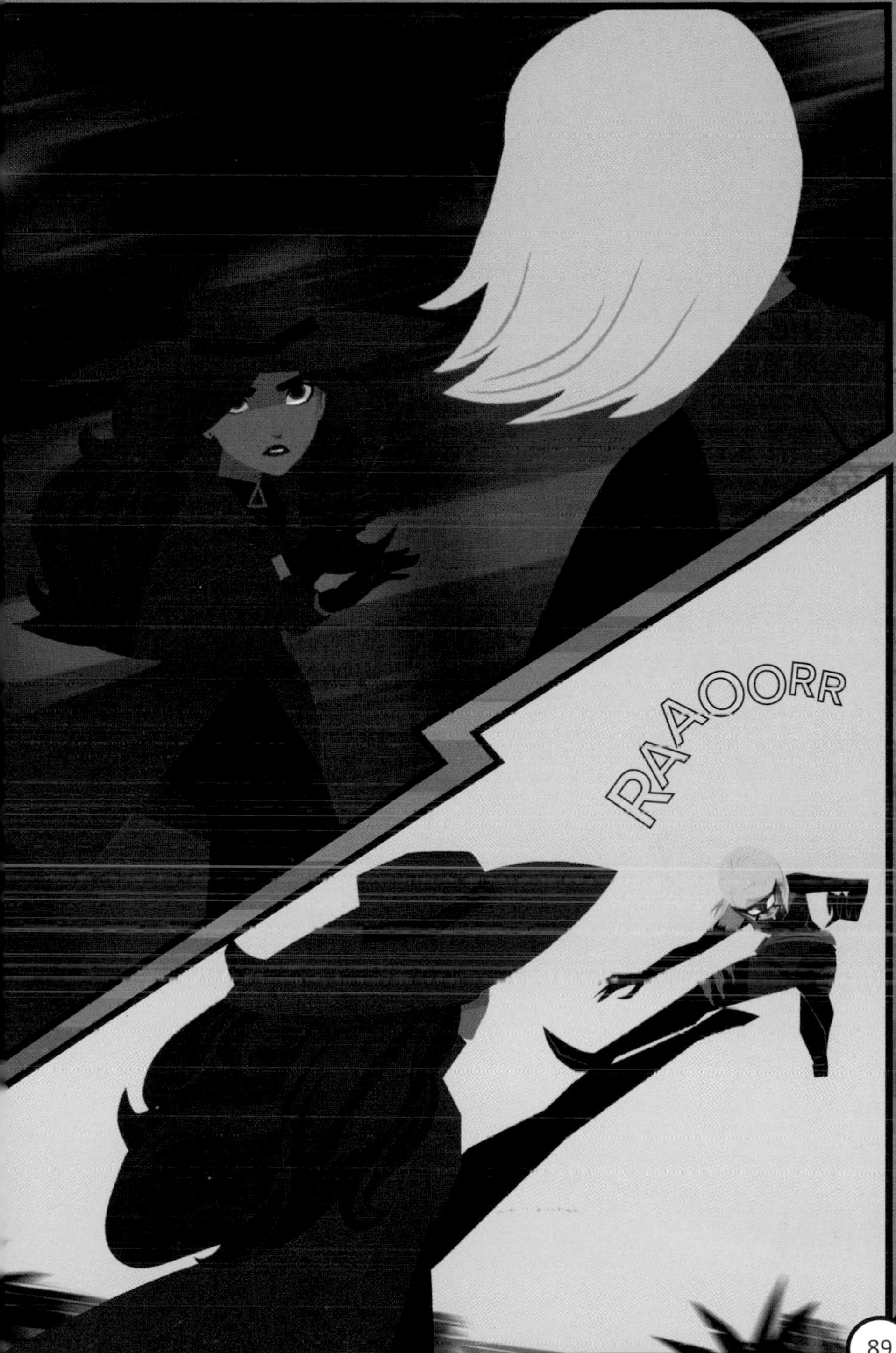
RAAOORR

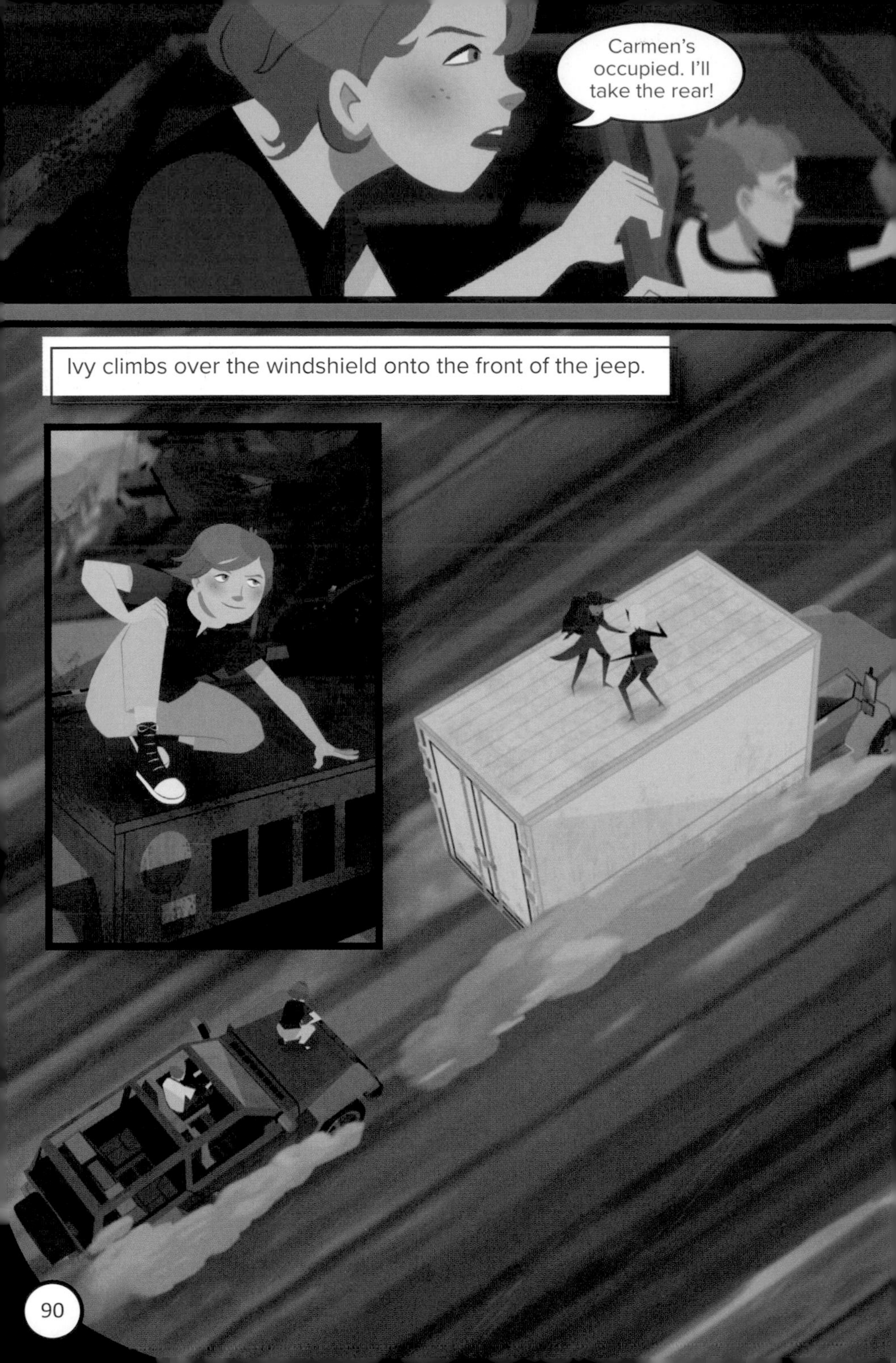
Carmen's
occupied. I'll
take the rear!
Ivy climbs over the windshield onto the front of the jeep.

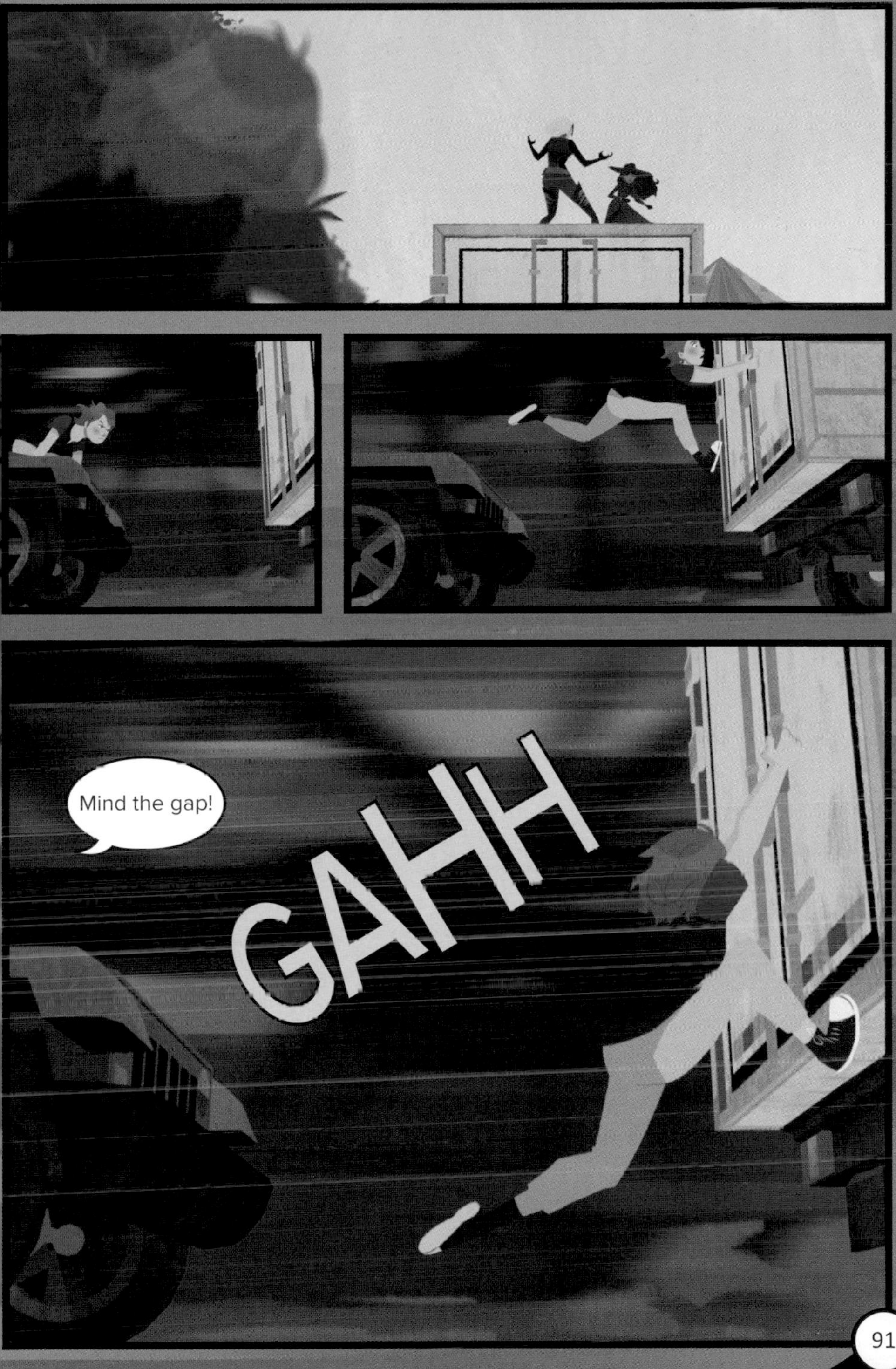
Mind the gap!
GAHH

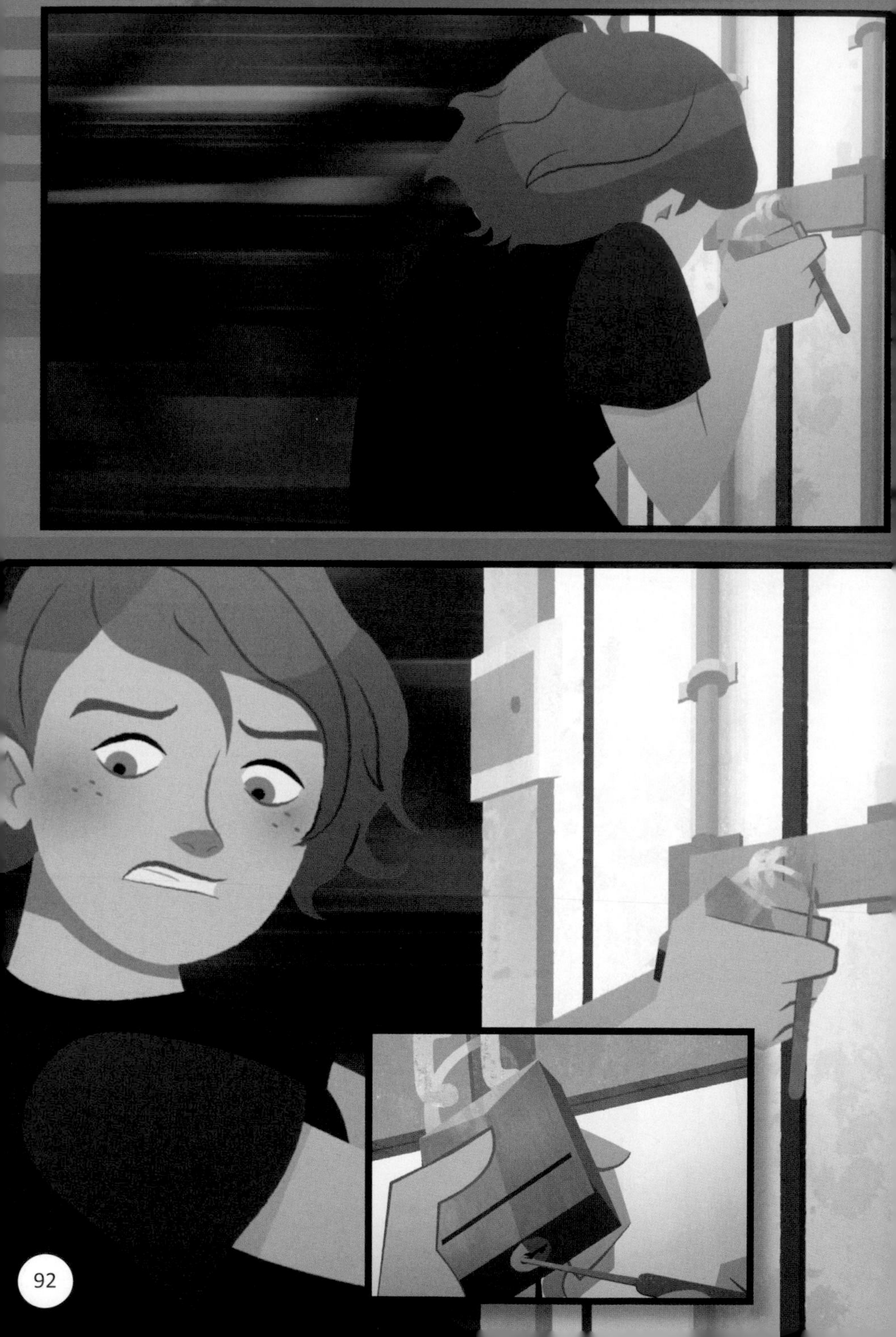

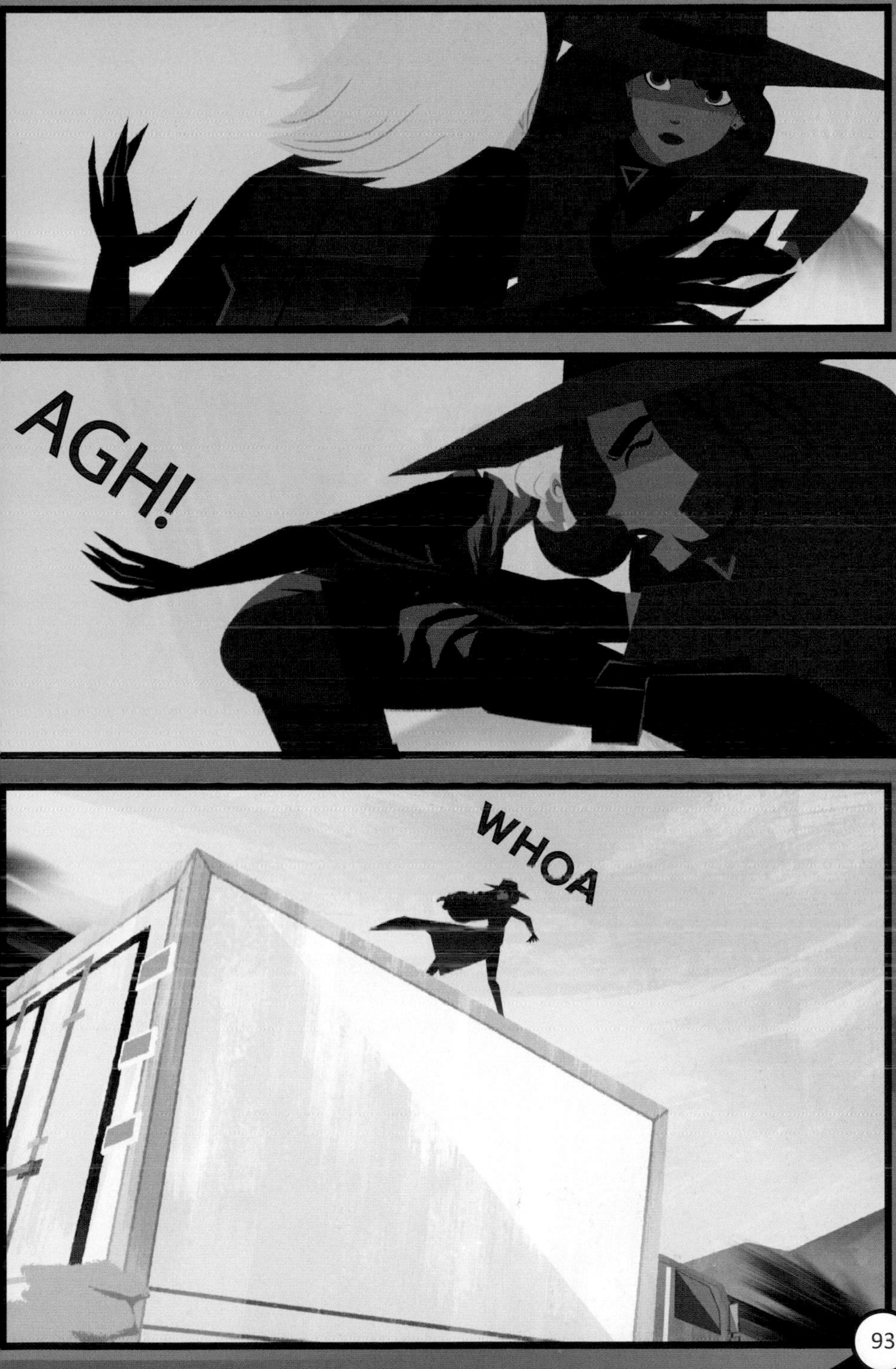
AGH!
WHOA

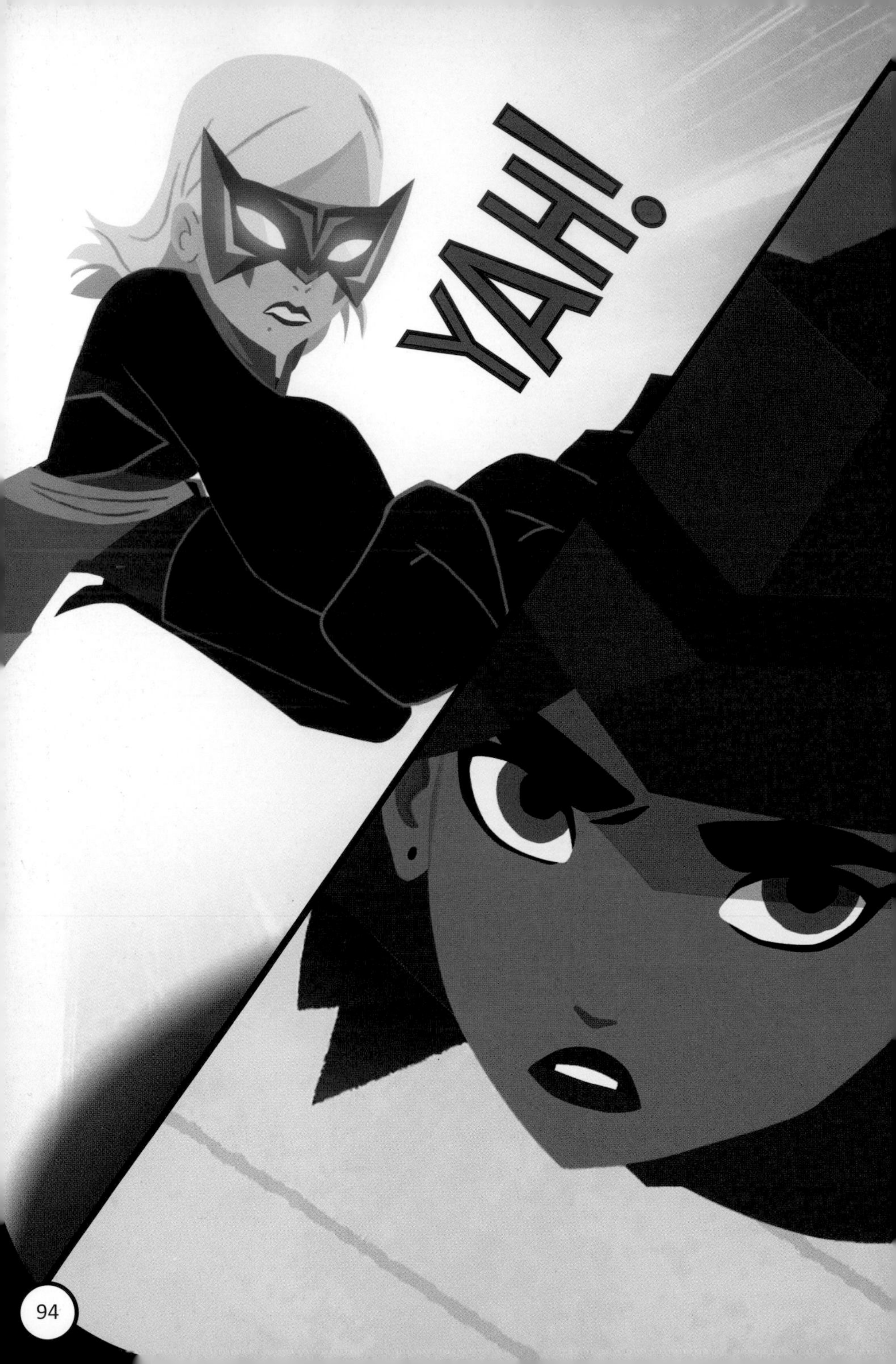
YAH!

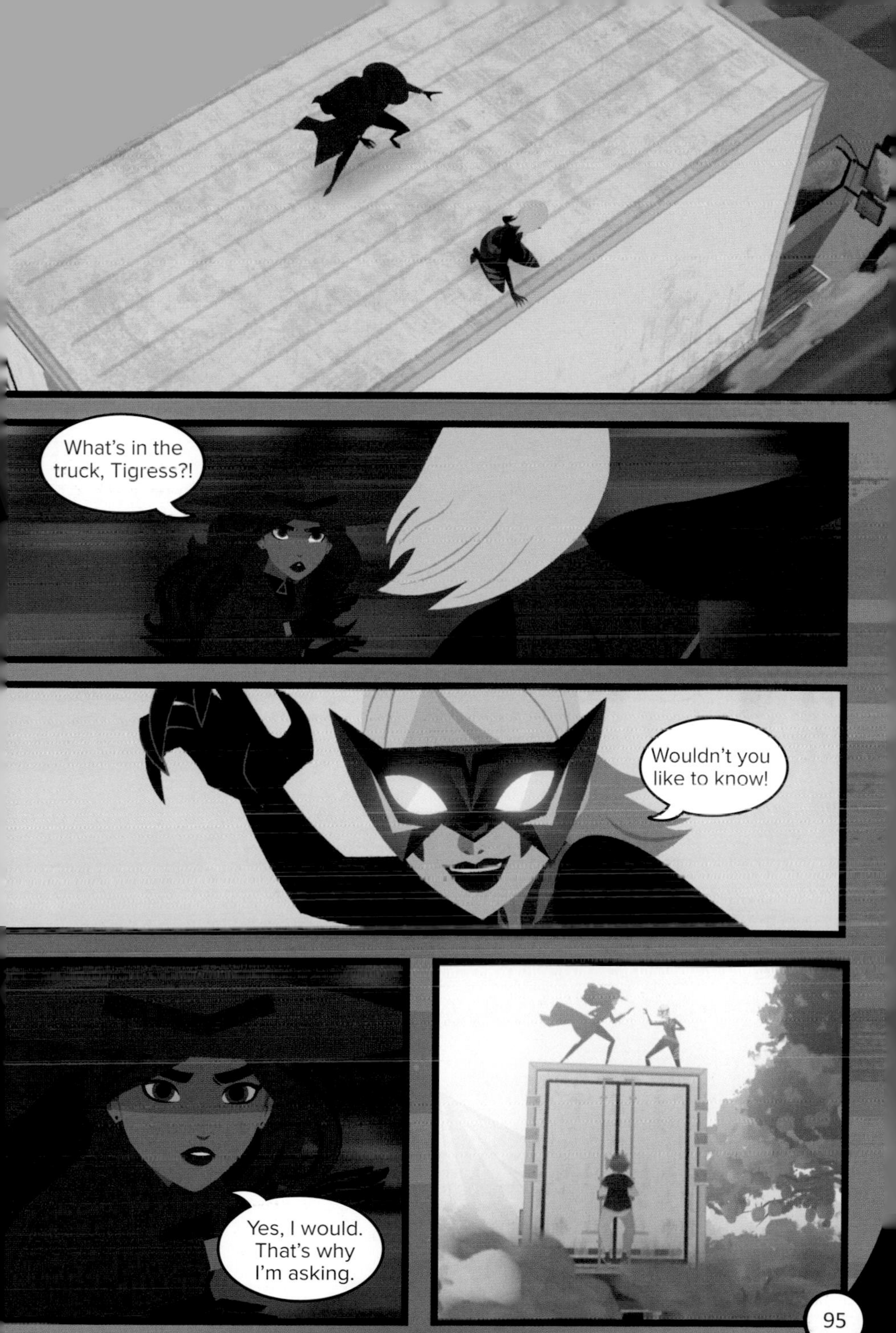
What's in the truck, Tigress?!
Wouldn't you like to know!
Yes, I would. That's why I'm asking.

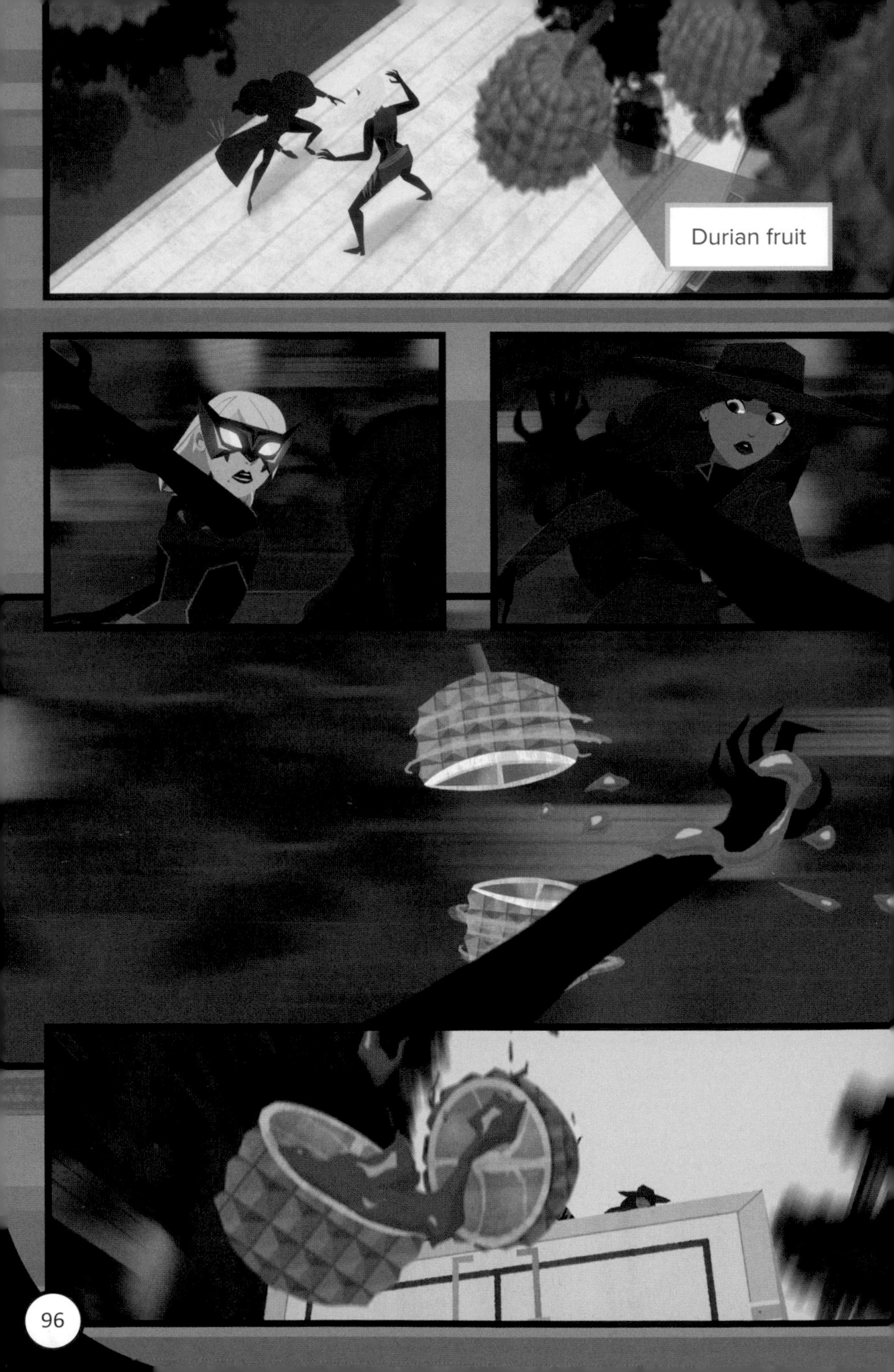
Durian fruit

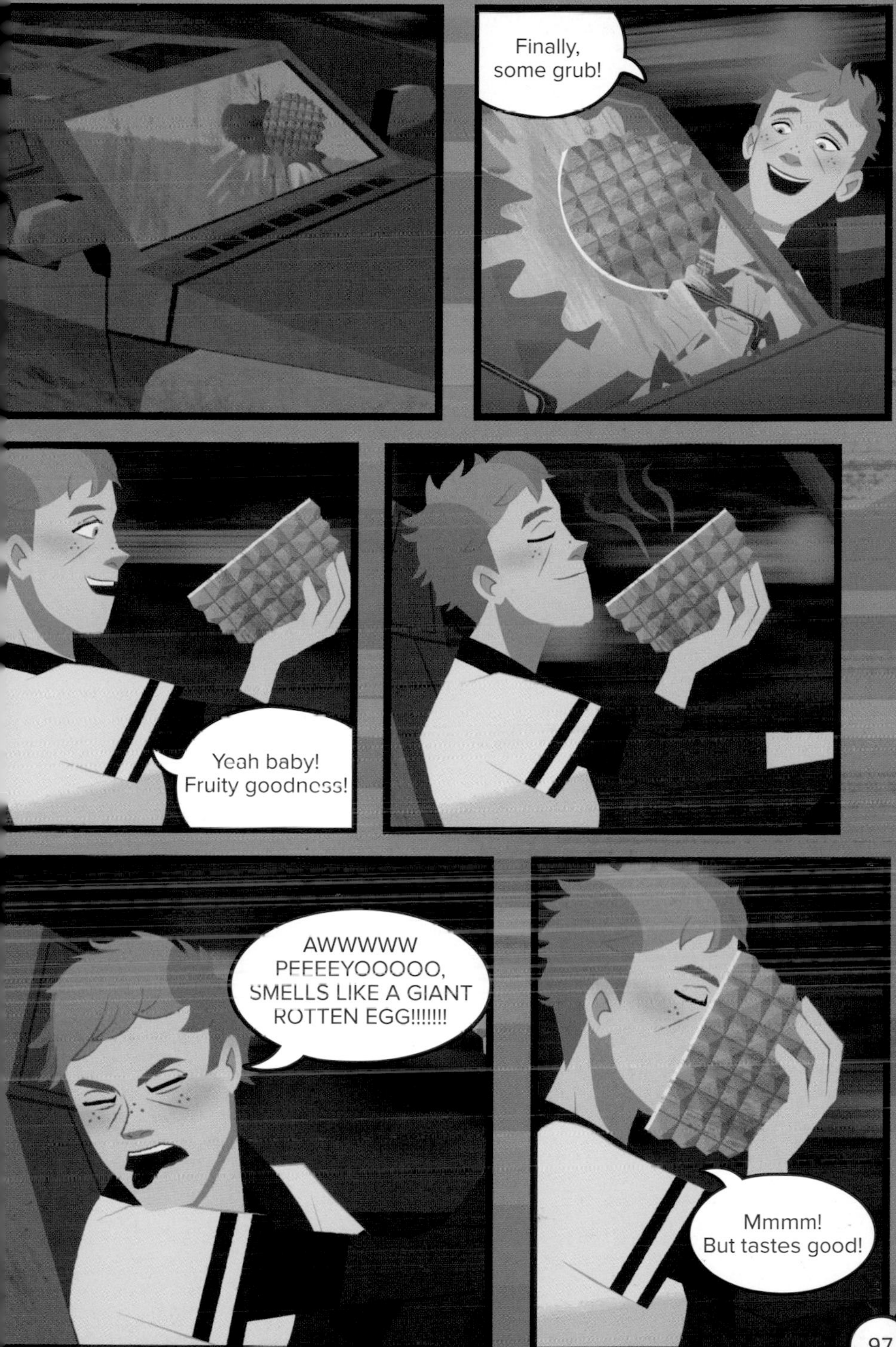
Finally, some grub!
Yeah baby! Fruity goodness!
AWWWWW PEEEEYOOOOO, SMELLS LIKE A GIANT ROTTEN EGG!!!!!!!
Mmmm! But tastes good!

Almost...

...got it!

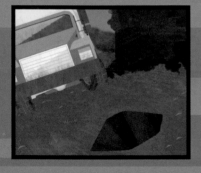

WAAAAAA

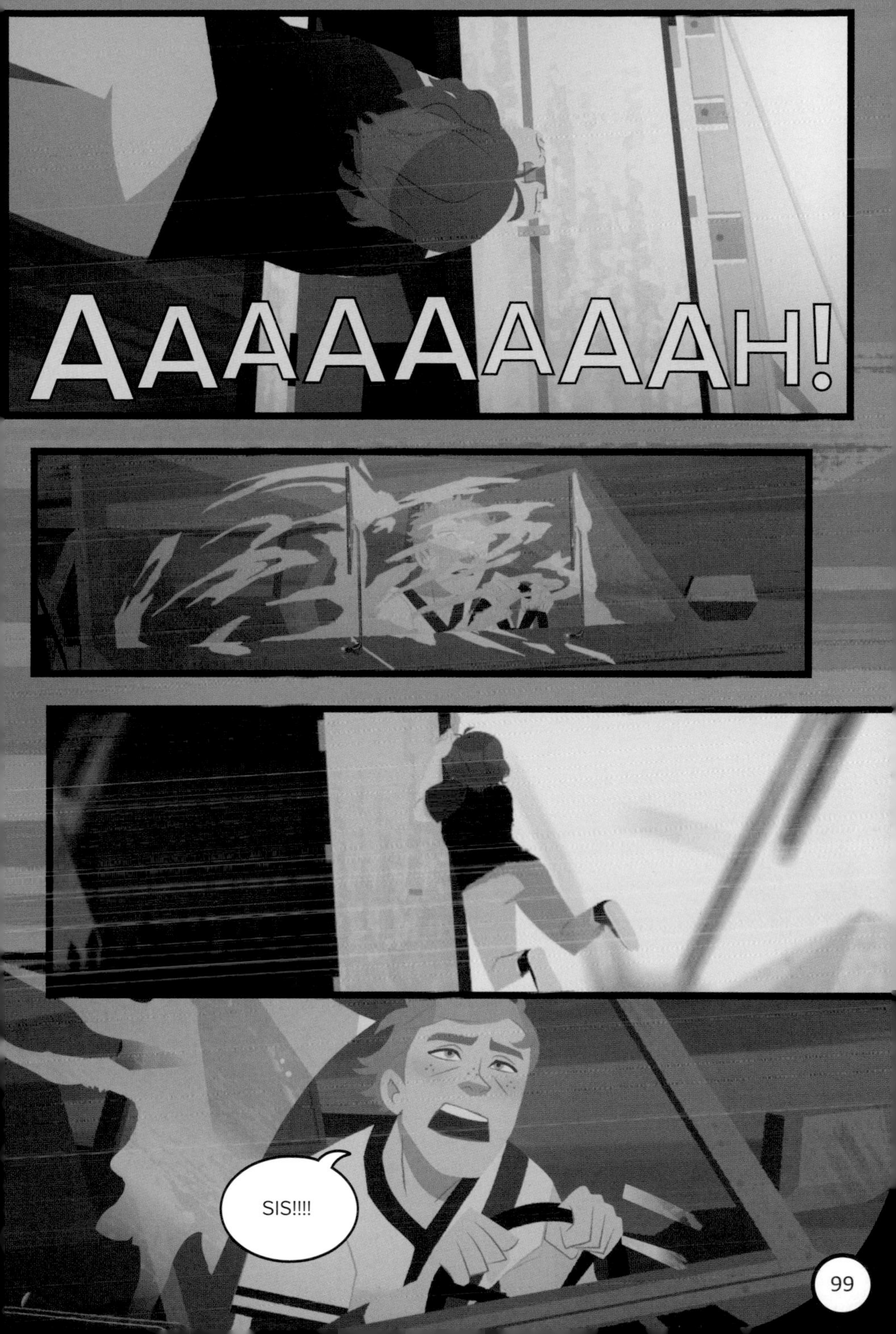
AAAAAAAAH!
SIS!!!!

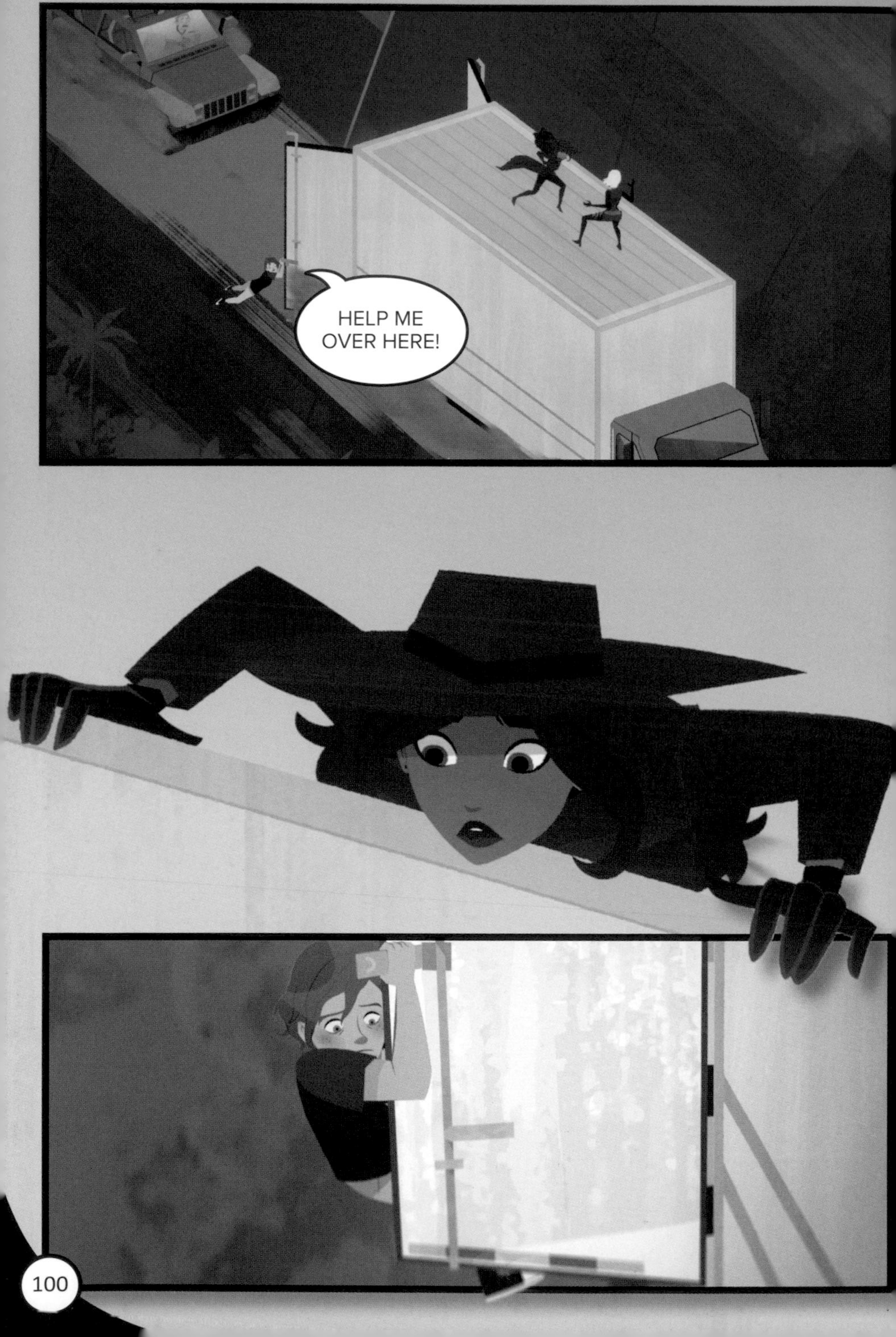
HELP ME
OVER HERE!

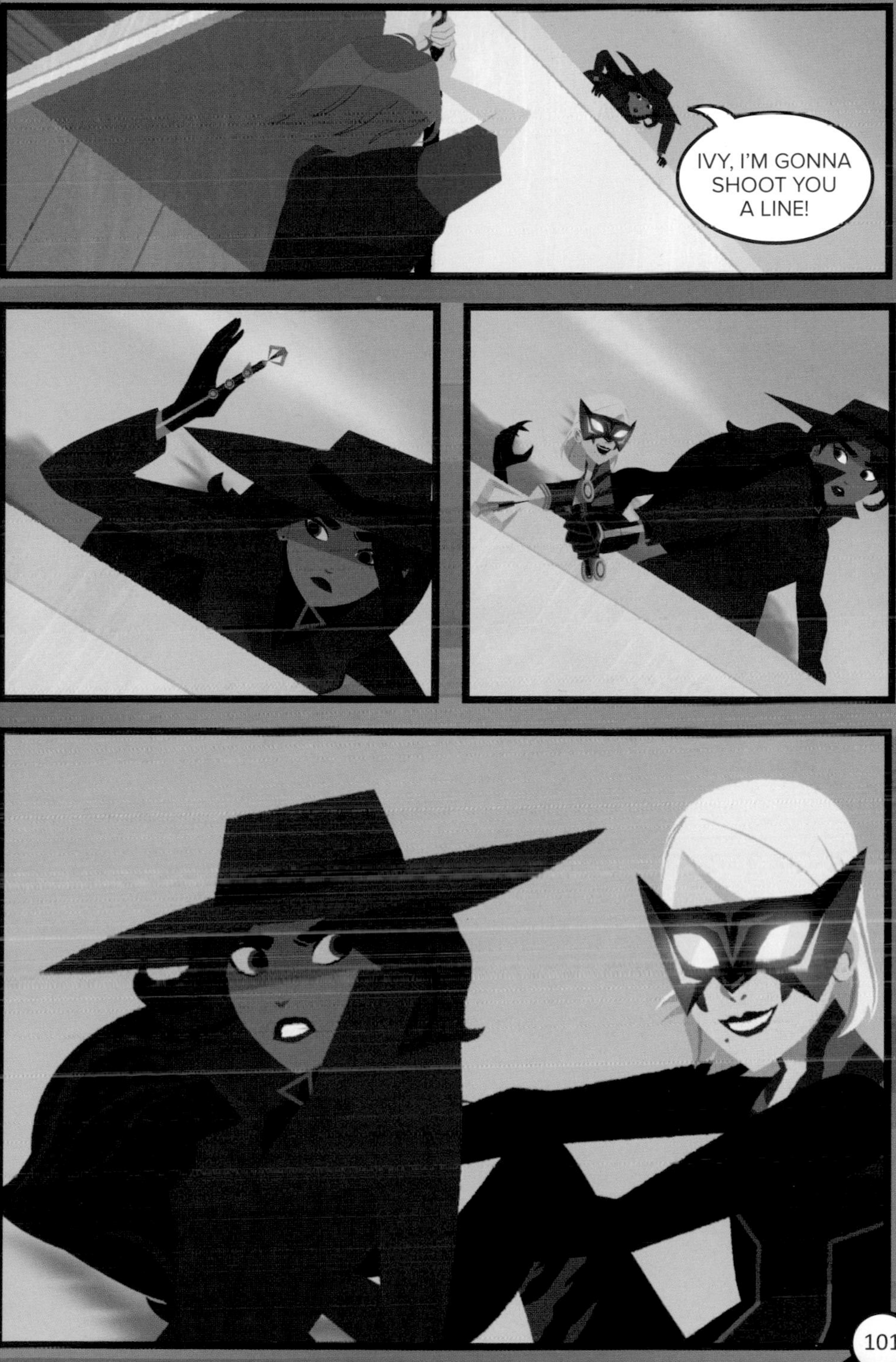
IVY, I'M GONNA SHOOT YOU A LINE!

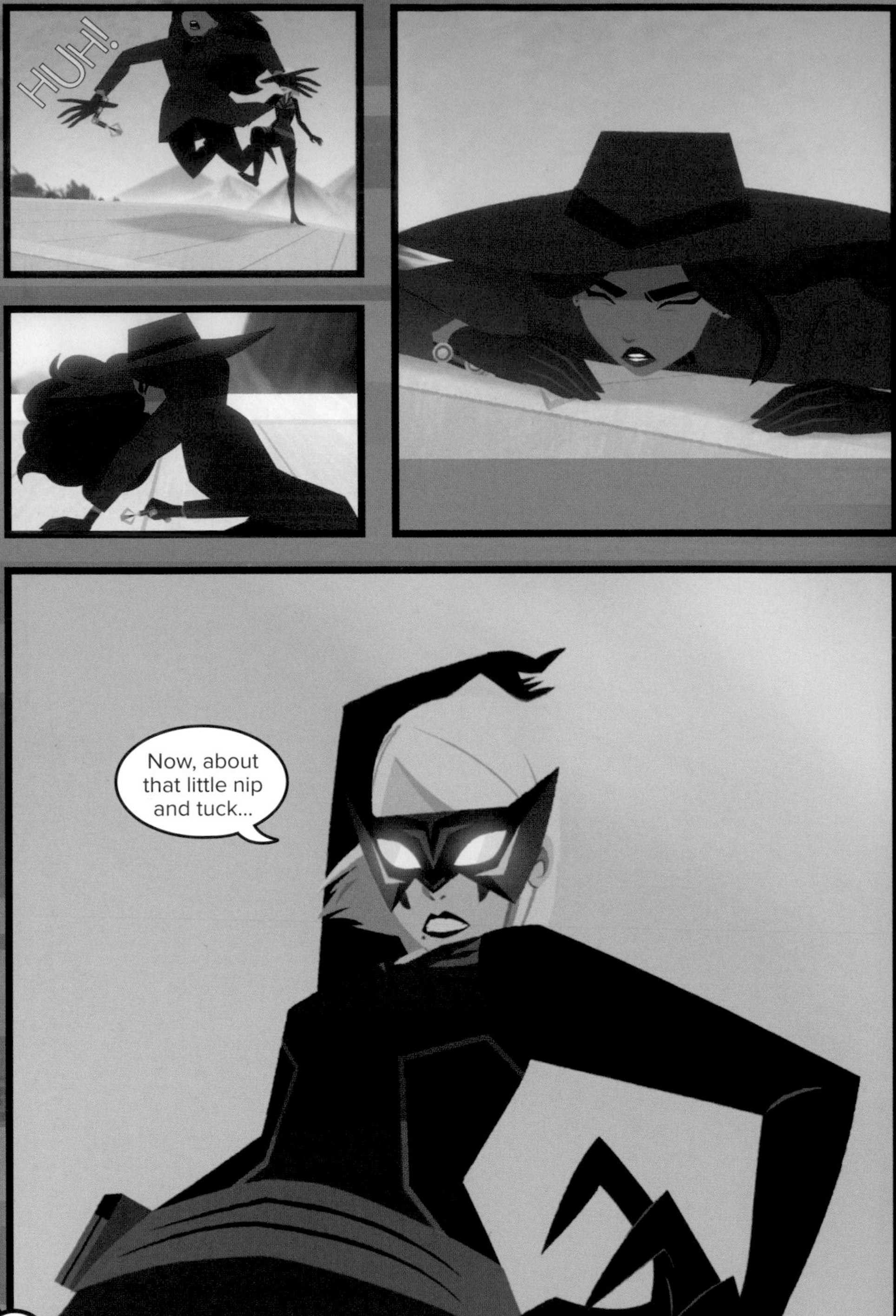
HUH!
Now, about that little nip and tuck...

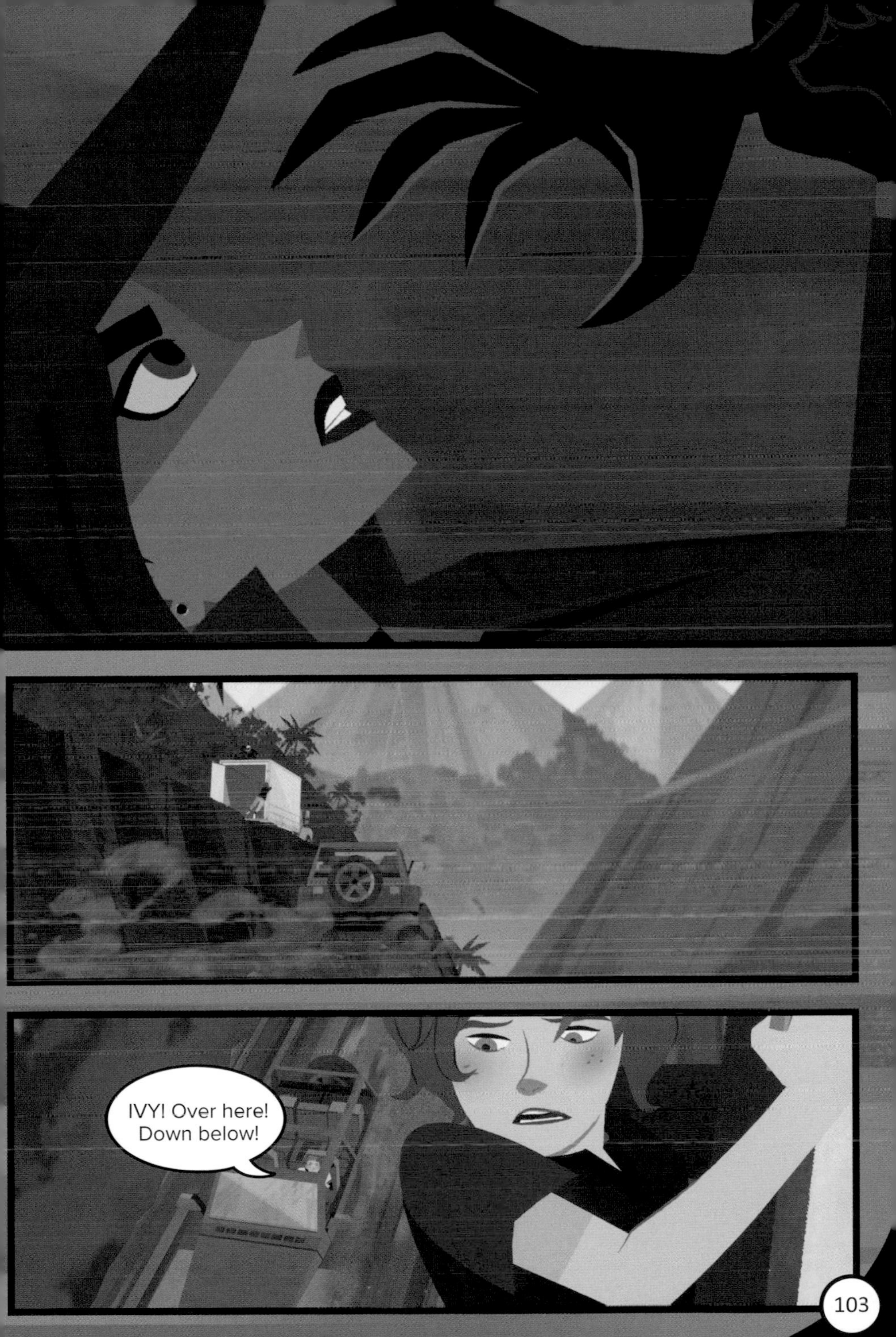
IVY! Over here!
Down below!

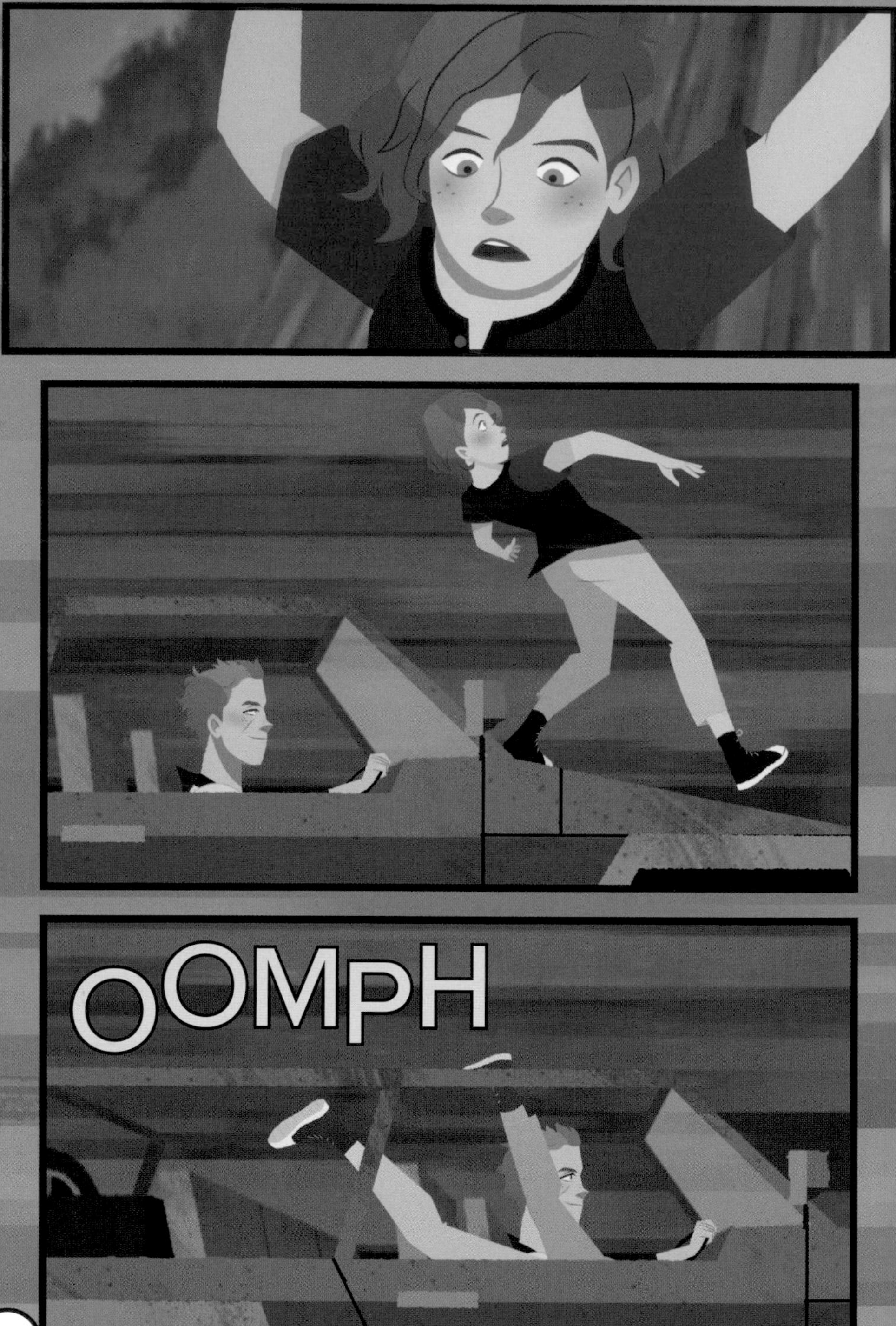
OOMPH

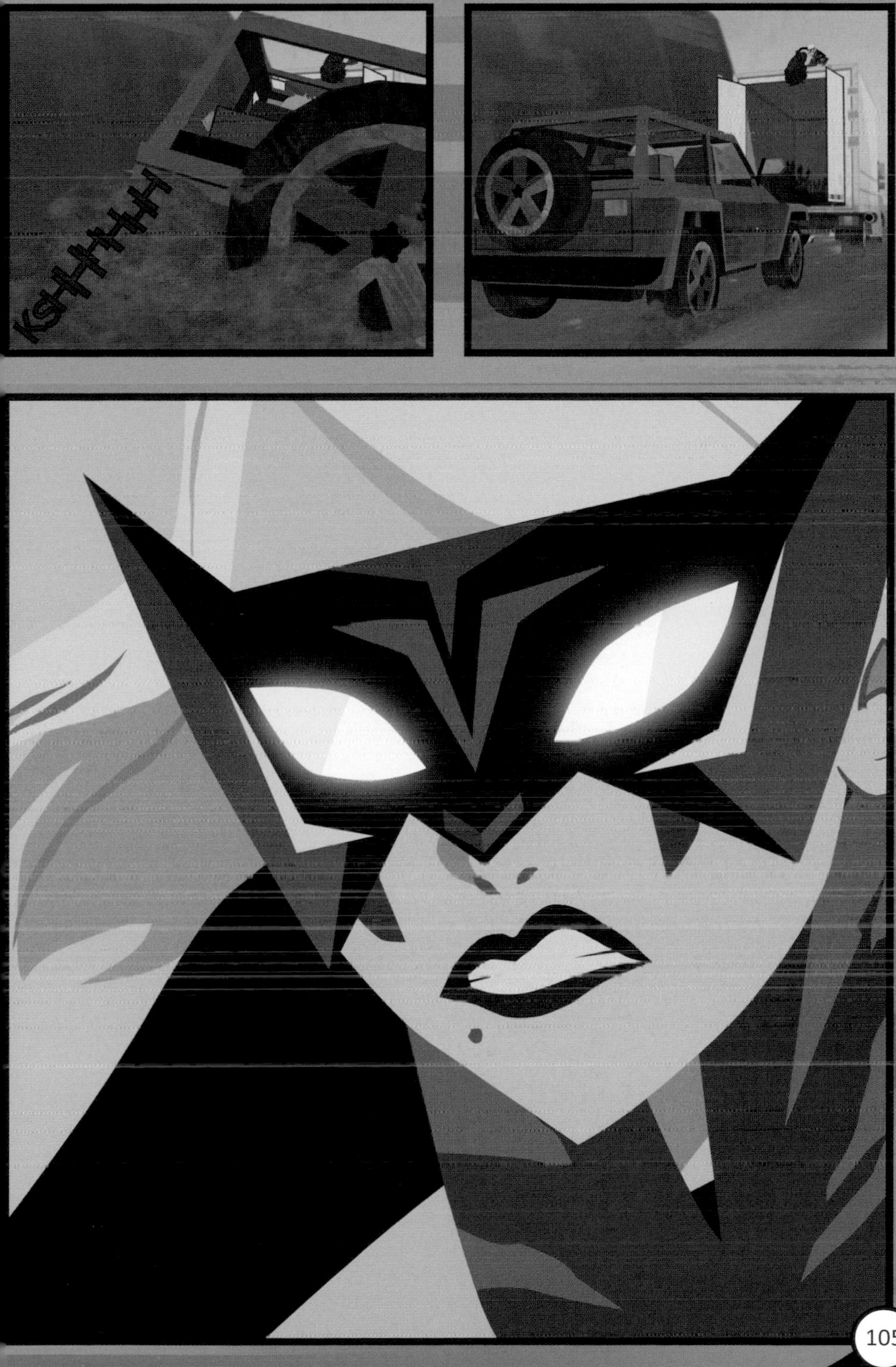
KSHHHHH

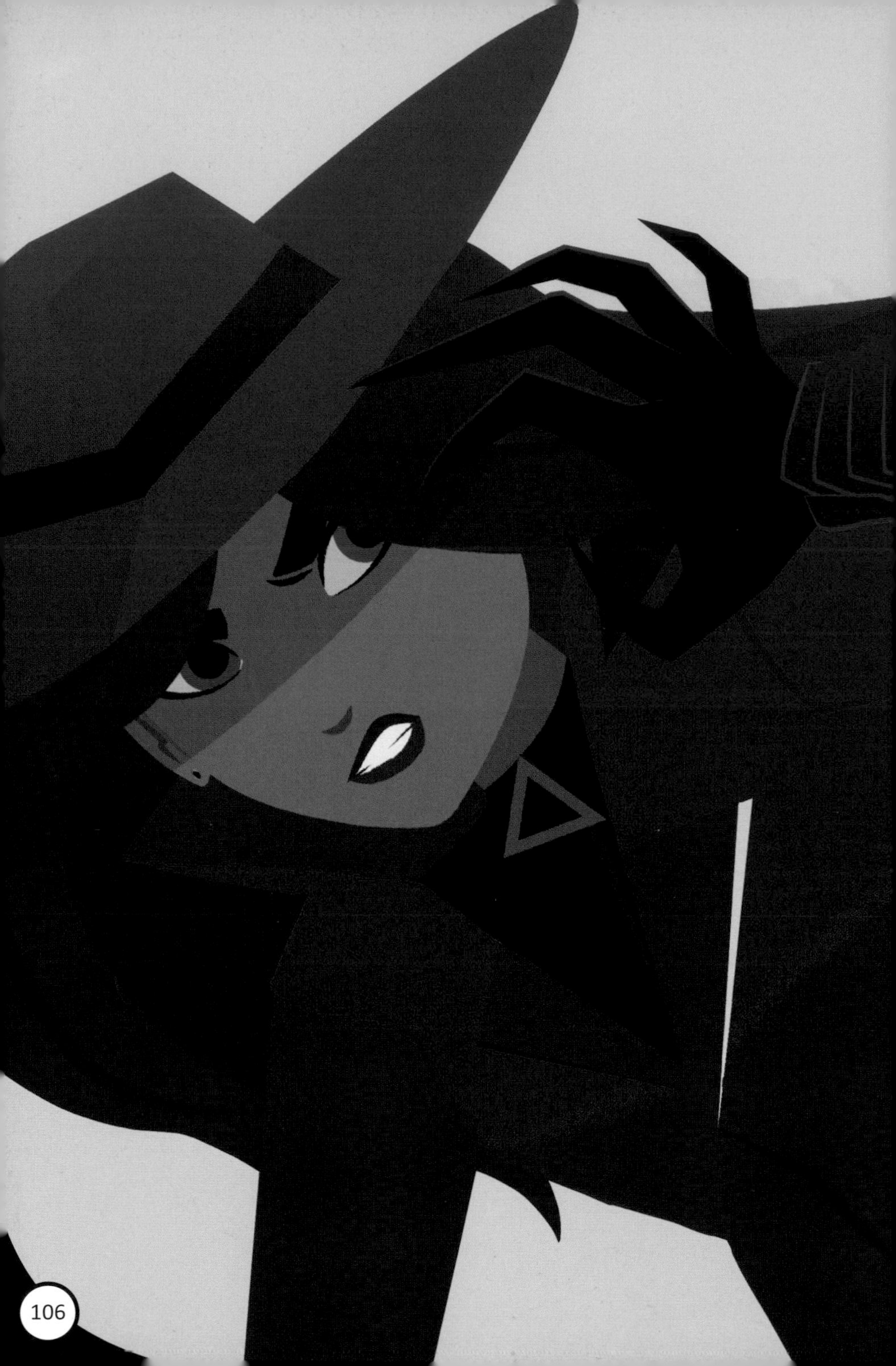

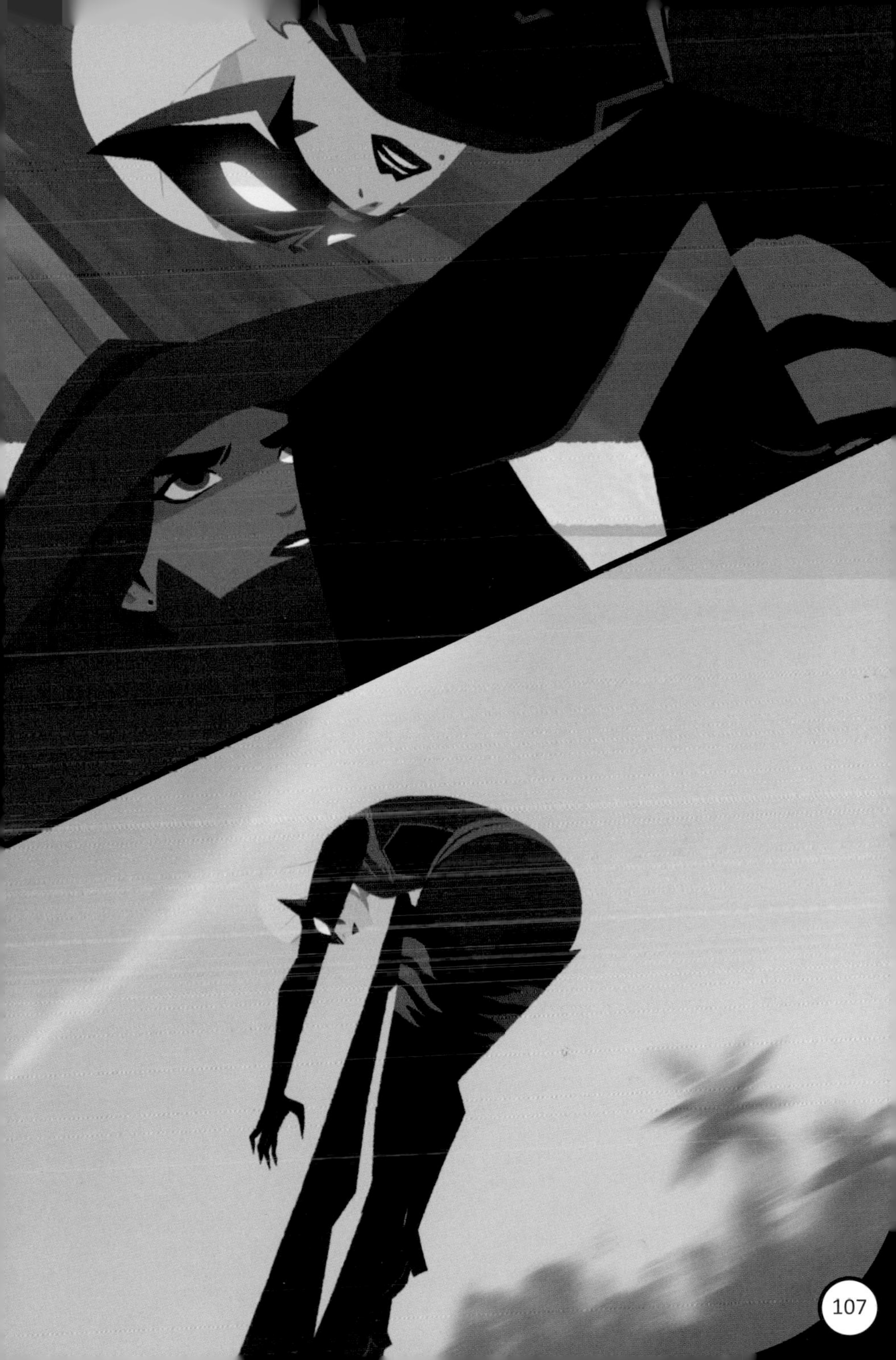

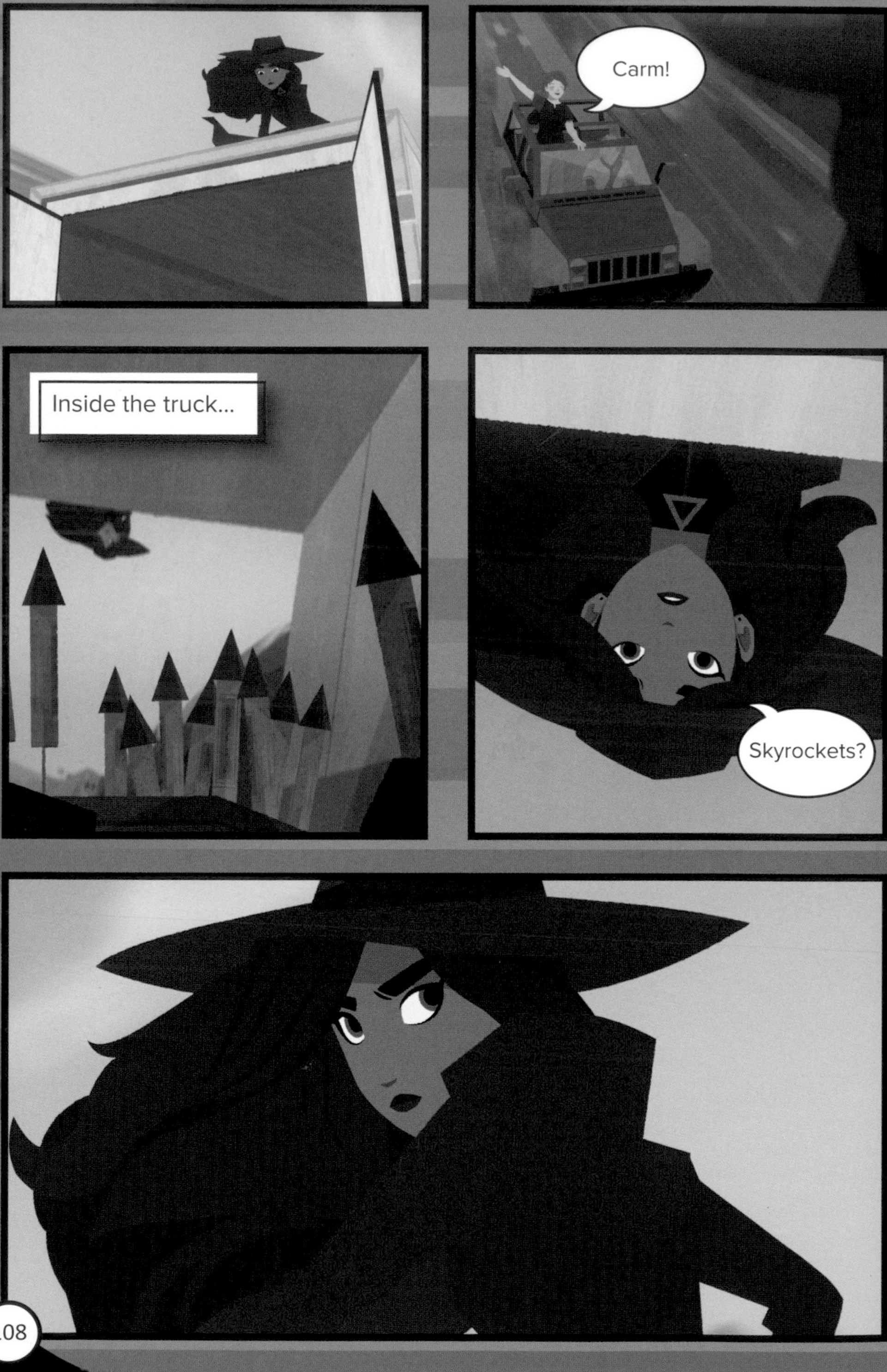
Carm!
Inside the truck...
Skyrockets?

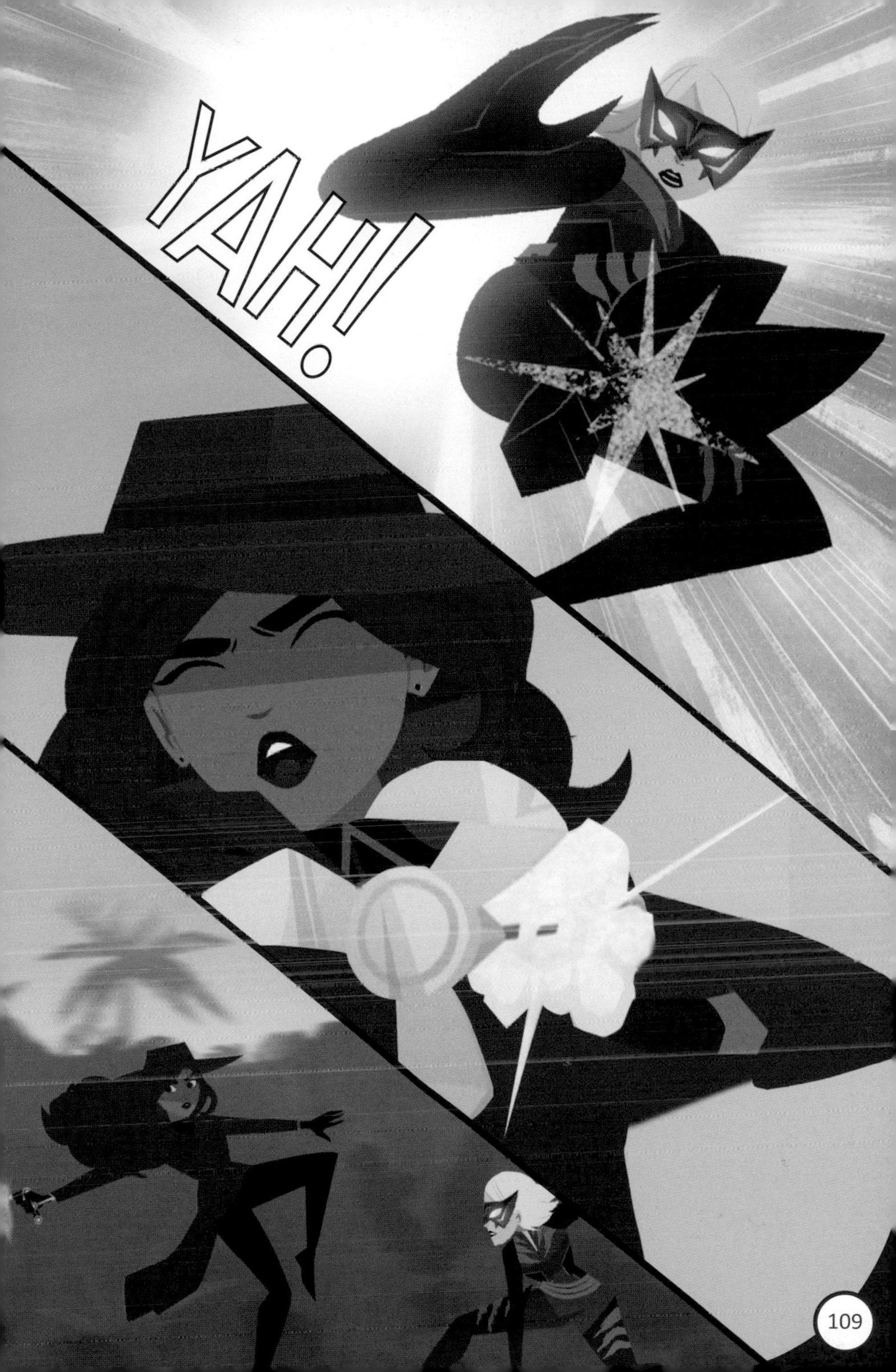
YAH!

Carmen's grappling hook accidentally punctures a tire.

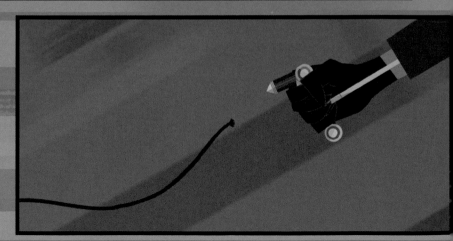

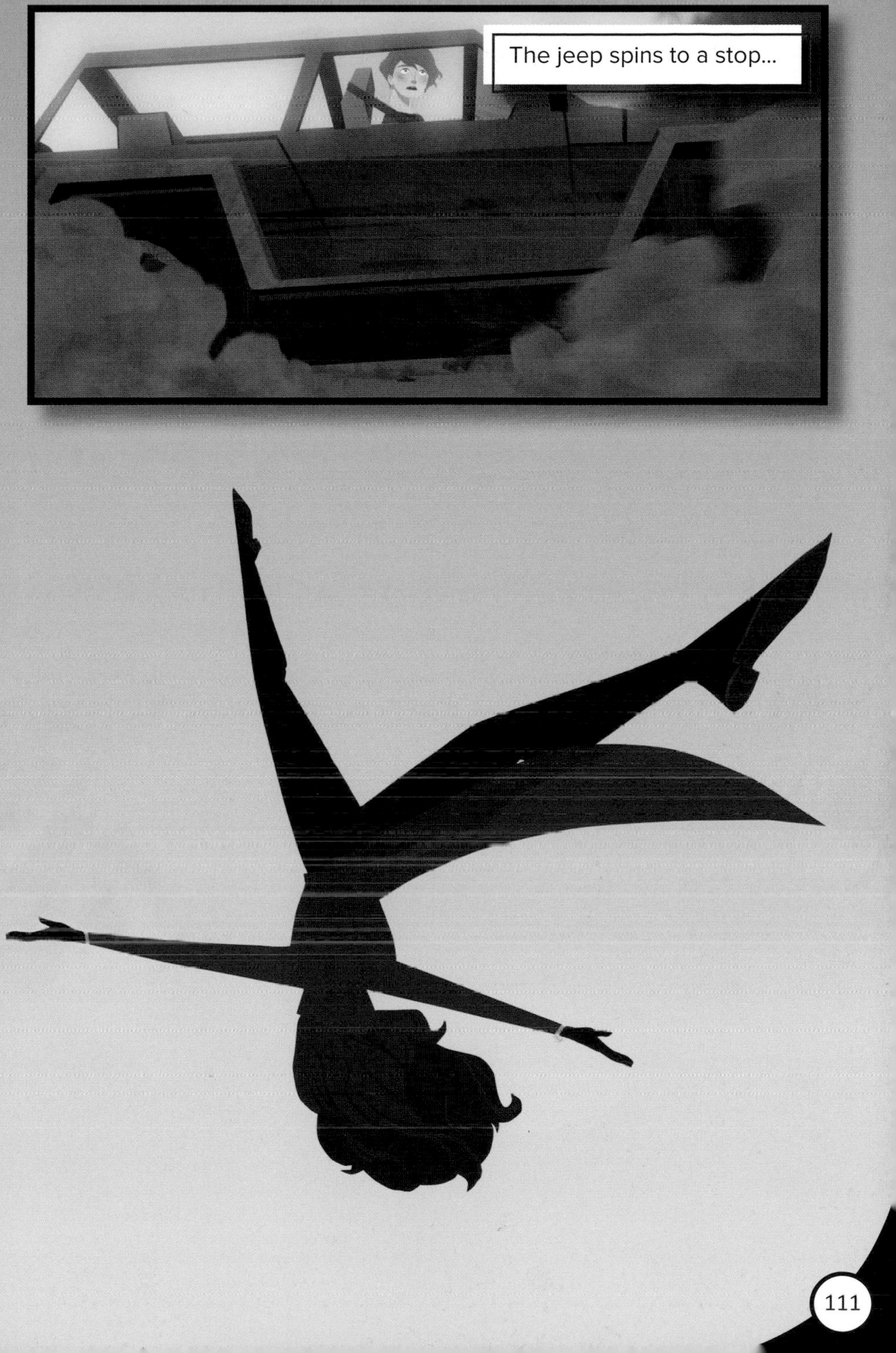
The jeep spins to a stop...

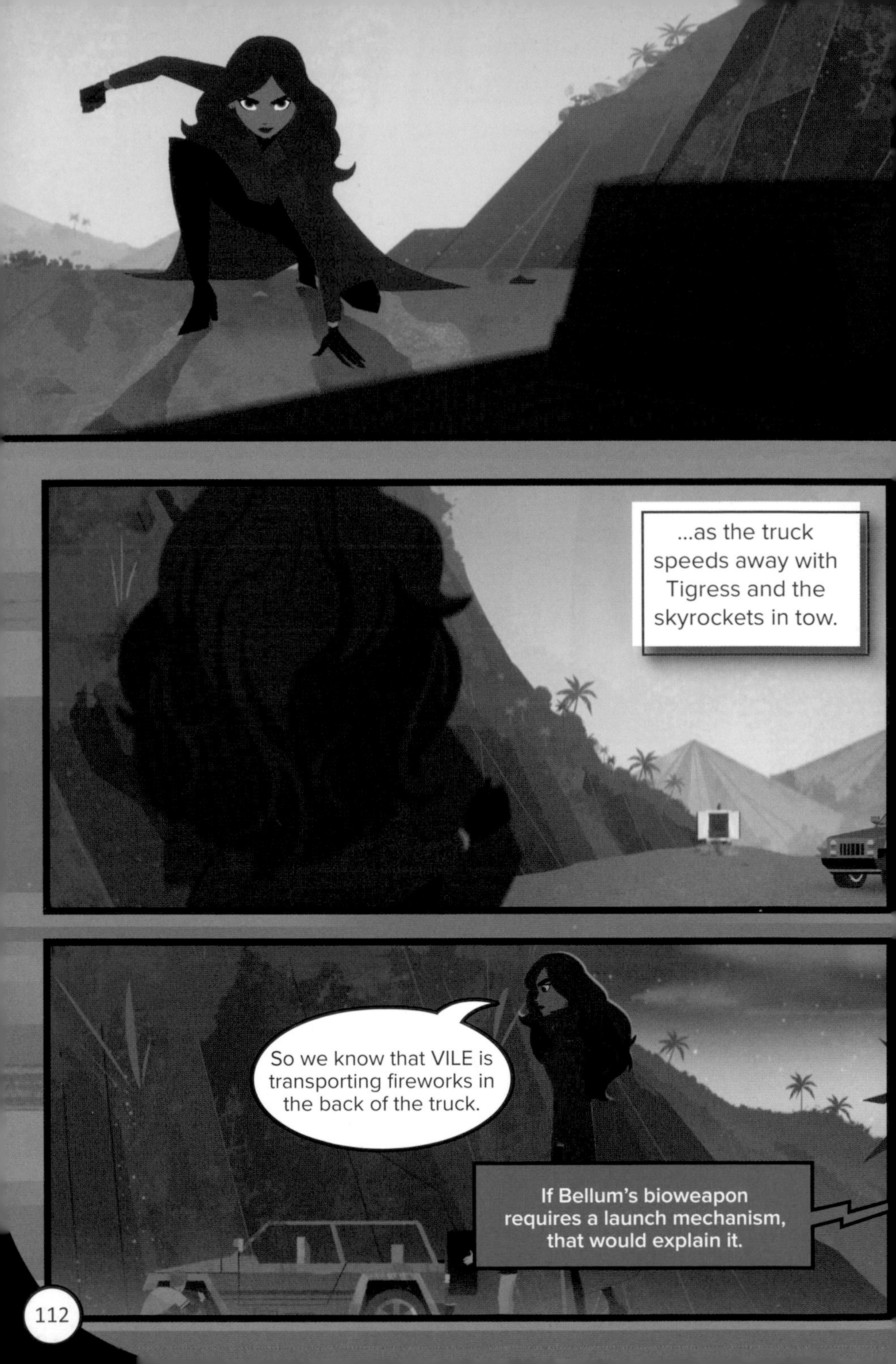
...as the truck speeds away with Tigress and the skyrockets in tow.
So we know that VILE is transporting fireworks in the back of the truck.
If Bellum's bioweapon requires a launch mechanism, that would explain it.

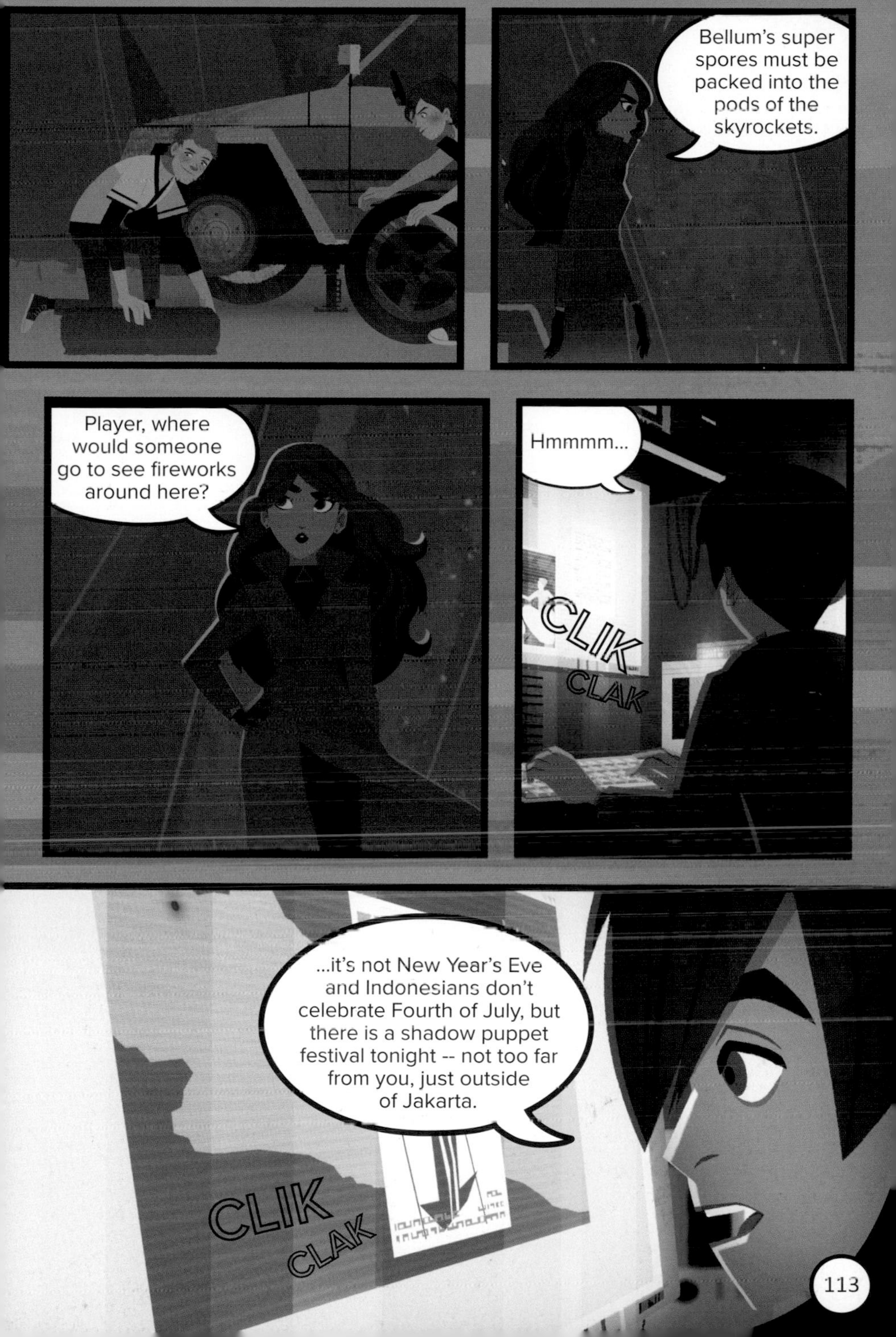

Bellum's super spores must be packed into the pods of the skyrockets.
Player, where would someone go to see fireworks around here?
Hmmmm...
CLIK
CLAK
...it's not New Year's Eve and Indonesians don't celebrate Fourth of July, but there is a shadow puppet festival tonight -- not too far from you, just outside of Jakarta.
CLIK
CLAK

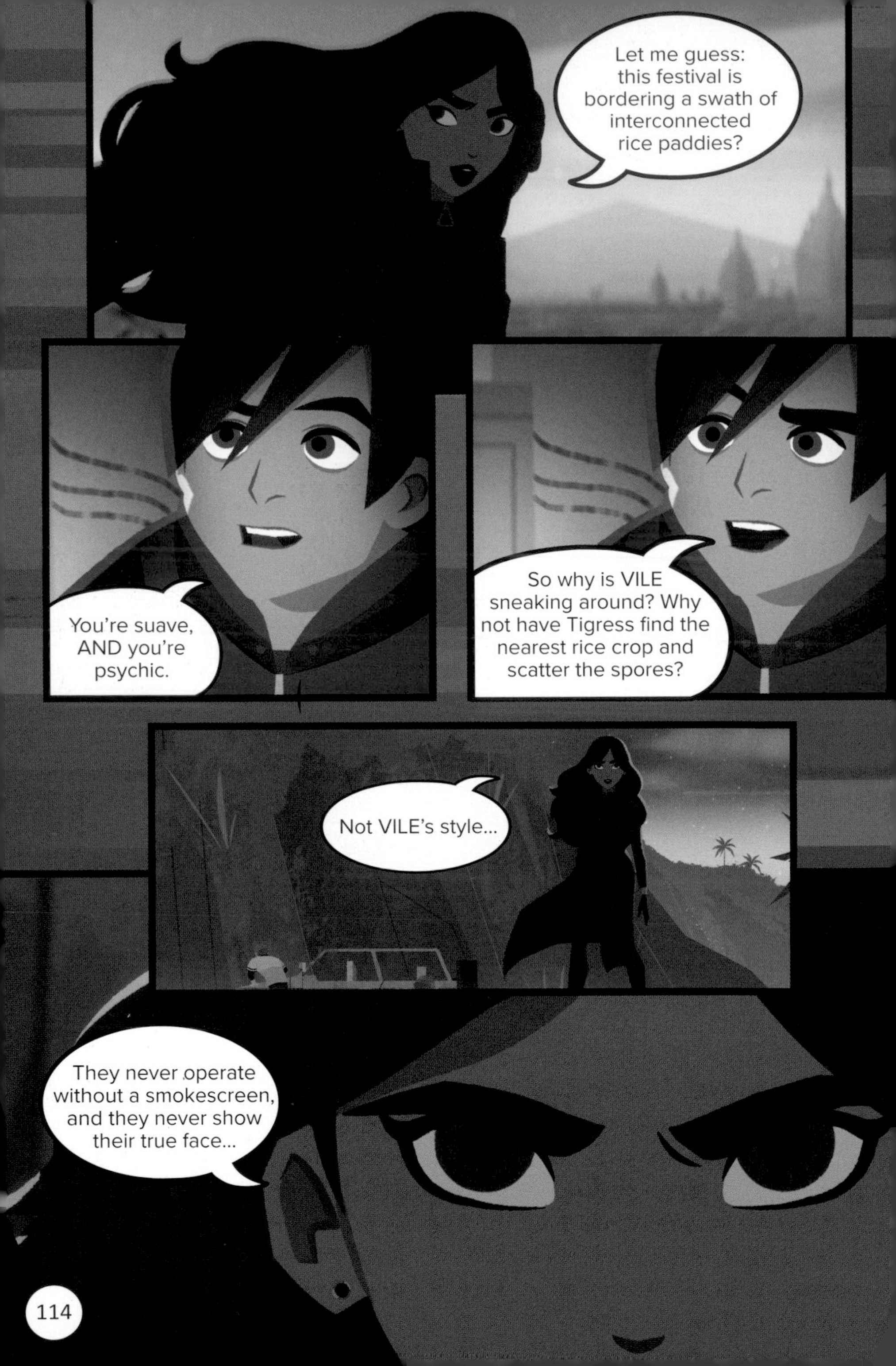
Let me guess: this festival is bordering a swath of interconnected rice paddies?
You're suave, AND you're psychic.
So why is VILE sneaking around? Why not have Tigress find the nearest rice crop and scatter the spores?
Not VILE's style...
They never operate without a smokescreen, and they never show their true face...

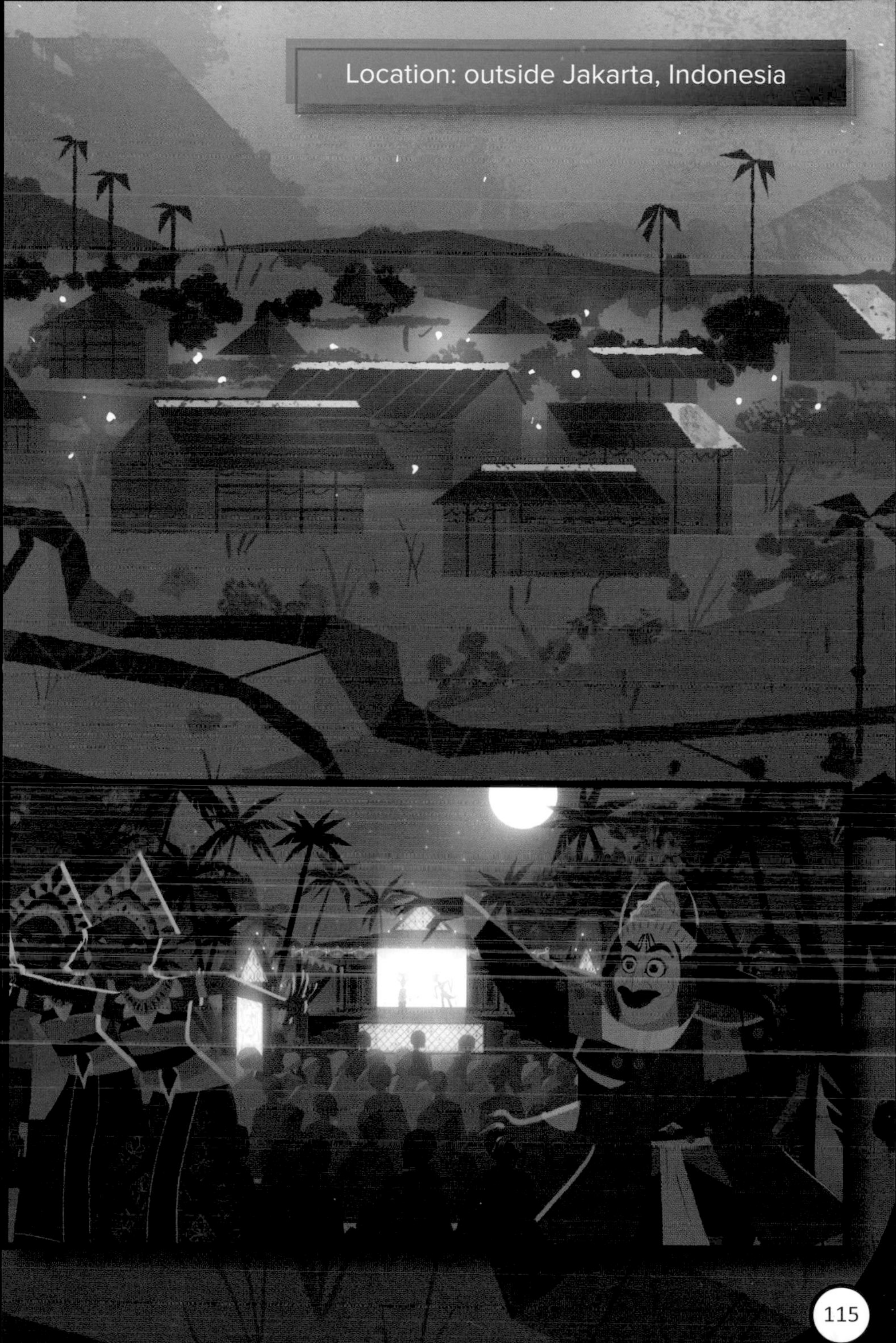
Location: outside Jakarta, Indonesia

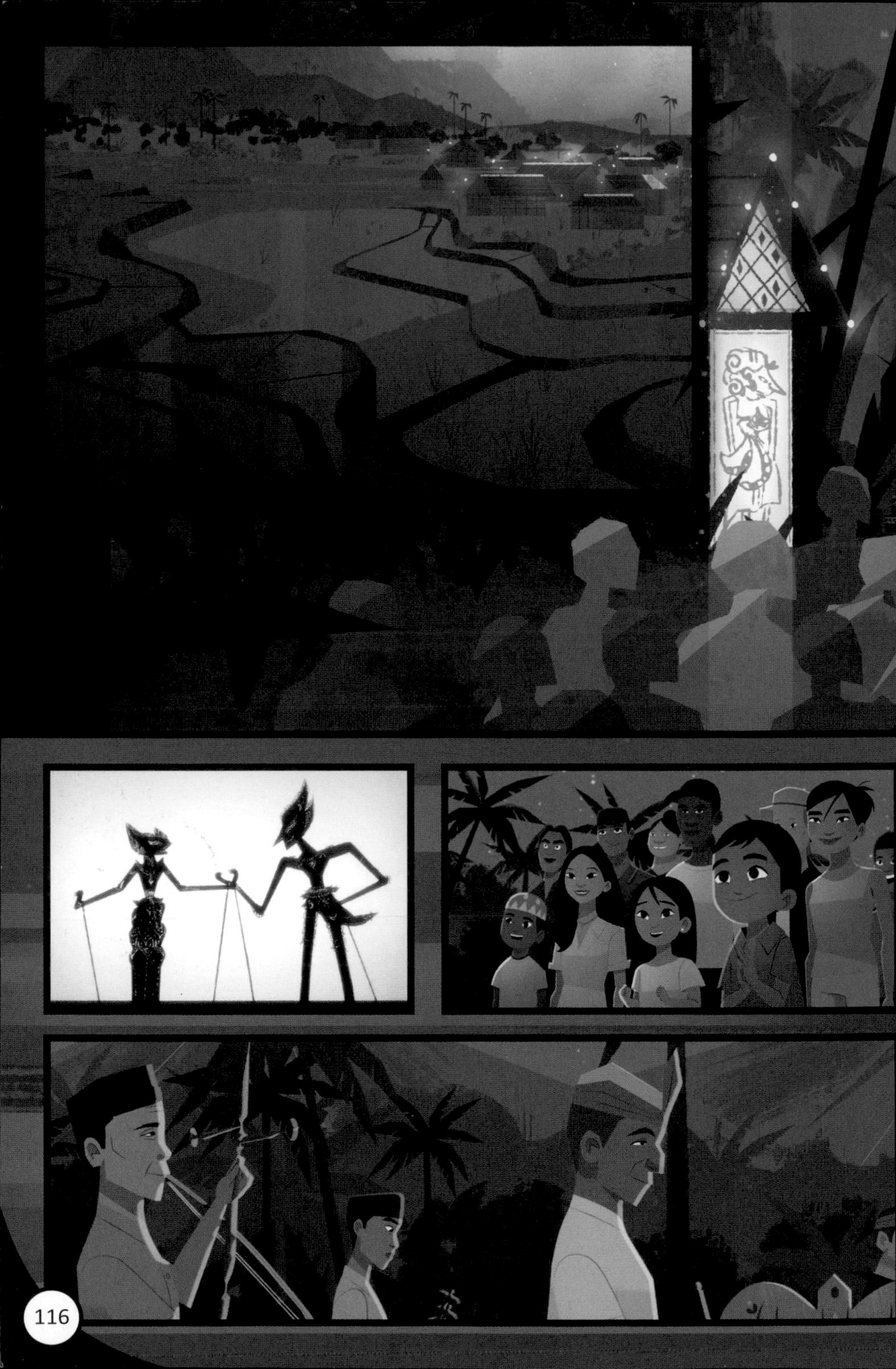

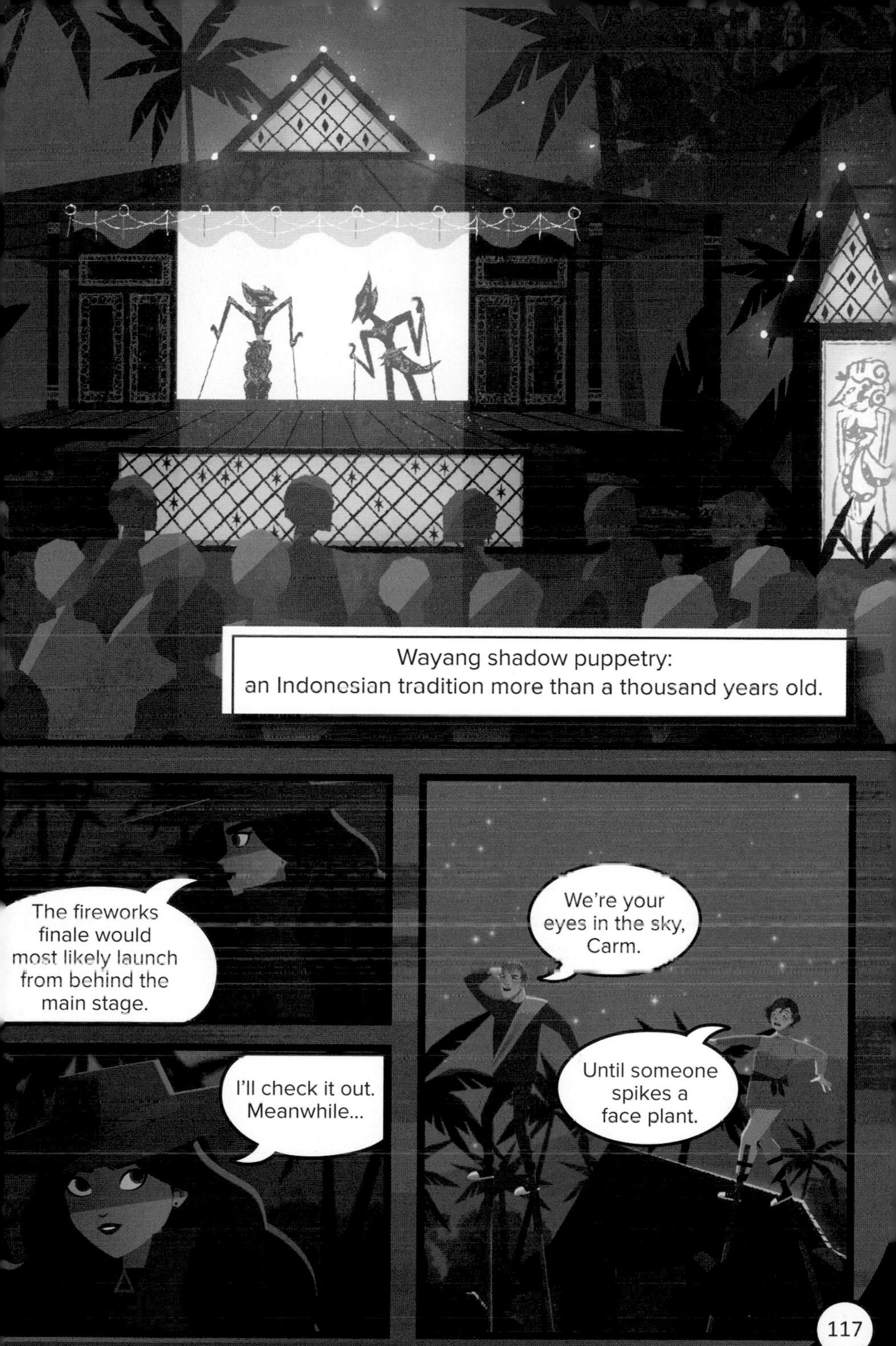
Wayang shadow puppetry:
an Indonesian tradition more than a thousand years old.
The fireworks finale would most likely launch from behind the main stage.
I'll check it out. Meanwhile...
We're your eyes in the sky, Carm.
Until someone spikes a face plant.

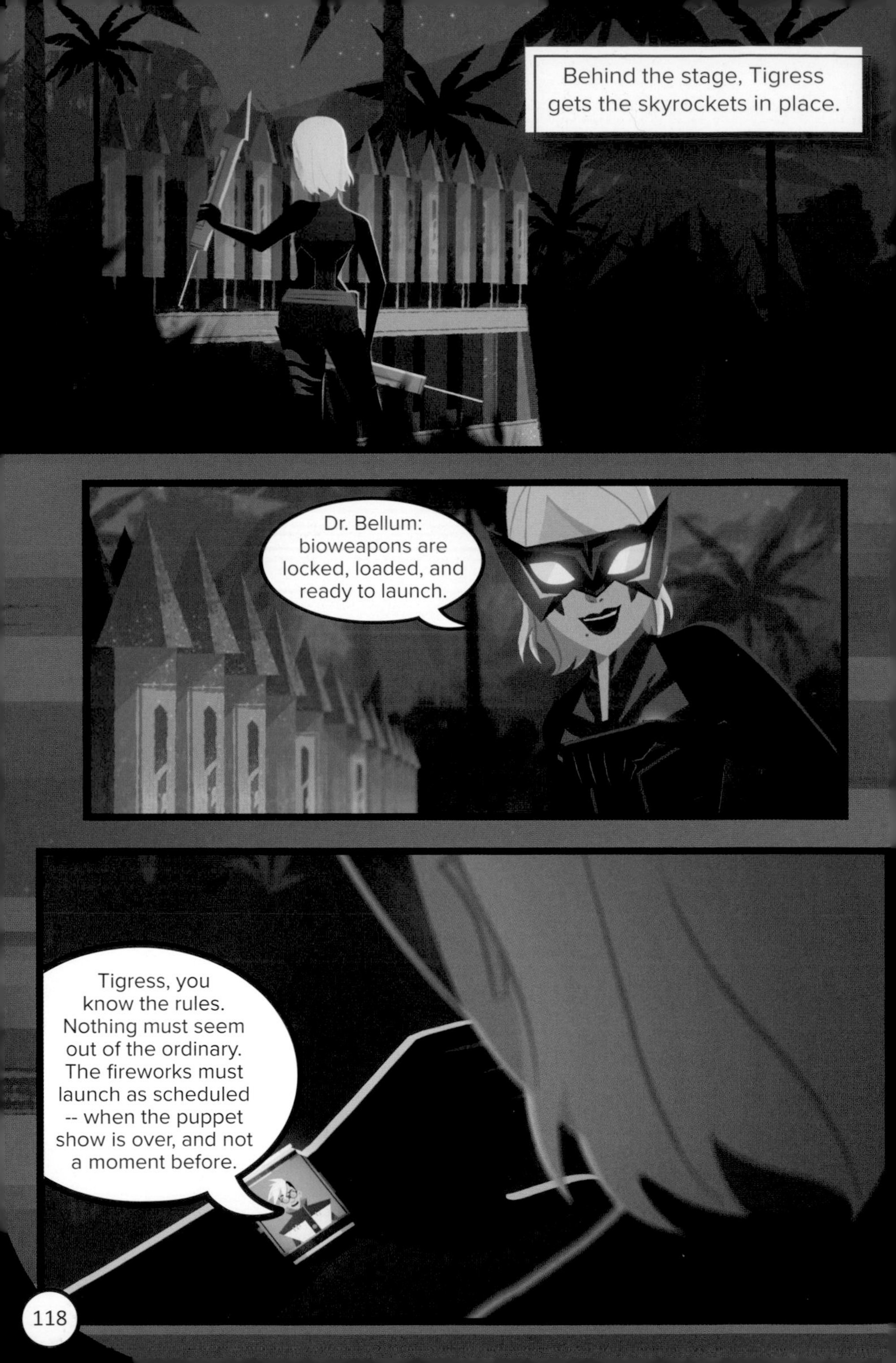

Behind the stage, Tigress gets the skyrockets in place.
Dr. Bellum: bioweapons are locked, loaded, and ready to launch.
Tigress, you know the rules. Nothing must seem out of the ordinary. The fireworks must launch as scheduled -- when the puppet show is over, and not a moment before.

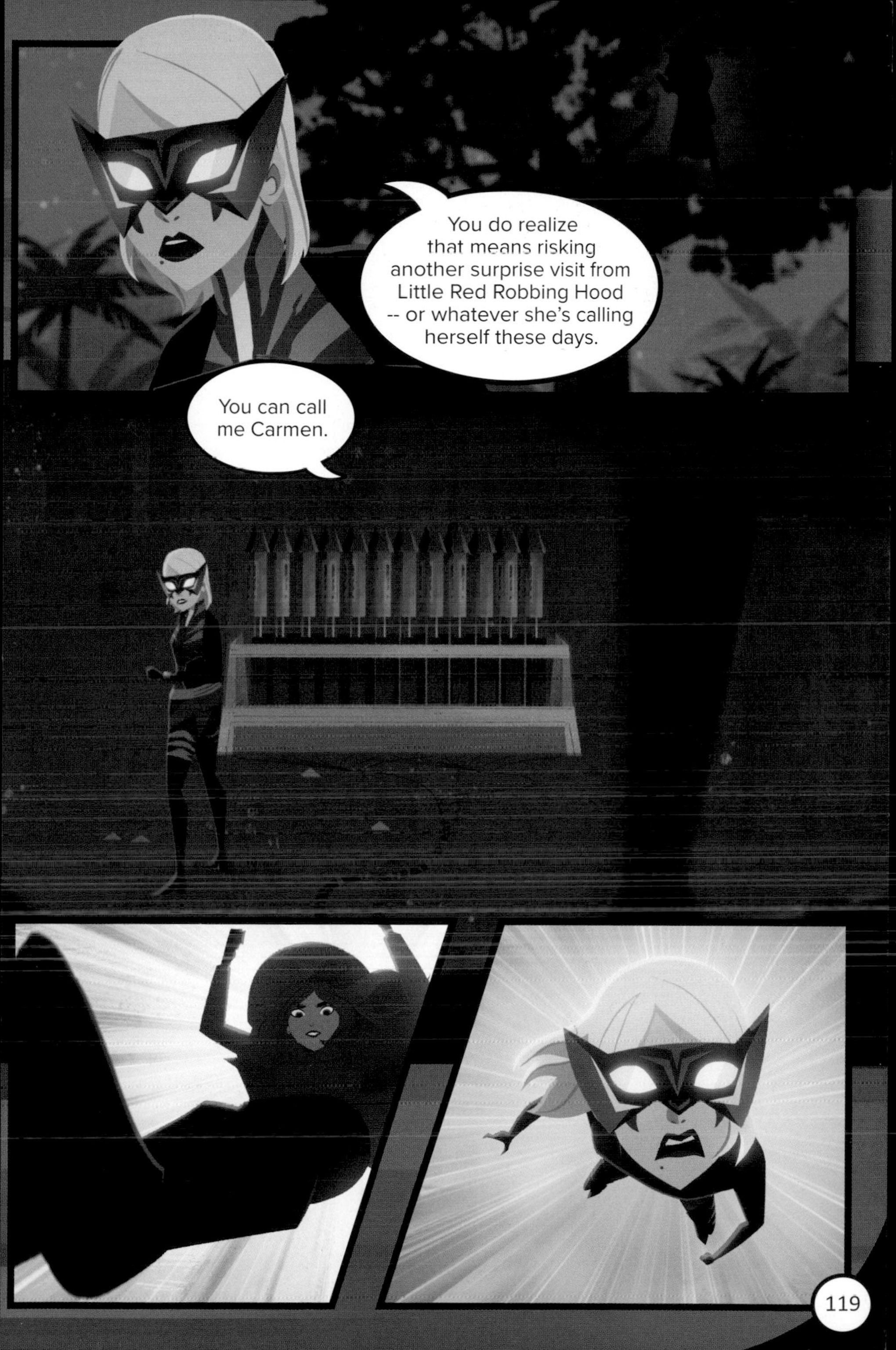
You do realize that means risking another surprise visit from Little Red Robbing Hood -- or whatever she's calling herself these days.
You can call me Carmen.

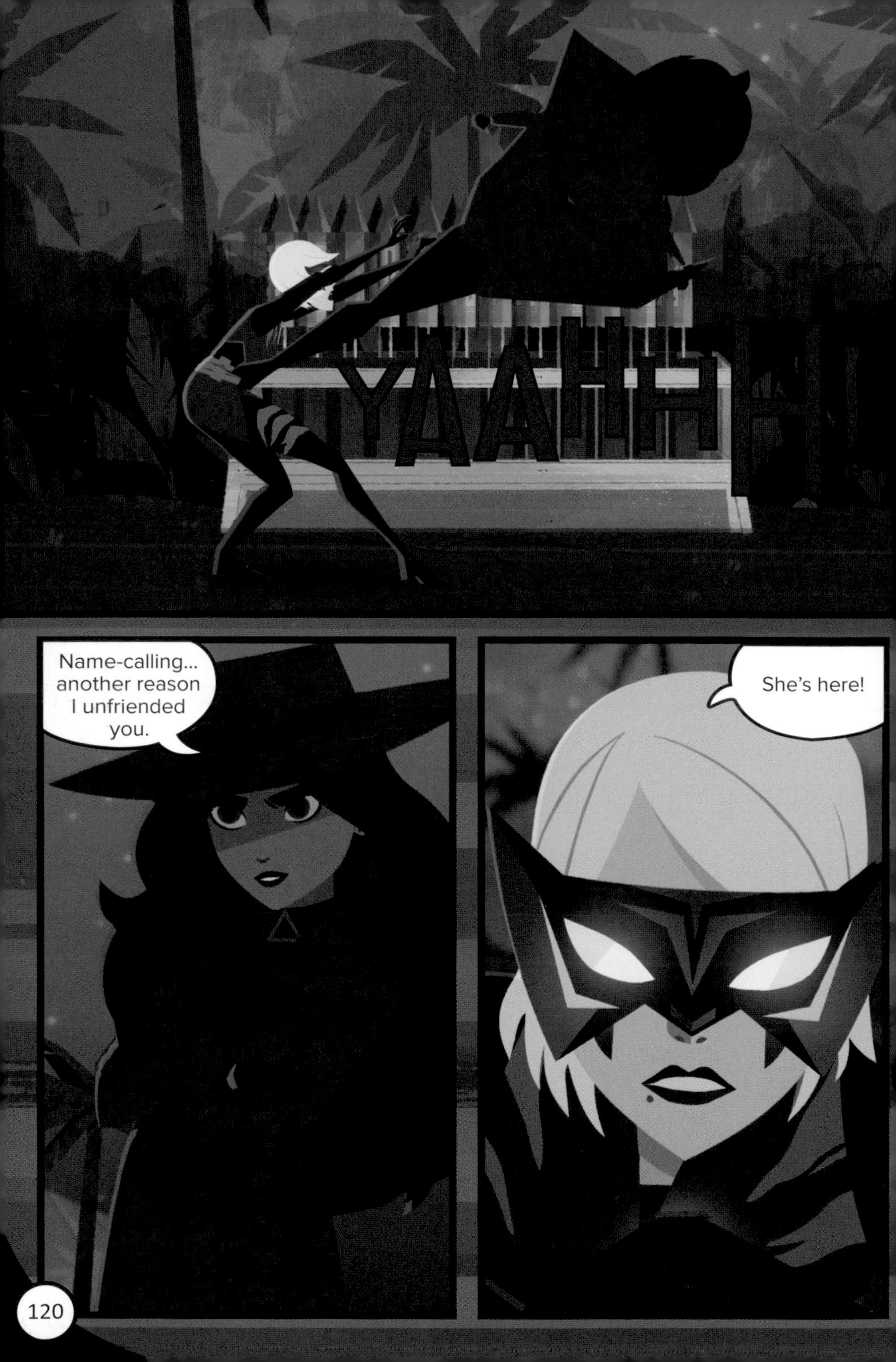
YAAHH!
Name-calling... another reason I unfriended you.
She's here!

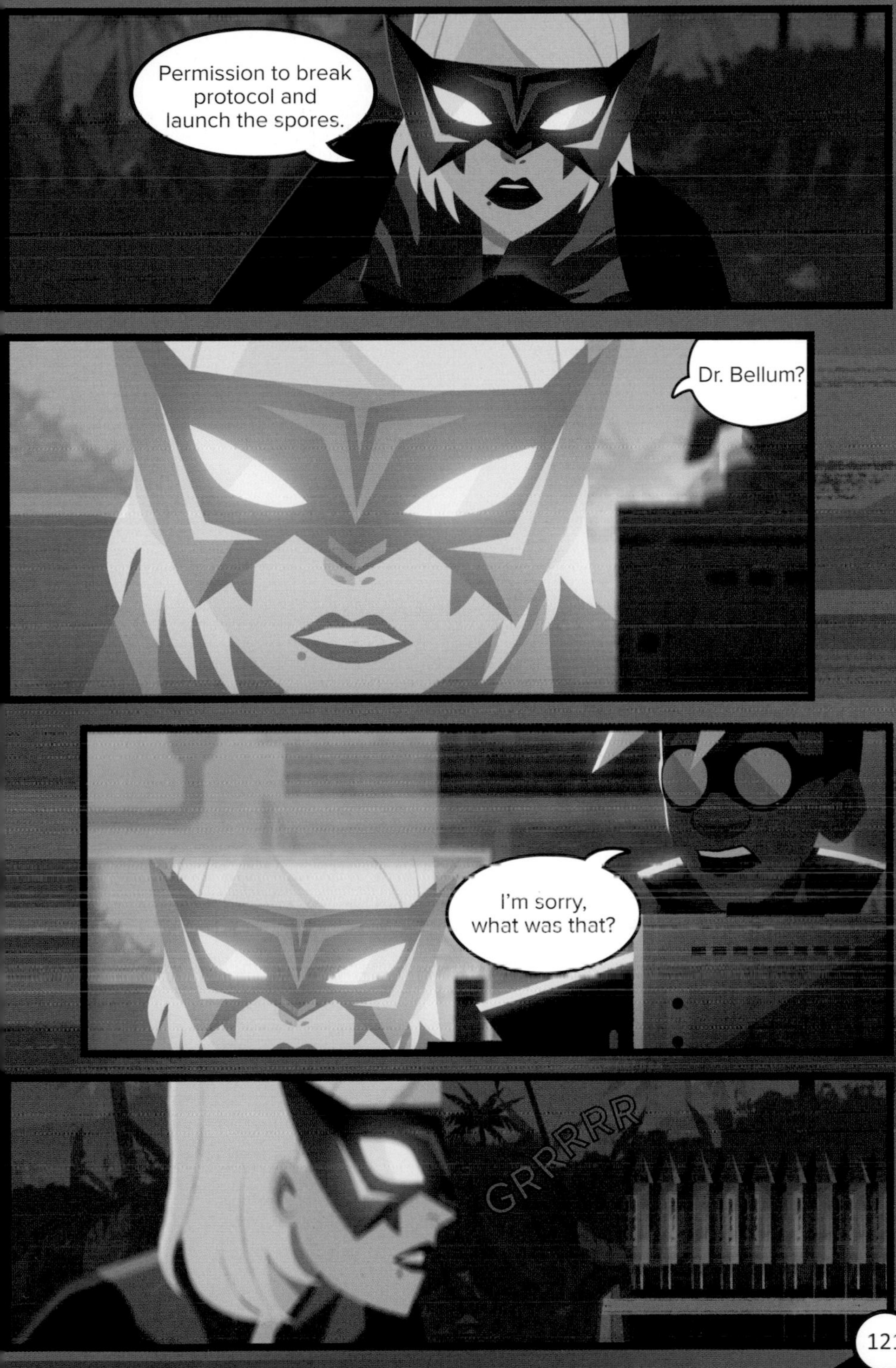
Permission to break protocol and launch the spores.
Dr. Bellum?
I'm sorry, what was that?
GRRRRR

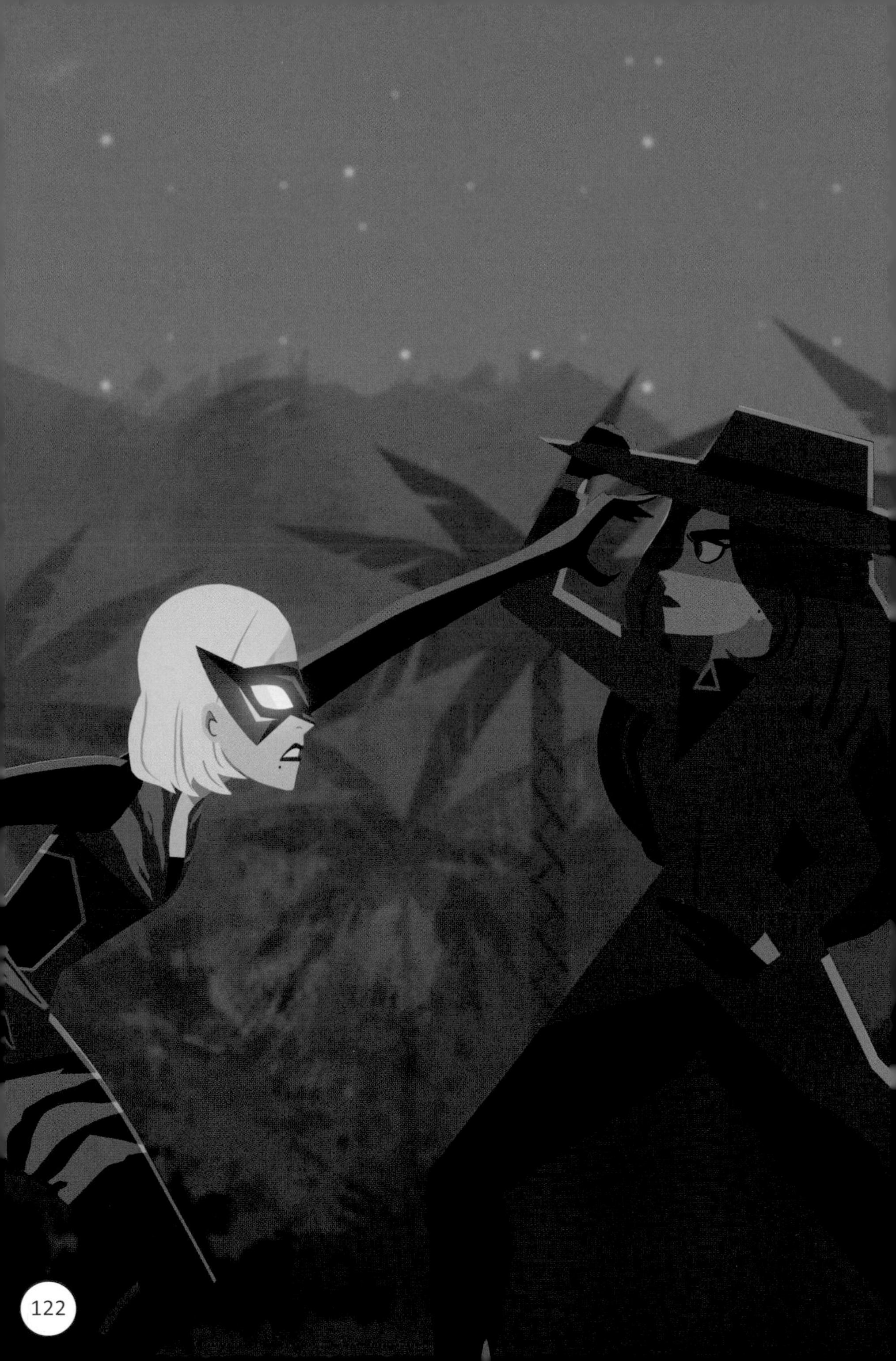

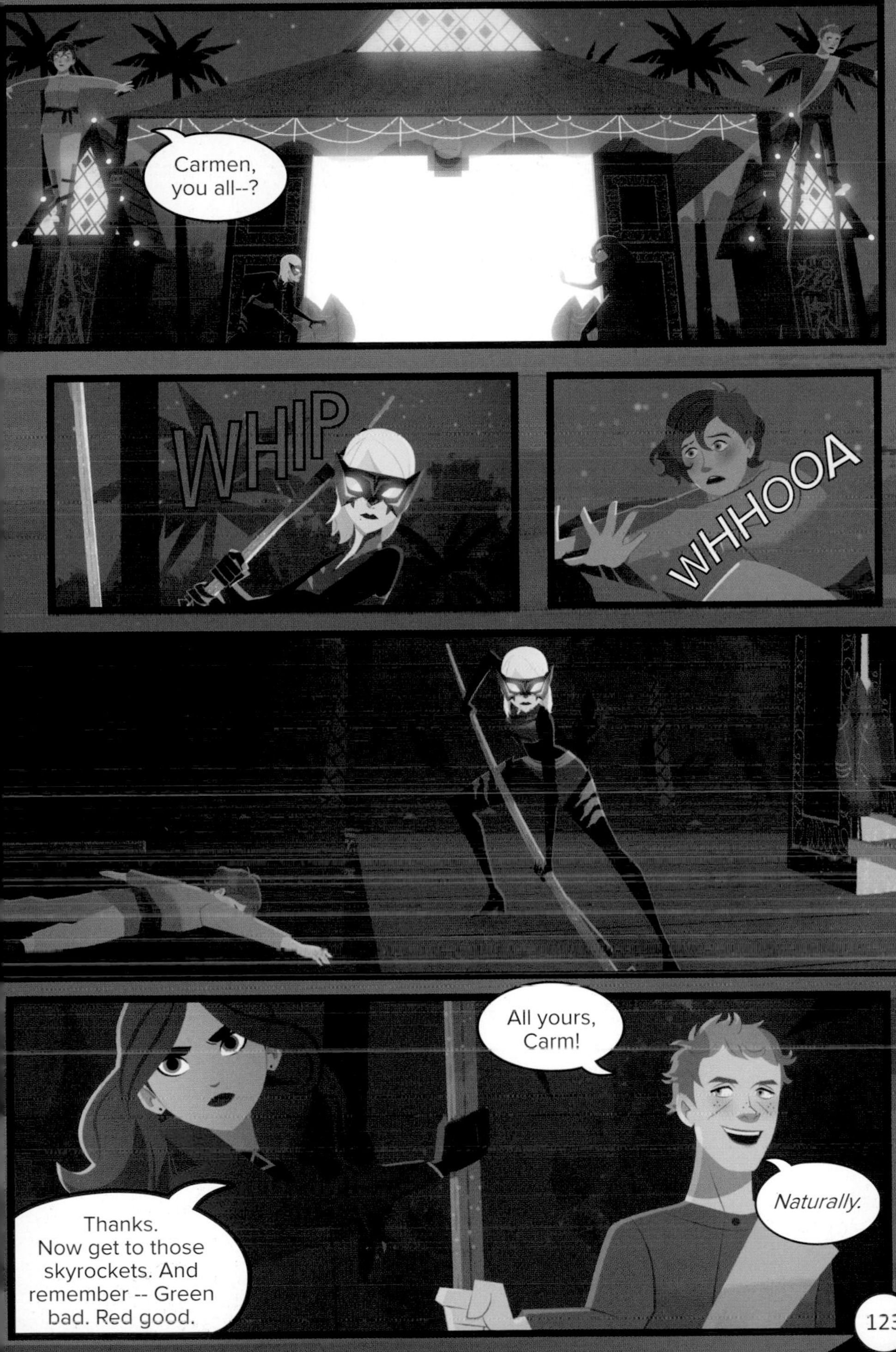
Carmen,
you all--?
WHIP
WHHOOA
All yours,
Carm!
Thanks.
Now get to those
skyrockets. And
remember -- Green
bad. Red good.
Naturally.

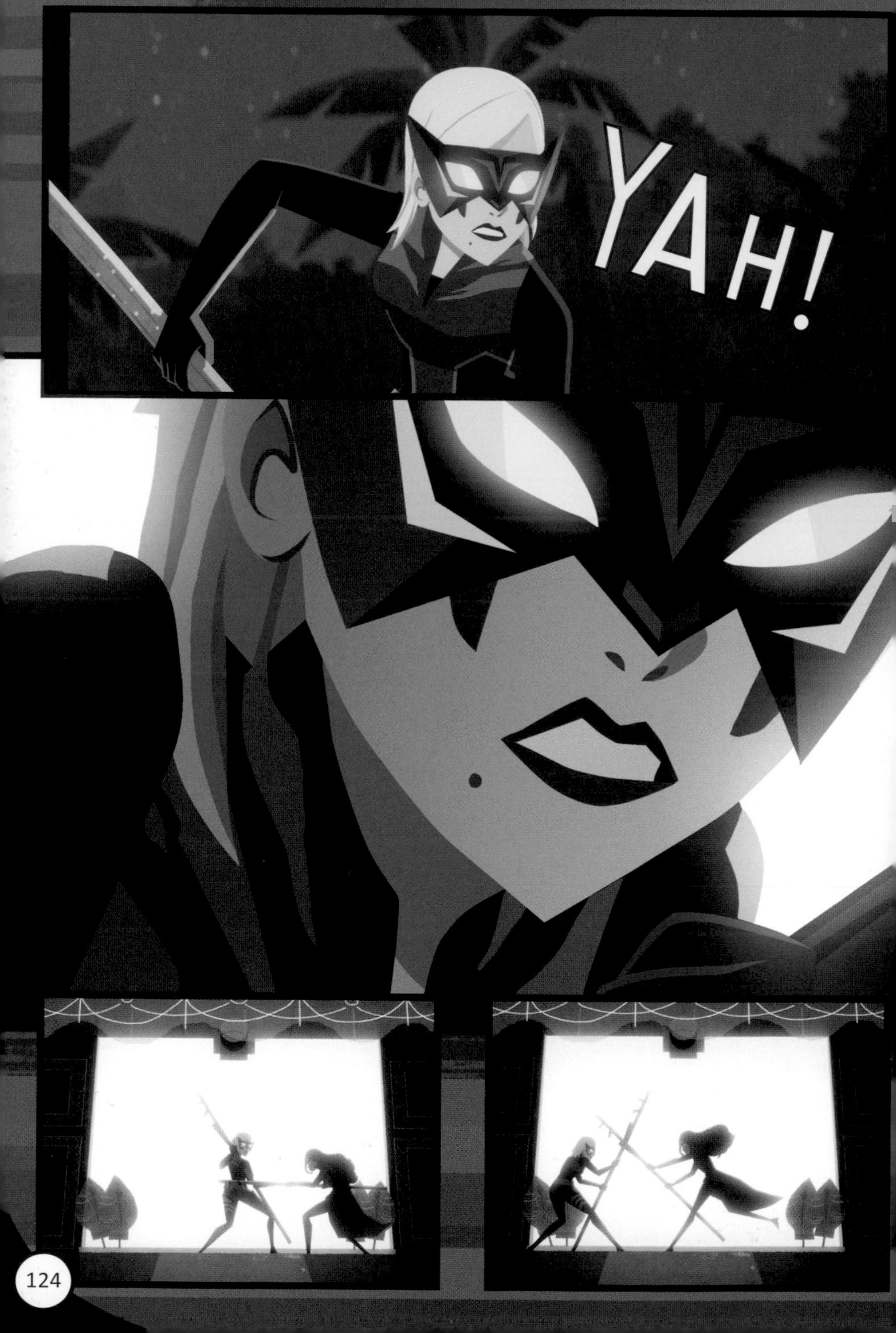
YAH!

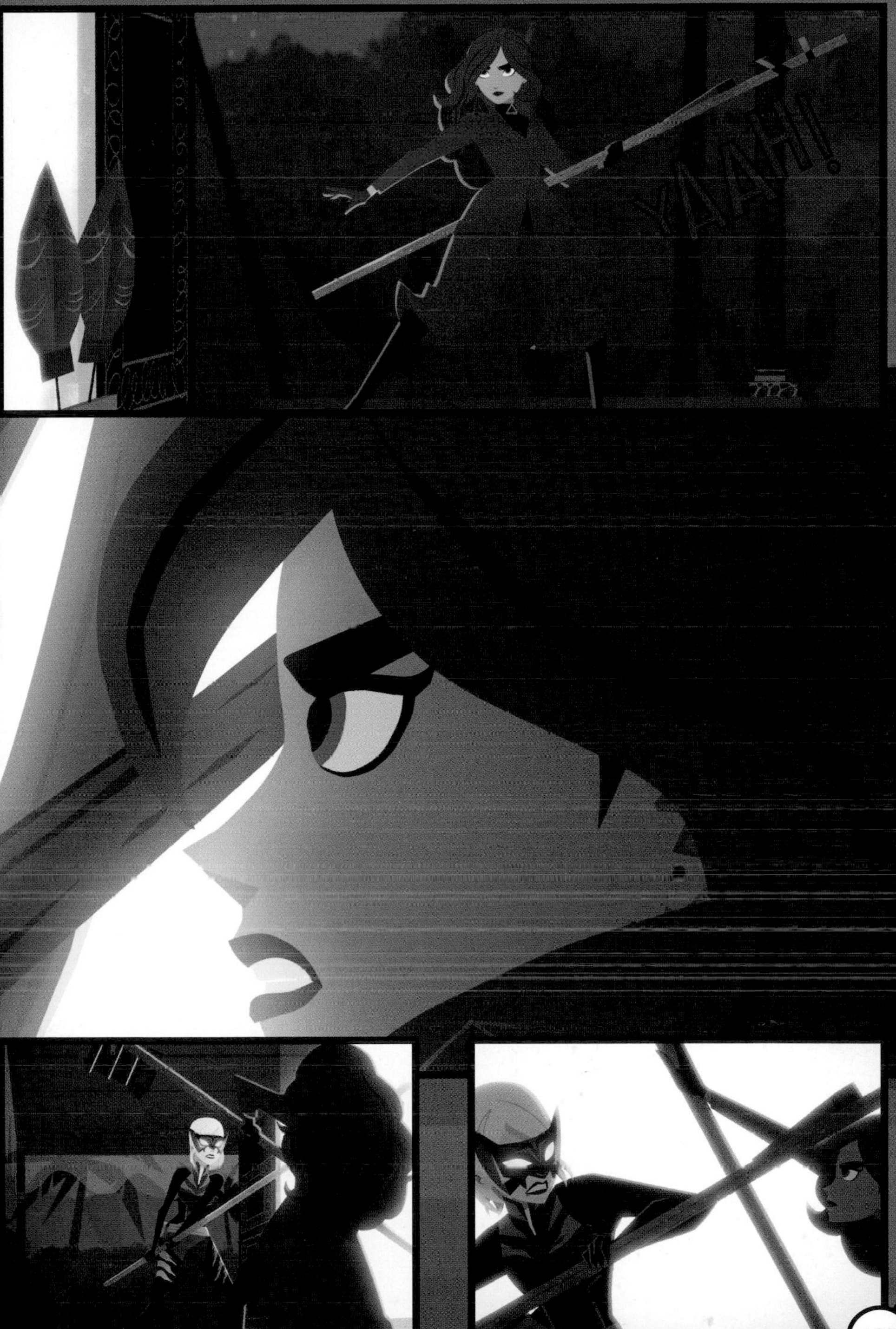
YAAAH!

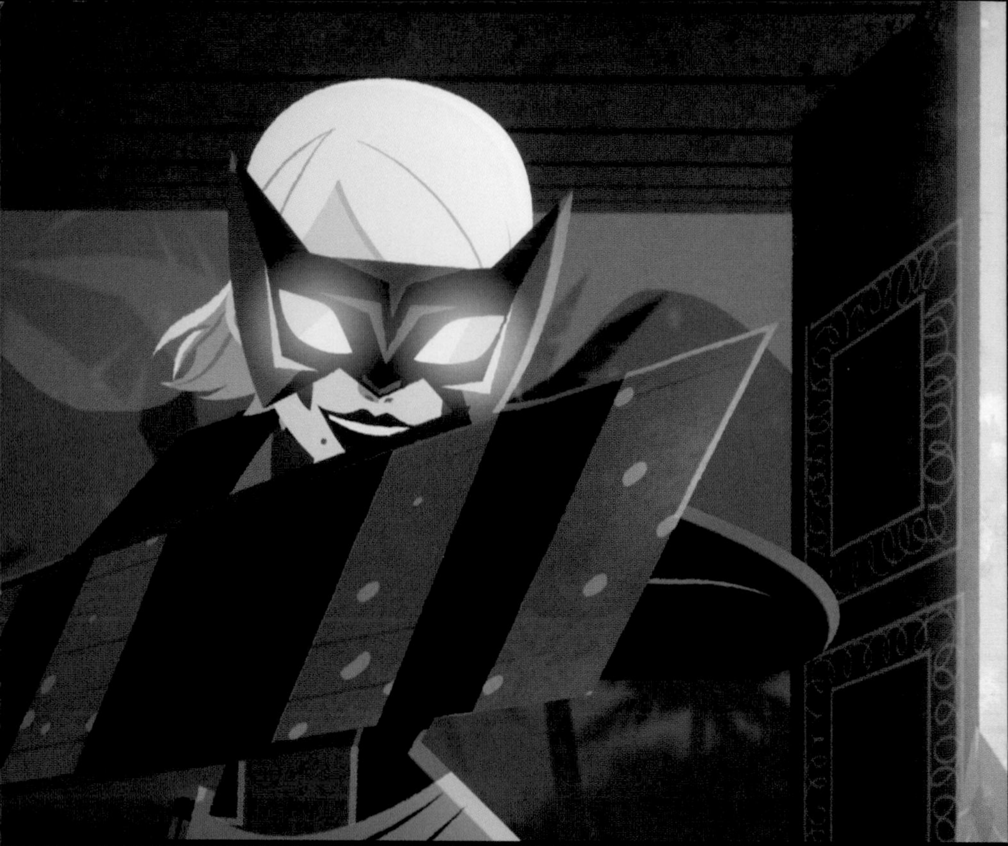
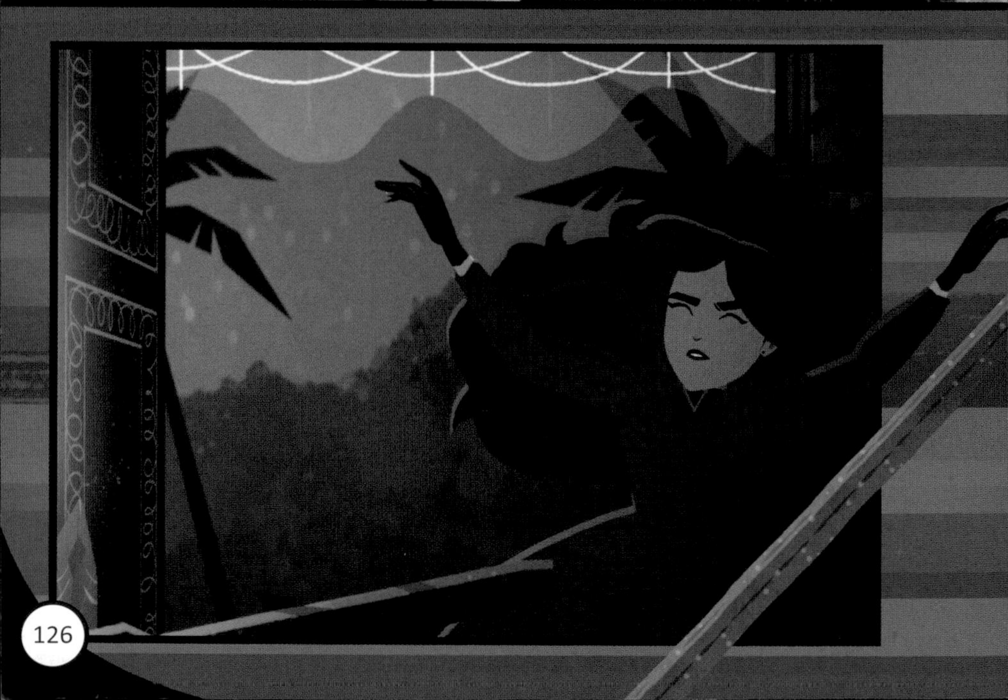

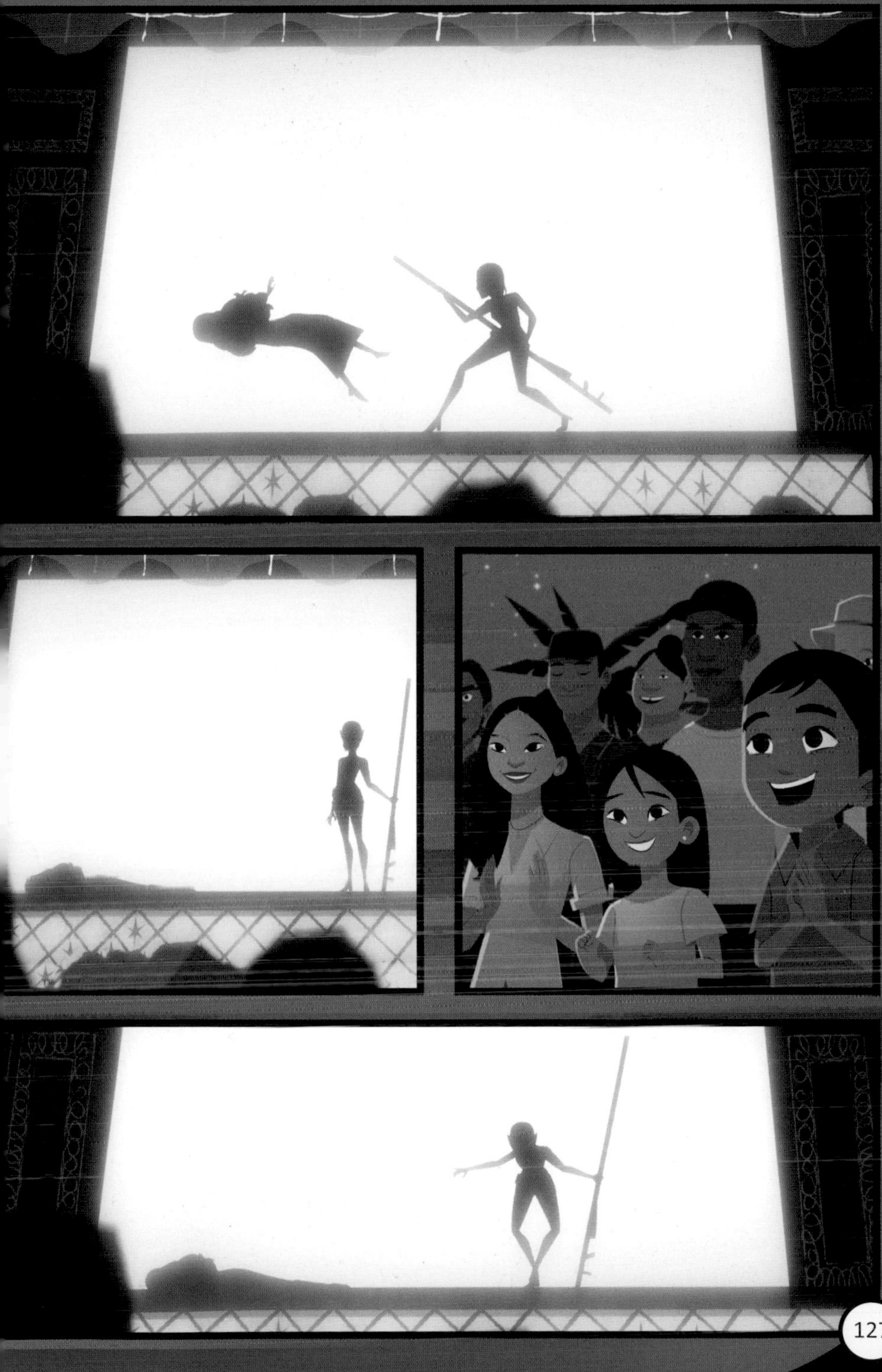

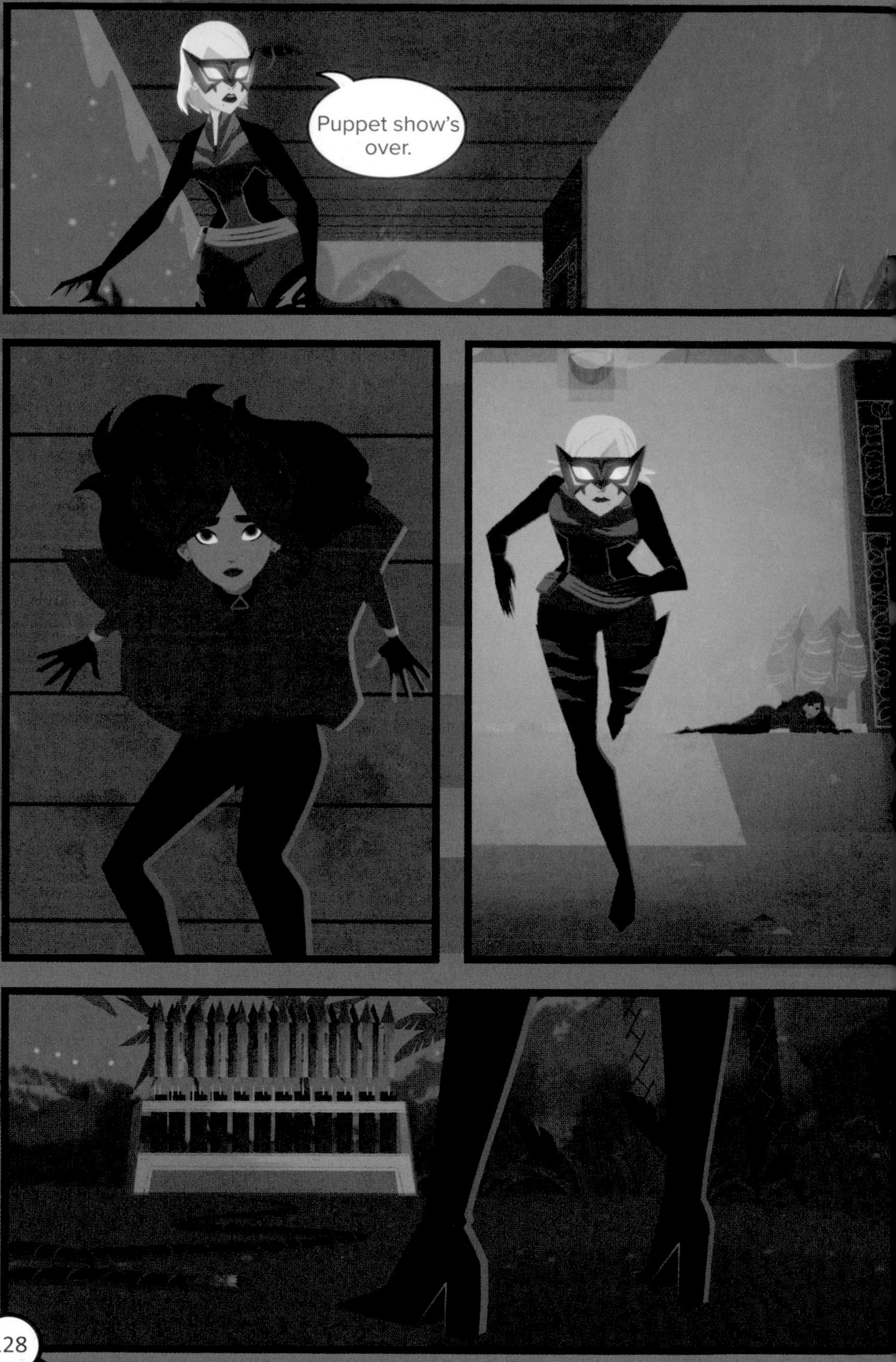
Puppet show's
over.

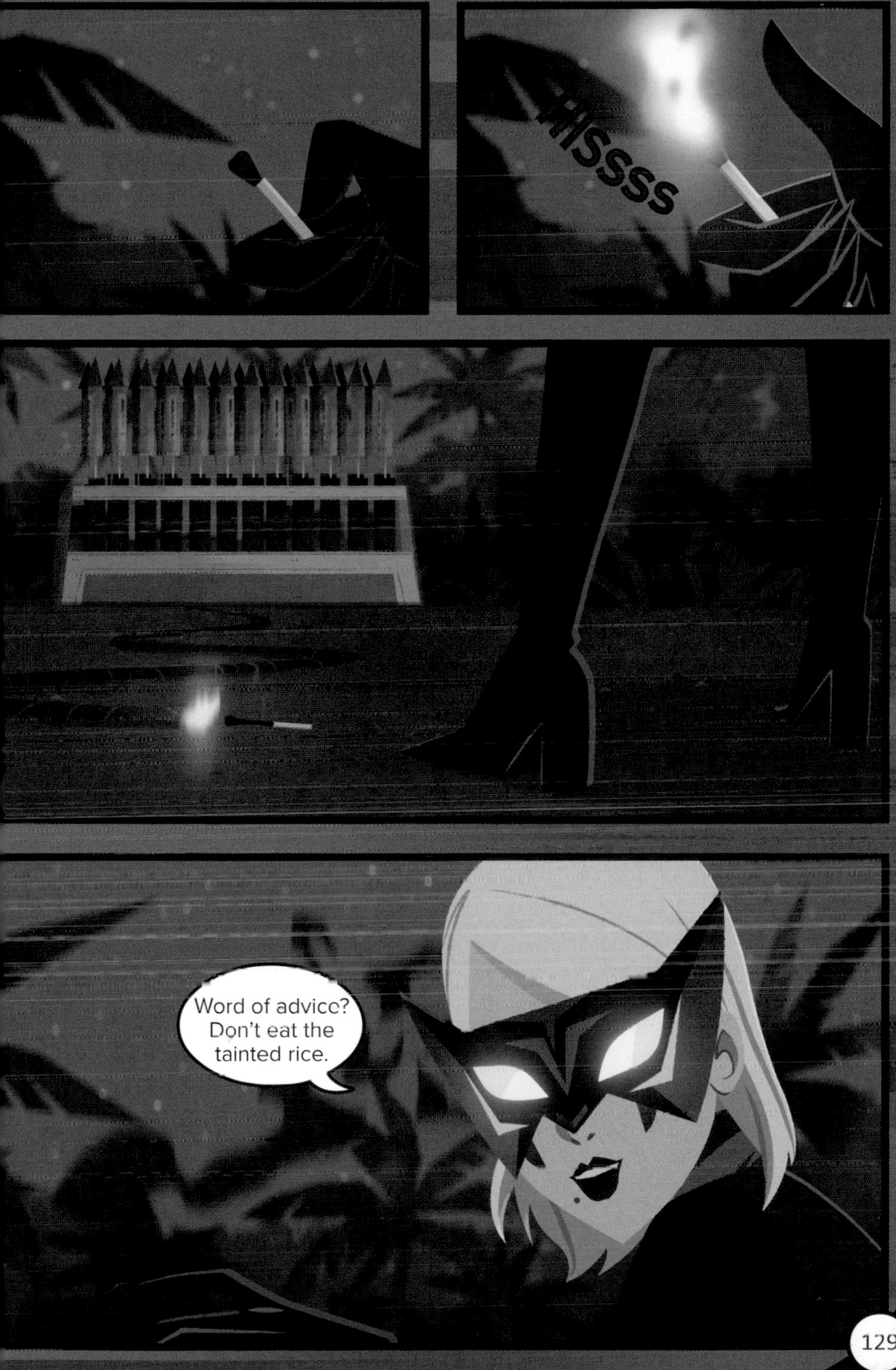
HISSSS
Word of advice? Don't eat the tainted rice.

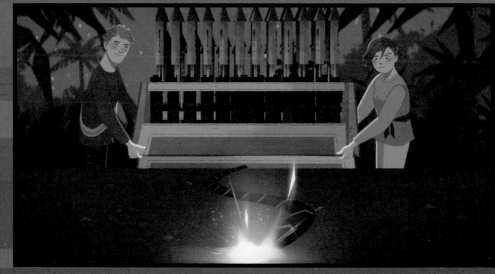

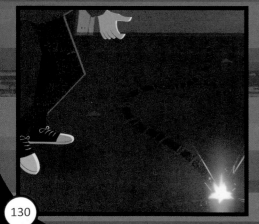

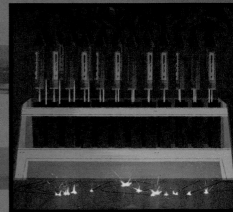

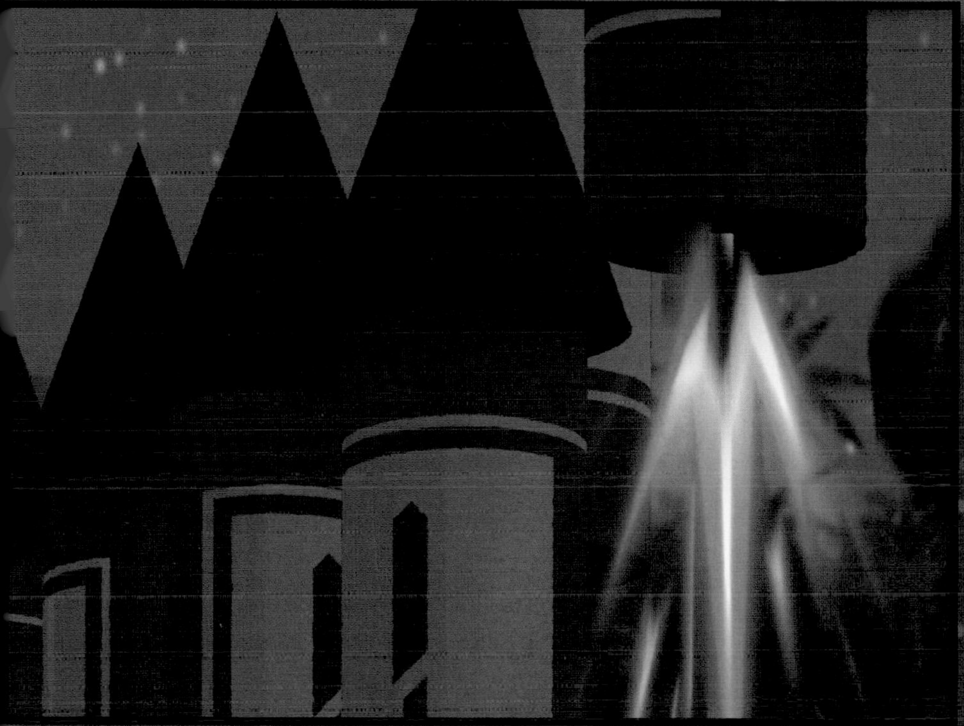

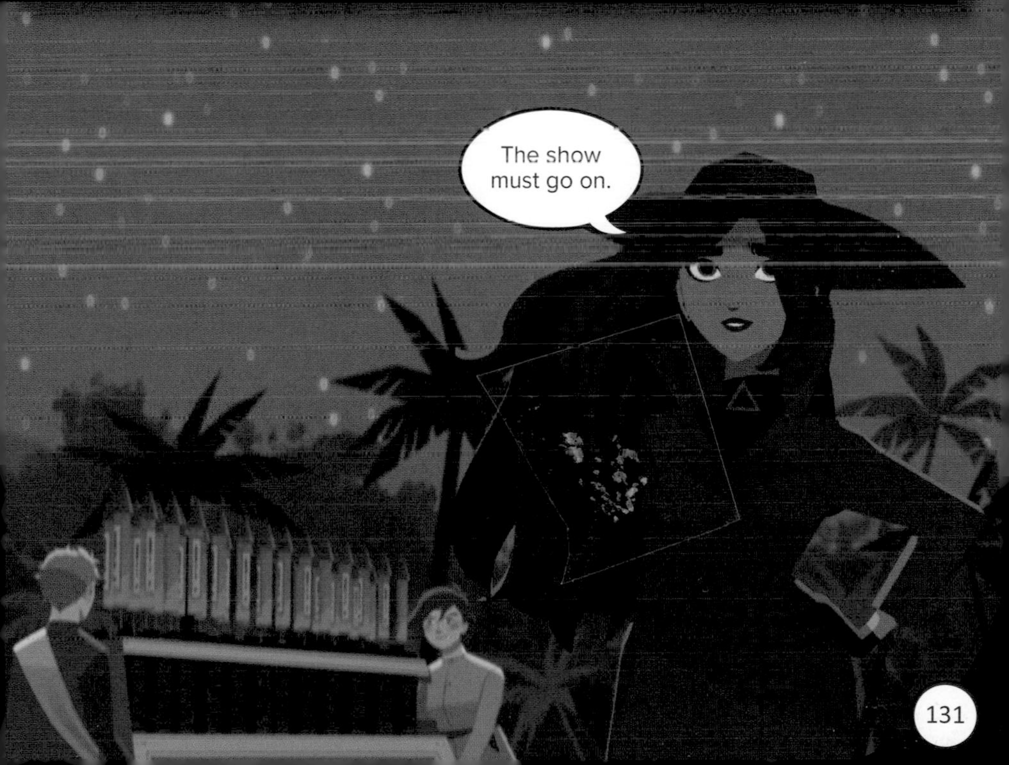
The show must go on.

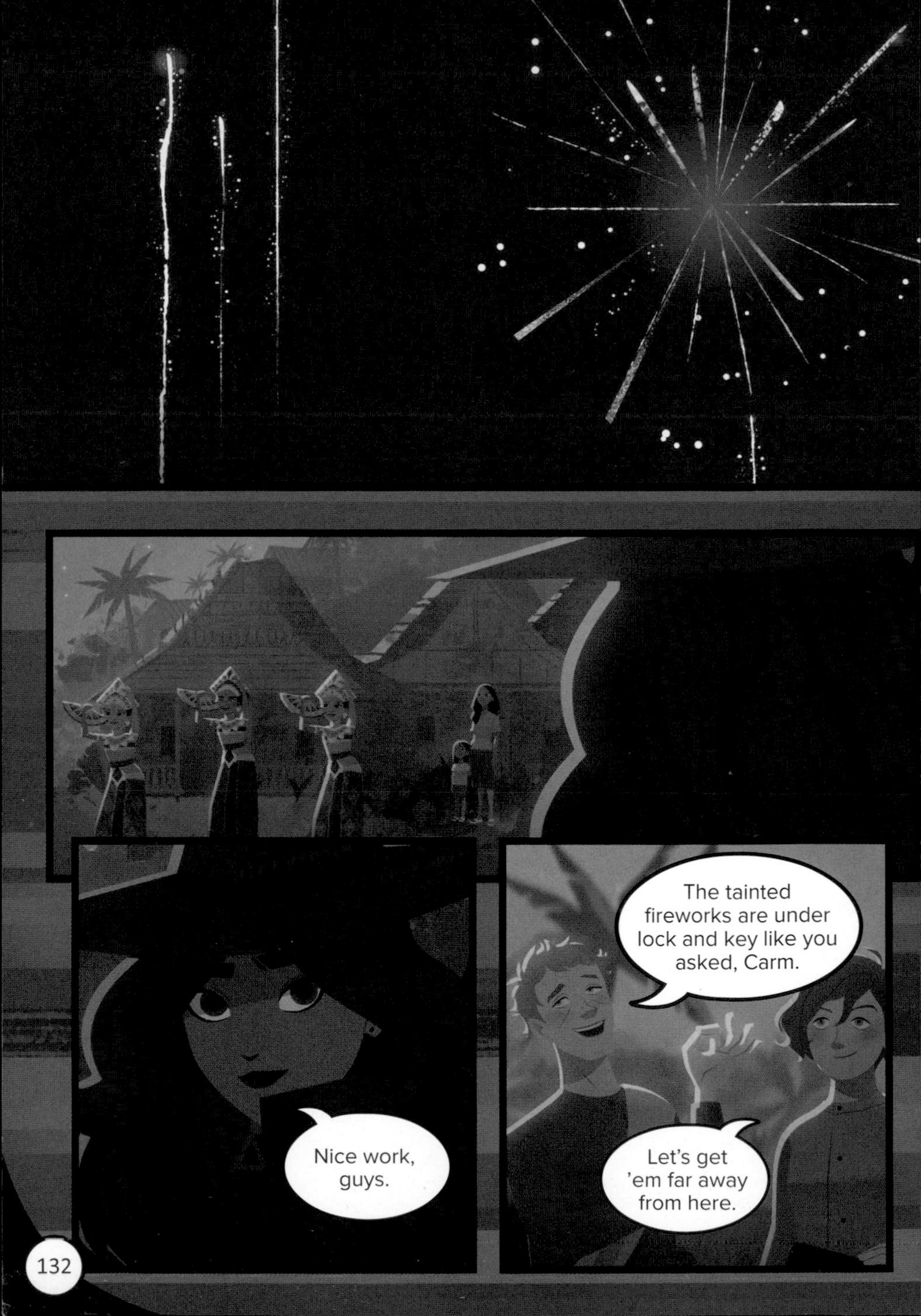
Nice work, guys.
The tainted fireworks are under lock and key like you asked, Carm.
Let's get 'em far away from here.

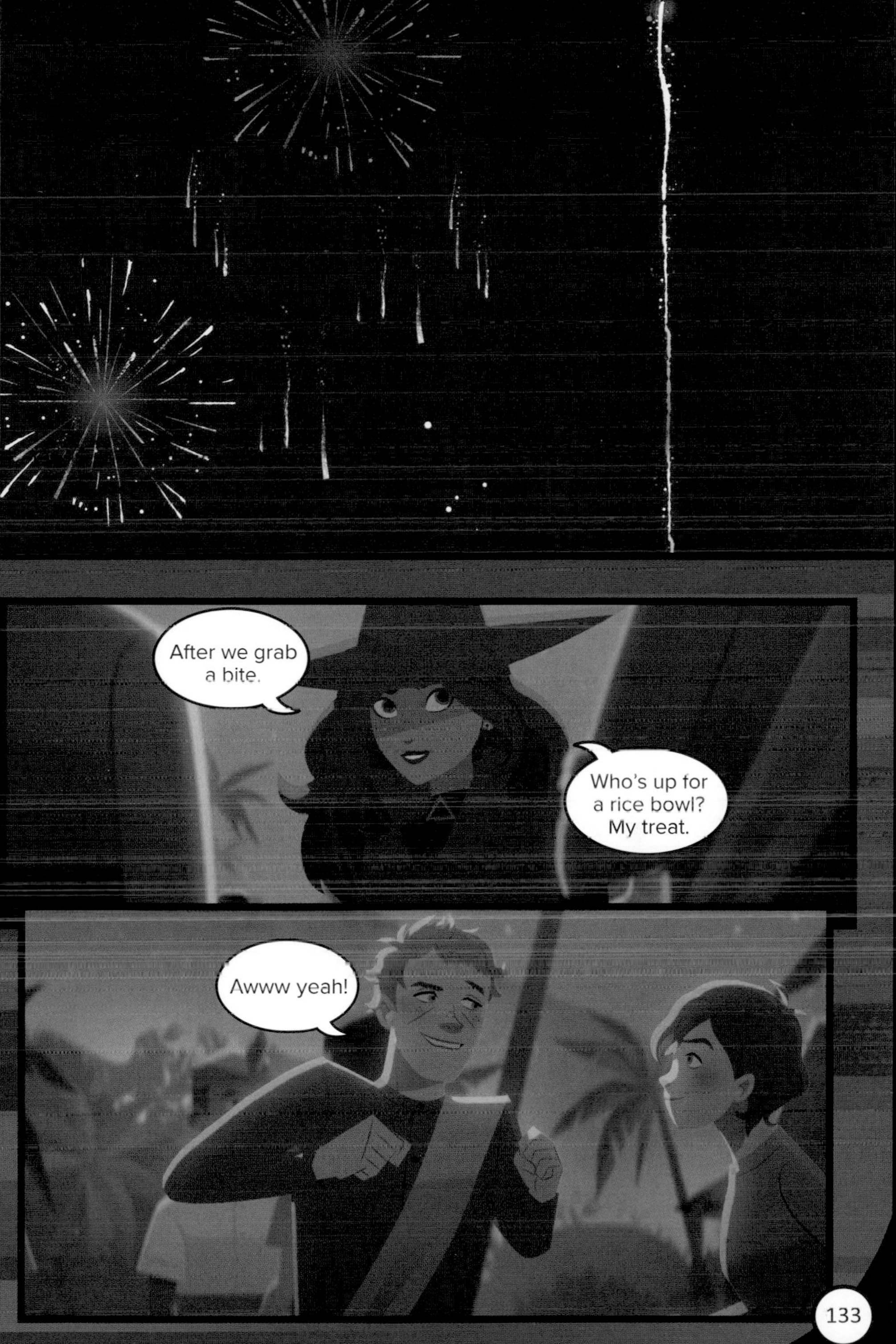
After we grab a bite.
Who's up for a rice bowl? My treat.
Awww yeah!

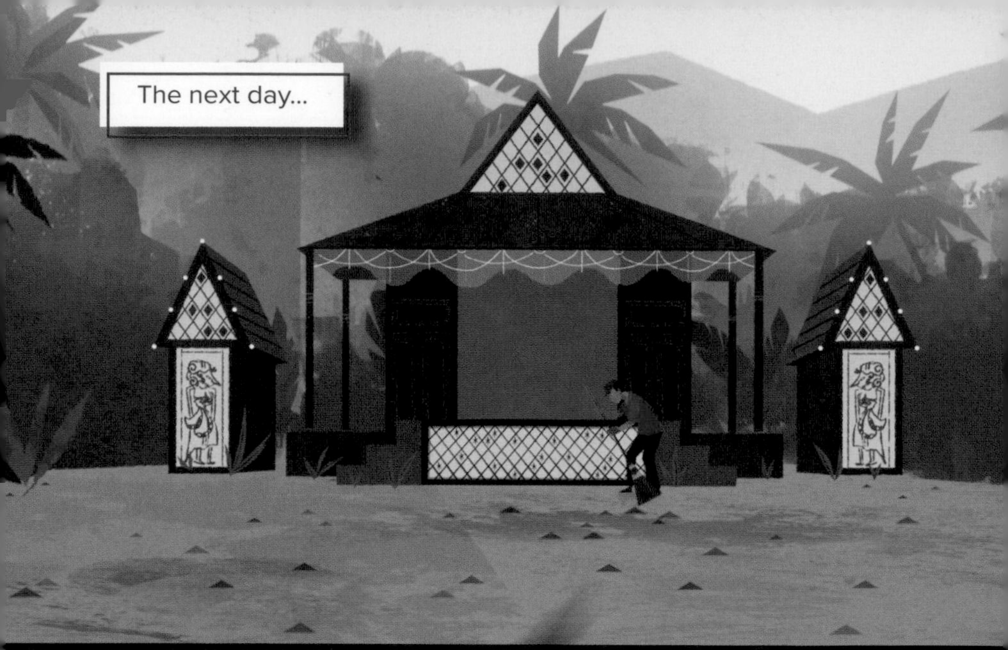

The next day...

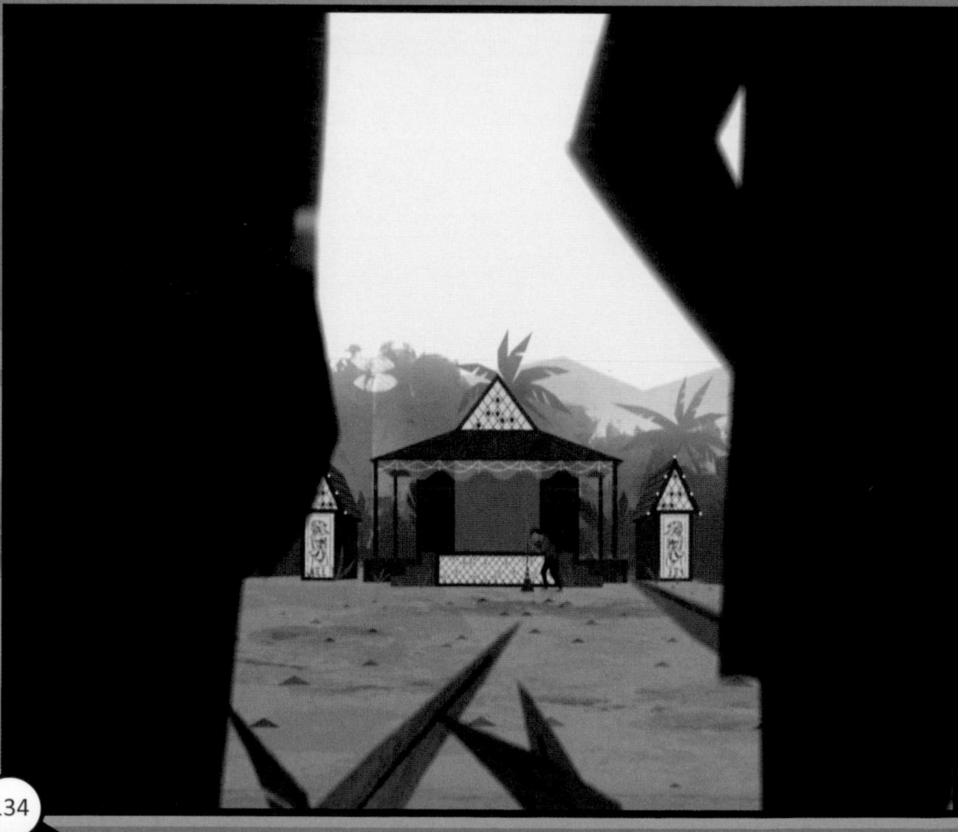

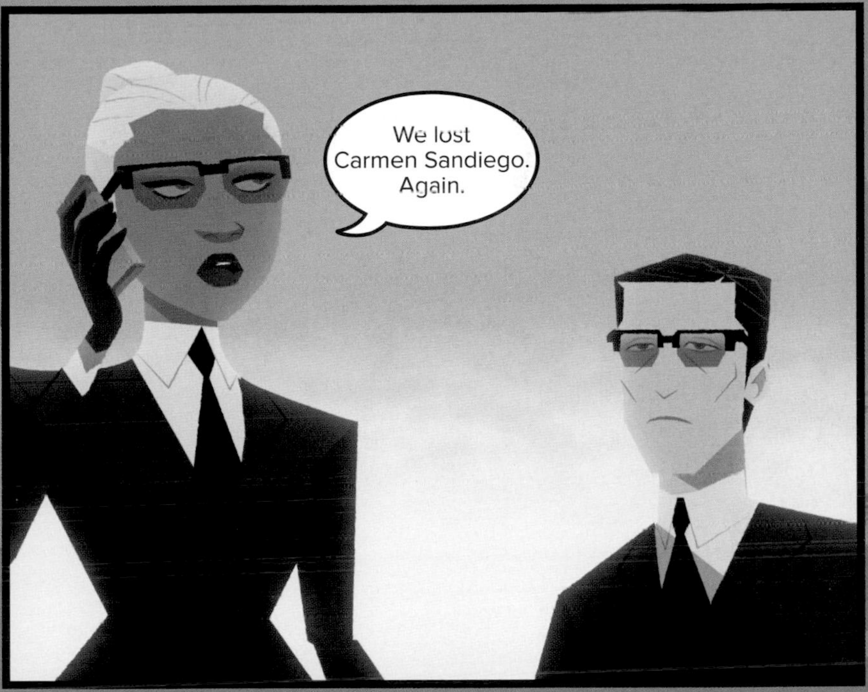
We lost
Carmen Sandiego.
Again.

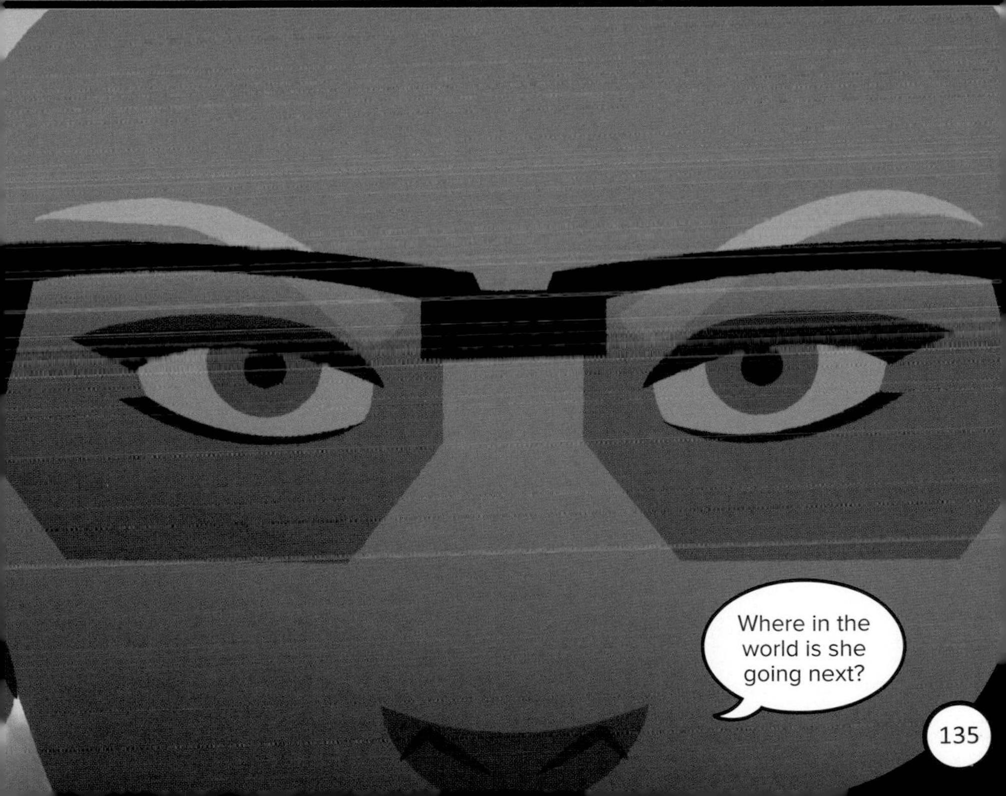
Where in the
world is she
going next?

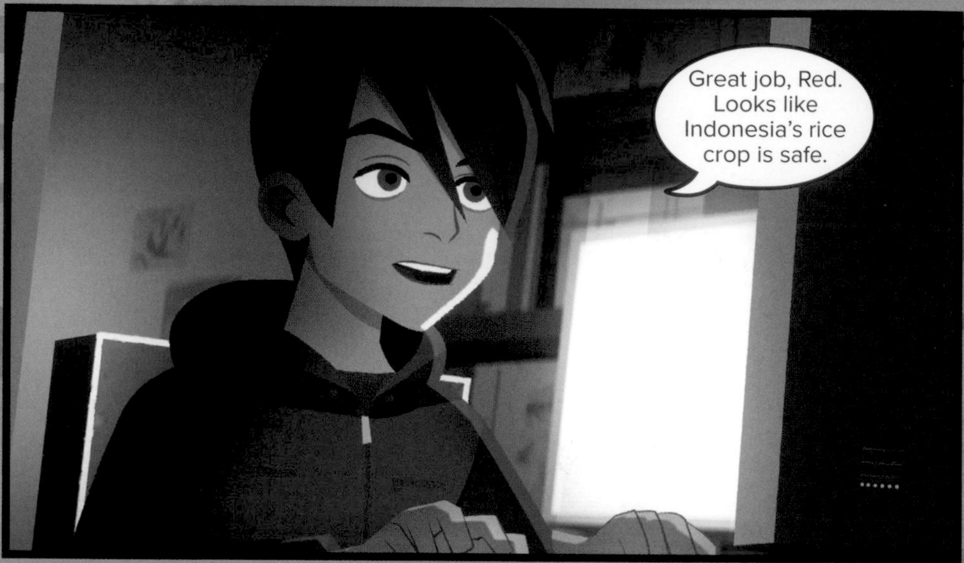
Great job, Red. Looks like Indonesia's rice crop is safe.

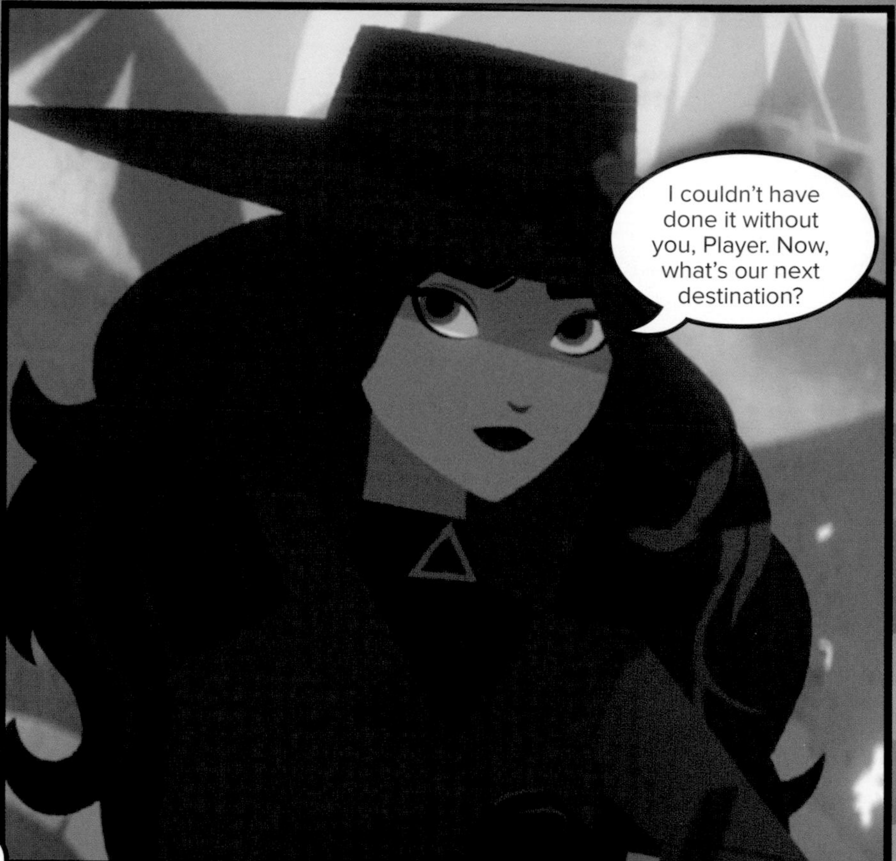
I couldn't have done it without you, Player. Now, what's our next destination?

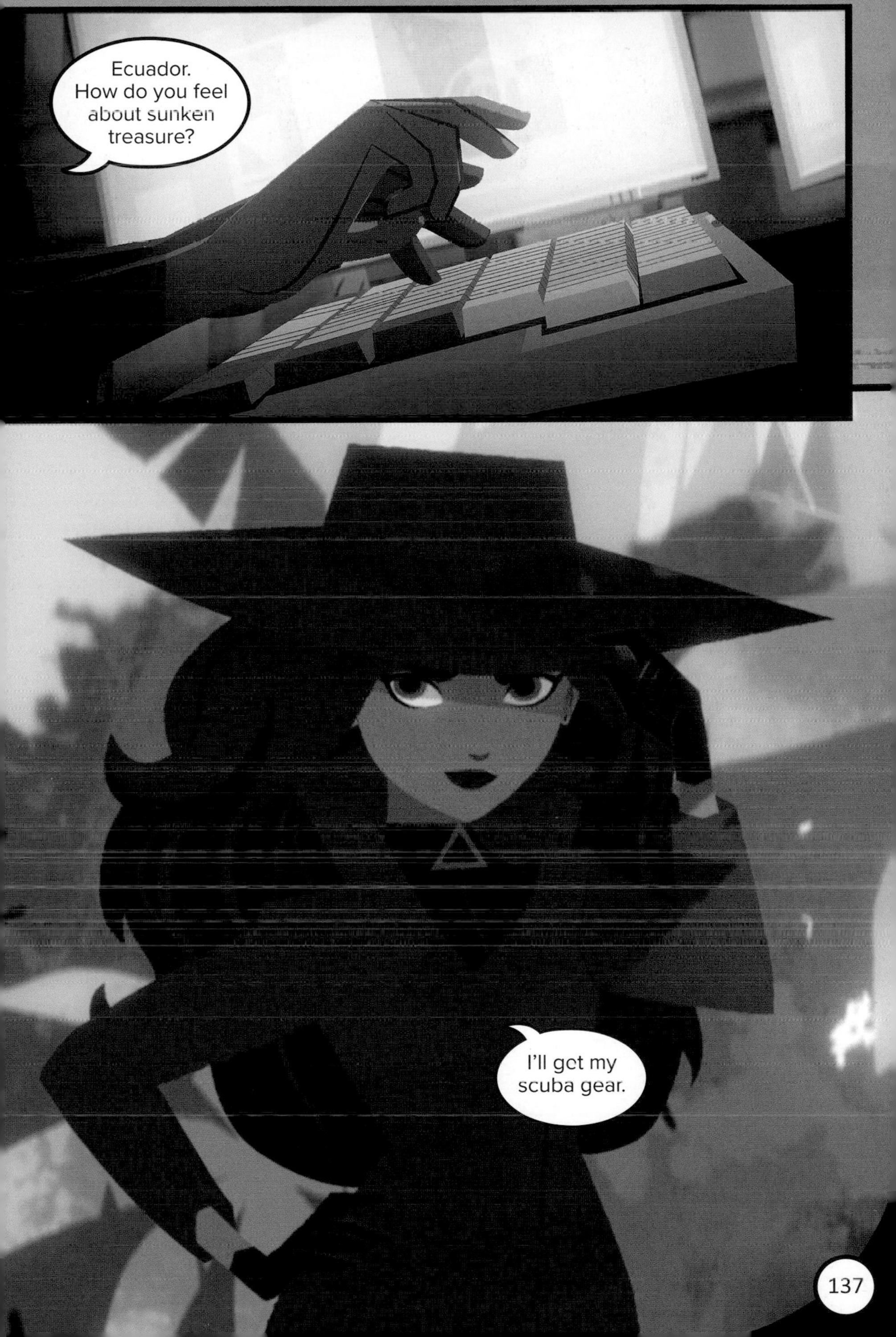
Ecuador. How do you feel about sunken treasure?
I'll get my scuba gear.

FRANCE

DID YOU KNOW . . .

Capital: Paris

Population: Over 62 million people (in Metropolitan France alone)

Official Language: French

Currency: Euro

Government: Semi-presidential republic

Climate: Cool winters and mild summers; warmer along the Mediterranean

Terrain: Mostly flat plains and rolling hills in the north and west; mountainous Pyrenees and Alps regions in the south and east

History: Monarchy abolished multiple times, the last time in 1870 with the fall of Emperor Napoleon III; varying forms of republican government culminated in the Constitution of 1958, which established the semi-presidential republic government of today

Flag:

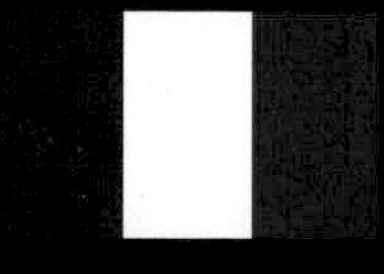

FUN FACTS:

In the early twenty-first century, five French overseas entities—French Guiana, Guadeloupe, Martinique, Mayotte, and Reunion—became French regions.

France is one of the oldest nations in the world.

Tour de France is an annual bike race that traverses 2,235 miles (3,600 km) over three weeks—it's the most difficult and highly regarded bike race in the world. It begins in different places, but always ends in Paris.

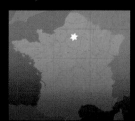

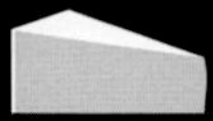

France is known for its cheese, both the quality and the quantity of it, with more than three hundred recognized varieties.

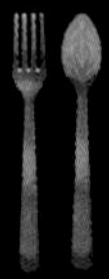

French culture is one of the most influential in the world in areas such as art, literature, dance, music, fashion, cuisine, and film.

The motion picture was invented by two French brothers, Auguste and Louis Lumière, in 1895. France has been at the forefront of cinema ever since, and to this day holds one of the most celebrated events in movies each year, the Cannes Film Festival.

The Eiffel Tower in Paris is one of the most recognized landmarks in the world. It was built over the course of two years, from 1887 to 1889, to celebrate the World's Fair of 1889. It was even the world's tallest building until 1930, when the Chrysler Building in New York City was completed.

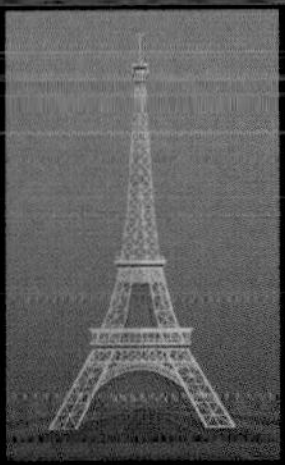

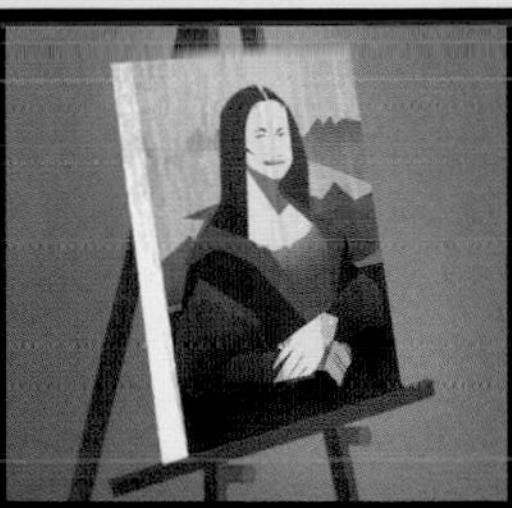

The Louvre Museum in Paris is the most visited art museum in the world, and has one of the world's greatest art collections. Perhaps the most famous work in its collection is the *Mona Lisa* by Leonardo da Vinci.

INDONESIA
DID YOU KNOW . . .

Capital: Jakarta

Population: Over 250 million people

Official Language: Indonesian

Currency: Rupiah

Government: Presidential republic

Climate: Tropical; hot, humid; more moderate in highlands

Terrain: Mostly coastal lowlands; larger islands have interior mountains

History: Ruled by the Netherlands until independence was declared in 1945

Flag:

FUN FACTS:

Badminton is one of the most popular sports in Indonesia.

The world's largest Muslim population is in Indonesia.

Indonesia has more volcanoes than any other country in the world.

Most meals are based around rice. Nasi goreng is considered the national dish: fried rice mixed with other ingredients such as eggs, vegetables, seafood, or meat and a thick, sweet soy sauce.

Indonesia is home to many jungles and exotic animals, like the Komodo dragon.

In addition to Indonesian, people also speak English, Dutch, and hundreds of regional dialects.

Indonesia is one of the world's largest coffee producers and exporters. Its Kopi Luwak coffee is one of the most expensive in the world, going for up to $600 per pound!

Wayang shadow puppetry is performed using puppets behind a screen, casting their shadow for the audience on the other side. It is often performed at festivals and accompanied by gamelan music, a traditional Indonesian ensemble of mostly brass percussion instruments.

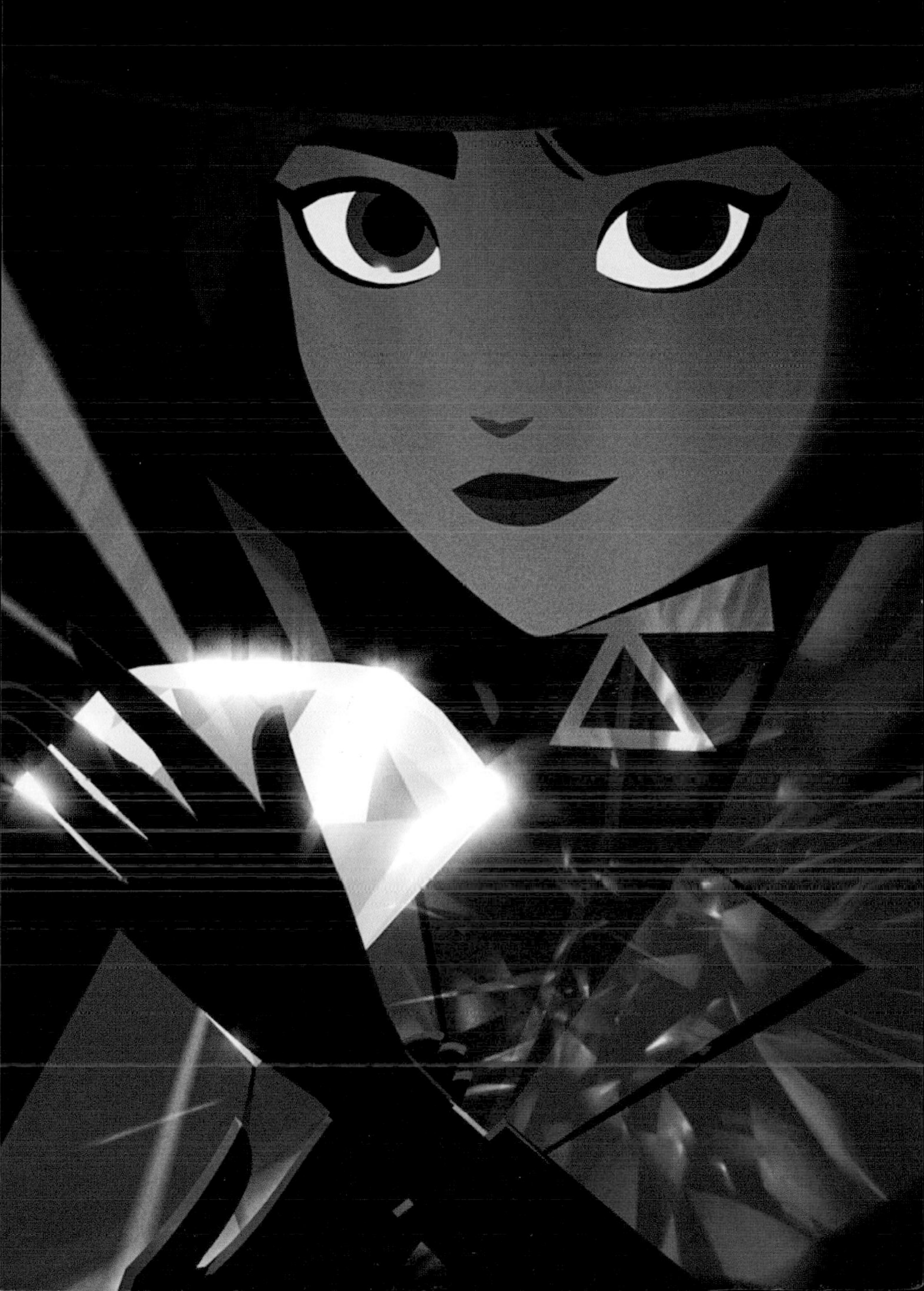

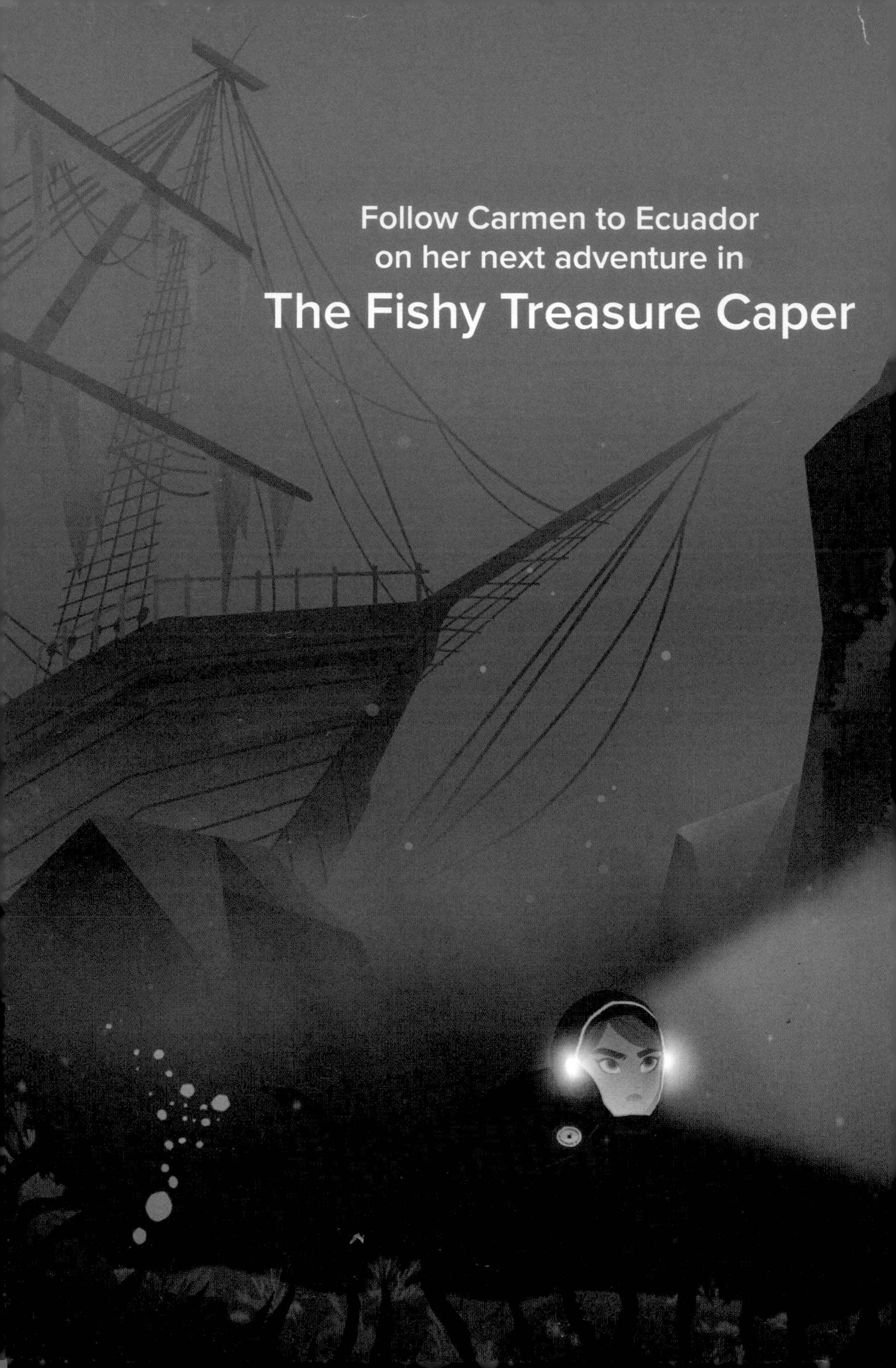
Follow Carmen to Ecuador
on her next adventure in
The Fishy Treasure Caper